WACCAMAW GOLD

A Novel

William Woodson

Waccamaw Gold is a work of fiction. Names, characters, places and incidents are the products of the author's imagination or are used fictitiously. Any resemblance to actual events or locales or to persons, living or dead, is coincidental.

Published in the United States by
CLASS
Publishing Division
P.O. Box 2884
Pawleys Island, SC 29585
www.ClassAtPawleys.com

ISBN 978-0-9911124-0-1

First Edition

Cover photograph by Mike Covington.
Cover design by OBD.

For
William, Harriett Jordan and Harrison

Chapter One

Beaufort Estes struggled down the thirty-foot embankment at Laurel Hill, silently cursing the unseasonal eighty degree heat and accompanying humidity on a March night. The young deputy that had summoned him to what looked like an ordinary automobile accident was catching some profanity as well. So were the extra pounds and inches Beaufort had added since his second marriage. Gone was the All American physique that had once helped bring football glory to the University of South Carolina. "Damn beer," he muttered, right as his feet slipped out from under him on the sandy bank.

Reaching the edge of the Waccamaw River, he glanced back up the embankment, wondering what could continue to delay the construction of a guardrail along the sharp eastward turn in the Kings River Road. "You'd think they'd get off their ass and build the damn thing," he muttered to himself, shaking his head in mild disgust as he thought of the number of prominent people traveling this road. Beaufort grimaced at his stained uniform and called to the young deputy standing ankle deep in the water, talking to an unseen colleague through the shoulder mike on his radio.

"You there. What's your name?"

The young officer felt more than heard the presence of his superior over the rush of the river and, turning toward Beaufort, said, "It's Sam Withers, sir. I called you out."

"So, what have you boys got here that needs a senior, off-duty deputy?" Beaufort replied, emphasizing off-duty perhaps a shade more than was necessary.

"Well, sir. Sorry, sir," young Withers replied. "It's just that … on account of …"

"Come on. Spit it out, son," Beaufort barked at him.

Withers pulled his shoulders back and took a deep breath. "Yessir. The river road comes from Oryzantia and tonight being the Inman Society dinner and with all the VIPs there … well, I just thought this might be … you know, it could be somebody important. It's only my second month and I … uh, I …"

Beaufort cut him off again. "What you got here, Sam? Somebody call you? Tell me, what are we doin' standin' round here with the bugs?"

"Dispatch got a 911 mobile phone call at 22:15 from some night fishermen. Thought they saw headlights go over the bluff and then disappear. I was the closest car. I got here at approximately 22:35."

"You got divers out there yet? A wrecker on the way?" Beaufort asked. He looked back up to the top of the bluff and then out across the black expanse of the Waccamaw. "Goddam," he muttered to no one in particular.

Functions at Oryzantia, for all their glamour, were a continuing source of anxiety for local law enforcement officials, representing as they did such an inordinate concentration of influential, well-connected people leaving the grounds late at night within a small window of time.

"The dive boat just got here, sir, and the first guy went down just as you walked up," Withers answered. "The wrecker should be only fifteen minutes away. They didn't want to come out until we confirmed we had a car in."

Beaufort hurried the young deputy back toward the river. "Go. GO. Get on it, man. Somebody's life might be depending on you. And get me a plate number!"

Sam Withers waded back into the shallow water at the edge of the river and punched his radio call switch, listening for a response from the dive boat. Beaufort could just barely make out the underwater gleam of a flashlight in the black water. Within two minutes the first diver surfaced, and Beaufort heard Withers calling to the dive boat.

"Car in the river, late model four-door…" was all he could make out in the exchange as the sound dispersed over the broad reach of the Waccamaw. Withers spoke into the shoulder mike of his radio, and Beaufort heard the beginning of a question that sounded like "passengers." He watched the diver re-submerging.

Beaufort Estes took several strides toward the river's edge, then turned back toward the embankment, kicking at a clump of oyster shells. "Sh…", and then he heard Withers repeating what sounded like a license plate number. Even though the young deputy was already moving out of the water up to where he stood, he yelled at him again "What you got, Sam?"

Withers felt the sweat breaking out under the band of his hat. "They say the plate number is…

"Call it in to DMV for crissakes … tell 'em we got a car in the river, and we need the ownership information. No. Wait. Don't tell 'em anything. Just get me the registration. What are the divers saying?" He watched Withers fumbling with his radio trying to reach the DMV emergency operations desk on the channel and heard Withers reply into the radio hand set, "that is correct, 'N'…" There was a pause. "… as in Nancy, 'L' as in Lima, 'J' as in Juliet, three-four-seven."

"N as in Nancy? Nancy? Godamighty, where'd you go to training school? What did they say?"

"Mercedes S420 sedan registered to a Martha Bradbury Commander, 555 Sabal Court, Georgetown."

"Say again." Beaufort removed his hat, slapping it against his thigh and running his fingers through his hair. He listened as Sam Withers repeated the information. "Sam, you got a mobile phone on you?"

The deputy reached for his cell phone in the carrier attached to his service belt and then dug his hand into his trouser pocket when he realized the leather holder was empty. "I must have…" he began to speak, clearing his throat when Beaufort cut him off.

"Listen to me," Beaufort ordered, grabbing the young officer by the arm, "get your cell. Call DMV and ask them for confirmation of the vehicle license plate you just called in. Write it down. Do not…" He half pulled, half pushed Withers toward his patrol cruiser at the top of the bluff. "Do NOT under any circumstances use your radio. Call the wrecker. Tell him I said to turn off his goddam radio. Do not use it to report back. Tell him I said that. I want silence on the channel. You hear me? You understand? Now go… GO."

Beaufort checked his watch and reached for his own mobile phone, hitting the auto dial for the Georgetown County Sheriff's Office dispatch desk.

"LaNita? That you? It's Beaufort. Listen, I need the sheriff. Hell, I know it's late." He listened for a moment. "I know he's going to kick my ass for waking him up. You think I'm happy about this? Just patch me through, would you?" Beaufort waited, trying to take his mind off the inevitable with the sounds of digital communication locating Sheriff Hugh Giles. "Yeah, Hugh. It's Beaufort. Yeah, I know it's late. Hugh, I'm out here on the river road south of Oryzantia at the Laurel Hill Bluff." He took a deep breath and looked out over the water. "I think we're pulling Molly Commander's car out of the river. Yes, sir. Yes, sir. I know. Right." Beaufort hit the disconnect button.

Chapter Two

Julia Pringle's mobile phone rang five minutes after she exited the main gates at Oryzantia. It was eleven-thirty. She was tired after four hours of intense conversation. The annual Inman Society dinner was typical of upper level donor functions at top tier American museums – those museums that by the weight of their artistic clout were able to assemble a constituency that extended far beyond a base of local support.

Survival, let alone prosperity, could be elusive for any arts organization and Julia knew it. One of the founders of the Society, himself a former Chairman of Oryzantia's Trustees, had put it quite bluntly, "We've got to have a minimum of five million dollars a year in unrestricted financial support to keep the gates open. Twice that to grow. So we round up all the old crowd. Twist some arms if we have to. Lean on the people we know to become charter members. Create some curb appeal. Then the new people will break their necks to get in. The corporate guys won't have any choice, they'll have to come along."

Of course, he was right. Membership in the Inman Society was by invitation only, albeit, in the early years, based on a relatively relaxed admission criteria. Exclusivity may have been at odds with the primary institutional purpose of creating a broad base of financial support for the museum, but the leadership of the museum's trustees had been right in the end. They understood the necessary marriage of business and the arts, and they knew that the men and women who ran big corporations typically preferred the golf course to the charity ball. An organization comprised of insiders, possessing the magnetic appeal of the old WASP elite, was able to reach deeply into the ranks of America's corporate aristocracy to consolidate the resources needed to become a powerhouse in the field of American art. Within ten years the original veneer of exclusivity had come full circle to a level of genuine exclusiveness that caused one Columbia matron to sniff that, in another year, it would be harder to get in the Inman Society than Augusta National.

Julia Pringle was a member of this highest level of donors of one of the most celebrated museums of its kind in the world, an inner circle of supporters that was itself a microcosm of power and influence in business and society. Her parents and most of their friends were members. Molly Commander herself had recommended Julia for membership, her application seconded by no less than two former governors of the State of South Carolina and three CEOs of Fortune 100 corporations. At twenty-nine, she was the youngest member of the Inman Society. She understood how this game was played.

While she was vaguely uncomfortable with many of the older members, she realized that it was only after she became a member of the Inman Society that she was asked to become a trustee of and the Associate General Counsel to the Winyah Bay Conservancy, the most influential environmental group in the area; and, that she was mentioned for membership in the previously all-male Sampit Gun Club, which in typically Lowcountry tradition was neither on the Sampit River nor had anything to do with guns.

Julia got it. She was just tired.

The insistent ring of her cell phone startled her. Noticing the home number of her administrative assistant, she quickly answered her phone.

"Susan. It's late. What…" she managed to say before she was interrupted.

"We just got a call from the Georgetown Hospital. Julia…" Julia heard the catch in her assistant's voice. "It's Mrs. Commander. She's been in an accident."

"Molly? Are you sure? That can't be. She was just at Oryzantia." Julia's voice momentarily trailed off as she tried to recall seeing Molly toward end of the evening. "Call them back and tell them I'm on the way to the hospital. I'm just passing the north causeway at Pawleys – so

I'm about twenty minutes away. Mrs. Commander is all right, isn't she?"

"Julia, I don't know. It scared the hell out of me. I didn't ask. I just called you."

"Call them back. Tell them I'm on the way. I'll call you when I know more," she said, disconnecting.

Twenty minutes later Julia strode quickly through the double glass doors of the emergency room section of the Georgetown Memorial Hospital and approached the nurses' station.

"I'm Julia Pringle. Someone called my office about Mrs. Commander. Please tell me…"

The duty nurse jumped to her feet. "Miss Pringle, Dr. Henning is waiting for you just inside the double doors at the end of this hall," pointing toward a short corridor to Julia's left.

Julia passed through the heavy hospital doors and found, waiting for her on the other side, a young doctor still in his surgical scrubs. His name tag identified him as Dr. Henning. His youthful appearance indicated that he was the resident in charge of weekend emergency operations while other more senior doctors were at the beach, the river or on the golf course.

"Odd. He looks like Billy," Julia thought.

"Miss Pringle?" The young doctor said. "It is Miss Pringle, correct?" Ordinarily, Julia might have detected a slight emphasis in the manner in which he said Miss, but under the circumstances she hardly noticed.

"Julia is fine," she replied, extending her right hand. "Tell me about Mrs. Commander."

"She was brought in about forty minutes ago with a severe closed head injury, lacerations to her face, a pneumothorax," He stopped in mid-sentence. "Forgive me. I'm over explaining. Look, let's sit down."

He led her to a cluster of metal chairs grouped in one corner of the room. "Apparently," he began again, "her car went into the river at the…," he looked down at his clipboard, "Laurel Hill Bluff. She sustained a concussion that rendered her unconscious as her car entered the water. The extent of her injuries and her advanced age made it impossible to revive..," his voice trailed off. "I'm terribly sorry… I… I'm not from here. I understand that she was quite highly regarded. Are you her lawyer?"

Julia could hardly hear him over the pounding in her head. "Lawyer?" she said after a moment. "Yes, one of them … no, not just … she is my… she was my great aunt." Oh God, she thought, this can't be happening.

The fluorescent lights, the sterility of the hospital surroundings, the clinical professionalism of strangers seemed somehow completely inappropriate for hearing the news that Molly Commander was gone. And yet, what surroundings could have been appropriate?

Chapter Three

Molly Commander had been a Main Line debutante, a cousin of the Wideners and the Cadwaladers, whose parents had found her a bit too straightforward for notoriously discreet Philadelphia society. She had been sent south for school at Ashley Hall and Converse College. After school, she gravitated toward the orbit of Pawleys Island and Georgetown, mixing comfortably with the remnants of the old plantation society and the new society developing in the late thirties along the Waccamaw Neck. Marrying into one of the oldest families in South Carolina, buttressed by her own family name and money, she became a fixture in South Carolina and Atlanta society, and, eventually, a mainstay of American banking.

Twice proposed by the President of the United States to become a governor of the Federal Reserve system, twice declined, she was said to have been the *eminence grise* behind Criswell Burnett's transformation of a handful of conservative, mostly small town southern banks into a financial colossus as he racked up acquisition after acquisition, ultimately assembling the third largest bank in the country. Molly Commander, with her signature Chanel suits, ash blonde hair, fire engine red lipstick and lacquered nails, at age seventy-five still drank bourbon on the rocks, occasionally smoked unfiltered cigarettes and loved a good joke with the boys.

The fifth largest individual shareholder of the Continental American Bank, she was one of the richest women in America. She had a head for business and an eye for talent and, some whispered, as it would never have been uttered in her presence, a tendency toward the dramatic. She also had a passion for the transforming power of education and opportunity.

"People come to us with the fiscal embodiment of their most cherished ideals – their lives, their dreams," she used to tell Criswell Burnett in the days when Continental American was being assembled. "We have a responsibility to participate in the building of communities that allow those dreams to flourish."

Gone. Julia tried to imagine their world without Molly Commander.

"I'm sorry. I am not prepared. No, that's not it. I'm not ready for this to happen."

Tommy Henning said, "We rarely are. It's the nature, I think, of accidental death."

"That's not what I..." she began. "Is there somewhere more private? I need to make some phone calls... somewhere other than the public waiting area perhaps. And, one more thing, if I may? Have you noticed any indications that the police channels may have been monitored? That others may know about this accident? The media?"

Not knowing which question to answer first, he dealt with the questions in order. "Sure. Let me take you down to the room we use while on duty. I haven't seen any reporters around, although I'm likely the wrong one to ask. The general public isn't allowed back here." He could not help thinking how strange it was that she had asked about reporters in the first minute of their conversation, prompting the fleeting, but unspoken, question, 'Who are these people?'

Julia followed him down the hall, already reaching for her cell phone. He showed her into a small lounge and had turned to leave her alone when she placed her hand on his arm.

Tommy noticed that her fingers were long, slender and perfectly formed, with short manicured nails, subtly polished. She was beautiful. Dressed simply, but in an expensively elegant manner that belied a small town, leading him to conclude that her orbit extended far beyond Georgetown, South Carolina. She wore a large square cut diamond on the hand that rested on his arm and a choker of pale grey – what were they called? His grandmother and his mother wore the same. South Sea pearls. That was it. Tall and clearly fit, although not obviously so, there was something restrained about her appearance, something that made her slightly untouchable, out of reach and yet was at the same time entirely… entirely what? 'Entirely, well… hot,' he thought. Maybe Georgetown would not be so bad. 'Christ, Tommy,' he told himself, 'get a hold of yourself. She's just lost someone of great personal significance and you're totally checking her out.'

"Please," Julia said, "if it's not too much trouble… could you… rather, would you mind staying for a moment?"

"Sure, nowhere I need to be right now," Tommy Henning replied. "Can I get you anything?"

But she had already turned away.

She had a way about her. A presence that bespoke a certain background and station, but, more than that, a subtle awareness of her position that created a self-assurance born of generations of occupying a constant place in society. He recognized it because his grandmother had it. His mother and his sister had it.

Later in the week, he would describe Julia and the night they met to his sister in St. Louis. "She had this hot pink kind of a jacket thing that was sheer but stiff with a collar that stood up."

"That's the first thing you noticed about her? Her jacket?" Celia Henning had laughed and said, "Sounds European, Tommy. Very big stuff for South Carolina, I would have thought. Who is this girl?"

"Julia Pringle. She was a relative of a woman who was killed in an automobile accident and brought in while I was on duty."

"Julia Pringle? Oh for god's sake, Tommy. Julia was at Chapel Hill with Stiles McPherson. She's Billy Commander's cousin. That's that whole Lucy Magrath crowd. You remember her. She was at Stanford with Susan. She went out with Alex Pearson for a while and was here about three years ago for the Veiled Prophet. Continental American Bank money, I think. You're in pretty serious company, bud. It doesn't get much bigger than that over there."

The door to the lounge opened quickly and Tommy signaled the young resident entering the room to leave them alone. He heard Julia say into her phone, "Walker? Of course, it's me. Are you in New York?" she asked. "What am I doing? That's hardly the point right now. You've got to listen to me." Julia heard the presence of another person in the background at Walker Evans Coggeshell's Upper East Side apartment, and realized he was speaking under his breath to whoever was there.

"WALKER."

"All right, Jules. Calm down. What is it? Talk. It's okay. I'm here. Although, to tell you the truth, I'd rather do this later. I'm kind of… well, I was in the middle of something."

Julia cut him off. "Molly had an accident leaving Oryzantia tonight and she's… Walker, Molly's dead."

There was silence at the other end of her call, "Walker? WALKER? Are you listening to me?"

Walker's voice staggered, "I hear you, Jules. When… what happened?"

"I'm at the hospital now. She had an accident. Her car went off the Laurel Hill Bluff into the river. Walker… I…," and Julia's voice broke.

She could hear Walker talking in the background to someone who, by the sound of it, was making plans for an earlier-than-expected departure.

"Julia," he said quietly, "one of us is going to have to call Billy. What do you want to do?"

And there it was. The moment Julia had been dreading most throughout the past twenty minutes. One of them would have to call Billy Commander, Molly's grandson, with the news of this second tragic death in only eight months.

Caroline Commander had been on the way to Georgetown from Atlanta to see her father when her car had been struck from the rear by a drunken driver at the wheel of a pulp wood hauler. She was killed instantly. She and Billy had been married one month short of two years when the accident occurred.

"Julia, I…," Walker began. She cut him off.

"Walker, I just can't. Molly sent me with John Harleston to get Billy after she called him about Caroline. I can't call him now and tell him about Molly. You're going to have to do it. I just can't."

Walker heard the catch in her voice and in his mind could see the tears beginning to collect in the corners of her eyes. Of course, she would not have a handkerchief. She never did.

"All right, Jules. It's…," Walker took his cell phone away from his ear to check the time, running his fingers through his hair as he tried to think what he should do next.

"Walker!" The strident tone in Julia's voice brought him back to the conversation.

"I'm here, Julia. I'll call Lucy. And Jane Ellen Atkinson, the head of the hospital. There'll be a fire storm there tomorrow – or rather this morning. Do you want me to call you back or wait 'til tomorrow? Let me call your dad to come get you. You probably need to try to get some sleep."

"Guys never cease to amaze me," she said. "I'm standing here in the emergency room of the Georgetown Hospital, alone mind you. Alone. Trying to figure out which of the six hundred things that need to happen I need to do first. And you think that now I'll just head on home and get some sleep. What then, Walker? A manicure maybe? Get my hair cut? God… call me after you talk to Lucy."

Walker pressed a programmed key on his phone. Within twenty seconds Lucy Magrath's unmistakable dusky voice answered, "Well, of course it's you, isn't it? Who else would be calling me from New York at one o'clock in the morning? So where have you boys been tonight and with whom? Did you hear that Charlotte Trapier is back from Paris and that…"

"Lucy." Walker broke in. "Stop."

Suddenly, she knew that something was gravely amiss. Walker, always the cheerful one, the glue that held them all together – Lucy, Billy, Julia, John Harleston Read. Walker the fixer, the arranger. Walker who always thought of others – especially Billy – before he ever seemed to think of himself. Something in his voice shattered the hope that he was calling merely to catch up.

"Lucy, Molly's dead."

She turned, instinctively looking out the window and saw Billy Commander in the distance at the round pen by the yearling barn, longeing a filly being prepped for the summer sales at Deauville.

Molly. Dead.

"What happened, Walker?" she asked.

"We're not sure yet, Luce. Julia just called me from the hospital in Georgetown. Apparently there was an accident leaving the Inman Society Dinner at Oryzantia."

Lucy's mind returned to the day, eight months before, when they had all stood side by side in the rain at St. Peter's Winyah and buried Caroline Coachman Commander. Billy, orphaned at age 19, widowed at 32. Now another fixture in his life was gone.

Molly Commander had come to her father's condominium at Pawleys Island the night after Caroline's funeral. Lucy had heard her at the door. "Morall, I am terribly sorry to intrude but I must speak with Lucy, if you do not mind."

Pacing up and down the living room, Molly had told her, "I fear this is too much for Billy. There are limits to that with which one can cope. I would like to send him back with you. To France. To get him away from this for a while."

Lucy could still hear Molly's elegant Main Line, slightly locked-jaw drawl, never lost after almost sixty years in South Carolina.

"Lucy, you must do this for me. It's the only thing I can think of that may rescue him from the crippling effect of despair that I fear will now set in. Had I had another alternative, I would have taken it, but I fear I do not."

Lucy had questioned the subtle qualification in Molly's request.

"Lucy, my dear, you have a history of running away from responsibility. It troubled your mother… it troubles your father." Molly held up her hand to silence Lucy, clearly indicating she would brook no dissent.

"I realize your current French enterprise seems to the rest of the world quite rational if not, in fact, business-like. You and I know differently. Yet, I remain devoted to you. I continue to hold out the hope that one day, quite soon, you will find yourself – and in some way become part of the legacy of contribution and service that characterizes your family. But for now, I ask you. May I send Billy back with you? Will you promise me that you will watch over him and bring him back to me after he is…," Molly had faltered, struggling with an uncharacteristic moment of uncertainty. "After he is restored?" she had concluded.

Of course, Lucy had consented.

Molly had continued, "If it's not terribly inconvenient, dear, and, of course, if your father has no objection, I would like you to leave in the next few days. I will see that all the necessary arrangements are made."

It was vintage Molly: calm, rational, controlled in a crisis, accustomed to decision-making authority. And yet, Lucy could instantly sense the anxiety – almost desperation – in her voice.

So Billy had come to France the next week – the plans orchestrated by Molly, the arrangements made by Walker and the Morgan Bank – and found himself inserted into the middle of Lucy's three-year, uneven relationship with Hubert de LaGardiere at her small breeding farm, ten kilometers from the sea between Deauville and Bayeux.

Lucy put the phone down when Walker had finished. He had told her they would miss the U.S. bound flights today. She would have to get Billy to Charles de Gaulle tomorrow to catch the eleven a.m. flight to Atlanta and then on to Charleston where Walker and John Harleston would meet him.

Eight months of watching Billy Commander struggle with what, she wondered? Grief? Sadness? Certainly. But it was something else. More like a sense of dislocation. Of being lost or unable to discover any meaningful purpose for his life.

"What is it with all of us?" she thought. "We have money. Education. Talent. We know everybody. We've been everywhere." But the pieces of the puzzle never quite fit. Billy had told her once that their lives seemed to be like Baroque music.

"Lots of activity. No real harmony," he had laughed.

And now this. Lucy looked out at Billy again and struggled with the start of a stream of tears. She never cried. She prided herself on her ability to control her emotions, especially in exigent circumstances, and derided the lack of that same ability in other girls of her acquaintance. Pulling her dark hair back into the ponytail that defined her daytime look, securing it with an elastic band from her wrist in one quick gesture, she shoved her hands into the pockets of her jeans and started down the slope to the round pen.

"Hold back the night, turn on the lights…" The strains of an old beach music song began to loop through her mind, as she looked over the grounds for her farm manager. She reached for the radio on her belt and paged him. "Billy has to go to the states tomorrow, and I need you to take him to Charles de Gaulle. Why don't you take my car and… Okay. *D'accord*," she finished in her grammatically flawless but American-accented French.

Lucy tried to focus on the arrangements Walker had made, tears again welling up in her eyes. "Hold back the night, turn on the lights… I want to dream"… the eleven a.m. Air France flight from Paris to Atlanta, connecting with the Delta flight to Charleston at 4:30. Someone. Who? Some government official would meet Billy and walk him through customs and passport control to avoid the lines. A Delta PSA in some kind of a jacket.

"Red," Walker had said. We can't be going through this again… a red jacket guy would take him in a car from the international concourse to the Charleston plane. Walker and John Harleston Read would be waiting in Charleston.

"Good god, all this has been arranged in New York in the middle of the night. The power of the Morgan Bank," she thought.

She watched Billy hand off the bay filly to a hot walker and shielding his eyes from the bright March morning sun, smiled at her as she approached. "When you left, you took the sun right out of my sky…"

"Billy. Walker just called." She detected the change in his expression immediately, caused by the tone of her voice. "Molly's been in an accident."

Chapter Four

Walker Coggeshell stood at the floor-to-ceiling windows on the B Concourse of the Charleston Airport watching the Delta 767 with Billy Commander on board move into position at the end gate. He had been staring blankly out the windows for twenty-five minutes since his own flight from LaGuardia had landed. He saw the ground crew at Gate 27 open the jet way door, and he knew that in less than five minutes Billy would exit the aircraft through that door. He knew because his office had made the arrangements. He knew the number of Billy's seat in the front cabin of the aircraft. He knew the name of the senior INS official who had walked Billy through passport control in Atlanta two and one half hours ago. It was his job.

Walker was a Morgan banker.

It had always irritated Hugo Lesesne, the Chairman of Continental American, that its Wealth Management Division did not manage for Molly. "Christ, Molly, you're one of the largest individual shareholders of the bank. You're the chairman of the Executive Committee. And, whatever the reality may be, conventional wisdom in the financial community is that Criswell could not have assembled CAB without you. How do you think it looks for a tight-assed outfit like Morgan to manage for you?"

His irritation seemed to grow over the years as Molly continued to demur politely when the topic came up, refusing even to discuss it with him, despite the interwoven nature of their financial affairs.

Molly's mother had been a Cadwalader, a cousin of the Wideners, whose forebears had made a fortune in coal and, later, steel and the railroads. Cadwalader Trust had been formed in 1910, primarily to manage the business affairs of the Cadwalader heirs. In 1978, Cadwalader Trust merged with the Morgan Brothers Bank in New York, itself having no relationship to J.P. Morgan and the banking companies that had descended from his enterprises. The new entity became the Morgan Brothers Cadwalader Trust, ultimately becoming known in financial circles simply as the Morgan Bank. The clients of the Morgan Bank – clients because they would never have been referred to as customers, let alone depositors – along with the clients of Philips Trust in New York, the South Coast Trust Bank of Palm Beach and the Stanford Bank in San Francisco represented the final accession – indeed acceptance – into the top two per cent of American business and society.

Walker Evans Coggeshell was a Morgan Banker, partly because of his education and ability and, in no short order as it was often observed, because of his personality. But, it was unavoidable that the door to Morgan had been opened by his grandmother, Mary Williams Fraser Coggeshell.

Mimi Coggeshell had inherited from her mother's family a fifty per cent interest in the Coca Cola Bottling plant serving northeastern South Carolina, including most of the bedroom communities south of Charlotte. In 1982, when the Coca Cola Company decided to consolidate its control over the bottling subsidiaries and bought back many of the independently owned bottling companies, the Williams family elected to receive shares in the new CCE, as well as Coca Cola common stock, in exchange for their former holdings. In the years since the Williams family had sold the bottling plant to Coke, the value of Mimi's CCE and Coke stock had increased fourfold to approximately sixty-two million dollars.

She had also inherited from her father a ten per cent interest in the Bank of Georgetown, which after multiple mergers and acquisitions left her with shares in the Continental American Bank, currently worth over twenty million dollars. Other ventures had added to the net worth of the Coggeshells over the years. Their story was typical; their involvement in the core industries and services that lay at the heart of economic growth was repeated all across the South. Grounded in conservatism, Southern families tended to hold on to property. Shares of stock in the companies they owned were not merely financial instruments but the tangible representation of the family's association with the building of an enterprise, which, while enriching the family, also contributed to the creation of jobs and the building of communities and opportunities for the people that lived in them. It was the mirror opposite of fortunes made in the financial markets that seemed to accumulate by, in the words of Molly Commander, "moving things around and constantly taking a piece out of the middle."

The Coggeshell story was characteristic of the client list of Morgan Brothers Cadwalader. Family fortunes at Morgan were sufficiently cloaked in privacy that the annual *Capital* magazine list of the 500 richest people in America was forced to observe the list did not include many of the clients of Morgan Brothers Cadwalader.

Walker had heard all the jokes when he went to work for the bank. Get the dog walked. The plants watered. Make sure there was fuel in the jet or the boat. But behind the passing derisiveness, Walker's colleagues in the upper reaches of the financial services community knew that Morgan had a client list that went beyond gold-plated. It was untouchable. As a result, the Morgan Bank prided itself on providing an array of services to its clients, services not typically associated with a bank. For many, to be able to say discreetly "the Morgan Bank manages for me" or "just send the bill to the Morgan Bank" were among the most enviable statements in American life.

Still, Morgan would not accept just anyone with money as a client. There were no clients with Silicon Valley money, for example. As one eager thirty-year-old California billionaire had been told: "It seems unlikely we have the level of understanding of your industry and the particular demands of your lifestyle that we could be of service."

So Walker had prospered in the rarefied world of Morgan Brothers Cadwalader, prospered because he was from that world, understood its demand for absolute discretion and understood the subtleties and nuances of life among these kinds of families. In the experience of the Morgan Bank, the ability to manage for its particular client base was not easily learned by those who came from outside that world.

Walker saw the top of Billy's head coming out of the jet way. Billy Commander had a look that caused people to take notice of him in a way that acknowledged something was different about him. He exhibited a dignified composure combined with a relaxed, open attitude, a warmth of companionability that made him at home in both the U.S. and Europe. With slightly wavy, dark hair and eyes that girls found remarkable – sort of a Baltic blue – his classic good looks seemed lifted from some lifestyle magazine catering to Palm Beach or the Hamptons. Billy was aware of how he looked, comfortable with his appearance. But his charm had nothing to do with his appearance.

Billy Commander filled up a room. He had a way of making everyone feel welcome, making men feel insightful, informed; making women feel beautiful, intelligent, essential. He had a way of moving a conversation to the next level without ever seeming to dominate the flow of talk. To look at him casually attired in a double-breasted navy blazer, pink oxford shirt, a worn pair of Levis, sockless feet in a pair of brown suede snaffle-bit loafers, an ancient monogrammed canvas backpack slung over his left shoulder, his eyes hidden behind Ray Ban aviators, no one would have ever surmised that he had had a hurried, grief-ridden departure from France earlier that same morning.

Walker could have been the blonde version of Billy Commander, in a way. Indeed, seeing the two of them together, people often inquired if there were a familial connection. Dressed in grey flannel, a Pink's shirt and an Hermès tie, Walker had a refined yet comfortably casual air about him that created an almost magnetic appeal. Picking up his briefcase and throwing the strap of an old Hunting World duffle bag over his shoulder, he tried to contain the rush of emotion that hit him as he saw his oldest friend walking up the concourse to where he was standing. The two friends embraced, not speaking, not needing to. It was characteristic of their public demeanor – discreet, quiet, never drawing attention to themselves in public places. Little could be said anyway that would not in some way trivialize the moment.

Walker turned and began walking toward the terminal exit, inclining his head slightly toward Billy at his right side, "John Harleston's outside with the car."

John Harleston Read's Volvo station wagon was parked at the curb outside the baggage claim area, engine running with the passenger side doors open. John Harleston greeted Billy in a familiar, casual embrace that the boys held a moment longer than strictly necessary.

"Billy," he said quietly, shaking his head slightly from side to side. "I don't..."

"Thanks for picking us up, man. I guess we'd better get going before the *gendarmes* get restless," Billy said, noticing the approach of an airport security officer.

The boys drove up Highway 17 from Charleston in relative silence. As they drove through the mostly empty streets of Georgetown, Walker had broached the topic of the arrangements that had been made for Molly's funeral services the next day.

"Julia thought it was better at St. Peter's Winyah. She said that she thought Christ Church Waccamaw was just too casual and there is that other matter of the difference between Christ Church and the Diocese, and it could be that Loudoun Smith would think Christ Church inappropriate." He continued reciting in a detached business-like manner the arrangements being discussed – the music, the seating, the interment, the reception after the funeral. As they went through the gates into the DeBordieu Colony, Walker asked, "Billy, have you heard anything I've said?"

The silence from the back seat indicated Billy was indeed paying no attention to Walker's monologue.

"Do you want to go to Mimi's? Why don't you stay with us tonight?"

Walker's voice intruded on his thoughts. Billy Commander removed his sunglasses in the gathering dusk and looked down the lane of live oaks stretching two miles into the distance to the Atlantic Ocean.

Billy moved to Molly's house at DeBordieu from Atlanta after his parents died twelve years ago.

Sixty-two members of the Atlanta Art Association, major supporters of the High Museum, had gone to Paris in May of that year for the reopening of the Gae Aulenti designed Musee d'Orsay. As the L1011 rolled down the runway at Paris' Orly Airport for the return trip to Atlanta, the nose of the Tri-Star lifted off the runway but the body of the jet had remained on the ground. The aircraft was consumed in the fireball that followed. The sixty-two donors on board, representing the cream of Atlanta's business leadership and society, had included Motte and Frances Commander.

John Harleston and Walker had been called to the office of Barclay

Tarver, the Headmaster at the St. Bartholomew School, that morning in May. "What's going on?," Walker had asked, noticing a black sedan and driver on the curb outside McKinley Hall. Tarver's assistant motioned the boys immediately through the open doors into his office where stood Molly Commander, quietly talking to Dr. Tarver. John Harleston remembered what a powerful figure she was, all in black, wearing a wide brim hat, slowly removing her gloves, casually dropping them over the top of her bag on a chair by the desk. They had crossed the room, and each kissed Molly on her cheek.

"Boys, there has been some bad news and I thought it might be good if you were here when we send for Billy." Molly had eventually walked alone down to the aquatic center where Billy was just finishing swim practice. Walker and John Harleston watched through the nineteenth century arched windows in the headmaster's office, as she had told him about his parents, putting her arms around him and holding him close to her in the aftermath. An hour later they were all on the bank's jet on the way back to Georgetown.

Chapter Five

Thomas Dirleton, Molly Commander's houseman, drove the old British racing green Jaguar sedan, which Molly would neither sell nor replace, to the curb outside the Episcopal Church of St. Peter's Winyah. He reached to open his door to go around and open the rear door where his passengers sat in the back seat when he heard Billy Commander say, "It's all right, Thomas. We've got it."

Billy reached for the handle, started to open the door and then suddenly felt as if he were unable to complete the motion. He put his head in his hands, elbows propped on his knees, and tried to control his breathing, contain the complex rush of emotions that washed over him. He felt Walker's hand on his left shoulder.

"Billy? Billy, c'mon. We gotta do this. There's at least seven hundred people out there that do not need to see you fall apart."

Billy did not respond, rocking his head slowly back and forth between his hands. "I can't. This is the second time in eight months. It's as though all we do any more is go to funerals, Walk. I can't do it again."

Leaning slightly forward, Walker put his hand gently on Thomas' shoulder. "Thomas, would you be good enough to step over there and ask the Bishop if he could please give me five minutes. Bishop Smith. Can you do that, Thomas?"

Thomas did not reply but got out of the car with a dignity and seriousness of purpose that characterized the manner in which he had done his job for twenty years.

Walker put his head back against the headrest, removed his sunglasses, rubbing his eyes with his forefinger and thumb in the process, trying to think what he could say that would get them through the moment.

"Billy," he said as calmly as he could, desperately trying to control the emotion he knew was apparent in his voice. "Part of me needs to be your friend right now, and part of me needs to fill some other role that I cannot quite articulate at the moment." He put his glasses back on, adjusting the temple straps behind his ears, trying to summon the right words.

"Very business-like, Walker. The Morgan Bank would be proud…"

"Billy," Walker said with resolve. "In an hour and ten minutes, I'll go back to being Walker, your best friend. We'll go away. We'll get drunk. I'll hold your ticket. I'll hold your head. But right now we have a job to do. And I can't make it go away despite the power of our friendship, my affection…," Walker's voice broke and he reached for the white linen handkerchief in the pocket of his suit jacket. "I stood right by you when we buried your parents, and we got through that."

Walker swallowed and continued. "I've been there through all the years since. I stood right by you when you married Caroline and I stood right by you when we buried her and…"

Walker had to stop.

"And we got through that. And, I will stand right by you today while we get through this. But get through it we must. Whatever we may think about this morning's proceedings, however we may wish today to be other than it is, this is not only a personal experience but also an event – an event at the center of which now stands Billy Commander."

Billy looked first at Walker, then turned to look at the crowd of people gathered in the courtyard of the church. He felt a rising sense of – what was it? Neither control nor resolve. Numbness. Almost as if he weren't present.

Walker took a deep breath and seemed to gather some strength. "I wish I could change that, Billy. But I can't. This is not just somebody who died – this is Molly Commander – whose death, while personal for you and me, has enormous, maybe even national, consequences. Everybody knows you went away after Caroline died. However much we might know it to be otherwise, that creates a perception of doubt about your emotional stability – your ability to make decisions. Many decisions about Molly's estate and your business interests, consequential matters affecting the lives of people other than you, other than us, will now unavoidably fall on your shoulders. And however much you just want to close the door on your life and shut it all out, you can't. At least not today, not right now."

The silence between the two friends was huge and felt to Walker as if it weighed three tons. He noticed Billy's right hand reach for the door handle, and, as he did, Walker opened the door on his side and got out of the car. He watched Bishop Smith, moving rather slowly under the weight of his vestments and symbols of office, begin to make his way over to the car when he saw Billy open his door. Billy got out of the car and stepped across the sidewalk into the churchyard, pausing briefly and glancing back over his left shoulder.

"Walker?"

Out of sight of the assembled crowds in the churchyard Walker put his right hand on Billy's left elbow and said quietly, "Right here."

The Bishop handed his staff to Ridley Clement, the verger of the Diocese, and when he got to Billy enveloped him with both arms.

"William. How we had all hoped this day would never come. How I had prayed that when this day finally came, I would be the one greeting your grandmother on the other side."

"Thank you for coming, sir," Billy responded when the Bishop stepped back from his embrace. "I know your schedule… and with Easter so close, I…"

The Bishop cut him off. "William, your grandmother and I were friends and colleagues for over forty years. I was at Sewanee with your father and baptized you and Walker… and Julia," noticing that Julia Pringle had just walked up. She slipped her hand into Billy's and kissed him on the cheek, holding his arm now with her other hand.

"Molly Commander kept half the mission churches in the Diocese open when there was no money for missions and provided the same money in scholarships when there was."

He paused momentarily to allow his voice to steady and then continued, "The priest celebrates the life of a singular servant of God and sends her home with great joy, but the man struggles with a broken heart. Today is not delegable."

Billy was unable to respond, and the Bishop, sensing the emotion of the moment, again put his arm around Billy's shoulders and, in a way that no one would have ever noticed, began to move the group toward the church door.

The churchyard was filled with blooms of the white camellia bushes that were part of the fame of St. Peter's Winyah. Some of the bushes, it was said, had been planted by eighteenth century rice planters. Like the church they surrounded and the community it served, they had survived hurricanes, pestilence, wars, and economic deprivation and continued to bloom season after season. Four hundred people were already packed inside the church and at least another three hundred outside in the churchyard would listen and follow along with the help of loudspeakers. The names of those in attendance on this sunny March afternoon read like a veritable roster of power, influence, continuity, position and connectivity from South Carolina, Atlanta, New York and Washington. The *Georgetown Times* would later report that so many private jets flew into the Georgetown airport that by mid-morning the ground crews were parking twenty million dollar aircraft in the grass fields surrounding the runways as if they were cars at the Carolina Cup.

The funeral of Martha Bradbury Commander was an unusual event. It represented the odd combination of genuine memoriam and significant opportunity. For many, it was inconceivable that they would not assemble in this way to say good-bye to one of their own. For others, it was an event not to be missed, the details of which would be recounted later to those not present with the clear implication that the speaker also belonged to an elevated part of society, a part of society to which only the few had access. This essential falsehood was part of the complexity of Southern society.

Billy, Walker and Julia followed the Bishop across the churchyard to the portico of the church. Waiting for them there to go into the church as a group was the family party: Julia's mother, Dorothy, and her father, Lowndes Pringle, whose mother Mary Brewton Commander Pringle was Molly's sister-in-law; Walker's grandmother, Mimi Coggeshell, arguably Molly's closest friend since they were at Converse College together in the thirties; Isabelle Barrett Collins, the former United States Ambassador to Argentina and a fellow Continental American director; Gardiner Blackwood, another of Molly's close friends from Converse, completing a group that was known *sotto voce* as the Ashley Hall-Converse mafia because of their pervasive influence in South Carolina and Atlanta corporations, educational and cultural institutions; John Harleston Read; and finally, Thomas Dirleton.

As Billy arrived at the steps of the portico, a slight shift in the small group allowed him to glimpse at the rear of the group, closest to the church, a classic profile creating an unmistakable figure in a fitted, long sleeve black dress and a flat brim black hat. Lucy stood with her father from Greenville, Judge Morall Cogden Magrath, talking quietly with Mimi Coggeshell.

Billy turned to Walker and asked with some surprise, "Lucy? How did you get Lucy here? I just left yesterday."

"Shhhh," Walker lightly admonished him. "She took the afternoon plane from Paris to New York after you left, and Mimi sent her plane last night to get her in New York, and they picked up the Judge on the way down to Georgetown this morning."

Lucy crossed the portico to Billy and kissed him on the cheek, her damp eyes saying more than words could express.

At that moment, Tommy Hasell, the senior usher at St. Peter's appeared, spoke quietly to those closest to the door, and then said to Billy, "Billy, when you're ready," motioning to the open doors of the church with his left hand. Billy took Julia by the hand, and, stopping briefly at the entrance doors to embrace Walker's grandmother while she pinned a small white camellia to his lapel, entered the church followed by the others in the family party.

At precisely twelve noon, the prelude music stopped and the huge, nineteenth century Alston bell began to toll the hour. Twelve mournful, ponderous tones reinforced the quiet dignity of the moment. At the twelfth ring, the Right Reverend William Loudoun Smith, twenty-second Bishop of the Episcopal Diocese of South Carolina, struck the marble floor at the head of the main aisle at St. Peters Winyah, three sharp sounds in succession invoking the Father, Son and Holy Ghost. Then began the traditional words by which generations of the faithful departed in South Carolina had been sent to join the Church Triumphant.

"I am the resurrection and the life, saith the Lord; he that believeth in me, though he were dead, yet shall he live; and whosoever liveth and believeth in me shall never die. I know that my redeemer liveth, and that he shall stand at the latter day upon the earth; and though this body be destroyed, yet shall I see God…"

And with each phrase, the procession of clergy and choir moved forward in regimented steps with a military precision, at once establishing and echoing the cadence of the liturgy, into the aisle of the church. Finally, the casket draped in a white shroud embroidered with gold and, in the only departure from Episcopal and St. Peter's tradition, topped with the white camellias that had been Molly's favorite flower, entered the church.

With the last phrase in the processional liturgy, the powerful Skinner organ struck the first chords of the majestic Haydn tune known in the Episcopal Church as "Austria." Slowly, the procession reached and then surrounded the altar, each participant taking his customary place. A momentary silence fell upon the church, seeming to rest there in the light filtering through the stained glass windows. Billy then heard the deeply sonorous voice of Loudoun Smith intoning, "O God, whose mercies cannot be numbered: Accept our prayers on behalf of thy servant Martha, and grant her an entrance into the land of light and joy, in the fellowship of thy saints…"

And so continued, page after page, the funeral office, following the same order and form by which it had been done in this place since 1737. Then, just as it had begun, it began to end, in reverse. The strains of "Hyfrydol," signifying both the finality and the ascendancy of the moment, filled the church. In orderly recessional, the earthly symbols of an heavenly scepter and throne retired from the church. And it was over. Over.

Billy sat in the pew for a moment, unaware that the entire assembly inside the church was waiting for him to leave. He felt Julia squeeze his left hand slightly and yet he seemed unable to move. Julia realized instantly that something was wrong; the carefully orchestrated proceedings on which the preservation of society's composure depended were threatened. Billy did not move. Julia could sense the rising apprehension in those around her, who also sensed that something was amiss. She reached to her left and grasped Walker's forearm in a way that no one behind them would notice.

Walker instantly realized from Julia's right hand on Billy's arm what was happening and leaned to his left, speaking quietly to his grandmother. Mimi Coggeshell stood up, turning to Julia's mother seated behind her, leaning over slightly, smiling and speaking. Dot Pringle also immediately stood up, and as she did, Morall Magrath rose, offering first Isabelle Collins and then Lucy his hand to stand. Others around them began to rise, and the moment that Billy needed to collect himself was created – created in a way that no one outside the tight circle that surrounded Julia and Walker would have ever known. The moment was bridged; the difficulty passed. Billy stood up and stepped into the aisle, waiting for Julia to precede him and for Walker to come out right behind him, and they began to move out of the church.

"Over," he thought. He remembered the night Molly had come into his room upstairs at Commander House after they had buried Caroline. Molly had told him that it must seem as if his life were over. That it was difficult to see what tomorrow could be like. She told him that she would never attempt to analogize her experiences to his, never attempt to tell him that she knew what he was going through because she didn't; she couldn't. She told him of the ranks of well-meaning but misguided well-wishers who would begin to crowd into his life and how they should be avoided. She told him that from her seventy-five years of experience she knew two principles that could be said to be unassailably true on this night.

"Billy," she said, tears uncharacteristically continuing to fill her eyes, "God will always grant you the strength to meet whatever trials come your way. He does not abandon His children in times of desperation. Living with that hope – no, that belief – as we do, the primary agent of restoration becomes time. You have heard a thousand times that in 'returning and rest, we shall be saved.'"

She had continued with gathering momentum, "I cannot bring Caroline back to you. You know that. But I can carve out the time to let you recover, find yourself and decide how you want to go on with your life when that sense of restoration comes. And that I will do. I want you to go back with Lucy. I've already talked to her and made the arrangements."

She put up her hand to stop him from talking. He remembered he was getting ready to protest. Protest the decision. Protest his lack of participation in a consequential decision affecting his life. But he let the moment pass.

"The bank's plane is taking both of you to Atlanta tomorrow at noon and you'll be able to make the early flight to Paris."

And so he went.

But Molly had missed one important point. Men tend to define themselves differently, he began to realize while at Haras du Bezelay.

"Part of a guy's hard wiring is tied up in career," he had told Lucy late one night over a bottle of local *eau de vie*. Billy had become something of an emotional invalid at Lucy's farm.

"But you are wonderful at prepping the fillies… and…," Lucy had argued, albeit somewhat feebly. "They're going to make boxcars of money at Deauville in August."

"Lucy!" he had said. "I can't even begin to talk about this. My sense of purposelessness is a direct insult to your generosity, your obvious concern for me. But the reality remains that I'm making a horse go around in a circle. Is anyone's life changed by that contribution? Is mine?" He paused, sighing, instantly regretting the judgment he seemed to make about Lucy's life. "I'm sorry… I… I feel as if my whole existence has somehow been invalidated… and I can't seem to find the energy to start over."

Chapter Six

Three days after Molly's funeral, Julia, Lucy, Walker and Billy sat in the morning room at Molly's DeBordieu house. Julia was trying to organize the notes memorializing the outpouring of sympathy and concern extended in the aftermath of Molly's death. And, with limited success, trying to get Walker and Billy – not to mention Lucy – to help. Every delivery of flowers, every expression of sympathy, each dish of food sent to the house would be recorded on four-by-six inch cards, indexed and categorized for response. Some would require only the engraved acknowledgment card from the family, others would require an acknowledgment card with a handwritten note from Julia or her mother, and some – the list Julia was working on at the moment – would require a handwritten note from Billy.

"Lucy, who are Sallie and Arthur Tomlinson? It says she sent a basket of orchids to the house."

Looking up from her own list, Lucy said, "You're asking me? I don't live here anymore."

"This says Chanel sent five dozen white camellias. Why would a store send Molly flowers?" asked Billy. Julia started to answer and then thought better of it.

"Can't we get someone to do this?" Lucy started. "I mean…"

Julia turned to her.

"Lucy, when your mother died, and you and your Aunt May and I sat in Greenville for three days organizing the cards, did you consider getting 'someone' to 'do this' then?"

"Well, actually, Julia, I did… but, of course you were there and we did it by the book. I'm sorry. You're right." And then, standing up, "You know what? We're going out tonight. We've been closed up in here for what seems like a lifetime. Walker call Eddie's and tell them we'll be four for dinner. No wait. John Harleston is comin' back from Atlanta for the weekend. Make it five… and why don't we ask the adorable young Dr. what's-his-name. The one Julia's oh-so-casually mentioned about fifteen times."

"Lucy," Julia said, laughing. "For god's sake. It was the hospital. It's hardly the kind of thing…"

"Here. Walker. Hand me a phone. I'll call him." She dialed 411 as it would never have occurred to Lucy to slow down the process of making dinner plans with a telephone book. After her call went through, she said "You'd think the hospital would be the last place to have one of those if-you-want-this-dial-that-things…," hitting the zero key in exasperation to summon an operator. "Real person is redundant, don't you think? Kind of like live audience … oh yes. Sorry." Lucy's somewhat mindless commentary was interrupted by the obvious response of a real person at the hospital.

"This is Lucy Magrath. I need to speak with Dr. Henning, one of the emergency… this is whom? Oh Shirley, how in the world are you? No, not since… Well, it's too many years indeed. So, can you get young Dr. Henning for me?" Lucy was fidgeting, having absolutely no patience with many of the conventional requirements of daily life. "Walker. Did you call yet? Shh. Dr. Henning. Tommy. This is Lucy Magrath. Billy Commander and some of us are going to dinner tonight, and we were hopeful you might be free to join us. You were so helpful throughout the situation with Mrs. Commander. Julia said she would not have been able to get through that night without you." Lucy paused, listened and then said with a tone of subtle surprise in her voice, "Well, yes. As a matter of fact, she will be there. We're joined at the hip, Julia and I. One never goes anywhere without the other."

Julia looking up from the desk where she was indexing cards, rolled her eyes at Billy and made a gesture to Lucy to cut off her conversation.

"Good. 7:30 then. We'll have drinks at… wait a minute," covering the phone, and now speaking to the group in Molly's morning room, "where do you want to have drinks. Billy?"

Billy shrugged his shoulders and looked up at the ceiling, clearly indicating he had no opinion and scant interest in this latest expedition being organized by Lucy.

"The beach?" Lucy shook her head in mild disgust at the lack of response she was getting and turned back to the phone. "We'll have drinks at Commander House at the beach… Pawleys, that is. You take the first causeway coming from Georgetown, and then turn right when you hit the beach road. Fifth house on the left. Very casual. Okay great. Of course, we as well," and pressing the disconnect key said, "Okay – so there you are. Walker, did you call them?"

"Lucy. Yes. I've answered you three times. Eight-thirty. Six of us. I called John Harleston. What else?"

Chapter Seven

It had been traditional for generations to identify most of the old beach houses at Pawleys Island by name rather than address or ownership. This custom dated from a time when there were no addresses – the designation of a numbered location on a named street was impossible when most of the old houses were built. Similarly, family names were not always helpful. To be told to go to the Weston house would elicit the inevitable response "which one?" So there developed a litany of place names – Summer Hill, the Respite, Tamerlane, Waccamaw Retreat and so on. Tradition notwithstanding, the Commanders had always been unpretentious people, and there being only one Commander family at the beach, their beach house had become known simply as Commander House. To those unfamiliar with the derivation, especially in the newer communities along the Litchfield beaches to the north, the designation always sounded quite grand; but the house had a simplicity and an honesty that belied the imposing sound of its name.

Walker and Billy drove up from DeBordieu in Molly's old Jaguar, dropped Lucy and the car at her father's condominium near the pier, and walked down the beach to Commander House. Molly had rarely come to Commander House since she had built her house on the beach at DeBordieu, preferring the more precisely organized interior of her Philip Trammell Schutze designed house to the ramshackle casualness of Commander House.

The original part of the Commander's beach house had been built in 1890 by Billy's great-great-grandfather. Resting on huge cedar pilings sunk deep into the sand, the house was built solidly of southern heart pine and had resisted damage by a century of hurricanes and nor'easters. Additional bedrooms and bathrooms, an attached kitchen and additions to the porches had been added over the years, all in keeping with the original hand crafted construction, lending the house a comfortable sense of meandering along the dune ridge. Once inside the house, Billy started across the living room back toward the kitchen on the creek side of the house. "I'll see what there is here to drink. Maybe you could open the doors onto the porch, hit the fans and unlatch the screen door at the stairs going down to the driveway?"

Billy gave a low whistle from the kitchen and walked back into the main room as Walker came in from the long screened porch, which wrapped three sides of the old house.

"You can count on Molly to leave us well-provisioned," he said with a bottle of Krug champagne in each hand. "And there's a bottle of Plymouth on the sideboard. Do you think you could call Julia or John Harleston and ask one of them to stop at the corner for a couple of limes and some tonic? Then we're set. I'll wash some glasses – everything looks pretty cloudy. Wonder when someone was over here last?"

Billy crossed the room, took six champagne flutes and some double old-fashioneds out of the pine sideboard in the dining area of the large room, and, placing them on a tarnished silver tray, went back out to the kitchen to rinse the glasses. Walker called Julia, and when he had finished went back to the kitchen to see if he could help. Billy was standing at the sink, motionless, staring out the window at the marsh, with water running over the champagne glass in his left hand, seemingly unaware of what he was doing.

Walker had been wondering when the events of the past six days would begin to hit Billy. He paused for a moment to collect himself. "Billy?"

"It seems wrong somehow. Going out to dinner, I mean. So soon after we buried Molly. I think my mother would be horrified," Billy said, pausing. "I wonder if Molly would?" he continued, more rhetorically than with any actual curiosity.

Walker knew it was inappropriate. His grandmother had already commented on it – and said something about Lucy clearly being behind this plan. Julia, too. But he wouldn't dream of disclosing this information to Billy.

"Gotta eat, bud. Don't think about it. Nobody else will."

Billy was leaning into the sink, very still.

"I've no more family left Walker. You thought about that? My parents, Caroline, now Molly."

"Billy, don't. It won't…"

"Molly's been like this constant force after Mother and Daddy died. After Caroline died. Molly was always there. Kicking ass, fixing things, making it seem somehow like I had a whole family. What now?"

"What now, Billy? Hell, I don't know. We get through tonight. Then I guess we'll get through next week. I think people spend most of their time any more just getting through. Why should we be any different?"

"I've spent the last eight months just getting through, Walker. Thinking next week would be different. Better somehow. That the ache at the pit of my stomach would go away. That I'd wake up one morning and have some sense of where I am headed or even what I'd like to be doing this time next year. I am as sick of the pain as I am the self-indulgence."

Walker walked across the room and took the last champagne glass from his friend's hand. Picking up a tea towel, he began to dry the glass.

Billy would not quit. Turning to face Walker, he continued, "Has anyone asked what Molly was doing driving home alone from Oryzantia at ten thirty at night? I know she seemed invincible to everyone but she was seventy-five for Christ's sake. Has anyone asked that son of a bitch Hugo Lesesne why he let her leave alone after driving her to Oryzantia? Has anyone dared asked the chairman and CEO of the Continental American Bank that question, Walker?"

"Billy – Julius Irving is going to look into all of this. It's been less than a week – give it some time."

They heard a car below the kitchen windows and, looking down, saw John Harleston Read getting out of his car, still talking on his cell phone.

Walker started placing the glasses back on the tray. "Let me finish this. Go open the wine. See what John is drinking." They heard another car in the drive and the screen door open, followed by "Julia!" and then immediately close as John Harleston Read apparently went back down the porch steps to greet Julia.

Billy watched his cousin close the door to her car and press the automatic door lock button on her key, a plastic grocery store bag in her other hand. John Harleston walked casually over to her and throwing his arms around her kissed her on each cheek.

Julia held him for a moment as though she were seriously examining something about him, although it was clear she was kidding.

"Why is it that I cannot seem to find a tall blonde, devastatingly handsome, witty, well-educated, well-traveled, single, polo playing guy who might also have an interest in me?"

"Julia, I swear if I hadn't given up on women, you would be first on my list. Maybe…," flinching and saying "nah" as she playfully pinched his stomach, Julia took him by the arm and walked up the steps onto the porch, unconsciously reaching back with her right foot to stop the door from slamming. Julia's mother and Molly each had a thing about doors slamming. Billy heard Julia calling him from the porch.

"Billy? Look who's here – John Harleston," and turning to Walker handed him the bag containing the items he had earlier called her to bring.

"John-o," Billy said. "It's good to see you, man."

Grinning, John Harleston embraced his friend with affection. "Billy… it was such a madhouse at the church after Molly's service. I had to leave straight from the funeral for New York to see the managing editress of the rag… and then, like an idiot, I realized I've been leaving messages on your French phone. You okay?"

"Well, I dunno," Billy replied, his easy characteristic aplomb beginning to return. "The two musketeers plus Lucy are doing a pretty good job of keeping me moving. How are your mom and dad?"

"They're fine. Everybody's fine. Mother sends her love and says she'll be 'round tomorrow to check on you… after all the obligatory condolence callers have gone she said, although I'm not supposed to repeat that part," John Harleston laughed.

The crunch of oyster shells under the tires of a car in the drive below indicated the arrival of another person. Seconds later the screen door on the porch slammed, causing Billy and Julia to laugh.

"Why is everyone laughing?" Lucy asked as she came into the house. Not waiting for a reply, she continued, "There's a sheriff's deputy down there, parked in a car behind Tamerlane. He was watching me as if I were coming up to steal the spoons."

"Nobody steals spoons any more Lucy. It's all TVs and DVD players. No spoon market at all."

"John Harleston!" Lucy exclaimed, standing on her tiptoes to kiss his cheek. "Where have you been?" overlooking, as she usually did, the central reality that she was the one absent from the normal circles of their society.

"Ah, Lucy," said John Harleston, feigning a tragic tone in his voice, "trying to get over you. Just trying to get over you."

Lucy laughed and said to no one in particular, "Well, that's certainly a lifetime's work. God, let's have a drink. Is Julia's new boyfriend here yet?"

"Lucy." Julia protested.

"Jules has a new boyfriend?" John Harleston asked, "and no one told me? Where did we find him, and does he know what he's in for?"

Lucy went over to the sideboard to pour the champagne, talking as she went through the motions.

"Julia's in love with a doctor. From St. Louis. Yale undergrad. Hopkins for med school. He's doing his residency in ER at the Georgetown Hospital. Maybe he thought the beach sounded simpler than Boston. I don't know. Anyway, his mother's from Raleigh and he used to come to Pawleys in the summers."

"Lucy. How on earth do you know all that?" said Julia.

Handing first Julia, then Billy a glass of champagne, she continued, "Lucy knows everything. John Harleston, do you want wine or would you prefer Walker to try to find you a real drink. Walker, fix him a gin and tonic, why don't you?"

Walker turning, looking at Billy and grinned as if to say, "And we wondered how tonight might go?"

Lucy continued, "I was at Stanford with Susan Henning from St. Louis, so, of course, I rang her up and asked about Dr. Tom. Turns out he's her first cousin. His mother is a Jackson from North Carolina. They had all those textile mills in Tryon… Shelby or someplace. His dad's a surgeon in St. Louis. Anyway…," sipping her champagne, "he was dating a girl from Baltimore pretty heavily, but she apparently broke it off when she found out he had chosen Georgetown over Mass General. So…"

"Actually, I broke it off when I found out she was sleeping with my roommate at Hopkins," they heard a deeply attractive voice say from the screened porch, "but that's a minor detail, I guess. This is Commander House, I hope," not yet noticing Julia, who was the only one of the group Tommy Henning had actually met. Turning to Billy, who was sitting closest to the door, the new arrival said, "Hi – I'm Tom Henning," with a surprisingly bright smile given the circumstances under which he had just entered the room.

"Billy Commander," Billy said quickly, standing up and extending his hand, "and you'll have to excuse my maid," jerking his thumb in Lucy's general direction with a big smile. "She'll be leaving as soon as she gets the drinks poured, isn't that right, Lucy?"

"Oh, good grief… all of you," she extended her hand to Tommy Henning and continued, "I'm so glad you could come. I was at school with…"

"I know. My cousin Susan." Turning again to Billy he said, now seriously, "I'm terribly sorry about your grandmother. I am told she was greatly admired and loved. What a remarkable woman she must have been."

"Thank you. Julia told me how much you did the night Molly di… the night she was brought in." Billy seemed to falter a bit before recovering. "You know, Julia, of course, and let me introduce to you my friends, Walker Coggeshell and John Harleston Read. We were all at school together off and on and spent most of our free time at the beach. Anyway, that's the group, such as we are."

Tommy Henning shook hands with Walker and John Harleston, saying to John, "It's Harleston like Charleston?"

"Without the C… it's nice to meet you," John replied.

"I have a hard time getting used to the Southern custom of binomials. It seems like half the people in South Carolina have two given names."

Lucy interrupted, "Sometimes I think if it weren't for bad manners, we wouldn't have any manners. What on earth can we get you to drink? There's champagne and likely Walker could produce another gin and tonic, if pressed."

"Champagne's great. Is there a celebration?" And then, just as suddenly recovering Tommy said, "Oh man, Bill, I'm really sorry. I just wasn't thinking. Long day and all that."

Walker cut in, "We only drink champagne because Lucy makes us. She lives in France now, went to school over there and is exceptionally cultivated. We poor South Carolina boys would be just as happy with a beer. Lucy also told us not to scratch our ass while you were here," he finished, smoothing over the embarrassing gaff that Tommy Henning felt he had made with Billy in a manner that was one of the hallmarks of his behavior.

Tommy grinned, taking a glass of champagne from Lucy, and then made his way across the room to the sofa where Julia sat. "Julia, how nice to see you again, and particularly under different circumstances."

"Thank you again for… well, for everything you did last week. We were all touched that you were kind enough to come to Molly's funeral." Almost imperceptibly changing the subject, she continued, "I had no idea your mother was from Raleigh. So, you've been to Pawleys, I take it?"

"Occasionally, in the summers, some holidays. My mother's family has a place at Morehead City, and that was usually our beach destination – but her roommate at St. Mary's has a house here – the Carters down on the south end."

"Julia," she heard Walker interrupt. "Time flies, and so must we. We have an eight thirty table and it is Saturday night." Looking around, he went on "we're going to need two cars."

Tommy Henning volunteered, "I'm in back, so let me take my car."

Lucy interjected, "Then take Julia because I'll need to keep a rein on these three. Otherwise they'll end up in some seafood place in Murrells Inlet drinking beer." Moving the group through the doors onto the porch, she said to Walker who was collecting the glasses, "Oh, just leave all that, someone will get it later."

"Typical Lucy," Walker muttered to John Harleston as they went down the steps. "The 'someone' who 'gets these later' will be Billy and me."

Chapter Eight

Dinner went as dinners go. Eddie Hazzard's had become the place to see and be seen. The desirability of coastal areas generally and the specific appeal of Pawleys Island had turned what had once been an unpretentious, summer colony into a white-hot resort destination.

"Twenty-five dollar entrees and wine at eight fifty a glass," Molly sniffed after her first visit. "I give him three months – tops."

For once Molly's business judgment had been wrong and Eddie's, as it quickly became known, flourished. Certainly because of the kitchen and wine cellar, but also because, as Walker had observed to his grandmother, "A man pays two and a half million dollars for a house he doesn't need, he wants to be noticed. He wants the people with him to be noticed."

Billy seemed to grow quiet at dinner, not pensive or reflective, but soulful, in a way almost beyond his control. Lucy was sitting next to him, and she gently put her right hand over his left, curling her fingers around his palm, and said quietly, out of earshot of the others, "What can we do?"

Billy looked up at the ceiling, a habit of his indicating he had heard and was processing his response. Lucy felt him begin to push back from the table, sensing that he was pulling away. She increased the pressure of her hand on Billy's, preventing him from leaving the table.

"Walker – where is Eddie? Do you see him? Or the waiter – that cute blonde boy."

Tommy Henning caught the attention of the young waiter as he was passing. He came over to the table attentively checking the wine glasses, beginning to remove used flatware and dishes with the cool efficiency that characterized Eddie Hazzard's staff.

Addressing the waiter, Lucy said, "Sweetheart. Put all this on my bill," which was greeted by a chorus of protest from everyone at the table, except Billy. She silenced them, raising her left hand. "My bill," she repeated. "Now tell me, what's going on out on the creek tonight."

Eddie's staff was trained to know the names of the restaurant's best customers, as well as to learn the names quickly of those who seemed to have promise, so when he replied he said, "Miss Magrath – it's a band from eastern North Carolina called the Sands of Time. Unremarkable name I'll admit, but I understand they've been pretty big on the fraternity circuit at Chapel Hill and UVA this year…"

"That's fine. Tell Eddie we need a table and something decent to drink back there for a change. Champagne. None of that California wedding stuff, ok?"

"And we'll be out in about twenty minutes." Turning back to the table, she said, "Coffee?" more to take stock of the group than to see if anyone really wanted an espresso after dinner.

Tommy Henning watched with curiosity the scene unfolding around him. He had always been a keen observer of behavior, sensitive to social mores by background, and sensitive to non-verbal behavior because of his medical training. He sensed an element of tension at the dinner table but noticed that it did not become visibly apparent until the waiter walked away.

When the waiter had moved out of earshot, Julia said to Lucy firmly, but in a voice that could not be overheard beyond the immediate group, "You're not serious about going back there, are you?"

"I am, Julia. I'm entirely serious about it. And, we are going…"

Julia replied, "I can't think it would be appropriate, Lucy. It's only been three…"

Walker interrupted, "Lucy. Let's just go back over to the beach…"

But Lucy had already turned to Billy.

"It has been only three days, Julia. You're right. And eight months before that. And twelve years before that."

"Luce, maybe Julia is right. Let's just go back to the beach and we can…," Walker said with greater insistency.

Lucy ignored Walker.

"Billy, my heart broke for you when your parents were killed. And if it could break again, it did when Caroline was killed. And now Molly. You've been in mourning in a way for fourteen years. And tonight it stops. It stops because it has to. I would never presume to channel messages from the deceased to the living. I don't know what Molly would want you to do with the rest of your life. All I know is that when Molly was still alive and did talk to me, she made me promise her that, in time, I would deliver you back to the land of the living. She was terrified – not that Caroline's death would cause you to do something rash like take your own life, but that it would result in something worse – your gradual retreat from living until some sort of mournful dysfunction consumed you. I promised I wouldn't let it happen."

Lucy spoke in a rapid staccato that allowed no room for interruption and little room for debate.

"I'm not as quietly polite as the rest of you. I'm from Greenville, for god's sake, but I have never broken a promise in my life. And I will not break the one I made Molly. So it's over. Tonight. We're going dancing. And besides," turning to look directly at Julia, "nobody here would dream of commenting on anything we do. Certainly not in a way that we would ever know about it. They never have. It won't start tonight."

She put her hands down on the table and began to stand up. At that moment Eddie Hazzard walked up to the table with a baleful look on his face, knowing that the tables out back where the bands played were all full. Lucy Magrath did not like to be told that her wishes could not be accommodated and he knew it.

"Lucy, there's kind of a problem with a table out back. Everything is full. We've got…"

"Full, Eddie? Well, we certainly don't intend to go out there and stand up."

"Lucy, you don't understand. We've got Miss America here tonight. Some photo shoot in Georgetown and the paper made arrangements for her. She came with fifteen people in tow – hairdresser, makeup people, camera guys, agents, you know – and took three tables. That on top of everything else…"

Lucy cut him off again.

"Miss America? Miss America?" she said pausing, with mock reflectiveness. "I see."

Julia unconsciously held her breath, knowing what was coming. Walker excused himself for the men's room and Billy just looked across the table at Eddie Hazzard, with a half-smile on his face and shook his head, sympathizing with the misstep he had just made.

Lucy stood up and gave Eddie a brilliant smile. "How's business, Ed?" Eddie Hazzard nodded positively and she continued. "Good? That's great... What's it been now? Four years?"

"Five this June, Lucy," Eddie replied the pride obvious in his voice, but still not realizing what was coming.

"That's right. I remember. We were here the night you opened: my dad, Molly Commander, Walker's grandmother, Julia and her mom and dad, John and his parents – all of us. And we've been here all the time since. You've been sending all of us bills most every month, haven't you, Eddie? A bill that gets paid before the ink is even dry with no deduction for credit cards and generous allowances for your boys."

"Lucy, of course, and I appreciate your business but..."

Lucy ignored his comment. "So you might say, might you not, that I've been your Miss America twelve months a year for the past five years." She stopped to allow her comment to sink in.

Billy looked at Eddie and noticed that, wisely, he was giving up.

"Okay, okay." Eddie seemed to recover his normally robust sense of humor. "I don't know what I was thinking. I need fifteen minutes, Lucy, Bill, if that's okay?"

Lucy smiled at Eddie and gave him a playful pat on his cheek, turned back to the table and sat down. "Well. There you are," she said.

Walker rejoined the small group, asking, "So what's going on?"

"Oh, not a lot," said John Harleston. "Let's see if I can recap it for you. We had a brief discussion about Billy's mourning period. Some touching reminiscence about Molly. Found out Miss America is out back but then it appears she just got her ass moved out of her table after Lucy gave Eddie a quick lesson in the facts of economic life at the beach. It looked for a moment like Julia was going to bolt. And, I'm guessing Dr. Henning is wondering why he was standing on the tracks when this freight train came by." Looking around, "I think that pretty much covers it."

"And the buzz saw strikes again," Walker muttered under his breath to no one in particular reaching for his wine glass as he sat down.

"You, I don't need," Lucy retorted with a glance in Walker's direction and then turning back to the rest of the table, "Billy?"

Billy looked at Lucy and then at his friends and shrugged his shoulders. A moment later a glimmer of amusement seemed to drift across his face, and he said with a brighter tone in his voice, "Let's go." And, partially mocking Lucy's American-accented French, "*Nous danserons*."

Tommy Henning noticed that no one seemed to wait or even expect the check and he caught himself two seconds before he said something, realizing that there must be some protocol at work here of which he was unaware. He held Lucy's chair as she got up and began to speak to a table full of people directly behind them. John Harleston gestured with his right hand to Tommy as if to show the way out of the restaurant.

"I'm sorry about the freight train comment," he began, verbally stumbling a bit, "there's some complicated history going on here, and I… well, let's head out back, shall we?"

Julia walked along with Billy behind Lucy, who had taken Tommy Henning by the arm as they walked across the parking lot.

"I saw Julius Irving on the way back from the ladies room. He asked, assuming you felt up to it, if maybe we could drop by his office tomorrow or the day after. It's really you he wants to talk with but he was polite enough to make it sound like I should be included. But I really…"

Billy interrupted, "Sure, let's maybe go Monday morning."

"Well, you really don't need…," Julia was going to say "me to go" when Billy said,

"Jules… Monday morning, both of us. I'd like to go check on my boat tomorrow."

"Okay… I'll call his office tomorrow and let him know."

Chapter Nine

As Billy and Walker got closer to the open air pavilion out back, they could hear the last measures of a classic beach music tune coming through the windows. Walker playfully took Julia by the hand and began walking and moving to the beat of the music imitating steps to the shag. Laughing, Julia, pushed him away just as they got to the door. Julia and Walker spoke to Ben Hazzard, Eddie's younger brother, who was working the door, as they went in followed by John Harleston Read and Lucy and Tommy Henning. Billy went in last and shook hands with Ben.

"Bill! 'Sup, man. They close Europe? You and Lucy both here." Ben said, laughing at his own joke, and then immediately realizing the circumstances of Billy's presence at the beach said hurriedly, "Billy, I am so sorry, man, I just completely forgot about your grandmother. God, what an ass… I…"

"It's okay. Forget it."

"Billy, I…"

"It's okay Ben. Forget it."

Billy felt Lucy grab his left hand and begin to guide him out to the dance floor, such as it was, there being no real demarcation between dance area and the rest of the room, as the strains of the eighties hit "Lady Soul" began to fill the room.

Walker, John Harleston and Tommy found the table Eddie Hazard had arranged for Lucy. It turned out that Miss America and her party had not been evicted but rather relocated so that Lucy's table was in front of the space used as a bandstand. Julia had stopped on her way across the room to speak to several friends. Tilting her head back slightly and laughing as Tommy Henning came toward her with a glass of champagne in his hand, she said, "Good grief, I think I need this. You don't think we stick out do you? Champagne in a beach joint. That's Lucy for you. Lucy can be something of a loose cannon when she gets rolling. It must seem to you as if you stumbled into a play at intermission."

Tommy smiled. "And without a Playbill? I don't know, Julia – I think Lucy knows exactly what she's doing," watching her with Billy on the dance floor. "Look, if you were ill, you'd take something, right? Medicine, a pill, a tonic? Look around. It pulls you back."

"What does?" Julia did not immediately understand.

"This place. Beach music. Undeniably one of the ultimate restorative tonics."

She turned to look at him, as he leaned against one of the wooden posts supporting the pavilion roof.

"Most outsiders see all this as part of the architecture of," he gestured at the environment around them, "these citadels of American prep – like pink shirts, seersucker, white bucks. But to us," winking at her, "this is more like the emotional tangibility of simpler times. Ocean breezes. The decadent smell of the marsh. A full moon rising over the beach." Turning slightly and putting his back to the post so he could survey the room, he looked directly at Julia, "First date, first kiss, first love." Tommy's left hand was unconsciously keeping time with the music against his thigh. "Listen," he said, singing along softly, "I always knew we'd end up together, right from the very start. I believe we'll make it forever, it's written right here in my heart… It pulls you back – I think she knows exactly what she's doing."

Looking back at the dance floor, he finished, "And so does he."

Julia was quiet for a moment and then said with amusement, "Dr. Henning – a sentimentalist. No, not even… a poet, in the white jacket and stethoscope of medical science? Isn't that against the rules?"

Tommy Henning smiled at her, deflecting the compliment. Placing his glass on a ledge surrounding the old post on which he had been leaning, and placing hers next to it, he extended his right hand, laughing. Dance?"

Chapter Ten

Walker looked up from the *New York Times* as Billy walked into the living room at Commander House, wearing only his boxers, pulling on the shirt he had worn to dinner the previous night. Pointing toward the kitchen, Walker said, "Coffee on the counter."

Billy padded down the narrow hallway out to the kitchen with bare feet, the sound of the creaking old floor boards resonating through the morning stillness, and a few minutes later returned with a mug of black coffee.

"Thanks," he said with a big grin, followed by a yawn. Stretching, he rubbed his eyes and then his chest. "What time is it? I put my watch down somewhere."

"9:30." Walter chuckled. "Lucy said to let you sleep."

"Lucy. Where is she?" Billy asked looking around the living room and then the porch visible through the living room windows.

"Gone."

"Gone?"

"Gone," Walker repeated.

"She's gone? But…"

"Billy," Walker said with mock seriousness, "what part of the 'gone' concept is eluding you this morning? I was up early and went out on the beach, and when I wandered back in, Lucy was coming out of the downstairs bedroom. I went up to grab a shirt, and, to my surprise, noticed no one in Billy's room and Billy's bed appeared to have been… well, vacant, shall we say? And now, here you come, wandering out of the same bedroom in which Lucy quite obviously spent the night, wondering where she is?" Walker finished, laughing again. "Lucy is on the way to Greenville with the Judge. Her dad's driver is taking her to Atlanta this afternoon to catch the late Paris flight and thence *a la Normandie*. You want to talk about it?"

Billy had walked over to the open doors onto the large screened porch facing the ocean. Staring at the Atlantic, visible over the sand dunes and sea oats, he said rather quietly, "Nah. Not right now."

Walker watched his friend. "Billy, what's this? Lucy has a history of running… she's left a string of broken hearts and frustrated guys from Palo Alto to Park Avenue." Walker decided not to push it. "Okay. Never mind. So, do we have plans? I've checked with the office, and it looks like they can keep things running for at least another day without me."

"Why don't we go over to Wampee and get *Convergent* back in the water? Check her out, maybe go down to River House and spend the night. Eat some oysters at Belin Landing maybe. No crowds. How would that be?"

"Sounds good. But I have to come back before supper. I promised Mimi I would take her to Fleming Bradshaw's for drinks tonight and dinner at the club. She'd be pissed if I ditched her – even for you, Billy Boy."

An hour later they drove into the Wampee Marina and Boatyard, as Billy's boat was being moved slowly to the river in a large canvas sling suspended from the rolling steel crane. The thirty-two foot Moreland racing cruiser had been a present from Molly when Billy graduated from the University of Virginia.

She was a fast boat, technologically modern, racing to a low handicap, and yet retaining some of the elegant lines associated with older racing yachts from the '20s and '30s. When the boat was delivered to Georgetown, Molly had instructed the boatyard to remove the old name of the boat and repaint the hull to allow Billy to name his boat as he chose. Billy, not normally enthusiastic about material things, had fallen instantly in love with the boat.

That summer, Walker had been going to New York for a Citibank internship and Billy had been headed to Europe with John Harleston and Lucy. As they sat in the fading sun outside Billy's room on the Lawn in Charlottesville during graduation weekend, Walker had observed, "I guess this is where our paths begin to diverge." A week later, when Billy saw the Moreland 32 for the first time, she became the *Convergent.*

Billy watched as the operator carefully swung the boat around and began to lower her into the river with the bow pointed upriver. Buddy Cleveland, the dock master at Wampee, walked up to the boys. "Billy, we've serviced the engine. There was a small leak on the water pump, so we changed the seals, which seemed to cure it. Both battery banks are charged. All the tanks are full. I checked the bilge and the pump system and everything is okay there. She's rigged with the cruising sails and carrying the racing sails and spinnakers below on the v-berth. What else?" He paused, glancing at his work order. "I think that's it. You should be ready to go."

"Thanks, Buddy," Billy said, as he turned to find Walker.

"You boys need ice, drinks, anything else?"

"Nah – we'll be okay. I'm just going to run down to Oyster Island this afternoon. Maybe spend the night at River House."

"If you tie up at Asylum, you might want to set an extra spring line or two. Looks like we could have some wind and rain tonight."

Walker walked up, "All set?"

Billy nodded and said, "You'll drop the car at the ferry dock? I'll pick you up and then we'll head downriver."

Twenty minutes later Billy pulled up to the Georgetown County dock used by the small river ferry that provided the only public connection between the mainland and Oyster Island. Walker was standing at the very end of the wooden dock. Billy brought the bow of the boat close enough to the dock for Walker to step quickly over the port lifeline and onto the deck as he pointed the boat back out into the river in one smooth movement. The remaining run downriver to the Commander's Asylum Plantation was calm. Walker was quiet for the trip down, remaining forward of the cockpit as he made adjustments to the sails and rigging.

"Everything okay?" Billy asked.

The strengthening breeze seemed to carry his words away as he heard no response from Walker. They weren't flying a spinnaker, and it made Billy wonder. Walker's conversation remained mostly perfunctory, until he left on foot to catch the six o'clock ferry run from the county dock on the west side of the river.

"You're leaving?" Billy had mildly protested.

"I told you. Mimi. Fleming Bradshaw. Drinks… any of this ringin' a bell?"

They'd had to break in. Well, not really. The back door into the kitchen had been jammed somehow, and the front porch doors had been latched from the inside. Walker had managed to pop one of the screen door latches with a credit card and then jimmy the bolt open on the double glass doors into the living room.

Billy sat on the screened porch of the house overlooking the Waccamaw River. They had always called this place simply River House. Billy's great grandfather had restored the structure in the forties, although the restoration hardly approached the level of what would be called historic preservation. Cleaned it up and made the plumbing and lights work would have been a more accurate description. His grandfather Commander had used it infrequently for fish fries and sometimes for weekend shooting parties. Its location was remote, reachable only by the Oyster Island ferry from the mainland or by private boat. Molly hated it. She had not liked boats and didn't care much for the river. The rustic character of the house, despite its beautiful setting, had not appealed to her.

"I don't care how beautiful it is at sunset," she was fond of saying to her friends that lived overlooking the river. "How can you possibly favor a place infested by snakes, alligators and mosquitoes?"

She loved to remind the extreme environmentalists that the rice planters themselves found conditions along the river so untenable that they left for the beach or the mountains in late April, not returning until after the first frost in October. Still, in typical Molly fashion, the house was looked after. She had a woman – Ella Wingfield, who lived in the tiny village of Ruinville on Oyster Island – go in periodically to clean, make sure the beds were made and fresh towels were in order. Ella's husband Mack, who had worked for Billy's grandfather, continued to perform regular maintenance and simple repairs on the aging house.

The book Billy had been reading – or rather looking at – lay open on his lap, a half-finished glass of scotch on the table next to his chair. Looking at the glass, he thought, "I never drink scotch. That was Molly's drink… and my dad's." Molly thought most wine was a silly affectation. Part of her essential incongruity he thought. She liked champagne though. Good champagne, not the stuff she used to call wedding champagne.

"Never know when your spirits will need a lift," she used to say, laughing as she parceled the bottles out among her several houses.

"Christ," Billy thought. "I'm losing my mind." Reaching for his mobile phone to call Walker or Julia, he realized that his phone was in France and that it was a European phone anyway.

He tossed the rest of his scotch dispiritedly through the screen into the hydrangeas and oleanders surrounding the porch. He stood up and wandered back into the house.

"Bed. I'll go to bed," he thought, heading down the hall toward the rear of the house to the bedrooms. Entering the room where he had stayed infrequently, he threw his clothes onto a chair by the door and pulled back the covers on the bed, collapsing in his boxers into the down pillows. Had he not fallen asleep so quickly, he might have been surprised at how easily sleep came.

Billy woke up suddenly, sitting up in the middle of the bed. He heard a loud crack that seemed to come from the kitchen and, putting his head back down on the pillows, he thought it must be the wind causing the fronds of the Palmetto trees that surrounded the back porch to strike the windows on that side of the house. Still half asleep, he lay in bed looking at the ceiling and saw in his peripheral vision light coming from the kitchen. He rolled back over, too tired to think about getting up and turning off the lights he had carelessly left on somewhere in the house.

But the smell. It was the smell he then noticed. The scent of… what was it… something burning. Wood, maybe.

"Good god," he thought, immediately fully awake.

He half-ran, half-stumbled into the main room of the house and saw the flames in the kitchen. Already creeping up the walls from the area around the back door, the flames began to gather intensity and momentum. The sight of fire had still not completely registered in Billy's mind. He instinctively began to look for a phone and then remembered there had never been a phone at River House. "No cell phone. Goddamit."

"The radio!" There were two hand-held VHF radios on board the boat, tied up at the small dock in front of the house. He had to get to the boat. Smoke had begun to fill the house, choking off the oxygen supply and making it harder and harder to breathe. Billy dropped to the floor and crawled on his hands and knees to the front doors opening out onto the porch. Reaching up, he grasped the doorknob, turning it and pulling the door to him. It wouldn't open. A growing sense of panic began to overtake his efforts to get out of the house.

"Was there a deadbolt?" he thought, now standing, unable to breathe, groping for a thumb latch that would indicate a dead bolt.

There was not one. He pulled on the door handle with both hands, throwing all the strength of his back and shoulders into the effort. The door would still not budge. The fire had burned through the walls separating the kitchen and living room, and was steadily engulfing the house. The heat felt as if it were searing his lungs, and the smoke made it impossible to see. Dropping back to the floor and trying to breathe at the crack between the floor and the door, he thought, stricken by panic, "The window. Raise the window." Crawling to the tall window to the left of the door and holding his breath, he raised himself off the floor high enough to release the old-fashioned pivoting latches, which he knew from childhood secured the windows. With his free hand he pulled up on the bottom sash of the triple hung window, but it wouldn't move. Redoubling his efforts, he tried again. The window would not budge.

The heat had now become unbearable, and he could not breathe. He felt consciousness begin to ebb away and thought, "I'm going to die. This can't be happening to me." As he fell back to the floor, his head hit the arm of a wooden chair sitting near the window. "The chair. Throw the chair through the window. No screens. It's the porch. Throw the chair."

He picked up the chair by the legs and swung it as hard as he could directly at the panes of the old window, shattering the glass as the chair crashed through the window. Billy fell through the window after the chair, hitting the porch with his right shoulder and rolling to the porch doors. He could see *Convergent* in the distance, bobbing up and down in the current of the Waccamaw at the dock one hundred yards away. "The radio. Get the radio."

He ran, falling over a bed of azaleas. He picked himself up only to fall again, rolling, then scrambling on all fours down the slope to the dock. He got to the boat, tripping over the lifeline and landing in the cockpit. Feeling his way in the darkness to the companionway, he realized that he had closed and locked the hatch. "The key. Where was the key to the lock?" Reaching into the sail pouch below the starboard cabin winch, he felt the hand-held VHF radio he had used the previous day while bringing the boat down from Wampee.

Keying the radio and switching from memory to the emergency Coast Guard channel, the last thing he remembered saying as he looked back toward the flames now engulfing River House was, "Mayday. Mayday. This is the Moreland 32 *Convergent* at Asylum Plantation on Oyster Island. Mayday…"

Chapter Eleven

Beaufort Estes walked around the smoking remains of the river cabin at Asylum.

"Godamighty, how much can one family take?" he muttered to himself.

The Coast Guard EMS squad was treating Billy Commander down at the dock. They had found him unconscious in the cockpit of the sailboat. Fearing the worst, the EMS tech had found a pulse and had immediately begun to administer oxygen. They now had Billy propped up against the cushions in the cockpit bandaging the cuts he had sustained getting out of the house.

Beaufort walked around the house, which had burned almost to the stone foundations. The rain that had begun minutes after Billy escaped the house had prevented the house from burning completely to the ground. From the broken glass and remains of the window, it appeared that Billy had thrown a chair through a window and escaped the fire. Why had he not used a door? These old houses were never very secure and the doors could not have, on their own, kept a big boy like Billy inside, if he had thrown his entire weight against the frame. Beaufort kicked the remains of the front door again with the toe of his boot.

"Old houses by the water. The wood swells. Doors and windows never work. Won't close and the bugs can get through. Get 'em closed and then you can't get 'em open again."

The toe of his boot had dislodged the charred embers and ashes that had collected in the corner of what had been the door frame, revealing the momentary gleam of a metallic object reflected in the beam of his flashlight. Pale silver not yet encrusted with rust from exposure to the humidity. He bent down and attempted to brush the debris aside, momentarily forgetting about the heat. "Sh…," he began, jerking his hand back and wiping it on his trouser leg. He picked up one of the broken legs of the chair Billy had thrown through the window and used it to clear away the rubble, revealing the head of a steel decking screw protruding from what must have been the very bottom of the door. Squatting down to get a closer look, he realized it was a new screw with no traces of exposure to the weather. He noticed another in the adjacent window frame, shattered by the chair.

"Odd," he thought. "Why would there be decking screws…" At that moment one of his deputies walked up and announced that they were getting ready to take Billy to the hospital. Beaufort walked across the lawn to the dock at the river, where now were moored not only Billy's boat but also a Coast Guard vessel and the Sheriff's Department river cruiser in which he had arrived.

Addressing the EMS technician, he said, "How is he, Sandy?"

Billy looked up from the seat on the cockpit as the paramedic said, "Smoke inhalation consistent with the incident, some superficial lacerations to the left shoulder, left parietal area, and dorsum of the left hand, some first degree burns on his right leg and hip. Sorry, Sheriff," catching himself, "he'll need some sutures when we get him to Georgetown but all in all looks like he'll live," grinning down at Billy. Placing his hand on Billy's shoulder, he continued, "although this is one lucky boy."

Billy said, "Thanks, Beaufort. Sorry for all the trouble in the middle of the night."

"Don't even think about it, Billy. Two questions though. Have y'all been doing any renovation work out here, shoring up the foundations, structural stuff?"

"None of us came over here much. I've been out of the country for eight months… my grandmother didn't care for this place, probably hadn't been over here in ten years. Other than keeping the place clean, I can't imagine she would have been doing anything over here."

"One more thing then, do you remember if you shut the propane off at the tank or just turned off the grill, when you used it last night?"

"Grill? What grill?"

"What looks like the remains of a grill is next to the house, out by the kitchen, although I'm not an expert at this kind of analysis. Probably nothing. Forget about it. Sandy, you boys get Mr. Commander downriver to the hospital," and with his right foot he edged the bow of the cruiser out into the Waccamaw, as a seaman gathered the last dock line and jumped onto the stern of the boat.

Chapter Twelve

Three days later, shortly after lunch, Thomas Dirleton came into Billy's room upstairs at Molly's house on the beach at DeBordieu. "Mr. Read's downstairs, Mr. Commander. Miss Julia wants to know if you need her to come back over? And, Dr. Henning called to check on you."

Billy looked up, grinning, "It's Billy, Thomas. Just Billy." He threw his hands up in a gesture of mock disgust. "I've just got bits and pieces here," throwing a pair of boxers into the top of the open canvas duffle on his bed. "This will have to do. I should only be gone a couple of days."

"Is there anything else you need, sir?"

Changing the subject, Billy continued, "Look Thomas – I want everything to go right on – just as before Molly died. I don't know what I am going to do but for right now can we have that arrangement?"

Nodding his assent, Thomas waited for him to finish. "The bank pays your salary, right? And what about the bills? How did you and my grandmother handle that?"

"Well… all the regular bills get paid by the bank in New York, I think. Some things came here and Mrs. Commander would initial them and then I would send them on to Mr. Coggeshell. I have a credit card I use for household expenses. I would give the receipts to Mrs. Commander. We kept about a thousand dollars in a box down in the kitchen – for incidental cash expenses."

"Okay. I'll call Julia and ask her to help get these details worked out. I don't want Molly's Mercedes repaired and brought back. Get some kind of station wagon that you and Julia think will be suitable. She'll know how to handle getting all this paid, I guess."

"Mr. Commander, I'll be glad to drive you to the airport."

"Nah. Thanks. I'll go with John Harleston. It's on his way back to Atlanta anyway. No problem."

"Mr. Commander." Billy sensed something else was bothering the old gentleman. "I'm sorry about Mrs. Commander. I heard her tell Mr. Lesesne when he called that I would drive her to Oryzantia just like always and she would just meet him there. But I guess he said he would drive because I heard Mrs. Commander say, 'Very well, Hugo, we'll talk about it on the way over then.'"

"Thomas, don't worry – it's not… where was Mr. Lesesne's car?"

"He didn't have his car. When I answered the door, he said that he had walked down from his villa so he could drive Mrs. Commander."

Billy thought about that for a minute. "It's okay. Don't give it another thought." Clapping him on the shoulder as he started toward the door, he said, "I'll see you in a few days" and then turning around, "Was Mr. Lesesne alone when he arrived?"

"Yes, sir. Mrs. Lesesne wasn't… uh… nobody was with him."

"Okay. Let's not keep John waiting." Billy zipped his bag closed and, stepping aside in the hall to allow Thomas to pass, followed him down the stairs into the glass loggia that joined the kitchen and morning room with the rest of the house, where he found John Harleston Read reading the morning's *New York Times.*

"Let me get him out of here, Thomas. Give you a few days respite." John Harleston quipped good-naturedly. I'm on the way to Atlanta and Walker says you boys are headed to New York."

Billy slipped a lightweight tweed jacket over the polo and grey flannels he was wearing. Picking up an unlined topcoat from a chair in the loggia and nodding to Thomas, he said to John Harleston, "I guess we're ready."

In the courtyard in front of Molly's house, he tossed his things into the rear compartment of John Harleston's Volvo wagon and got in the front passenger seat. They rode in silence for a while until Billy said, "John, I feel rather irresponsible, but do you suppose you could look in on our…," Billy stopped with a catch in his throat, "… uh, my apartment when you get back. I left things sort of in a… I'm not sure I can…"

John Harleston began, "Are you kidding me?" and then abruptly caught himself. "It's okay, Bill," he said in a calmer tone. "I've already looked after things. When Molly came over to talk to Bunky Sanderson."

Billy glanced at John Harleston with some surprise. "Molly went to Atlanta to see Bunky," thinking of the senior partner at Howell, Raines and Sanderson.

"You didn't know?"

"Bunky called me at Lucy's and said they wanted me to take as long as I needed after Caroline died. My client files had been temporarily reassigned… I need to call him. It's just that I am no longer sure I want to go back to that whole Buckhead lawyer thing you know. How did you know Molly talked to…"

"She was in my office, Billy."

"In your office?"

"Molly came over on the bank's plane the week after you left with Lucy. She asked me to do whatever was needed to look after your house, see about the car, stuff like that. She called Bunky from my office. She said she didn't want to go to your apartment or the bank, and for some reason she did not want to see him face to face."

Confront him was more like it. John Harleston's mind went back to the morning the receptionist paged him in the editorial meeting for the upcoming issue of *American Interiors* to say that a Mrs. Commander was in the lobby to see him. Excusing himself immediately from the meeting, he rushed to the reception area to find Molly, thumbing through the galley proofs of an article from the next issue of the magazine.

"Molly! What an entirely pleasant surprise."

"All I can say, John Harleston Read, is that if you and that managing editress of yours in New York don't have anything better to put in your magazine than Fanny Burwell's house in France, you may be headed for oblivion. Authentic Provençal my… well, never mind. Her house has Atlanta decorator written all over it."

John Harleston laughed good-naturedly and, attempting to deflect Molly's attention from the magazine article, remarked, "I didn't realize you knew Diana Brennan."

"John, my dear. I need to use your phone and then you can take me to lunch. Somewhere nice, mind you. Not one of those dreadful

Buckhead places where the waiters introduce themselves as if they are going to become your newest friend. Now, let's go back to your office, shall we?"

Molly Commander had walked around behind his desk and placed the call herself to Bunky Sanderson at the law firm.

"Bunky. This is Molly Commander. Yes. Thank you. It's a very difficult time as you might imagine. You and Lydia were so dear to come all the way to Georgetown for Caroline's funeral."

Molly paused, and John Harleston sat down in one of the leather guest chairs in front of his desk and began proofing article copy for the upcoming issue, thinking what a dysfunctional monologue was created in overhearing only one-half of a conversation and how one's mind inevitably tried to fill in the missing part of the dialogue.

"Well, that's why I am calling," he heard Molly continue. "I need a small favor. I think Billy needs some time. I've sent him, somewhat against his wishes I might add, to Lucy Magrath's in France. They left a couple of days ago. I would really appreciate it if you could arrange some sort of leave of absence, sabbatical, call it what you will… or I suppose what you need to… say, six months or so."

John heard Bunky's voice suddenly fill his office, and he thought at first Molly had pressed the speaker phone button inadvertently. He arose from his chair to see if he could help and realized by her posture – one hand planted firmly on the surface of his desk and the other quietly replacing the receiver in the cradle on the phone set – that her action had been deliberate. He initially wondered why she had wanted him to hear the conversation and then realized that she wanted a witness to what she was saying.

"Molly, it's a difficult time for us to consider such an action. The firm is growing rapidly. We have added six new associates this year alone just to keep up. I don't know how I can justify such special treatment under any circumstances…"

"Umm… I see." Molly followed along with his remarks. "Busy." She paused. "Bunky, I have never called upon you for any sort of consideration, despite the special relationship that exists between Howell, Raines and me. Ordinarily I wouldn't. But this is not an ordinary situation and I am asking you to do this for me… personally.

And you have my assurance that I will also personally absorb any additional expense you might determine to be appropriate because of this arrangement."

"Molly, I fully appreciate your concern for Billy and understand what you are trying to do. Believe me I do. But firm policy is to permit a leave of absence in a situation like this of one week. You must understand – I have a business to run."

"I see." John Harleston remembered her saying as she smoothed her skirt and walked around the desk.

"Correct me if I am wrong, Bunky, but has not a large part of the growth Howell Raines has experienced recently come from the bank's business?" Silence ensued. "Is that not correct, Bunky?" she repeated. She waited for his response and not receiving it immediately, pressed on. "Do this for me, Bunky. I would prefer not to be forced to ask again."

"Molly, I have to say this is very close to an inappropriate exercise of your position at the bank. I don't want to have to talk to Hugo about this. Let's just…"

John Harleston had known Molly Commander since he was a child. She was like a second grandmother to them all. But he had never seen the Molly Commander that turned to face the speaker phone on the desk – or heard the tone in her voice that began to emanate from the conversation.

"Hugo? You want to talk to Hugo? Go ahead, Bunky. I dare you. In the meantime, while one of your two assistants, whom I am told are paid twenty per cent more than market wages for Atlanta firms of your size and with one of whom I am told your association is far more than professional, and whose charges are undoubtedly passed along somehow to the bank, to my own account and to the accounts of the other ten clients I have brought your way in the past three years – while one of them is trying to track Hugo down in Europe where he is traveling this week, you will have time to draft the memo announcing that Billy Commander, with the full support of the partnership, is taking a six-month leave of absence. And, you are temporarily re-assigning his client files, the most sensitive of which you and Crawford Raines will be pleased to assume personal responsibility for. I would prefer that you leave his office and his assistant just as they are. Any cost associated with our new program that you feel is in any way unwarranted in view of the client relationships you have with my business and my friends, you send the bill to me and I'll see that it's paid. Are we clear?"

"Molly, I…"

"You are going to do this because, if you don't, I will move one hundred per cent of the bank's business to O'Connor, Petersen before tomorrow afternoon. Are we clear?"

"Molly you can't…," Bunky Sanderson began.

"Can't? Try me. Just try me, Bunky." There was a hard demanding edge to her voice. "I don't often have conversations of this kind, and rarely find the need to stand on my position. But you just try me, if you want a lesson in law practice economics. You write Billy at Lucy's farm in Normandy. Some of your people are bound to be clever enough to find the address. You just completed the estate plan for her father and you sent Lucy copies of the correspondence. I know because I sent the Judge to you and he showed me copies of all the work you did. And you send me a copy of the letter. And Hugo Lesesne. And send Lucy two dozen – no, make that three dozen white Calais roses. They're her favorite, and tomorrow is her birthday."

And with that she hung up.

Chapter Thirteen

"John?" Billy's voice intruded upon his reflection. John Harleston looked across the small parking lot at the Georgetown Airport and saw Walker standing in the doorway of the Citation jet parked in front of the FBO terminal, talking to a uniformed cabin attendant. Looking up from his instructions, he waved to his two friends still sitting in the station wagon, curious after a moment when he received no response.

"We're here." John Harleston put his right hand on Billy's left knee. "You gonna' be okay?"

Billy sank back in the seat momentarily, removed his Ray Bans, and rubbing his eyes said, "Yeah. I guess. Who knows?"

The stillness and quiet between them was heavy for a moment.

"Billy… I… I know this is not the time," John seemed to hesitate.

Billy knew instinctively where the conversation was headed. It had to come up eventually. The night three years ago was still embedded in his mind, although they had never discussed it since. John Harleston had told him, to use John's words, that he didn't see "girls in his future." They had been at Harrison's on Peachtree for drinks after work and gone on to Fishtail's for dinner. John Harleston had followed Billy back to his Habersham Road condominium to pick up two books and a sweater he had left there the week before. Billy was checking his messages while John Harleston seemed to be rooting around the kitchen for something. He walked back into the living room, a glass of wine in each hand. "I have something to tell you." And the whole story had come pouring out. "Struggled with it. Always some attraction to guys. Tired of the marginal dishonesty." Billy listened calmly and remembered desperately trying to construct the appropriate response. "I know what you're telling me seems huge. I'm not sure what you think happens next. I'm not sure what you need to hear from me right now. I won't be so blithe as to say 'so what', but…" He paused to let John Harleston respond, but instead he stood up abruptly and started back toward the kitchen.

John finished the bottle of wine and, in an excess of caution, Billy had sent him to bed in one of the guest rooms. Billy couldn't sleep, and in the middle of the night, he rolled over in his bed and saw John standing in the door to his bedroom. Without saying a word, he had climbed up into Billy's four-poster bed and rolled over on his right side. Billy placed his hand on his friend's shoulder for a moment. "It's going to be all right," he had said, not knowing if his statement was a lie or had some ring of truth. "It'll be fine."

John was gone the next morning when Billy got up, and that night had never come up between them again. Eleven months later, Billy Commander married Caroline Coachman in a relatively small ceremony at St. Peter's Winyah given the significance of the nuptials – and John Harleston Read had been a groomsman.

"John Harleston, it was three years ago," Billy began. "It was a moment." Silence again hung rather heavily in the air. "I gotta go, man." Smiling now, he attempted to sound light hearted, "It's a big taxi to keep waiting. Come up this weekend?"

Opening his door, John said, "I have a meeting in Miami tomorrow, but I need to see Diana in New York, so maybe I'll run up Saturday morning, hang out with you guys and see her Monday morning." He lifted the tailgate of the wagon to let Billy get his coat and bag and clapped Billy on the shoulder. "I'll call you."

As Billy crossed the tarmac to the waiting jet, the cabin attendant came out part of the way to meet him, his hand extended to take Billy's bag.

"Thanks. We all set?" Billy said, handing him his bag and topcoat.

"Yes, sir. Mr. Coggeshell's already on board, sir. He says we're ready to be wheels up as soon as you give the word." Billy started to reply as the attendant continued. "Mr. Commander, if I may say, sir, I'm terribly sorry about your grandmother. I fly a lot with Mrs. Coggeshell and whenever Mrs. Commander was on board… well, the old girls, excuse me for saying that, were kind of a favorite of mine. I could never have been obvious about it, but the two of them had me laughing all to hell most of the time. It's a… a heartbreaker. I'm sorry, sir."

Billy glanced down with a quick practiced look at the young man's name tag. With no noticeable gap in the conversation, he replied, "Thank you, Robert. They had me laughing all to hell a lot of the time, too. Let's go to New York, shall we?" extending his right arm indicating the attendant should precede him into the plane. Billy turned momentarily to look back at John Harleston and saw only the rear of the station wagon leaving the airport.

Billy ducked into the jet, sliding into a leather seat across the small aisle and facing Walker.

"Window or aisle?" said Walker jokingly.

"Is this first class? It looks like coach to me."

"Funny. You really crack me up. I'll be sure to let Mimi know. It's her ride." Lifting the intercom handset, Walker said to the Captain, "Let's rock and roll, boys. We have Mr. Commander on board."

The heavy insulation on the jet meant that Billy could feel, rather than really hear, the twin turbines spin up. The plane began to taxi and, as it turned, the small terminal and the maintenance hangar at the Georgetown Airport came into view through the windows on his side of the aircraft. Billy noticed Beaufort Estes standing next to a younger deputy, leaning on a Sheriff's department cruiser parked on the tarmac. His head was slightly lowered talking to a handsome, well dressed young black man watching the plane taxi, whose hands were shoved into the pockets of his grey suit. Billy could see all three men intently watching the jet and, as it turned onto the runway and the terminal began to recede from view, he noticed the young black man pull a mobile phone from his pocket and begin dialing.

Billy said nothing and putting his head back against the deep cushions of the seat, closed his eyes for a minute. The jet climbed to the northeast, out over the Atlantic, at the rate of three thousand feet per minute and within ten minutes began to level off and change direction to a more northerly heading. He heard Walker say from across the aisle, "Beer?"

"Diet coke for me." And within minutes Robert was there with the soft drink for Billy and a Coors Light for Walker.

"You wanna' tell me now, what's going on?" Billy asked, speaking quietly but with a determination that gave his voice an edge.

Walker took a drink from the glass in his hand, swallowing deliberately, "What?" not naively, but clearly attempting to avoid the question.

Playing the scene at St. Peter's Winyah the day of Molly's funeral back through his mind, Billy said, "Walker, there was security all over the church. Georgetown Police. Sheriff's deputies. The suits with earphones had to be state law enforcement, if not FBI. My house at the river burns down after surviving a hundred and fifty years of hurricanes, lightning, god knows how many vandals – and with me in it, unable to get out of doors and windows with rusted, sixty-year-old locks. I barely get out of the hospital and suddenly you decide that we have to go to New York – and that we have to go this afternoon. We get to the airport, and Beaufort Estes and his boys are watching our every move. And, if I am not mistaken, that was Dinny Washington, erstwhile football star and Fulbright Scholar, recently appointed Assistant District Attorney for Georgetown County, who also seems to have developed a sudden very intense interest in our movements. Walker?"

Walker put his head back, closed his eyes, and took another drink from the beer he was holding.

"Walker?"

Looking Billy directly in the eye, he said, "There are some indications that Molly's accident may not have been – well, accidental."

"Some indications?" Billy queried.

"Apparently the rear bumper was severely damaged on the far left side – and the glass in the rear view mirror on the driver's side was missing…"

"Broken, you mean?"

"No. Missing. Gone. The fluid levels in her Mercedes were exceptionally low, including the hydraulic fluids in the braking system." Walker took another drink from his beer, wiping his lips with a linen napkin as if to buy additional time for his response. "Beaufort Estes found the propane lines at River House had been tampered with, and the doors and window you thought were jammed had apparently been sealed with decking screws."

"What?" Billy began, incredulously. "You're telling me they think Molly's car was forced over the bluff at Laurel Hill and that someone tried to kill me at Asylum? There's some plot or…"

Walker said nothing.

"Are you crazy, Walker? Why? You're saying Molly was murdered, and now they are trying to kill me?" Billy stood up, frantically turning left and then right in the narrow aisle. "What the fu… how did you know all this? And when?"

"Dinny Washington called Julius Irving last night when they began to piece all this together. Julius called Mimi this morning and told her that I had to get you out of town for a while."

Billy felt as if his head were going to explode. "Walker. I'm just some guy. I've been in France for the last eight months for god's sake. And before that I was just another Atlanta lawyer. This makes no sense, Walker."

"Sit down, please." Picking up the intercom handset he said, "Robert, Mr. Commander needs a drink – scotch if there is some, on the rocks will be fine. Billy, did you tell anyone where we are going?"

"I don't want a drink. Damn, Walker. John Harleston brought me to the airport."

"It's okay. I sent John to get you. What about Thomas?"

"I told him I would be gone a few days. He knows I am with you. He probably heard John talking about New York."

"Anyone else other than Julia know where we are? Think, Billy. Did you mention to anyone else where we are going?"

"You think I'm seeing a lot of people these days Walker?" Billy said, the sarcasm evident in his tone of voice. "No. Of course not. But someone had to know we were leaving. I note that we have a flight crew, some of whom knew my name."

"I called AmeriJet flight ops myself," Walker paused for a minute.

"Good lord… Walker, what is all this?" Billy asked.

Walker spoke with growing frustration, "Bill. I don't know, man. I've been at Morgan three years now and we've never had a non-medical, life-threatening situation with a client – so there's…"

Billy broke in, "Well, that certainly sanitizes the whole experience of getting my ass roasted and Molly dumped in the river with the crabs.

A non-medical life-threatening situation? With a client? They taught you to talk like that at Morgan?"

Walker reached down and flipped open the top of a well-worn leather satchel resting against the base of his seat. He pulled out the issue of Financial Week magazine that had hit the newsstands two weeks before Molly's accident. Pictured on the cover was Hugo Lesesne and behind him was Molly, half-seated on the edge of the boardroom table at Continental American's new Atlanta headquarters tower. The headline read "Continental American Bank Reaches for the Stars."

Tossing the magazine to Billy he said, "Page 42," his voice sounding suddenly tired.

Billy opened the magazine.

The new Santiago Llurillo designed Continental American Bank tower sits astride an entire block of midtown Atlanta. At the time of its completion a year ago, the legendary Richard Goldstein, writing for the New York Times said "like the gracious ladies who once inhabited Peachtree Road, who brought a civilizing influence to a brawling commercial center, who more than once brought a quiet dignity and strength of purpose to a city beset with trouble, the Llurillo Continental American building addresses midtown Atlanta with a serene presence that belies the obvious energy and determination just beneath its skin."

At the top of the CAB tower, in perhaps the most unusual partnership in American banking, sit Hugo Lesesne, the Chairman and CEO, and Molly Commander, the Chairman of the Executive Committee. The head of this house is clearly the talented and determined Lesesne. However, in the corridors of power and influence in the U.S. and Europe, it is also commonly regarded that, like those gracious ladies of old, the mistress of this house is Molly Commander.

Molly Commander (neé Bradbury) was born into the rarefied atmosphere of Philadelphia society, into a family whose holdings included a major stake in the Bank of Pennsylvania. Her arrival at the pinnacle of the U.S. financial system was not entirely coincidental. The only child of activist parents, she appeared in South Carolina in the 1930s…

The story went on, tracing the intersection of the Bradbury and Commander interests, accurately placing Billy's family in the 1950s at the confluence of all of the re-emerging initiatives in coastal South Carolina. The article elegantly intertwined the themes of her family's love for the South, its belief in a purposeful life exemplified by service, and her particular passion for the opportunity created by economic development. The story traced her association with Criswell Burnett, beginning with the merger of the FirstSouth National Bank and the North Carolina and Atlantic National Bank, continuing through the bold national acquisition strategy that he had undertaken and that she had helped implement. The author described the career of Hugo Lesesne from a small eastern North Carolina river town to Chapel Hill, then the Harvard Business School, his rise through the ranks of the bank, ultimately to the chairmanship. The article was a bold paean to a woman of privilege who worked because she had been taught to… because she believed that the efforts of one person, working in community could, in the end, make a difference.

"All right. What's the point here, Walk? It's reasonably well-researched, reasonably well-written. Parts of it are quite lyrical even. Molly as mistress of Hugo's 'house' is bound to have rankled some on the fifty-second floor. But it's more info-tainment than journalism – in a magazine known for its feature coverage of business – not hard news. The cover was shot by a photographer whose reputation rests on his fashion work, not financial journalism. It seems hard to conclude that harm to Molly, to me, could arise because of this article. It's fluff. That's all you've got?"

Billy handed the magazine back to Walker.

"You're serious about this, aren't you?" Billy asked again. "Some nefarious activity behind Molly's death because she was prominent? Stretches credibility, Walk, even for your creative mind."

"Look, Billy, maybe everything that's happened in the past two weeks is just coincidence," Walker said. "We're going to disappear in New York for a few days, and let them sort this out. It's the best place in the world to get lost." He checked his watch and continued, "We'll be in town by 7:30, drop your bag at my place and then go grab a drink and dinner somewhere."

Billy stared out the left side of the aircraft watching the farmland of New Jersey give way to the industrial landscape of Bayonne, Jersey City, and Secaucus. The jet turned slightly east and then back northwest to line up the approach to Teterboro. Closing his eyes for a minute, Billy tried to visualize some rational end point to the confusion that engulfed him. In some remote corner of his mind, he heard Walker talking, "... come on man... best place in New York for a drink on Friday night in March?"

It was a game that they – Billy, Walker, John Harleston and Lucy – had been playing for years, a competition of superlatives, arcane historical trivia and cultural information based on their shared passion for reading and traveling.

"Best place in New York for a drink on Friday night in March? Come on."

Billy gave a small grim chuckle, turned, signaled the cabin attendant with his right hand for a beer, and then said, "Uptown or down?"

"Up."

"East Side or West?"

Walker paused for a minute and then, he, too, grinned. "East."

"The Ravelled Sleave," Billy said.

"Got to be. Best place for dinner after drinks on the Upper East Side on a Friday night in March."

And so it went. The two of them bounced places and experiences back and forth like so many verbal volleyballs. But it filled up space that would otherwise have been heavy with tension, if not anxiety.

Chapter Fourteen

An hour and fifteen minutes later Walker and Billy went through the double Third Avenue doors of the Raveled Sleave, shed their topcoats at the coat check, and made their way through the crowd gathered in the bar.

"Walker. Walker!"

Walker looked across the room and saw Hardin Murrah standing at the bar. He had been a third former at St. Bart's their last year and then overlapped with Walker again at Chapel Hill where he had dated Julia for a while. Despite the fact that he was now trading European bonds for a French investment bank, Hardin retained much of the natural ebullience attributable to his Houston background and his descent from the legendary wildcatter, whose name he bore.

"Walk – and good god, who's that with you? Billy boy!" he said. "Bill – I can't tell you how sorry I am to hear about your grandmother. Man, what a blow. Sudden and so sad. You doin' okay?"

Billy shook Hardin's proffered hand. "Thanks Hardy. Yeah, I'm okay. I just let Walker tell me what to do and everything seems to go along fine," he said, laughing.

Hardin signaled the bartender. "Let's get you boys a drink. What's it gonna be? Walker?" Dispensing with the drink orders quickly, he turned back to Billy and Walker.

"Billy, you know everybody in Houston loved Molly. When Continental American bought First Texas, she was out there a lot with Criswell. My dad always said it was Molly behind the scenes kicking butt and getting the deal done. 'Course it's different when you get your butt kicked with a nine hundred dollar shoe, I guess," he said. "She was wonderful. I sat next to her at dinner at River Oaks one night. Drank straight scotch and laughed my ass off. Said she hadn't come all the way to Texas to drink some silly French wine and could I find us a real drink. She was great."

Billy put his hand on Hardin's shoulder. Hardin realized he had said enough. "Hey, guess what? Nancy Randolph's here somewhere. She's just back from Paris, working on some art thing the Met's gonna' do with the Louvre next year. Charlotte Trapier is on her way uptown to meet me, believe it or not, and I saw Stiles McPherson in the gym at the Empire Club. I'll call him and we'll make a night of it. What dya say?" He spotted the elegant profile of Nancy Randolph, re-knotting an Hermès scarf around her neck as she turned to survey the crowd at the bar. "Nancy. Nance," and motioned her over.

Billy turned to Walker as Hardin continued his orchestration of the night. "Good call. Disappear in New York for a few days. That worked well. Five minutes, and half the Upper East Side knows we're in town."

"Ah, come on," Walker laughed. "None of them wants you dead. Although there was that thing with Nancy once upon a time. But she's bound to be past the murderous recrimination stage."

They ended up as six for dinner: Hardin, Walker, Billy, Nancy Randolph, Lucy's roommate at Stanford, Charlotte Trapier from Georgetown, and Stiles McPherson from St. Louis, who had also dated Julia for a while in college.

Billy listened to the dinner table conversation floating around the table at Jim McMullen's on Second Avenue. Charlotte put her arm around his shoulders, said, "Reading a book in your mind, big guy? I talked to Lucy yesterday."

"Lucy? She went back to France after Molly's funeral. I haven't really talked to her."

"Ummmm, so she said. So what's up? She sounded… I don't know. I've wondered if this thing with Lagardiere would survive," rolling her eyes. "Those Franco-American relationships rarely seem to make it under the best of circumstances. And Lucy and relationships were never what you might call the best of circumstances."

"Well, would you look at this?" Nancy said under her breath across the table. "Billy, don't turn around, but Hugo Lesesne just walked in with a group. Yep. Here we go. He just spotted Hardy, and now he's coming over."

The chairman of the Continental American Bank excused himself from his group and approached the table. "Hardin, Walker, Charlotte… and Nancy Randolph, I believe – we've met," His smile and handshake were consummately well-practiced. "A meeting of the most elite financial and cultural organizations in New York… *les jeunesses doreé*, as it were. Well, well, well. Billy! I didn't see you with your back to the door. How are you?"

Folding his napkin, Billy stood up to shake hands. "Fine, Hugo. Hope you are."

"Beautiful service in Georgetown, Bill. Beautiful. Big crowd, too. Everybody seemed to be there."

Billy started to respond but was interrupted. "We need to talk," said Hugo. "How long are you in town? Perhaps, you could come by the offices tomorrow morning and we can have a little chat?"

Out of the corner of his eye, Billy saw Walker, who uncharacteristically had not risen when Lesesne approached their table, shake his head.

"Maybe another time, Hugo? Tomorrow's kind of up and down. And then tomorrow afternoon, we're…," Billy paused, a moment too long, and a dark look crossed Hugo Lesesne's face.

"We're going to mother's place up in the country," Nancy offered. Laughing brightly she continued, "Good grief, Billy. It's Dutchess County, not Peru!"

Hugo's smile, his charm was back. "Sit, sit… please. Another time then. Thank you for letting me interrupt for a moment. Walker, tell your grandmother hello for me. Hardin – I saw your dad at the Houston Club last week. Wonderful to see all of you."

"You too, Hugo," Billy concluded. "Give Georgia my best. Is she with you?" He turned to look for Georgia Lesesne but Hugo had already begun to walk away.

"Thanks, Nance," Billy muttered as he sat down.

Leaning forward on her elbows as she watched Lesesne depart,

Nancy commented, "He's certainly become very grand. The CEO-ishness of it all. He and Georgia lived near my father in Charlotte when Hugo was just one of many bank vice-presidents. Not so grand back then, as I recall."

"Look at that group, would you?" Walker interjected. The chairman of the bank. Richy Concannon, the head of their chop shop… their… what do they call it Hardy?"

"Structured Financial Products Group, I think. Risley Lawrence, the head of Alderlay Development," continued Hardy. "Who's the blonde?"

"Oh that's… umm. What's her name, Charlotte? I used to see her at Chapel Hill… but I think she may have actually gone to Virginia," Nancy commented, watching the group being seated in the rear of the restaurant.

Casually looking to her left, "Cynthia Morelli," Charlotte supplied. "You're right. She was at Virginia when I was. Grad school, I think, at Yale. Ambitious. Her family is from someplace like Rhode Island, or maybe Roanoke Rapids. I don't know. What does it matter? Her father owns some kind of trucking company." She turned back to the table, "She's down there with you now, Billy Boy. Running development at Oryzantia I heard. Mind you, she'll be no fan of yours."

Billy laughed. "How's that?"

"Fallout from Lucy," Nancy commented. "Guilt by association maybe?"

Charlotte continued, "Lucy was at Chapel Hill with Julia for a big weekend. Jubilee or Germans. Cynthia was there, at the Deke house and apparently made some snippy remark to Julia about seeing her there – Julia, that is – and didn't she practically live at the St. A's house at Virginia. Lucy was standing there when it happened and then later told someone that Cynthia would walk naked from Vinegar Hill all the way to Rugby Road, if she thought she could darken the door at the St. A's house for even one night. It got back to Cynthia. She's made it clear what she thinks about 'Lucy's crowd'. I don't know – so many of Lucy's actions seem to end up like a dark cloud around someone else's head."

"Do you think it could be because she is usually on a plane before the fallout hits?" Nancy laughed, watching Charlotte ruffling Billy's hair.

"Somebody figure," Stiles interjected reflectively, "what would be they be doing together – the chairman of Continental American, the head of development for the largest museum in South Carolina, one of the largest resort developers in the east, a big shot financial gunslinger – and who is that fourth guy, the one who looks lost? A meeting of the 'Oddfellows' society – southern division?"

"Recruiting the developer guy for the Oryzantia Board, I'd say," Nancy concluded. "Walker! Do you own the wine tonight?" She fingered her empty glass with a laugh.

Seeing that Billy could not seem to divert his attention from the Lesesne table, Walker said, "Billy. Forget about it." He saw Billy folding his napkin and without taking his eyes off his friend he launched into a story. "I remember when I used to get all twisted up over some issue or perceived slight from someone and, railing and ranting to my mother, would finally demand, 'Don't you agree?' And she'd say 'I do, darling. In my heart I do – it's just that… that's not a hill I'm prepared to fight on today.'"

A few seconds of quiet fell over the table as the point of Walker's anecdote became obvious. "Oh, hell," Hardy said. "What say we blast outta here and hit the bar at the Four Seasons? May see some models or Euro trash or something."

Billy stood up and held Charlotte's chair. "Odd comment from the European bond voice of Rémond Moncrif," he said with a broad smile. "Let's go."

Chapter Fifteen

The next morning Walker found Billy drinking coffee on the small terrace overlooking Central Park, his bare feet propped on the railing.

"Some view," Billy said. "This was Mimi's place, wasn't it?"

"Yep. You haven't been here since I moved."

"Remind me. How did you get so lucky?"

"Remember about three years ago, right after you moved to Atlanta, I called you late one night and asked you to go out to the airport to see about Mimi?"

"She was on the way back from San Francisco – the opera, wasn't it – and missed her connection."

"That's it. Got really confused and a bit lost. The situation could have gotten out of hand but for you. After that, my dad wanted to make her stop traveling alone. Said she was too old to be flying about and that it would just get more dangerous. That's when I did the AmeriJet deal for her. She gave me this place last year for my birthday to say thanks for keeping her out of 'old people's jail' as she put it. She bought it back in the seventies for practically nothing in a condo conversion gone bad. Kind of a modest pied-a-terre, except of course for its million dollar view. She stays at the Harriman Club anyway – just as Molly did. They like having room service and the sense of security. Anyway, here I am. Look, I gotta go to the office – will you be okay?"

"Fine. Fine. Gonna run down to Brooks, Paulie's. Meet Charlotte and Nancy at the Empire Club for lunch. John Harleston said he may come up tomorrow morning. Maybe we can get Yankees tickets for tomorrow – opening day I think? Oh, and I need to run back down to Georgetown, Monday. Julia and I are supposed to see Julius Irving."

"I'll check on the tickets and a flight at the office. You can probably grab a ride on one of the bank's planes Monday morning, if you don't mind getting up early."

"Walker – I can go to LaGuardia. Not a big deal."

"No need. I'll see who's headed down that way. There's always someone going to Atlanta or Florida. Georgetown is a twenty-minute detour. I'm running. See you tonight."

"Walker, really I can…"

"Ah, Billy," Walker ran his hands through his hair, the sardonic tone in his voice unexpectedly obvious, "it's not a problem. I mean what would life be like if I were unable to pick up my annual Oscar for best supporting actor in the continuing saga of life in Commanderland?"

Billy stood up abruptly and turned to face his friend.

"Where in the hell did that come from? Are you…"

Walker picked up his suit jacket from the chair by the door. "Not now. I've got to run. I'll call you later."

Billy nodded, confused. "Walker… I…" but the door to the apartment had already closed behind him.

Chapter Sixteen

"There's your boy, Julia," Sam Gregory said, pointing out over the ocean to the outline of the Morgan jet. "He's going to bank through a 180-degree turn and land to the north on the main runway."

"This is so much easier than Atlanta," Julia laughed, shielding her eyes from the bright, morning sun as they watched the plane approach the Georgetown airport. Sam put on his headphones and walked out onto the tarmac to help guide the pilot into position as the small jet landed and began to taxi toward the terminal. The plane's engines began to wind down as the pilot brought the port side of the aircraft around to face them. Within minutes, the door opened, and Billy was smiling at Julia as he descended the steps and walked across the tarmac.

"Everything okay?" she asked, reaching up to kiss him on the cheek.

"Yep. Okay. Everybody missed you. Hardy – Stiles McPherson, that was kind of weird – them at opposite ends of the table. Kind of like a meeting of the ex-boyfriends of Julia." Julia slapped him playfully on the arm as he continued. "Charlotte was there. Nancy Randolph, too. It was fun. I dunno… I felt, well, almost alive. So how was your weekend? You and the doc hang out?"

Julia deflected his question, becoming serious as they reached her car. "Billy, you need to put on your game face. This may not be easy with Julius. You've done this with clients, as I have. Facts following the death of someone we love have a way of sounding horrifyingly realistic. I don't know what they know."

"It's cool, Julia. It's okay. Besides, it's probably time don't you think?"

Julia could not see his eyes behind his sunglasses. She quickly ran her fingers through his hair and kissed him on the cheek again, causing Billy to laugh and step back slightly. "So. How do I look?"

As they hit the Sampit River Bridge going into Georgetown, Billy could see the spire and belfry of St. Peter's Winyah and the sweeping porches of the early nineteenth century houses facing Winyah Bay in the distance. "Do you know a girl named Cynthia Morelli?" he asked.

"She's the new chief advancement officer at Oryzantia. Why?"

"She was at McMullen's Thursday night with Hugo Lesesne and some financial types. Stiles referred to them as 'oddfellows.' I just… Never mind. Forget it. We're almost there," noticing that Julia had turned onto Front Street next to the waterfront.

The Honorable Julius Middleton Irving, retired Federal judge for the Northeast Circuit of South Carolina, partner in the Charleston law firm of Montagu, Savage and Bird, resident in the Georgetown offices since he had stepped down from the bench three years ago, was running late.

"I doubt his luncheon began on time – they rarely do," his assistant had explained as he showed them into the judge's office. "Julia, can I get you anything? Coffee, soft drinks?"

"No, I think we're all right," she said, noticing Billy looking closely at the framed pictures covering the office wall opposite the door.

Julia heard Julius Irving's dignified voice from behind them. "Julia! William! I am so sorry to have kept you waiting."

"Judge, how are you sir?" Billy said, walking across the room to meet him, hand outstretched.

"Thank you for seeing us, Julius. I'm sorry we had to reschedule twice," Julia said, picking up the conversation.

"My pleasure. My pleasure. They offered you something, did they not? Coffee?"

Shaking his head Billy asked, "Judge Irving, this photograph," indicating a framed black and white photograph on the wall. "This is you and my grandmother at what appears to be a graduation?"

"Yes, it is, William. That was taken at my law school graduation. I shudder to recall the year."

"I'm sorry sir. I didn't mean to sound… Molly was there?"

"Sit down, won't you?" indicating two leather chairs in front of his desk. "Thomas Dirleton's mother is my great-aunt. She grew up on Oyster Island and worked for the bank as a cleaning lady for forty years. My last year in high school my aunt got me a job at the bank. Running errands, putting up the mail, helping with some of the heavier maintenance tasks. I met your grandmother." Julius leaned back in his desk chair as he recalled the moment. "She was leaving the employee lounge with a cup of coffee. 'I'm Molly Commander' she announced, in that funny lock-jawed Philadelphia accent of hers. 'Who are you?' We shook hands... talked. She asked me about school, asked me where I was going to college. I told her I had no plans to go to college. 'Why is that?' she sort of barked at me in that way she sometimes had. 'Are you lazy?' I told her I was plenty motivated but that my family could not afford to send me to school. That I wanted to go to the university in Columbia not S.C. State or another all-black school. And, that it was unlikely I would get in anyway.

Smiling broadly, he went on. "'Are you smart?' she said to me. This was all transpiring in the hall, mind you. 'And, what did you mean you wouldn't get in?' To make a long story short, I went to the University of South Carolina as the first James Motte Commander Scholar. Five years later I entered the law school as the first Martha Bradbury Commander Scholar. Molly came to my graduation. She introduced me to Chandler Cleveland, who was then the Chief Justice of the Fourth Circuit of Appeals, whose law clerk I became. The rest of the story you likely know."

"I never knew any of that," Billy said. "Why is that? I didn't even know there was a Commander Scholars program at Carolina."

"The scholars program is funded out of the Commander Foundation. The foundation by-laws provide that all trustees must be at least thirty years old to serve. You weren't even born when Molly and your grandfather set up the foundation. Later, when you became old enough to know more about your family's affairs, your parents were not... well, not available. You were away at school. Molly saw you less frequently than she would have otherwise wished. The business of your family's business had to go on."

"I never knew any... was I so completely useless in Molly's eyes?"

Julius Irving cleared his throat, not exactly sure how to proceed.

"Billy, maybe this is not the time for this?" Julia said, placing her right hand lightly on his left forearm.

"Not the time? When is…"

She continued, "Mother said once that Molly was never able to mourn the loss of her own child, such was her concern for you after your parents died. Her maternal, protective instinct led her to build a…," Julia struggled to find the right word. "A sort of… wall around you," she said with resignation. "To keep bad things out. When Caroline died, she became frantic. She was terrified that she might lose you. All of us were to some degree co-opted into shielding you from anything Molly thought might upset you further." Julia felt the muscles in Billy's forearm tense.

"Walls can protect, Julia and also isolate, cut you off from the real world."

Julia, now at a loss to know how to go on, stood up and walked around behind his chair with her hands on her hips. Billy looked over his shoulder at Julia. She had tears in her eyes and looked straight at him, shrugging her shoulders as if to say, "what do you want me to do?"

"William, perhaps we can work through the details of your financial and business situation at a later time." Julius Irving interjected. "There is another matter, however, that I consider to be more critical at the moment."

"Please," Billy said, indicating he should proceed.

"Are you all right? Are you sure we can't get you a coffee or something?" said the Judge, trying to assess the possible impact of the information he was about to divulge on Julia and particularly on Billy. "I realize this is not a pleasant discussion."

"Julius, I think I would love a coffee…," putting her hands on Billy's shoulders.

"A coffee for me as well, Judge, if it's not a problem."

Julius Irving dispatched the request into the speaker phone on his desk and continued, "There are some indications that your grandmother's accident may not have been accidental. I know Walker has discussed some of this with you previously," he said.

"Upon further inquiry about the fire at Asylum, it appears that colleagues of your grandfather have continued to use the grounds surrounding River House for fish fries and other social gatherings – the remnants of the old Hot n' Hot Fish Club, I think. Henry Casteel confirmed that they installed the fish cooker – the grill, as it were – outside the kitchen porch. Here's the curious thing. The propane lines installed by Henry and his cohorts never entered the house – they ran underground from the nearby propane tank to the cooker itself. Now, we have talked to Mack Wingfield, who did some light repair and maintenance tasks from time to time. He confirmed that the old locks on the kitchen door had rusted and would no longer keep the door closed securely. He used decking screws to secure the kitchen door while they were waiting for your grandmother to tell them how she wanted the door repaired and to have the new locks sent over to the island."

"They just screwed the door shut?"

"No one goes over there and apparently the kitchen door was being blown open by the wind. They did what seemed to them appropriate at the time and under the circumstances. The problematic part of all this is that Beaufort Estes believes more of the doors and windows were screwed shut than the one Mack told them about. However, Beaufort did caution me by reminding me that Mack is now almost eighty years old and his specific recall is not as exact as one might hope. There remains, of course, the issue of the propane line leading into the house."

"So my grandmother's accident and the fire at Asylum might be nothing more than two oddly coincidental events?" questioned Billy, shaking his head somewhat in confusion.

"I'm saying that based on the evidence and analysis from Hugh Giles' office, the prosecutor's office sees no connection, let alone a criminal intent, between the two," said Julius Irving, turning his palms upward in mild frustration.

Billy stood up, a bit too abruptly Julia thought. "Judge Irving, while I deeply appreciate your time and the new information, I'm not sure I understand the point of this conversation. Is there something – or some further information - you think that you need from me?"

"No, William. Not at all. Only an update on developments here, in the aftermath of our concern for your safety that led to your recent trip to New York. In another, unrelated matter, I have had made copies of your grandmother's will, the trust instrument that established the Commander Trust, and the organization documents and by-laws of the Commander Foundation for you to review. I'll have them sent around to your grandmother's house. Excuse me, William. To your house. When you've had a chance to look through these papers and collect your thoughts, call me and we will get together again. As I told you, Nothing is particularly pressing. We have begun the process of probate on your behalf. Walker and the Morgan Bank continue to manage for you and, for the moment, for the estate."

Billy paused, "Walker manages for me?"

"Well, yes. Walker is the relationship manager assigned to the Commander accounts. Were you unaware of that?"

"I guess I just didn't realize the professional connection was that direct."

"You are aware, I am sure, that you have a number of accounts at Morgan. One of those accounts, as you know, was set up when you were born; others, later on by your father and your grandmother." Billy sat back down in front of the Judge's desk. "Your accounts were maintained in your name, but as management accounts over which, after the death of your parents, Molly held the specific decision-making prerogative. The direction of your own accounts now passes immediately to you with no probate issues involved. With the exception of a bequest to Julia and certain retirement benefits for Thomas Dirleton, your grandmother's property, as well as the direction of the Trust and the Foundation, will also pass to you. I am summarizing tremendously, as you can tell. But yes, it is clear that Walker now will take his instructions from you."

"When we were in New York, Walker said to me one morning…" Billy stopped, seemingly confused, struggling for words. "He made some crack about being a bit player in the Billy Commander show… I don't…"

Julia, sensing the need to get Billy out of this discussion, extended her hand to the Judge, changing the subject abruptly. A bit too abruptly, Billy noticed.

"Billy, we should go. Julius, thank you for everything. Are you going to the opening at Oryzantia Thursday evening?"

"I have to be in Charleston, Julia, but you and Billy should go – I hear it is something of a tour de force and another feather in Inness Chapman's crowded cap of accomplishments," he said laughing, shaking hands with Julia and then with Billy. "Call me for anything, all right." He concluded with obvious affection in his voice.

Turning as he reached the door, Billy said, "The attorney in the prosecutor's office who has been investigating Molly's death and the fire… would it be Dinny Washington by any chance?"

Looking up from his calendar, Julius Irving nodded, "Why yes, it certainly would."

Chapter Seventeen

"Billy! Billy!" Billy turned to see Inness Chapman, one of the curators at Oryzantia, making his way across the crowded gallery.

"Great opening, Inness. Big crowd for a Thursday night, don't you think? The new painting galleries look terrific," he said, indicating the enfilade of exhibition spaces stretching almost to the banks of the old rice fields.

Kissing Julia on the cheek, Inness said, "Thanks. You know Oryzantia is the only place other than the Huntington Library that you'll be able to see these paintings."

"How'd you pull this off? Seventeenth and early eighteenth century Spanish paintings of America. Fascinating. Florida. One even of the Carolinas."

"We worked on it for over a year. The Huntington has a significant collection of Latin American paintings that provided the starting point. We assembled the exhibition from twelve museums in the U.S., Mexico and Spain. They were all out there – no one ever thought of it before. Betsy Drake at the Huntington did most of the work. She brought me in primarily to write the catalogue. None of the other American museums seemed very interested in the show, but we obtained funding from Banamex and the Kearney Foundation and here we are," he laughed.

"You know," Julia began, "I'm sure you've already thought of this, but the Museum of the Indies in Seville just re-opened after several years of renovation and conservation. One would think they would have a big interest in this. It would be quite a coup for Oryzantia to travel a show internationally. Anyway, congratulations again. Call me if

I can help. We were actually on our way down the hall to hear Alabama Deas' lecture on the history of the Waccamaw Neck."

Inness tapped his watch good-naturedly, saying "you better hustle then. She always packs the house."

Billy and Julia walked into the rear of the crowded lecture hall, on the other side of the painting galleries from the exhibition, just as the scheduled presentation was beginning.

"The Waccamaw River is almost one hundred miles long from its headwaters in Brunswick County, North Carolina to Winyah Bay at Georgetown, South Carolina." They heard Dr. Deas struggling to make herself heard over the cocktail fueled chatter among patrons who seemed reluctant to turn their attention to the distinguished looking, elderly African American woman at the front of the room.

The soft, lilting tones of her cultivated speech, still redolent of the flavors and patterns of her native Gullah culture, began to have their affect. As her voice crept through the crowd, Julia heard several patrons standing near her whisper, "shhhhhhh, I want to hear her."

Thus it had been through a thousand story hours at the Georgetown Library, countless days in the classroom and later, meeting after meeting as she mentored dozens of other teachers who followed her into the classrooms of Georgetown County.

Alabama watched the process of captivating an audience take hold yet again. Opening young minds to the world around them had been her singular passion since she returned to the Lowcountry over forty years ago. Their parents, however, especially at Oryzantia, seemed always to present a particular challenge.

"Can we stand near the back in case we want to leave?" Billy whispered to Julia. " I'm pretty tired after today." Julia nodded her assent as people near them began to find a seat and Alabama continued.

"You know, this was once the land of the Indians. The land of the Cherokee, the Muskhogean, the Tuscarora. The tribes of the Eastern Sioux – the Sewee, the Sampit, the Winyah, the Pee Dee and the Waccamaw.

For Alabama, the sounds of her culture were operatic. She had them now. "I've been asked to tell you a little about the Waccamaw Neck and Oyster Island tonight as we celebrate these perfectly marvelous paintings, and particularly this one of the confluence of the Pee Dee and the Waccamaw," indicating a painting over her right shoulder. "The first white man ever to see this area was a Spaniard. His name was Luca Vasquez de Allyon, we think. In the early sixteenth century, the Spanish settled briefly on the shore of Winyah Bay but the colony did not last. Soon the English came, pushing north from Charleston to trade with the Indians, flooding into the area in search of opportunity." She paused for a moment and shifted her posture, leaning heavily on the podium.

"In time, it became apparent that the Waccamaw Neck was uniquely suited to produce two products in great demand in London, and throughout the British empire – indigo and rice. Overproduction in the Caribbean in the early eighteenth century caused the price of indigo to collapse and the cultivation of the plant in the Carolinas to disappear, but the demand for rice continued to grow."

"Now, unlike other cash crops of that era, the cultivation of rice took a certain amount of skill – a skill that the white man, at first, did not have. Moreover, growing rice was hot, dirty work that required being knee deep in brackish water with crabs, snakes, sometimes alligators. The men who owned the land brought people from the West coast of Africa to work here because they were experts at the cultivation of rice in their native land."

Julia glanced at her cousin, leaning against the wall, listening intently to Dr. Deas' story, but the strain of the day was showing in his eyes.

"By 1852, sixty per cent of the rice production for the entire United States came from right here – Georgetown County. The rice we grew and sold was called Carolina Big Gold and the money that flowed into South Carolina from the sale of rice supported an incredibly rich, cultivated lifestyle that had no equal anywhere else in the country. But this lifestyle lasted for only a brief moment in time. The Emancipation of the Negro work force in 1863 by President Lincoln spelled the end of the rice culture."

Alabama paused to take a sip of water from the glass under the podium and continued. "Hard times settled in across the South, across Georgetown County. People – white and black – didn't have enough money to live, sometimes not enough money to eat. It was almost a hundred and forty years before gold again flowed into the Waccamaw Neck as it did when we were growing rice." She gazed out over the crowd of white faces in her audience and thought "and flows as disproportionately today as it did in 1852."

"Why don't we slip out now?" Julia whispered to her cousin.

Billy and Julia made their way out of the main galleries onto the plaza surrounding the entrance to the museum grounds. Billy gave the parking ticket to the valet attendant and rejoined Julia where she was chatting with several other museum patrons awaiting their automobiles.

"Julia," he said excusing himself and gesturing to the black Lexus which had just been brought up to the curb, "I think this is us."

Julia walked around to the driver's side where the young parking attendant was holding the door open. Instinctively checking the back seat before she got in, she saw a red sweater and a brown briefcase that were not hers. Turning to the parking attendant, she began, "I don't think this is my...," and immediately noticed another black Lexus ES being pulled up to the other side of the median dividing the driveway.

Billy had been watching the security officer in charge talking into his mobile phone rather than attempting to resolve the confusion and was about to say something when he heard a voice behind him.

"Looks as if your wife and I have similar taste in automobiles." Turning, Billy saw a couple in their mid-forties, whom he did not recognize. "Sorry. Jack Evans. My wife Susan," said the man extending his hand.

"Yes, it looks as though you and Julia did make the same choice last year. Billy Commander," he said extending his hand and chuckling. "Enjoy the exhibition?"

"We did, actually. We just moved from Atlanta and it's our first function at Oryzantia. Great place and great exhibition. Do you live here?"

"Excuse me just a minute. Jules," he said gesturing to Julia, "we're over there on the outside curb."

At that moment, Inness Chapman came out of the gallery, calling Julia. Julia smiled and walked back over to the plaza which was now beginning to fill up with patrons leaving the galleries and coming out for their cars. Billy looked around for the security officer to ask him to have

Julia's car moved out of the way, while she went back to talk to Inness Chapman. 'Odd,' he thought. 'He was standing right there.'

He heard the Evanses saying something about "nice to have met you," and he mumbled a response and walked over to move Julia's car out of the lane to avoid delaying other patrons whose cars were now being brought up by the valet staff. By the time he walked back to the plaza to get Julia, the couple in the other black Lexus had gone.

He overheard Julia saying, "All right. I'll see what I can do. Call me next week. Come into town for a drink after work maybe?"

"Sorry," she said, slipping her arm casually through his. "He seemed to like the idea of the Seville connection. Probably should have kept my mouth shut. Did you straighten out the car business?"

"Yeah. No problem. Some guy from Atlanta and his wife. Seemed nice enough. New. First time here. Want me to drive?"

The traffic seemed to be backing up as Billy and Julia reached the main gates to Oryzantia. "You hungry? We could grab something at the bar at Eddie's or go by the new fish place next to the library that John-o was talking about."

"That fish place is dreadful. I can't think John Harleston's actually been there. Let's go to Eddie's. I'll call and let them know," she said reaching in her bag for her mobile phone.

"Good god, what's all this?"

Julia looked up and saw a Sheriff's department cruiser and two of the Oryzantia security vehicles, creating a blaze of flashing blue and yellow lights in the green space outside the gates. A security guard in the entrance circle was attempting to direct traffic onto the highway. In the distance, she heard the scream of an ambulance.

"Billy, that's Odell Carter," indicating the security guard. "I know him. Ask him what happened – if there is anything we can do."

Billy rolled the window down as he approached the security guard. Carter recognized Julia in the reflection of the lights and walked over to the car. "Bad wreck, Miss Pringle, really bad."

"What happened Odell?"

"Not sure yet. It looks as if a car comin' down the highway hit a car leavin' the museum. Must have been flyin'. The car coming out of here flipped and hit a tree. It doesn't look good. The car who hit him just kept goin'. Didn't even stop."

"Odell, is there anything we can do? I'm sure you've already called the duty officer for the museum tonight?"

"Yes, m'am. It's the director himself. He's on the way over now. Ya'll be careful now," waving Billy toward the highway. "Try to pull into that far left lane and get around all this."

As Billy moved the car slowly out onto the highway, Julia could not avoid looking at the wreckage of the car to her right. "Billy, oh no. It's those people from Atlanta."

"Who? You mean the ones with the car like yours?"

"Yes. I can see the car and just make out the Georgia plates. How awful."

Billy noticed out of the corner of his eye the security guard from the reception area talking again into his cell phone.

Chapter Eighteen

The next morning Billy was awakened by knocking on his bedroom door.

"Mr. Commander," followed by more knocking. He groggily recognized Thomas' voice and made a garbled, sleepy reply. "Mr. Commander, may I come in? It's important."

"Come… come," Billy said as he rolled over.

"Mr. Commander. Judge Julius Irving is downstairs. "He says he needs to see you now, sir."

Thomas Dirleton was standing by the bed holding a robe he had retrieved from Billy's closet.

"Okay, Thomas. Let me throw some water on my face and brush my teeth. Maybe you could make some coffee."

Ten minutes later, Thomas handed him a cup of coffee as he walked barefooted into the glass loggia that Molly had always used as a morning room.

"Billy, do you know Dinny Washington?" indicating the attractive young black man that had accompanied him that morning.

Billy shook hands as Julius Irving continued. "There's been a development. Perhaps, we could sit down."

"Of course. Can we get you anything? Coffee? Thomas…," Billy said looking back toward the kitchen.

"No. We're fine. There was an accident last night leaving Oryzantia."

"I know," Billy began. "Julia and I were just…," he was going to say "leaving" when the Judge cut him off abruptly.

"A car carrying two passengers – a man and a woman – was struck by a larger vehicle speeding south on Highway 17. The man died as a result of injuries sustained in the accident and the woman remains in critical condition."

"Yessir, but why… " Billy started to say.

"Mr. Commander," Dinny Washington began. "The Sheriff's deputies have located what we believe to be the vehicle that struck the car leaving Oryzantia, a recent model Ford Excursion reported this morning as stolen. The car it struck is identical to the car you and your cousin were driving last night." He paused, and went on with difficulty. "We retrieved from the floor of the SUV a handwritten note bearing the exact description of the car – and Miss Pringle's license plate number and home address. There was a pre-paid, non-traceable cell phone under the floor mat on the driver's side."

"Wait a minute. This hit-and-run guy had the description and plate number for Julia's car?" Billy said incredulously. "You think someone was trying to hurt Julia?"

"No sir. We think someone may have been trying to hurt you. This is the third…"

"The guy died you said?"

"Yes sir."

"Are you telling me that now you think that it was supposed to be me?"

"William. Let's try to remain calm."

"Calm. Julius. Am I going crazy? What the f…?"

"Mr. Commander. Billy. We now have specific reason to be concerned about your well-being. We are continuing to investigate."

"So some guy steals a car goes for a joyride up the beach, kills a guy from Atlanta and just happens to have Julia's license plate number written down in his car. Can I ask if anything else could happen to make you 'concerned about my well-being'? I'm sorry," Billy said getting up for more coffee. "Thomas!"

Dinny continued, trying to effect a calm tone in his voice. "It is somewhat disturbing but I feel I should tell you that, while the Sheriff's investigation is not yet complete, there is no evidence that the vehicle was hot-wired."

"They had a key?" his incredulity growing. "They had a key to a car, truck – whatever – to a 'stolen vehicle'? Where'd they get it? The valet lot at Eddie's?"

Dinny exchanged glances with Judge Irving and continued. "The SUV was removed from a secured lot in south Georgetown used to store repossessed vehicles awaiting liquidation."

Billy almost stammered he was so upset. "They just took the key off the goddam board out in the parking lot? Sh… this is unbelievable! You guys are…"

Billy heard familiar footsteps coming down the hall from the front entrance and a few seconds later, Julia entered the room. "I called Walker and they are checking. He has my mobile number and the number here and as soon as… Dinny, good morning," she interrupted herself to shake hands with the young assistant district attorney. "Thank you for coming with Julius. I could not even begin to tell you how much we appreciate this."

"Will someone please tell me what in the hell is going on around here," Billy said with rising anger.

"Billy. Sit down," said Julia firmly. "This is serious. This situation is becoming increasingly dangerous. Julius wants to bring in an executive protection service. I went so far as to call Walker and to have him identify some options through the bank's resources.

Julia's mobile phone rang. Putting the phone to her ear, she said bluntly, "What?" Listening for a moment, they heard her respond, "$2500 an hour to assess the threat? Are you crazy Walker? I'll get back to you about the bodyguards," she said, disconnecting the call.

"Walker says they have an executive protection service they have used a number of times, which includes, as a first step, an assessment of the threat. Imagine that? They evaluate the threat," she said. "Somebody killed Molly. Now somebody's trying to kill Billy. I'm standing here in the way while they try to do it. There's the threat analysis. God, I'm going to get a coffee and some ibuprofen," she almost spit the words out as she started down the loggia to the rear of the house.

Billy was stunned by the speed with which the situation was rocketing out of control. And particularly stunned by the content and tone of Julia's comments. "Give me a minute here, if you would?" he said, getting up to find Julia.

She was standing in the kitchen, facing the wall, with her hands resting on the countertop, a cup of coffee in the middle of a large spill next to her left hand. He walked up behind her and put his arms around her, holding her tightly.

"Do you remember the summer after you were in the third grade when Robby Marion pushed you off the diving board at the beach club?"

"You beat him up," she half-laughed, "and your mom wouldn't let you go out of the house for a week."

"I'm not going to let anything happen to you, Jules."

"Billy, these aren't third grade bullies…"

"I'm not going to let anything happen to you. You're my only family. I'm sorry I've been such a worthless, dysfunctional piece of…"

She turned around, interrupting him, putting her right hand on his cheek. "Forget it. I'm just really tired and…," she stopped in mid-sentence.

"What? Tell me."

"I'm terrified. I seem to go to more funerals than cocktail parties these days." Trying to control herself, she wiped her eyes. "I have no coping skills for this. I stay at Mother's now because I am afraid to go home. I'm tired of being forced into the role of the strong, capable one in this family. I'm afraid that if something were to happen to you – that the mantle of Molly Commander would somehow end up draped around my shoulders."

"Jules, I don't know what to say. I …"

Julia refilled her coffee cup and, wiping up the earlier spill on the counter, said "Come on, let's go re-join them and try to get this over with."

Dinny and the Judge stood up as Julia and Billy walked back into the loggia. When they sat down, Dinny Washington said, "I clerked for Morall Magrath. Did you know that?"

"No. I had no idea." Billy found himself surprised that Lucy was brought so quickly to mind by the reference to her father.

"One of the first cases assigned to me was a securities fraud case that came up to the Fourth Circuit on appeal from the Eastern District of North Carolina. Fifteen appellants had been joined by the trial judge as co-plaintiffs. The respondents included a savings and loan, three of its officers, two brokerage firms and an accounting firm. The trial had lasted five weeks. The transcript, together with the pleadings and discovery, filled a small conference room. I struggled with the file for two days, trying to make sense of it. Getting nowhere, I could barely understand the allegations, let alone the substance of the lawsuit.

"Judge Magrath came into the conference room one afternoon to ask how it was going. After listening to me verbally wander around for about five minutes, he said, 'Follow the money, son. Follow the money.'"

Dinny continued, "As a prosecutor I have observed that, if you lay aside truly pathological behavior for a moment, three things tend to lay at the source of personal violence." Ticking them off on his fingers, he continued. "One: Carelessness. Bunch of guys get drunk at the river and beat up one another or someone outside the group. Two: Love. Crimes of passion. And, three: Money," He said with finality. "That's where I'd start unraveling this story, if I were you. Follow the money."

"If you were me?" Billy asked in disbelief.

"Look, Mr. Commander. Billy. Unofficially, I'm concerned. I think there is a connection among these events and that you – and possibly even Julia – could be in harm's way. Officially, I have a one-vehicle automobile accident with fatalities, a fire in an old house during a thunderstorm, and a hit-and-run with fatalities, which did not involve anyone even remotely connected to you or your grandmother. I have nothing to take to a grand jury. I'm neither an investigative reporter nor a P.I. Follow the money."

Standing up, he came over next to Billy and put his hand on his shoulder. "I'm sorry."

Julius Irving also stood up to leave. "William, I want you to think seriously about a protection service. At least for a while."

"A bodyguard. You can't be serious, Judge?"

"I am, my boy. I am. Let's at least bring them down for a conversation."

"To what end, sir? Are you suggesting that I will live the rest of my life with bodyguards. That Julia will be looking over her shoulder everywhere she goes for the rest of hers or that she, too, lives under the protection of a security detail. And why? Because we have money? That seems a high price to pay for…"

Julius shook Billy's hand, somewhat sadly Julia thought. "Think about it, William, please."

Julia walked the two men to the door, while Billy stood staring out the windows. A peaceful breeze rippled the surface of the Atlantic seen in the distance. Georgetown and Pawleys had always seemed to him a safe place. The anxiety swelling up in him threatened to create its own paralysis of action. He shook his head and turned to find Julia tidying up the morning room.

"Leave it, Jules. We have work to do. It's time I begin to understand Molly's business – my business – and I need your help."

Chapter Nineteen

Billy and Julia sat in a small conference room on the second floor of Julia's law firm. Staring at a platted map of the Waccamaw Neck thumb-tacked to one wall, he twisted in his chair to look again at the diagram on a dry erase board on the opposite wall of Molly's – and his, he realized – investments in Continental American and other corporations.

"So other than the ten million dollar bequest to you and the pension benefit to Thomas, there are no other specifically designated bequests in Molly's will?" he asked.

"Maybe to the Boy's School out on the Black River... Converse. But it's been two years since I actually read her will."

"And is it safe to assume, Miss Pringle," he said mocking the formality of a trial lawyer, "that you did not shove Mrs. Commander in the river to get at the ten mil?"

She threw an empty styrofoam coffee cup at him.

Looking at the land map again, Billy said, "Okay. Go back over the land ownership."

Julia looked at him silently for a moment.

"Billy – the bequest from Molly. I never..."

Billy leaned across the table and put his hand over hers.

"Stop. She told me when she did it, Julia. I know you have your own money. I think Molly wanted to be sure that, if anything ever happened to me, you had the means at your disposal outside the courts to look after the Commander land. It sounds on the surface very parochial. I told her at the time that ten million or a hundred million was okay with me."

He held up his hand as she started to protest.

"You have your mom and dad. I have only you."

Pausing, he studied her face as she turned back to the maps, caught in a moment of time he wanted to remember, savor.

"Come on," clearing the emotion from his throat. "Highway 17…," he gestured toward the maps.

"Highway 17," she said tracing the north-south axis with her finger. "The Waccamaw. The Pee Dee. Meet the Black River," moving her finger south toward Georgetown, "to form Winyah Bay. Oyster Island," indicating the large barrier island that separated the Waccamaw and the Pee Dee Rivers. "The yellow areas are all residential development. Litchfield and Pawleys from here south," indicating an imaginary east-west line. "Wachesaw from here north," indicating another east-west line.

"And the green areas?" Billy asked.

"Undeveloped land."

Billy took notes as Julia talked, although he knew bits and pieces of the story from childhood.

"Moving up the river, north of Litchfield are Sewee Hill, Oak Lawn, Tuscarora Wood and Hasell Hill. The first two are the Commander plantations, acquired in the late-nineteenth century by our great grandfather and now owned by you and my dad. The last two, here and here," she said indicating plats on the map, were bought by your grandfather Bradbury in 1931."

"Remind me of that story again."

"Radcliff Bradbury was a buddy of Henry Simons – I think they were at school together. Simons, also from Philadelphia, was close to both Bernard Baruch and Harrison Inman. Baruch owned all of the land south of Craven…"

"Hobcaw," Billy supplied.

"Right. Inman had assembled what is now Oryzantia from four eighteenth century rice plantations. Simons bought Litchfield Plantation for a hunting preserve at about the same time. Rad Bradbury came down to shoot ducks with Simons and Inman, and they showed him Tuscarora Wood and Hasell Hill. These were desperate times in the economic fortunes of the old Waccamaw Neck families. Money from rice production had long since dried up. Poverty had settled in everywhere in the midst of what had once been unbelievable luxury. Your grandfather bought almost 3,000 acres for about $125 an acre."

"All four of the Commander – Bradbury plantations included land on Oyster Island", Julia continued. "The Bradbury land on the island has always been known anecdotally as Asylum Plantation. That's the piece here, just north of Ruinville and that's the boat dock at the site of Molly's – rather your - River House."

"The rest of this on the mainland side is Oryzantia, which also includes about two thousand acres on Oyster Island. The piece here," she said again pointing to the relevant parcel on the map.

"Okay. What are those two tracts on the north end of the island, north of the Oryzantia land?" Billy asked looking back over his notes.

"The small piece in the northwest corner is actually Bradbury land. The larger tract, here, is owned by a private investment group. Some lawyer in Atlanta manages for them. They say they bought the land for hunting and for the timber stands. The speculation is that they bought it to flip it to a developer."

"Wide-scale development will certainly be difficult without road access. There's no bridge."

"True. But if there were a bridge. Just look at it." Julia leaned back on the edge of the conference table looking at the map of Oyster Island. "Fourteen thousand acres, much of it in virgin timber, surrounded by deep water, navigable rivers – one side being the Intracoastal Waterway itself," pointing to the Waccamaw River side of the island. "Five miles from the headwaters of Winyah Bay, and thence the Atlantic Ocean."

Billy gave a low whistle. "Condomania."

Julia laughed and replied, "Yachtomania. It's the perfect adjunct to Georgetown's drive to become a sailing destination and a permanent home to yachtsmen."

"But it can't happen. We wouldn't sell. Oryzantia can't." Billy stood up, going to the map. "That creates a – two, four, six thousand acre non-developable buffer," he said, pointing to the Commander, Bradbury and Oryzantia tracts as he spoke, "separating all of the potential marina sites here around Ruinville and the southern tip of the island from the higher ground here in this tract you said the Atlanta lawyer manages.

The million dollar views on these bluffs have no access to the yacht basin. Hard sell. Also makes the infrastructure development impossible.

Julia studied her cousin's face for a moment, and then said, "Wow. Where did that come from?"

Billy grinned. "Real estate finance course in law school. Plus, I worked on the zoning appeal for Three Sisters Development when they were trying to re-zone that thousand acre tract on the Chattahoochee north of Alpharetta. "Isn't this the route of the proposed Cypress Bay Parkway?" Billy asked, tracing a line across the map.

"Close."

"So any bridgehead on the island would have to be here, on Commander – or Bradbury, I think you said – land, which, of course would be subject to the state's right of eminent domain."

"Only if the bridge were public," Julia added reflectively.

"A private bridge?" Billy remarked, mentally processing the ramifications of her statement.

"Gibson Island in Maryland, Maiden's Island in Connecticut, Ketcher Island out in Seattle. Those two new ones below Sanibel and Gasparilla," she said thinking, "where the developer got in trouble over the manatees. What were the names?"

Sitting down, Billy laced his fingers behind his head, leaning back in his chair and continuing to gaze at the map. "How on earth do you know all this, Jules?"

"I'm a trustee of and associate counsel to the Winyah Bay Conservancy. It's our business to understand the land ownership in the Winyah Basin, as well as be familiar with threats to other similar ecosystems. And I was one of Molly's lawyers. She had me copied on most of the correspondence dealing with the land."

"There must be volumes of correspondence from developers. Especially those Atlanta guys."

"Odd. You'd think so, but that's not the case.

Billy rocked back and forth on the rear legs of the chair and then, remembering the strict dicta of his family, put the chair abruptly down on its four legs.

"Julia?" he heard the intercom on the phone interrupt.

"Yes, Susan."

"John Harleston Read is on line three for you."

Smiling at Billy as she picked up the phone, "John. What an entirely pleasant surprise. Are you in town? Wonderful," she said after a slight pause. "No real plans. I was going to meet Tommy after work. I also have my difficult and tiresome cousin in tow," she continued, laughing. "Why don't you meet us? I can't imagine Tommy would mind," she said, pausing again. "It's a new place on the water downtown. Directly in front of the old Bank of South Carolina building. Cypress Grill or Cedar Grill, something like that. Oh, I don't know forty-five minutes or so. Where are you?" Glancing quickly at her watch, Julia said "Perfect, we'll just meet you there."

"John Harleston's on the way into town from Atlanta. Says he needs to stay with you. His mother has a crowd at the beach house." She noticed that Billy was still staring at the map. "I need just a minute to check in with Susan."

Billy stood up, stretching. "So we're off to meet the doc? I don't have a car. I forgot I rode in with you."

Taking several pink message slips from her assistant, she said, "You can ride back to the beach with John Harleston," while she looked through the stack. "These can all wait until tomorrow morning. Thank you, Susan."

Chapter Twenty

"Beautiful," John Harleston said as they settled into their table by the windows overlooking Georgetown Harbor. "Portofino-on-the-Winyah."

"It will be," replied Julia, "if they are able to clear the industrial development from down there," pointing generally in a westward direction. "It's not hard to imagine the entire waterfront bordered by six- and seven-figure condominiums. Billy needs to come on or we're going to order the wine without him," looking across the room where Billy was still talking to a table of Molly's DeBordieu neighbors.

Glancing sideways at her and attempting rather quickly to take the pulse of the proceedings, Tommy Henning said, "Ill-advised as it might otherwise be, maybe we should try to drink these blues away?" As he began to look over the wine list, he asked "John Harleston, would you…?" courteously extending the wine card toward him.

"Oh, good lord Tommy. Just order something."

"Julia, I'm hurt," John Harleston said good-naturedly.

Billy finally walked over to the table and sat down, making a wry comment about the chatty familiarity of the wait staff. "Hi, I'm Billy, and I'll be your server tonight…'

"Ok. That's it. Give me that," Julia said as she took the wine list from Tommy. "That's all we need tonight: a bunch of lame comedians."

Tommy Henning dispatched the waiter with the drinks order and, turning his attention back to the table, said, "Sad about that couple leaving Oryzantia last night. You were there weren't you," looking first at Billy then Julia. "They were brought in while I was on duty."

He noticed an immediate awkward silence at the table. "Is something wrong?"

Julia stood up abruptly saying, "Excuse me for a minute, will you?"

Tommy half rose from his chair to help her out.

"What's going on?"

"Their car was identical to Julia's," John Harleston began. "And the sheriff's deputies found a piece of paper with her name and license plate number in the front seat of the hit-and-run vehicle."

"Holy sh…," Tommy muttered under his breath.

"How did you know all this?" Billy asked.

"Walker called me this morning at seven o'clock."

"And, how did Walker… never mind. So Walker called, and here you are?" Billy said querulously.

"Well, we're shooting a house at Prince William and… you know what? Screw it. Yeah. Walker called me and here I am. What is it that strikes you as odd about that, Billy?"

"Oh good," Tommy Henning interjected. "The wine. No, just pour it. I'm sure it's fine," he added, rising again to hold Julia's chair as she returned. "Looks like everybody's had a long week," he said raising his glass.

"Billy?" John Harleston said, tipping his glass toward Billy's.

"Thanks, Tommy," Billy said acknowledging the wine. "We're all a little over the top today. An actual threat to one's safety is hard to reconcile with the way in which we have always lived. It seems vaguely surreal somehow."

The events of the past few days did not come up again at dinner as the conversation lapsed comfortably into topics of mutual interest, shared experiences and common associations.

Sometime later, Julia said, "Do you really think we need another bottle of…?"

"I don't know, Jules. I've almost been killed twice in the past twelve days. The brightest minds in the Georgetown criminal justice system can't seem to figure out why. One of the most distinguished jurists from the federal bench thinks that now, at the ripe old ages of thirty-one and twenty-nine, you and I need to live the rest of our lives under the watchful eye of a security detail."

Julia began to realize the toll the past three weeks had taken on Billy.

"... and now, with any luck, I can get my cousin killed, too. But that's okay because she can't have a life or a boyfriend anyway because of me. My best friend has to drop whatever he's doing because my other best friend, whom I now find out is also my banker, called. So, yeah. I thought I'd drink a little wine," he said holding up his glass and, forcing himself to laugh, "I don't have to drive because I don't even have a car."

Julia locked eyes with John Harleston and held his gaze for a moment. Billy didn't seem to notice.

"Oh, come on, Julia. Loosen up. It's not like we're dancing on a table or throwing things. Maybe you need to get somebody to drive you home. Like the doc. He looks pretty responsible. And, we haven't scared him away yet," said Billy, laughing again.

"Billy, that's enough," Julia said but she had already started to smile, wishing something would make her own anxiety go away. She studied John Harleston as he refilled her glass.

"In that case, I have a toast," Tommy Henning began as the waiter cleared the last of the dinner dishes and re-filled the wine glasses. "An invitation. Can you do that?" They all laughed.

Billy said, "Make a toasted invitation. But then you have to get someone to drive you home."

"Well, I can walk. I'm one of those condominium desecrators of the harborscape that Julia mentioned. You guys have been great since I met you. The Indigo Ball is the third week in May. Would you consider coming as my guests? It's the first year the hospital has tried a charity fund raiser like this, and I'd like to help."

"No better way to help than with a glamorous crowd at your table," John Harleston joked. And then, laughing aloud, "I'm definitely in."

"There's a small problem, though. The tables seat ten."

"I do hate ten tops at a gala," Julia intervened. "The flowers rarely work... inhibit conversation. It's just a mess..."

"That's not the problem. Well, maybe it is." Tommy seemed momentarily confused by Julia's comments. He continued, "You are the only people in Georgetown I know."

A moment of silence fell across the table that left Tommy Henning wondering if he has made a misstep of some kind. Then Billy, Julia and John Harleston burst out laughing.

"Ten?" Julia pondered. "Well… there's the four of us. Walker. I'm sure Charlotte and Nancy would come down. That's seven."

"Hardy," Billy added. "That's eight."

"I've got it," John Harleston added. "Mimi Coggeshell and Julius Irving."

"Perfect!" said Julia. "Good choice, John."

"Terrific. You can get me the names to send to the invitation committee?"

"Would you like me to do it for you? I know Kathryn quite well actually," Julia volunteered.

Tommy looked at her quizzically.

"LaBruce. Kathryn LaBruce, the ball chair. I'll get Susan to send the names 'round tomorrow. She'll have everything the committee needs except… I'm embarrassed to say, I don't know your full name?"

"Waterman. Thomas Waterman…"

"From New Orleans?" Julia asked, as Billy looked up abruptly at the same time.

"My grandmother was, yes. How did you… never mind."

Billy leaned across the table toward Julia, teasing her in a voice only she could hear, "broad are the shoulders which bear the mantle of Molly Commander."

"Oh, shut up, Billy," she said pushing her chair back from the table.

"We're clear here. What dya say we go?" Billy heard Tommy Henning saying.

"Okay. Let's get the check then" John Harleston offered.

Tommy held up his hand, silencing the flood of protest he anticipated would follow, "It's done."

As they reached the street, Billy noticed, buzzed as he was, that Julia seemed to linger a moment longer than necessary on the sidewalk as he and John Harleston said goodnight. Billy brought things to a close, joking, "Take me home, John."

Billy and John Harleston rode toward DeBordieu mostly in silence. As they turned off Highway 17 and slowed at the security gate, John Harleston looked sideways at Billy, "You okay?"

"On what level? The excess of wine we – or rather I – drank? The turn my life seems to have taken?" And then, surprisingly, "or me and you?"

John Harleston nodded to the security guard as the car rolled slowly under the porte cochere, gripping the wheel tightly with both hands. "How about all three?"

Billy put his head back on the headrest, rubbing his eyes and saying nothing. They pulled into the driveway at Molly's in what John Harleston was beginning to sense was a heavy, if not uncomfortable, silence. When the car stopped in front of the steps, Billy got out without a word, unlocked the front door, and went into the house, leaving the door open. John Harleston retrieved his bag and his briefcase from the rear of the station wagon and followed Billy into the house, closing the door with the toe of his left foot.

"Billy? Billy?" he called as he walked down the glass loggia toward the rear of the house. He noticed Billy's jacket and shoes on the floor and the door to the terrace open. John Harleston walked out onto the terrace toward the pool, tripping on Billy's pants and shirt in the semi-darkness. At the edge of the pool, he saw a pair of boxers and at the far end of the pool the dark curls on Billy's head, his arms resting on the apron of the pool deck, his naked body silhouetted by the underwater lights.

"Coming in?"

"Billy…"

"What? Aw… come on. It's just Molly's pool. We've been in here naked and drunk before," Billy seemed to taunt John Harleston.

"What are you doing?

"What is it? Afraid now to face the music? That it?"

John Harleston replied, "You're a lousy drunk. Anybody ever tell you that?" Kicking his loafers off, he sat down on the apron of the pool dangling his legs in the water.

Billy squirted a stream of water at his friend from between the palms of his clasped hands. Laughing, he repeated the gesture as he watched John Harleston rolling up the now soaking wet legs of his pants. "You remember the night you stayed at my place in Atlanta?"

John Harleston nodded.

"You slept in my bed."

John Harleston swallowed visibly, not knowing where the conversation was headed. He looked straight at Billy. "It's your party…"

"And you want to know two things. What did it mean? And where might it go?"

"Fair enough."

"That night was for you, I perceived, a fairly cataclysmic event in the overall scheme of things. You tell your best friend you're gay. No more hiding behind something on that one. Great risk. Maximum uncertainty. Huge downside potential in the disclosure. But gutsy. So like you. Incapable of even a moment's dishonesty. If ever there was a moment for a meltdown, that was it. Too old for your mom to hold. No girlfriend around for…"

"Obvious reasons," John Harleston supplied with a chuckle.

"I was the available shoulder. You and Walker are my oldest friends, John Harleston. I can't imagine my life without you in it – not even for a day. We… I'm sorry. I may be overreaching. I can't… I can't get this out unselfishly."

"Just say it."

"I don't want there to be any barriers between us – me and you. I'm standing here naked telling you that as tangible proof. But here's the thing. I'm straight – whatever that means these days. I don't want to feel as if I am walking on glass around my best friend because some action or comment might be misinterpreted. And I don't want you to let the chance of some relationship pass you by because of…," Billy paused, carefully considering his words. "We gotta square this up between us. Now. Tonight."

John Harleston laughed, "I thought you were drunk. I forgot for a moment. The mind never clouds over with you."

"Speaking of," Billy said in a brightening tone of voice. "Go dig something up from the kitchen. Go. Couple of beers or something?"

John Harleston paused at the terrace doors. He heard Billy behind him, laughing. "Get your ass moving."

Chapter Twenty-One

The next afternoon Billy and Julia were again seated in the small, second floor conference room at her firm. Billy looked across the table at his cousin who was uncharacteristically twisting a strand of her hair with the fingers of her left hand.

"Jules?"

She looked up abruptly.

"You want to tell me about last night? You and the doc?"

"You want to tell me about last night? You and John Harleston?" she shot back at him.

"Let's say we resolved some outstanding issues, eased some tensions. Tried to establish a new plane for communication."

"Cryptic," Julia replied.

"*Et toi?*"

"I stayed with him Billy, okay?" she said in a way that curtailed further discussion.

"Okay," Billy said. "We'll come back to that one."

The land maps from the previous day were still hanging on the conference room walls. Billy studied the land plats over the top of his coffee mug.

Billy turned to the dry erase board outlining Molly's corporate investments.

"Ok. Walk me through this chart?"

"Motte Commander, our great-grandfather, after whom your dad was named, was one of six founders of the Bank of Georgetown. Motte held," Julia glanced down to check her notes, "a twenty per cent interest in the bank until 1931. In 1931, the bank was close to failing – in fact, it was the only bank in Georgetown that had not failed. Henry Simons," she indicated Litchfield on the land maps on the opposite wall, "a Philadelphia banker, put together a group of northern investors with South Carolina ties to shore up the bank."

She paused to pick up her coffee.

"The group included your grandfather, Radcliff Bradbury, who put up close to a million dollars. Three years later Rad Bradbury bought out Simons and the others who had become disenchanted with economic recovery in the South – to say the least – for another million dollars. He ended up with seventy per cent ownership of the bank. Motte Commander retained twenty per cent, and the remaining ten per cent was held, interestingly enough, by Mimi Coggeshell's father, Hugh Fraser. Most people thought Rad was nuts including, Molly always said, your grandmother. Your grandmother had Bank of Pennsylvania money through her mother's family, the Wideners. Molly said she always called your grandfather's participation in the Bank of Georgetown his 'patriarchal southern folly.' As it turned out, she could not have been more wrong."

"The bank survived and began to ride the rising economic tide of the region in the early '60s, acquiring other small local banks, ultimately merging with the Peninsula Bank of Charleston, and, in the process, changing its name to Coastal Carolina National Bank. The new bank enjoyed a financial prominence somewhat larger than its actual size for two reasons: First, it was the regional bank for all the major timber and forestry products companies, which have a huge presence in the Lowcountry; and second, it was one of the few sub-regionals in the country with a competent, sophisticated trust department."

"Sorry. The significance of that?"

"Banks tend to grow and prosper in two ways: retail banking – individual deposits, credit cards, auto loans and leases, mortgages and so on; and, corporate banking – one of the most important functions of which can be cash management and institutional funds management – for which, back then, you needed the administrative services and fiduciary relationships normally associated with a trust department. The Bank of Georgetown had both and, thus, became the dominant partner in the Peninsula merger.

"In 1980, Coastal Carolina acquired the First National Bank of South Carolina, a bank with a greater presence in retail banking with offices primarily in Columbia, Greenville and Spartanburg, changing its name again to the First Carolina National Bank. First Carolina subsequently acquired the First Georgia National Bank in Atlanta and the Peninsula National Bank of Savannah, changing its name again to FirstSouth. In 1997, Criswell Burnett, the chairman of the Atlantic National Bank in North Carolina, came to see Molly, whose Bradbury and Commander inheritance made her the third largest individual shareholder in FirstSouth, after the Wright brothers in Charleston, whose family had owned the Peninsula banks. Are you following this – you look dazed?"

"I was just calculating in my mind the money spent in the past twenty years on new signs and stationery in the banking business," Billy said, laughing.

"Exactly. But the face of banking was changing rapidly, you must remember. The advent first of state-wide banking, then banking across state lines. The Riegle-Neal Act in 1994 permitted bank holding companies to acquire banks in any state and then, after 1997, allowed interstate bank mergers. Gramm-Leach in 1999 tore down the walls that had previously existed among banking, securities and insurance."

"Okay, push on."

"Seeing the impact of both Riegle-Neal and Gramm-Leach, Criswell came to see Molly to ask for her support in persuading the Wright brothers to consider a merger with North Carolina Atlantic, then the largest bank in North Carolina and Virginia. The chairman of FirstSouth was the elder of the two Wright brothers, McCallie Evander Wright. Mac Wright was a visionary corporate leader but compromised by an ego the size of Montana, Molly used to say. The merger of the two principal banks in the South made perfect sense, combining traditional strengths in both retail and corporate banking. Molly and Criswell saw the synergies long before anyone else."

"And, the rest, as they say…," Billy offered.

"Not so fast. Mac Wright was sixty-three at the time the discussions began and was resistant to a merger or acquisition in which his bank would be the lesser partner. But the numbers were such that ANB had to come out on top. Molly got Criswell and Mac out on the beach in front of her house at DeBordieu one afternoon – it's reported with a bucket of ice and a bottle of scotch – and told the boys they were not going back in until they hammered out a deal. One thing about Molly – she could smell opportunity. The boys finally shook hands at six o'clock. Mac would become the Chairman of the new organization with certain lifetime perks and in eighteen months, at his normal retirement age of 65, he would step down in favor of Criswell Burnett. The new bank became known as Continental American. The rest then…"

"Is history," Billy finished.

"Criswell, with Molly's active participation, acquired major banks in Texas, Missouri, Maryland, and Florida, culminating two years ago with the acquisition of First America in California. When CAB acquired the Bank of Pennsylvania, Molly, who had inherited her mother's shares, became the fifth largest individual shareholder in the bank, which distinction you now hold."

"Impressive."

Julia nodded. "Along with Walter Wriston and John Reed at Citibank, and David Rockefeller at Chase Manhattan, they changed the face of American banking," she said, glancing over the chart on the wall, as if she might have missed something.

"I meant your grasp of the history and what it means strategically."

"The rest of the story," she began, pointing to the second tier of corporate diagrams. "Rad Bradbury and Motte Commander were part of a consortium of local business men and investors that partnered with the Columbia and South Coast Railway after World War II to get railheads into Georgetown County that enabled the shipment of timber and forest products. The old CSCR line was acquired by the Baltimore and East Coast Line, which, in turn merged with the Piedmont and Southern Railway and then was acquired by MidAmerica Railway in the mid-eighties. That's the MidAmerica stock you see here, indicating a maze of red intersecting lines.

"Okay. And the green lines?"

"Lumber. Forest products. As early as 1952, Motte Commander and a group of other Georgetown County timber owners began consolidating timber cutting and hauling operations, and assembled what we would today call an economic cooperative. By 1960 the co-op had developed sufficient critical mass that Southern Atlantic Paper Products offered to buy the operation along with over a million acres of timberland in coastal South Carolina and Georgia. Our great-grandfather took stock instead of cash, which proved to be a wise decision. The year after the acquisition was completed, SAPP spun off some toxic assets that had been the subject of the ongoing dispute with the FTC into Central Pacific Timber and its stock began to recover. The stock has split eight times since 1964. The Commander stock, approximately 100,000 shares at the time is now 800,000 shares worth over 19 million dollars."

"They were at the confluence of all the pieces of the re-emerging economy in this part of the Lowcountry," observed Billy.

"Except tourism. Both your grandfathers hated resort development. Very old school, they."

"So Molly was a director of Southern Atlantic, MidAmerica and Continental American, a trustee of Oryzantia, and a trustee at the Baker Endowment. What else?"

Julia rubbed her temples with her fingers. "She served two terms with the National Endowment for the Arts. She and Walker's grandmother were both on the board at Converse. She had some Diocesan responsibilities, but that's most of it. The Black River School," she said as an afterthought.

"What's the Black River School?"

"I don't know much about it, Billy. It's a small school for young at-risk African-American boys. Molly loved its mission. She called it a 'beacon of light in the darkness of Lowcountry swamps.'"

"Colorful," Billy mumbled.

Billy sat down on the corner of the conference room table as Julia continued.

"You know about the Fed – twice asked, twice declined. That said, you pretty much have the whole picture."

"So, Molly managed the land herself, and Morgan manages the portfolio holdings."

Julia nodded.

Billy shook his head. "Then how, or maybe why, in the world

would anyone get crossways with a rich old lady, or her heir, neither of whom appear to be involved in anything remotely controversial? And what do you suppose Dinny is talking about: 'follow the money'? I don't see a money trail here other than the income produced by Molly's property that we live on or donate to charitable causes. I don't get it." Billy rubbed his bridge of his nose. "Let's grab some lunch, what do you say?" Billy asked. "I've got a splitting headache."

As they walked out of Julia's building onto Front Street, Julia's mobile phone rang. Looking down at the screen, then laughing, she slid her finger across the phone's screen. "Walker. You need to get down here. Your best friend is wearing me out."

They paused on the sidewalk, as she removed the earring from her right ear, continuing to listen to Walker. Billy shoved his hands into the pockets of his trousers, waiting patiently in the afternoon sunshine to see what the conversation between Walker and Julia would yield.

Julia moved the phone slightly away from her ear. "Walker says he has a meeting in Atlanta on Friday morning. Do we want to meet him and make a weekend of it?"

Billy said, "Sure, I guess. I need to get my car, and some clothes. I could do that. What's the doc doing this weekend? You guys want to go to Atlanta?"

"Tommy's not on call, as far as I know. I can call him. I have to get a dress for the hospital ball at some point anyway."

"But let's fly over. I hate that drive."

Laughing again, Julia said "No, Walker, I haven't forgotten that you're there. And you're wrong. It's not that I suspect you have nothing more important to do than talk to me. I'm certain of it," humorously emphasizing 'certain.' "Thursday night then. Do you have a key and the alarm code? Okay. You, too."

"Walker said to be there for dinner and he said to get a mobile phone."

Billy chuckled, "Kind of a repetitive concept with Walk."

Chapter Twenty-Two

Tommy Henning walked into the waiting area for the Delta flight from Charleston to Atlanta, after dropping Billy and Julia at the curb with the bags and parking his car. He paused for a moment as he spotted them. Billy was dozing with his head on Julia's shoulder as she leafed through the pages of the current issue of Vogue.

He walked up to Julia who straightened imperceptibly and moved to awaken Billy. Tommy shook his head placing the first two fingers of his left hand on his lips and then on hers, shaking his head to say "It's okay."

Just at that moment the gate attendant began announcing the Atlanta flight, and Billy stirred. Julia looked sideways at her cousin and tugged a lock of his hair gently.

"I'm putting you to bed as soon as we get in."

Billy seemed groggy as they checked in at the gate, and the minute he was in his seat across the aisle from Julia and Tommy, he went back to sleep. When the plane reached its cruising altitude, Julia took a pashmina from her bag, stepped across the aisle and placed it around Billy's shoulders, turning out the cabin light above his seat. Tommy Henning could see the traces of a smile flicker across Billy's face as he settled deeper into the leather seat.

He watched Julia as she returned to her seat, the smile on his face belying the intensity of his gaze. Leaning his head against the window, he dozed lightly until he heard Julia say to the flight attendant, "A glass of Chardonnay, please,"

"Nothing for me right now, thanks," Tommy responded as he

stirred in his seat. Tommy watched her as she reached down to retrieve from the cabin floor the magazine she had been reading, and yawning, turned slightly in his seat to face her.

"You two are a lot of fun," she chided him.

"Notwithstanding my North Carolina antecedents," he began with mock seriousness, "I fear I have a certain Midwestern directness."

Julia waited, unsure where he might be headed.

"There's a substantial chance that I am falling in love with you."

Julia looked up abruptly at Tommy and then at the flight attendant, saying "thank you" as she took her glass. "I am certain that Dr. Henning will have the same, if you don't mind? Tommy, I… it's only been…"

"Just listen, okay? I get it."

"Get it?"

"You and Billy. The wall you call family and friends, behind which you have lived your entire life. The connectivity that runs through every moment you spend with Walker, John Harleston, even, I suspect, the inimitable Lucy Magrath." He looked out the window of the jet, pausing. "The night we went to Eddie Hazzard's – the ill-fated Miss America incident – I thought it would be… no, that's not right. I thought you and your group would be perfectly solidified…" Shaking his head and obviously struggling, he said "Preserved. That's it. If you were with Walker or John Harleston."

Julia laughed aloud, putting her head back against the seat and looking up at the cabin ceiling while she fingered the strand of pearls around her neck.

"Good lord, Tommy. You make me sound like the subject of some treaty negotiation. John Harleston's gay. Did you miss that part? Not to mention confused. Walker and I would be like Billy and me – kissing your brother or something." Turning to look at him, she went on, "but I'll admit the constancy and maybe even the apparent sufficiency of our companionship is part of our pathology."

"Julia. I love you. With all of your pathology." She started to speak and he stopped her. "And, it's not like I'm some second-stringer," he finished with a solemn wink.

"Oh, good grief, Tommy, that's not it. Your grandmother is Sadie Waterman for god's sake. Your name is plastered on half the containers in the Port of Charleston. Yale. Hopkins…"

"Yeah, yeah, yeah," Tommy teased her. "You're a résumé girl. Here's the thing. I began falling in love with you the night you walked into my ER. I can't explain it. I remember every detail of the way you looked, what you wore, your perfume. I told Celia…"

"Perfume?"

"I recognized the fragrance. It's distinctive. I've known only two women who wore it, and I've loved them both."

"Just for curiosity's sake, who was the other?"

He laughed. "My grandmother Waterman."

"I thought girls were meant to be the romantic ones."

Laughing, he said "I'm a romance guy. So, what's it going to be, Miss Pringle?"

Unbuckling her seat belt, she said "What it's going to be, Dr. Henning, is that I'm going to wash my hands before we land. Put my bag under your seat and I'll wake Billy up when I come back."

An hour and a half later, Billy unlocked the door to his Habersham Road apartment for the first time in nine months. The lights were on in the living room and the hall, and they could hear the strains of a familiar Cornelius Brothers song coming from the kitchen.

"'Bout time you guys showed up," Walker said as he walked out into the front hall. "Dr. Tom!" Walker laughed. "Julia's favorite house call."

Grabbing Julia and spinning her around, he continued, mocking the song playing in the background, "It's too late to turn back now… I believe, I believe I'm falling in love…"

"You have no idea what a bad choice of songs that is," Julia muttered. "Let me go."

Walker winked at Billy over her shoulder as she extracted herself from his arms. "So what's the plan, Jules?"

"Oh lord Walker. You boys decide where we are going. I'm starving. I need a minute to freshen up." Starting down the hall toward the rear of the apartment, she put her left hand lightly on Tommy's forearm and, reaching up, kissed him on the cheek. "Fifteen minutes actually," she said, glancing back at Walker.

Billy glanced at Tommy Henning, saying nothing.

The start of what might otherwise have been a blush began to creep up Tommy's cheeks. He seemed to recover himself, then shrugged his shoulders and laughed quietly.

Walker continued. "It's not without reason that Julia occupied a prominent niche in the pantheon of ice queens at the Deke house at Chapel Hill. Gorgeous. Qualified. Unbelievably in. Unbelievably unapproachable. Almost put Hardin, among others, over the edge."

"Hardin?" Tommy began.

"Walker," Billy said with unexpected sharpness.

Tommy watched the subtle change between Billy and Walker. Walker looked at Billy intently for a moment, and then, without breaking eye contact, said, "How about a glass of wine? Or a real drink? I was able to sneak two bottles of this totally superlative Sancerre by the gendarmes at LaGuardia and it's in the cooler. Gimme a sec," he said, as he headed to the kitchen.

"Why don't you take the guest room, second door on the left down the hall?" Billy said. "I haven't been here in a while but John Harleston swears everything is in order."

"Everything?" he heard Tommy say in a questioning tone of voice as he started into the kitchen.

Billy turned back, running his fingers through his hair to buy a moment. "Look. It takes a while, with all of us," he paused, searching for the right words. "She's worth it. It's complicated," he paused again, shaking his head.

"I know." Tommy laughed softly as he shouldered his bag.

Billy watched for a second as Tommy walked down the hall. Then turning, snapping his fingers to the beat of the music, went to find Walker.

"I feel the need to dance," he said, walking into the kitchen where Walker was opening the wine.

"Now? With me?"

"No, ass," Billy said, picking up one of the bottles with a low whistle. "Big stuff, even for Mimi."

"Closed a big deal. She knew about it."

"What's the deal?"

"Half billion dollar account. Some guy in the car business. Owns twenty Toyota dealerships in Southern California."

"Car dealers in the rarefied atmosphere of the Morgan Bank? The times, they are a changin'."

"He races out there. Mimi and Molly knew him in the horse business," Walker said raising his eyebrows. "CAB was trying to land him in their new wealth management division. I played the 'we've-got-more-members-of-the-Jockey-Club-than-they-do' card at Mimi's suggestion. It worked. Hence, the wine."

"Good man. Congrats. But why are we not sending Mimi wine?"

"You know Mimi. I sent her a basket of orchids and four tickets to the opening of the new Billy Budd thing at the Met, the one with the hot new baritone. Thought we would get John Harleston to go with us. Hear the baritone doesn't wear a shirt for the whole opera. Anyway, she sent the wine and said to find you and Julia and drink it. So I did. Oops," he said quickly grabbing a napkin off the tray as he spilled some of his wine. "Said she'd meet us next Saturday night in front of the Met, unless we needed her to pick us up."

Walker looked up at Billy. Billy noticed the slightest traces of dampness beginning to collect uncharacteristically in Walker's eyes. He picked up a glass from the tray Walker had carefully arranged.

"She'll go on forever. Just like Molly."

Walker touched the rim of his glass to Billy's. "*In pectore*," lightly thumping his closed right hand to his chest. "Now, about that dancing thing, we have a problem," Walker said, picking up the tray and moving toward the living room.

"A problem. What kind of a problem?" Billy said playing along.

"Well… you and I have no dates, and, I can't shag backwards, cute as you are, so to speak."

"Cute as I am…," Billy snapped his fingers as if to say 'I've got it.' "The Five Paces Inn!"

"You're not serious? Tell me you're not serious."

"It's right around the corner. We could crawl home after if we had to."

"Julia will have a fit."

"Hey. She rode around the parking lot in a shopping cart after the steeplechase, not us. We didn't make her."

"She'll have a fit," Walker repeated.

"She's over it. Everybody will be there."

"Everyone seven years younger than we."

"And?"

"Okay. How about we first hit the bar at Chops? Then dinner at that new Catalan place up on the corner, then the Five Paces. You go tell Julia."

"Better idea. Make it a surprise of sorts," Billy said, continuing to craft the subterfuge. "Dinner. Somebody called… and said it's kind of a… uh, thing. Blitz the Five Paces late. Thursday night and all that."

"Weak. Really weak."

"Ansley Boykin called."

"From the Trust Company?"

"Well, she would've if she'd known," Billy defended his fabricated story.

"Okay. Ansley Boykin called and said, 'Five Paces blah blah blah…'"

"Why does the word 'incorrigible' spring to mind?" they heard Tommy say from the entrance to the room. Picking up a glass from the tray, he continued, "Of course, Ansley was at Hollins with my sister Celia. I called Celia to tell her where I was going and she said she'd kick my ass if I didn't call Ansley while I was here because they were so close…"

Walker and Billy looked at one another with a touch of sheepishness and then burst out laughing.

"Well, you should. You should, Tommy, my man. Never let a sister down, I always say," Walker said, laughing.

"Liars," they heard Julia say as she entered the room. "Walker, hand me a glass of wine and move over. Mimi must have sent this. You would have never picked this wine," she said looking at the three boys in turn. "Has anyone called John Harleston? Let me guess, you've cooked up some evening plans to which I might ordinarily object."

Billy started to speak.

"Oh, please," she laughed. "Tommy's away from the ER for the first time in what must seem like years. Walker has likely concluded some major deal, as evidenced by the wine. Billy is back in Atlanta. So we're feeling flush, as perhaps we should, and you boys want to kick it up somewhere, only the two of you don't have dates," she said, looking pointedly at Billy and Walker, "and no real prospects. And since it's Thursday night, I'm guessing you have it in mind that we'll end up at the Five Paces. Have I missed anything so far, sugar?" she said, playfully pinching Billy's cheek, imitating Lucy. "But can't find the guts to make a clean breast of it because of the shopping cart thing with Hardy."

"Julia…," Billy began.

Julia looked at him. "Fine. Walker? The wine," she said, reminding him of her empty glass, "I'll forgive you for the ice queen comment."

"How did you…," he sputtered.

"You forget. Billy nabbed this place on the cheap because the developer was going under. You think they spent a lot on insulation while the ship was sinking? That's probably John Harleston at the door."

Billy got up to answer the door, chuckling to himself as he listened to the undercurrent of conversation kick in behind him. "Thursday night and the lights are low, lookin' out for a place to go," he sang under his breath, amusing himself with the paraphrasing.

Chapter Twenty-Three

The next morning, Julia pulled Billy's silver Mercedes up to the curb in front of the Continental American tower in Midtown. Gazing up at the tower through the open sun roof, she said, "How long do you think you'll be?"

"I'll meet you for lunch. How's that? Where will you be?"

"I have to drop a strand of pearls at Charles Willis to be re-strung for mother. Then to Neimans. We could eat there."

"Shoot me first. How about Savannah?" Billy suggested. "12:30?"

Julia nodded her assent as he leaned over and kissed her lightly on the cheek. "Keep your wits about you. Need anything at Neimans?" She said as he started to get out of the car.

"How about a new Rolex?" he said, laughing.

"Get out."

Billy watched Julia pull out into the traffic, signaling a left turn to head back uptown toward Buckhead. Turning, he glanced up at the fifty-two story Continental American Bank tower, reaching into his jacket pocket to retrieve the office number of Mildred Ferguson, the administrative assistant to the chairman of the Board's Executive Committee, a post momentarily vacant following the death of Molly Commander. Ten minutes later he presented himself in the reception area of the bank's executive offices. The attractive young African American man behind the desk stood up to shake hands.

"Mr. Commander, Mrs. Ferguson is expecting you. She's coming out right now, sir. Can we get you anything? Coffee? Juice…"

"No. I'm fine. Really."

"William!" he heard a voice from behind him. "How perfectly wonderful to see you. And, how perfectly wonderful you look."

"Mildred. It's been a long time…," he began.

"Let's go back to your grand-…," catching herself, she continued, "to our offices."

"Thank you for seeing me, Mildred. Particularly on such short notice. I just came over last night from the beach."

"Dear boy. I would have rearranged my entire day to see you," she said taking his arm lightly and guiding him into the suite of offices used by the outside directors of the bank. "Although, to be truthful, it's been rather quiet here for the past few weeks and likely to remain so until Mrs. Commander's successor is named."

"And who do you think that will be, Mildred?"

"Well, no one knows, and the Board won't meet again for another two weeks. Still, we've heard it said that Mr. Lesesne would like to see Richard Carlton in that spot," referring to the young, iconoclastic former chairman of the First New England National Bank, recently acquired by Continental, and known to be a protégé of Hugo Lesesne.

"Um. I see," Billy volunteered noncommittally, not sure of Mildred's implication, if any. "Well, that would shake things up a bit, would it not?" he said, raising his eyebrows quizzically.

Mildred smiled at him and said humorously, "There'll be no comment from me, Mr. Commander. I'm just a working girl. Way below the radar screen of bank presidents… and lawyers," she finished with a wink.

"Mildred. Can we talk seriously for a minute?"

"Of course. Sit here," indicating a sofa and two French chairs in Molly's office. "May I pour you some coffee?" she asked, gesturing to the small bar in the corner of the office.

"No. I'm fine, really. Julia and I stopped for breakfast on the way downtown this morning."

Mildred sat down in one of the chairs opposite Billy, unconsciously smoothing her skirt. "Julia is well, I hope? She's such a lovely girl. Mrs. Commander was devoted to her and as time went on, came to rely increasingly on her." Patting Billy on the knee, she said, "Give her my love."

"I will. I will indeed." Billy paused briefly. "I'm interested in what my grandmother may have been doing… uh, involved in the last several months of her…" Billy paused to collect himself.

Mildred straightened up noticeably, cocking her head slightly to one side. "Go on."

"I'd like our conversation to remain off the record. We are trying to reconstruct my grandmother's activities in the weeks preceding her accident. It may be helpful to…," he paused, searching for the appropriate way to phrase his request. "Look through, or have someone Molly trusted look through her correspondence, messages, meeting records and the like. We're searching for anything that might help us understand in what matters she was involved during that period."

"I assume you mean bank records?" Mildred asked, with a certain discreet emphasis on bank.

Billy nodded.

"William, this is a complicated area, especially so in the wake of 9/11 and the El Paso Pipeline and GlobalPetro debacles." Mildred seemed momentarily unsure how to best proceed. "Bank procedure is that any correspondence that comes in for one of the directors is first cleared through security – like all mail to the executive officers of the bank. Then it comes here. I open the mail and make a copy that goes immediately into a file we call the daily file, along with copies of any intra-bank memos, records of telephone calls and minutes of any meetings in which a director was involved. The originals go to the director pursuant to his or her particular instructions. Once every sixty days, the twenty-one daily files for a given month are consolidated and transferred to a monthly file. Every six months, the oldest monthly files are indexed, recorded on a storage log and sent down to records storage on the sixth floor. Internally generated documents follow pretty much the same guidelines."

"And the procedure for recalling one or more of those boxes?"

"Recall requires the signature of the director whose files were stored – or in his or her absence, the signature of one of the executive officers of the bank."

"I see. Which in this case would be certain to raise some eyebrows?"

"The bank has a very strict protocol covering the movement of documents internally, influenced undoubtedly by the involvement over the past several years of outside accounting firms in document custody and control issues."

Not to mention the activities of the big banks in the same mess, Billy thought.

"If I may ask, why do you ask? I might be more helpful if I knew."

"You worked with my grandmother for a long time, didn't you? You used to put little notes in with the checks and other things Molly would send me while I was in school."

A trace of dampness began to appear in Mildred's eyes.

"Yes, sir. I staffed Mrs. Commander from the very beginning when First South and North Carolina Atlantic came together to form Continental American. I was one of several assistants to the elder Mr. Wright. When he took the chairmanship of the new organization, he asked me to come with him as liaison to the Board."

Billy let Mildred continue to reminisce, although he began feeling slightly impatient with the direction of the conversation.

"… but your grandmother had been a First South director for years," he heard her continuing. "Mrs. Commander did not chair one of the principal committees right after the merger, although it was clear from the first day that Mr. Burnett, in particular, depended heavily on her advice, not to mention her contacts. But, she sat on more committees than most and…," leaning toward Billy and lowering her voice, "worked harder than most of the men, if you want to know my opinion. Mr. Burnett said Mrs. Commander would play an important role in the future growth of the bank and in developing its image in the financial community. He said she would need her own office and staff support. She became my responsibility – my only responsibility – the month after Mr. Burnett assumed the Chairmanship," she finished, now dabbing her eyes with a handkerchief.

"Mildred, we're grasping at straws here," speaking quietly, he went on. "There is increasing reason to believe that my grandmother's death may not have been accidental."

The cool professionalism in her voice was at odds with the startled look in her eyes when she answered Billy.

"I hadn't heard that."

Chapter Twenty-Four

Billy noticed her gaze shift over his shoulder to the entrance into Molly's suite of offices. Turning casually, as if he were about to leave, he saw two men, whom he assumed were senior bank officers because of their appearance, their familiarity with the surroundings and their sense of authority, coming in from the corridor.

Mildred stood up, extending her hand to shake his, and said in a voice that would be easily overheard by the two bank officers, "Mr. Commander, thank you so much for dropping by. I was devoted, as were we all, to your grandmother and you have no idea what your comments and kind sentiments have meant to me."

Taking his elbow firmly, she continued, "I am just on the way out to an early lunch. May I show you down?"

Billy was slightly confused.

"I've taken way too much of your time already…"

He felt her grip tighten as she said, "It's no trouble, really."

As they reached the outer offices, she paused.

"Mr. Dillon. Mr. Asbury. I am sure you must know Mrs. Commander's grandson, William?"

Billy shook hands with the two men as Mildred continued, "Mr. Dillon is in charge of the bank's derivatives trading division and Mr. Asbury has recently been named to head up the new Wealth Management office in New York."

"Yes. Of course. My pleasure," he said. Declining their invitation to lunch in the bank's private dining room, he said, "Another time perhaps. I am already running late for another meeting nearby. I just popped in to say hello to Mildred."

As they descended in the elevator to the lobby plaza, Mildred kept up a polite, but distant conversation, as if she were escorting a distinguished guest of the bank to his next appointment. When they reached the street level, she immediately steered him across the bank plaza to Peachtree Street, which was already crowded with other midtown professionals on the way to lunch or moving between morning meetings.

"Mr. Commander, I've worked for the bank, in one capacity or another, for almost thirty years. Because of an anomaly in the pension vesting rules due to so many mergers and acquisitions, my pension will not fully vest for another year. If I am terminated for cause… it's… well, let me just say it would be disastrous for me."

"Mildred… I…"

She cut him off. "When your grandmother turned seventy, she told me she was concerned that she might not have the energy… might not be able to get to Atlanta as frequently as she once had. You probably remember when she sold her apartment and began staying at the Ritz."

Billy nodded. Molly had, indeed, sold her apartment at the Reid House on Peachtree Street after his parents were killed and had begun staying at the new Ritz-Carlton Buckhead. He had always assumed the move had more to do with his parents' death than her personal situation. He listened to Mildred continue.

"She was also concerned that as she became older she might miss something… something significant."

"Miss something? Excuse me, but would you like to sit down and perhaps have a coffee?" Billy asked, indicating an outdoor café at the corner of the next block.

Billy noticed that she glanced casually around herself, taking notice of her surroundings and other people on the sidewalk.

"Perhaps, we could continue walking, if you don't mind. It's a lovely day. As I said, over the past several years, your grandmother became increasingly concerned that she might miss something."

"Go on," Billy encouraged her.

"When Mrs. Commander took the chairmanship of the Executive

Committee, there was already some talk about her age. As a matter of fact, it came up in her presence at a board meeting when she was nominated by Mr. Burnett. I was taking the minutes."

Her mind went back to the meeting. She could still see Molly sitting at the far end of the table, her blonde head slightly inclined to her right, listening to something said by Isabelle Collins, the chairman of Barrett Media, which owned, among other things, the Miami and Raleigh newspapers, thirteen mid-western radio stations and two CBS television stations. She was a year younger than Molly at the time. They looked up simultaneously.

"Age?" Molly questioned to no one in particular. "Is that what he said? Too old? Criswell, please tell me that I did not just hear the distinguished general counsel to the bank suggest that a director should decline responsibility because of age? Perhaps, Mr. Gregory, you would like to add to that indictment that I am a woman? And, ask me to step down?"

"Molly, that's not what I…"

She cut him off.

"And perhaps you would like to ask my distinguished colleague and fellow director, the Honorable Isabelle Barrett Collins, the former United States Ambassador to Argentina, to step down as well. I seem to recall we are not far apart in age. I wonder how that will resound in the board rooms at Coca Cola and Emory University when it is known that this bank has asked one of its directors – a director, mind you, whom the Coca-Cola Company holds in sufficiently high regard to entrust her with the leadership of its own Executive Committee – to relinquish her responsibilities after she has acquired and made available to this bank the experience, the vision, the compassion, the leadership ability, the contacts commensurate with leading a global enterprise in these uncertain times because she is… what was the phraseology you chose, Hartford? Oh, yes. Eloquently put. Too old. How will that resound? Perhaps you could also prevail upon Henry Harkness at the Trust Company of Georgia to ask Gardiner Arrington to step down. She's my age. We were at school together. Maybe you could get us a group rate or a suite at Bishop Ellison?" referring to the Episcopal retirement home near Emory University.

"May I ask you this, Mr. Gregory, as general counsel to the bank? While you were in law school, did you by chance become exposed to the sensitivity modern companies are required to have with regard to matters of age, race and sex? Or, were you just absent the day they taught that part of the law?"

Mildred remembered the embarrassed indignation that clouded the face of Hartford Gregory; the discretion with which Isabelle Collins had lightly placed her hand on Molly's arm. Molly turned and looked at her friend of fifty years, who nodded slightly. Turning back to the board room table, rising from her chair, Molly looked straight at Criswell Burnett at the far end of the room.

"Mr. Chairman, I would be delighted to accept the chairmanship of the Executive Committee, if that is the wish of this Board, and it will be my great honor to bring to that position not only my full energies and attention but also the collected experience and contacts of thirty-five years in the financial community."

She was of course elected by acclamation.

"Mildred… Mildred?"

"Oh. Sorry."

"Molly was concerned that she might miss something?"

"Mrs. Commander saw herself, in addition to her specifically assigned role within the bank, as part of the conscience of the organization, something of a reminder of the bank's roots, heritage and responsibility to the communities it served. She was passionate about it. You must remember this was back in the go-go days of mergers and acquisitions when companies and their employees were being shuffled about like so many pieces on a game board. I think she mistrusted the motives of some of the young guns – as she used to call them – who were beginning to emerge as important figures within the bank."

"Like Hugo Lesesne?" Billy inquired.

"Specifically Hugo Lesesne."

Noticing they had reached the High Museum, Mildred said, "Perhaps I would enjoy a coffee now. Have you seen the new terrace at the museum? It's beautiful on a sunny day. I've never understood why people from the bank do not come here for lunch."

Billy, grasping the significance of her statement, said, "Of course, lead the way."

When they were settled into a corner table on the terrace with a clear view of both the entrance and the forecourt of the museum on Peachtree Street, Billy asked, "We began by talking about internal bank protocols… I'm afraid I've lost the thread."

"When Mrs. Commander turned seventy, I began sending copies of all correspondence that came into her, as well as all correspondence that concerned areas of bank activities that fell within the purview of her committee, over to her at the bank in Georgetown."

"I don't see…"

"It violates bank protocol."

Trying to get the conversation focused, Billy asked "So you mailed Molly copies of…"

"No, sir. That's what I am trying to tell you. Everything went in the overnight bag."

"The overnight bag?"

"Yes, sir. The way checks clear has changed in this age of electronic clearing. However, for years, checks clearing through the system eventually had to get routed back to the city centers and then sorted and included in a customer's monthly statement. Those checks were distributed overnight by small air couriers."

"I'm lost."

"I know it seems unbelievable that we once sent the checks written by Georgetown area customers to the city center there to be sorted, stored and mailed monthly to customers."

"And these checks went overnight every night via FedEx or UPS?"

"No, sir. FinAir."

"Finn Air?" Billy replied, not completely understanding.

"Yes, sir. A network of small planes that transported bank items every night. I think it may have been regulated by the Fed somehow. Anyway, the plane was going and for the same nickel we could throw another parcel on board, so to speak. We called it the overnight bag – sort of like a diplomatic pouch, I guess."

Light suddenly began to dawn. "Wait a minute. Let me see if I've got this right. You mean for over five years you were sending – below the bank's radar screen – copies of everything in which my grandmother was involved?"

"Or in which she had an interest."

"In which she had an interest?"

"As you might expect, the chairman of the bank's Executive Committee had access to whatever documents and correspondence she found germane to the discharge of her duties."

"So Molly gave you a list of topics, deals, matters…," Billy looked at Mildred searching for feedback.

She was attentive, nodding her assent.

"… that she wanted to…"

"About which she wanted to stay abreast, yes. And, people."

"People?"

"Yes, sir. Whose activities she thought affected the discharge of her duties, I guess."

"You mean that she wanted to keep an eye on? Every week, for at least five years?"

"Yes, sir. Mr. Burnett told me – not long before he died – that Mrs. Commander was the soul of the bank and that as long as she was active in the management of the bank, there was only one response to a request of hers."

"Which was?"

"'Yes m'am. It would be my pleasure.'"

Billy was momentarily overcome with the implications of the information he had just received.

"Mr. Commander, I have to go."

Billy was searching in his pockets for a business card, forgetting for the moment that he had none. "Mildred, you know Mr. Coggeshell at the Morgan bank in New York, do you not?"

"Yes, of course."

"Mr. Coggeshell can find me twenty-four hours a day, seven days a week. If you need anything… anything at all, get in touch with him. You have his contact information?"

"Yes, sir. On my rolodex."

"Copy it. Take it home. I'm a mess right now. No cards. No cell phone. But if anything adverse happens at the bank… call Walker. Now Mildred, we had coffee. Talked about old times. Shed some tears for Molly. I thanked you for all you had done for her and for me while I was in school. You walked me out, and we shook hands and said good-bye. That's what happened."

As they crossed the terrace on their way out of the museum, Billy noticed the vaguely familiar profile of a man standing at the gift shop kiosk just inside the terrace doors. A sudden sense of discomfort came over Billy as he recalled having seen the man before.

"Mildred," he said quietly. "Do you by any chance recognize the man in the light blue golf jacket, standing by the postcard rack just inside the doors?"

Pausing, as if looking for something in the pocket of his jacket, Billy turned away from the entrance to the museum. Mildred, sensing the change in his demeanor, glanced quickly toward the museum and then toward Billy as if she were assisting him in some way.

"I don't know his name. I've seen him at the bank. Something makes me think he works on the second floor, off the main reception lobby."

Billy raised his eyebrows, listening attentively.

"What's in those offices?"

"Building security primarily. Some bank security officers and personnel. And the asset recovery offices," she added as an afterthought.

"Asset recovery?" Billy asked.

"You know – collateral recovery – repossessions. A loan goes bad and the bank takes possession of certain collateral as part of a work-out prior to liquidating the loan."

"Like cars, for example?"

Mildred laughed softly at what she perceived to be Billy's naiveté. "Well, we don't actually repossess automobiles at corporate headquarters, but that is where policy is made, guidelines are set and the process by which that part of the bank's function is administered."

"Mildred, is there another way out of the museum?"

She studied him coolly. Without comment she reached into her bag and retrieved a laminated blue card from one of the inside pockets. Staring into his eyes, she said, without question, "This way, quickly. An elevator in the corridor goes up to the members' reception rooms, and from there. Never mind. Come on," she said already moving toward the elevator.

"William, are you all right?" She asked when the elevator doors closed behind them.

"I'm okay. I'm just overly sensitive these days to things that seem… overly coincidental. The man I asked you about – the one you said worked in the bank's security office. I've seen him before. He was part of Oryzantia's security force, on the night an innocent man from Atlanta was killed by someone driving a car removed from the repossession lot of the bank in Georgetown."

"Perhaps it was an after-hours job," she began without conviction. "He could have…"

"Three hundred and twenty-five miles away? On a Thursday night?"

"I see your point. Follow me."

The doors opened on the fourth floor of the museum. Mildred glanced quickly to the left and right and, taking Billy by the arm, walked briskly across the empty members' lobby to a pair of lacquered white doors marked "Private."

"Wait here." She went through the double doors and returned in less than three minutes with an attractive woman in her mid-fifties, beautifully dressed in a beige silk suit. The woman nodded at Billy courteously, but without speaking, and motioned them both down a service corridor behind the bar in the members' lobby where they found another smaller elevator with key entry pad instead of conventional buttons. She punched in a numeric code on the pad, and the doors opened.

"Internationally famous architects," she said with obvious sarcasm. "Two million dollars for the design schematics for the new addition, and we end up with a private elevator to the MARTA station. I guess today that's all right, though. As the doors opened, she held one side back with her left hand, indicating Mildred and Billy should enter the car. "Take the elevator down to the second basement – that button. The one that reads -2. When you step off, turn right, end of the hall through the double doors and you are in the concourse leading to the Arts Center MARTA Station. The bank is the first southbound stop. Is everything okay, Millie?"

"Fine, dear, everything is fine. We're just running late, that's all. Lunch next week?"

"Of course. Call me. Take care," was the last thing Billy heard as the doors closed.

"Some kind of administrative assistants' mafia?" Billy grinned, relief beginning to flood over him.

"Something like that," Mildred smiled.

Several minutes later, as they approached the escalators down to the train platforms, Billy said, "Mildred, I'm taking the northbound train to Lenox, to meet Julia for lunch. Thank you. For everything." He leaned in and kissed her on the cheek.

"Mr. Commander, someday – I hope sooner rather than later – you'll be able to tell me what is going on."

"Mildred, when I know the story, I'll share it with you."

"I will see what I might quietly learn about the man you saw – sub rosa, your grandmother used to say." She laughed. "'No one looks under the roses, Mildred,' she'd say. 'The blooms themselves distract your attention, and if you put your hand underneath, you get stuck.' Your grandmother loved you. More than life itself. Dear boy, take care of yourself. I will be in touch with Mr. Coggeshell." She touched his cheek briefly with her hand and turned abruptly to step onto the escalator.

Chapter Twenty-Five

Billy descended to the northbound platform of the MARTA line and stepped onto the train which, fortuitously, was waiting. Twenty minutes later he walked into Savannah, adjacent to Lenox Square, where he found Julia in the waiting area, reading that morning's *Atlanta Journal-Constitution*. As he walked in, she stood up, closing the paper and leaving it on the bench behind her.

"It's not crowded yet – we can sit down anytime." Julia took stock of her cousin's facial expression and attitude even as they crossed the small lobby to the maître d' stand. Recognizing a certain tension in Billy's demeanor, she said to the hostess, "You know – I think that the table there in the corner," indicating a table normally used for larger parties, "would be ideal. We have some business to discuss and papers to review and I would not wish to disturb other patrons, if you know what I mean."

"Of course. Please…," indicating the way to the table Julia requested.

When the young waiter came to their table, Julia efficiently dispatched him with the lunch orders so that she could talk to Billy without interruption. "What happened? You look as if you were dragged behind the MARTA train instead of being on it."

"You remember that night leaving Oryzantia."

"Yes."

"They brought the wrong car. You walked off and left it to talk with Inness. I tried to get the security officer in charge to move your car, and, then I had to do it myself?"

"Billy?"

"He just happened to be buying postcards at the museum today while I was having coffee with Molly's administrative assistant from the bank."

"Who?"

"The security guy."

"Thank you," Julia said, acknowledging the waiter as he placed their drinks on the table.

"And," he said with finality, "he works for the bank. Security."

"An Oryzantia security guard works for the Morgan Bank?" Julia queried, momentarily failing to follow Billy's narration of the morning's events.

"No, Julia. Continental American. In Atlanta. In the security office. Which is on the same floor as the corporate Asset Recovery offices. Asset Recovery. Which manages the process by which the bank's branches repossess, among other things, cars."

Julia looked at him in frank disbelief.

"In Atlanta. On the bank's payroll. In an Oryzantia uniform the night Mr. … what's his name? Oh, how horrible, Billy. I can't recall his name."

"Evans. Jack Evans."

"In an Oryzantia uniform." Julia toyed with the rim of her glass, thinking. "Billy, are you sure you could not have been mistaken? It's likely unwise to look for…"

Billy cut her off. "Trouble? I think trouble has already found us, Julia."

"Maybe you need to tell me what happened with Mildred," Julia replied.

"Mildred's been sending copies of correspondence, memos of meetings and who knows what else over to Molly in Georgetown on some small private air carrier that specializes in financial records. For five years. Two senior officers of the bank dropped in while I was there, ostensibly to say hello, but I had the feeling they had been sent down to see what was going on with Mildred. And then the guy from Oryzantia… and it appears he works for the bank and at least would have access to information about repossessed automobiles. I don't know. I feel like I'm seeing conspiracy all around me when rationally one would think that the activities of the third largest bank in the country with respect to its own insiders are completely above reproach, let alone suspicion."

He lowered his voice. "We assume the integrity of the institutions that service our lives, don't we? I mean we expect that the power company will deliver power safely. We assume that the market will sell fresh fish or chicken and not something besotted with mercury or toxic chemicals. We assume that when we have the oil changed in our car that the oil is actually changed. Have you ever seen anyone actually change the oil in your car?"

"I leave my car next door every so often when I go to Eddie's for lunch. They could replace the oil with glue for all I know."

"That's my point Julia. We assume the integrity of the institutions to which we entrust these things – the phone company, the cable company, the gas station, the grocery store – the bank."

"The bank?" she questioned, not immediately following his logic.

Billy continued, "Molly finds out – or begins to have reason to believe – that the fundamental confidence people have always placed in the bank she helped build is misplaced."

"Misplaced?"

"Yes."

Julia leaned back against the leather banquette, studying Billy's face.

"And, that whatever the underlying circumstances may have been, someone in a very powerful position in the organization realizes that one of the most visible, respected members of the Board who – oh, by the way – just happens to be the Chairman of the Executive Committee, who enjoys status not unlike that which would be accorded a founder of the bank itself – has wind of… conduct unbecoming. What do you do?"

"What do you do?" Julia responded. "You attempt to marginalize the effectiveness of the director. Change his – or her – committee assignments. Ultimately, hope, he will step down or end up as an ineffective force within the organization."

"Yes. But this was Molly Commander. The largest individual shareholder of the bank on the Board. Present at the creation. The inheritor of the mantle of Criswell Burnett. Held sufficiently high in the esteem of two Presidents of the United States to be twice nominated to become a trustee of the American banking system itself. Marginalize that? I don't think so."

"You're making a case for the bank – or someone high up in the bank organization – wanting to get rid of Molly? And wanting it badly enough to engage in foul play? Why? What possible reason could there..."

"That's the hard part isn't it? I'm probably overreaching, trying to find some connection?"

"The bank involved in Molly's death? In the attempts on your life? Impossible hypothesis. Impossible," she said again for emphasis. "Look. You're exhausted. You need to take some time..."

"Time? What do you think I've been doing for that past eight months, Julia? Working on a PhD?... or trying some complicated anti-trust matter in Europe? I've been sitting on my ass, largely feeling sorry for myself. I don't need any more time. I need resolution of the chaos that has become my life."

Chapter Twenty-Six

"Where's the doc, anyway?" Billy asked, abruptly changing the subject.

"Emory. Tommy left this morning before you and Walker made a sound. Connecting with his medical buds."

"So, you and the doc…?"

"Billy, I told you before. Leave it. This is different. It's not like Hardy or Stiles and another debutante weekend. It's different."

"Are you paying?" He said good-humoredly, as the waiter brought the check to their table.

Julia reached for her bag. "I'm sure you don't have any money. How do you do that? Go through life with no money?"

Billy leaned back into the leather cushions of the banquette. "I have money. I just forget where I keep it. I'll get organized while we are over here. Let's go get me a mobile phone." He said brightly. "Get you and Walker off my ass."

Billy stood up first, extending his hand to help Julia out of the banquette. He took her arm, guiding her through the restaurant out to the curb to retrieve the car.

"Different? Why, or rather how?"

"What…"

"You and the doc. You said it was different. I'm asking how?"

"Oh lord, Billy. Let's don't have this conversation now. I didn't quiz you about Lucy."

"Lucy?"

"Do you think Walker didn't tell me the next morning that she'd… that it seemed…"

The parking attendant at that moment brought Billy's car to the curb where they were standing.

"You drive. Here...," he said, discreetly pressing several dollar bills into her hand for the attendant.

"I love how you have tip money but not lunch money," she laughed, getting into the driver's side of the car.

Billy got into the car and fastened his seat belt.

"That I slept with her?"

"Who?"

"Lucy."

"Right."

"Are you going to explain to me why we can't have this conversation? About Lucy. About the doc? Christ, Julia. I almost got you killed. Isn't there some middle ground where we can talk about emotions? Involvement? Our dreams?" he finished in an obviously teasing tone of voice.

Julia stopped the car at the exit onto Lenox Road, taking a deeper than normal breath, her hands tightly clasping the wheel.

"Sure. You want to have a real conversation. No wait. You want to have a real relationship. One that we don't hide from because somebody died. Relationships where we face things instead of getting on another airplane to another place? You want to have that conversation? That level of involvement?"

Julia put on the turn indicator and moved the car out into the stream of traffic, heading back toward Billy's apartment.

"Yes," he said.

"What?" Julia said, the irritation clear in her voice.

"Yes."

"I'm not sure I follow..."

"Yes. Julia, those are the relationships I want. That's the conversation I want to have. That's exactly the conversation I want to have. The conversations we used to have... the relationship we used to have...," Billy's voice trembled slightly.

"Before...," he stopped, unable to finish his sentence. "Before Caroline..."

"Died?"

"No, before Caroline came into the…"

"Billy, I'm sorry. I should not have…"

"No, you're right, Jules. Lucy was right. John Harleston. And probably even Walker."

Billy put his head back against the headrest, characteristically rubbing the bridge of his nose with two fingers.

"Maybe it's not time. Maybe I'm not ready to have this conversation today."

Julia said nothing, waiting to get some sense where Billy was headed.

"Let's go get the doc."

"But he may not be…"

"You have his cell, don't you? Well, call him and tell him we're on the way. Walker, too. And call John Harleston. Tell them we are going to have a drink at my place, and then we're going to dinner."

Julia finally burst out laughing, searching in her bag on the floor by Billy's leg. "Here," she handed him her mobile phone. "Call three people and make drinks and dinner plans in the middle of the most lethal traffic in existence. You do it. It will help you with that whole relationship thing you're after."

"Ouch. Shades of Lucy's sarcasm. Why'd you say that?" Billy said, mocking a heavy southern accent. Billy picked up her right hand, kissing it lightly. "It's me and you, babe. 'Til the wheels fall off. The doc's gonna have to sign off on that program."

Billy slid the icon to open Julia's phone and started to search for the numbers he needed. Looking out of the corner of his eye at Julia while he was calling Walker, it occurred to him he was completely in the moment. "Nice," he thought. "Nice." For a moment the memory of Caroline, of Molly, of his parents seemed to slip away.

"Billy. Billy!" he heard the voice in the telephone saying insistently. "Here, Walk. Sorry. Okay. You call John then. Six-thirty back at my place. We'll think of something. Julia says she bought this outrageous dress today and shoes from some Asian shoe guy – so she is all set to go somewhere splashy. John will know where better than I. Walker, I don't have my book with me. Can you get the car service? I like the one that drives my car better than the other one, but a town car will be okay. Do you mind?"

Billy chuckled as he listened to Walker. "No. Are you kidding me? That's great. We'll just get two cars. Okay, man."

Disconnecting Julia's phone, Billy said, "Walker said Charlotte's in town and she's going with us. Do you think the doc's got a suit? I mean, with him?"

"He's not that much different from you. I haven't snooped around in his bag, but, on the other hand, I've never seen him not turned out appropriately. One of his friends from Hopkins was going to run him back over this way. I guess he could run by Neimans and pick up something if need be."

Billy located the number for Tommy Henning's mobile phone in Julia's contact list and pressed the call button. "Hey, Doc. Before you say anything too revealing, it's Billy Commander."

Julia heard Billy laughing and then begin to explain the plans for the evening that were developing.

"Okay. We'll see you when we do. Oh, yeah, she's driving me crazy and around town simultaneously. You need to talk to her? Okay. That's good. I'll tell her." Disconnecting the call, he said to Julia, "the doc says he's set in the clothing department, and he said to tell you there's a chance he may need to stay another day."

Julia laughed.

Billy watched her with increasing amusement. "Omigosh. Turn right, here. On West Paces. You've got it," he said looking quickly back over his right shoulder.

"Billy," she said with exasperation "Across two lanes of .."

"Now, right again into the parking lot, just there. Crawford's. The wine place. I'm going to get champagne. Pull up there right in front. I'm just going to run in for a second."

Julia reached down by her right leg to retrieve her bag. "Here." She offered him several bills.

"No need, " Billy grinned, making the gesture of a signature in the air with his right hand as he got out of the car. "House account."

Julia rolled her eyes, replacing the wallet in her handbag. "Give me my phone. I'll check my messages. Get another bottle of Sancerre. Charlotte loves Sancerre. Might be the start of something big, you never know," she said, looking at him with a sly amusement in her eyes.

Billy stuck his head back into the car. "What do you have up your sleeve, sugar?"

"It's a sleeveless dress," she said matter-of-factly, refusing to be drawn in by Billy. Holding her hand up while she listened to her messages, she continued, "Wait a minute. Walker says tonight is the members' party at the Peachtree Club downtown and then…," she paused for a moment, listening further, "… and then we could go on to the Fulton Club for dinner… he thinks there may be a band."

"A band? At the Fulton Club? Is he sure?"

"Okay. That's it. Give me your driver's license."

"What?"

"Give me your driver's license right now. I'm going into the store right there," indicating the wireless telephone store next door to the wine shop, "and getting you a phone."

"But…"

"But nothing. Their phones work in the U.S. and in Europe. It's the one Walker and all the Wall Street cowboys have. Give me your driver's license."

Julia got out of the car, locked the car doors and took Billy's driver's license, which he offered with a sheepish grin. "Come in and sign the papers when you're through in the wine shop. Boys," she muttered in mock disgust, as she shouldered her bag and walked off.

Chapter Twenty-Seven

Billy walked into the living room and saw Julia, alone, sitting on a small sofa staring out the window onto the terrace.

"It's dark in here," he said, turning on the table lamp next to her and then moving to turn on the other lamps in the room. "Let me pour you a glass of champagne?"

Billy sensed something was wrong with his cousin. As she turned slightly toward him he could see an unwrapped present on her lap. He noticed a trace of tears in her eyes. 'Take it easy here, Billy boy,' he said to himself, buying time by fooling with the iPod in the dock. He queued up a Harold Melvin CD, and the sounds of "The Love I Lost" softly began to fill the room. Pouring Julia and himself a glass of champagne, he walked across the room to where she was sitting. Extending his hand with her champagne, he said, "That dress oughta be outlawed, Jules… you're gorgeous." She took the glass without really looking at him. "Christmas come early for you?"

She put the glass down on the table next to her and began tidying up the wrapping and ribbon, placing a flask of perfume, still in its box, on the sofa cushion next to her.

"It's from Tommy."

"Looks… uh, French," Billy said, still unsure what was troubling Julia.

"He's in love with me. Or, at least says he is."

"Ummm…"

"He had an interview at Emory today. He didn't tell me that. He says we have a shared history."

"A shared history?" Billy asked. He sensed Walker come into the room behind him and tried to catch his attention before he blustered into the conversation unaware of the context.

"Who has a shared history?" Walker inquired brightly, pouring himself a glass of champagne, not yet fully understanding Billy's pointed look.

Julia turned to look at him. "We do. You, me, Billy, John Harleston. Even Lucy, he said."

"Who said?" asked Walker.

"The doc," supplied Billy. "He coughed up the big 'L' word."

"Anybody could see that."

"He told her, Walker."

All of a sudden Walker understood the quietness that filled the room when he walked in. "Jules…"

Billy picked up the perfume box and wrappings and sat down next to Julia on the sofa, while Walker pulled up a side chair close to her knees.

"He had an interview at Emory today, didn't he?" asked Walker.

"Yes. How did you know?" she said with an almost exasperated emphasis on 'you.'

"Instincts. And now he says he loves you…"

"He says we live behind a wall, a wall we call friends and family, but a wall nonetheless…"

"And he wonders if he can ever be part of our shared history," John Harleston commented. They had not heard him enter the room. He poured himself a drink at the bar. "I wonder the same thing sometimes," he said leaning against the entrance into the living room rather than joining his friends by the windows. "He thinks you'll never… never ditch us and likely the thought of life without you makes him as despondent as it would any one of us."

"What's the point? This is a train wreck. How did I get myself involved in this?" Julia said.

"Jules. Stop. Be quiet." Billy put his arm loosely around her shoulders.

"It's a live-by-the-sword, die-by-the-sword argument," John Harleston continued from across the room. "Tommy is smart enough to realize it and face it head on. He was a doctor doing his job and one night a patient was brought in, the arrival of whom caused things to change in his emergency room in a way he did not entirely understand. And then you arrive. Not only a vision but probably a couture vision – and I am willing to bet you unconsciously co-opted not only his time but also the manner in which the emergency room operated. Again, without explanation. And if that's not enough of an introduction to Lowcountry life, he next wanders into Commander House into the midst of… how shall we describe it?"

"Delightful chaos?" offered Walker.

"… the delightful chaos that seems to attend upon Lucy. He thinks the two of you have a chance – but he realizes that, however you come at it, you come encumbered with all this marginally dysfunctional male baggage."

"I'd like to take issue with the dysfunctional part," said Walker, good-naturedly.

"John, we're thirsty here except for Julia," Billy winked at her, noticing she had not touched her champagne. Billy put his head against the back of the sofa, regarding his friends contemplatively. "It seems that we are outgrowing the option of being… what is the word?" he queried, looking at Walker.

"I dunno. What?" Walker responded brightly. "Dinner ornaments?"

Billy gave him a dark look.

"Here's the thing," John Harleston began. "Three weeks ago Billy inherited not only 6,000 acres of irreplaceable coastal estuarine land but also a huge interest in the third largest bank in the country. Walker manages more money than the… the…"

"The Vatican?" Billy supplied, somewhat illogically.

"The Vatican. And has the responsibility to recommend how to vote the shares of corporations that define the future of this country. Amusingly enough, I've been given the chance to speak with a voice of taste and discretion on a national stage."

Billy sat up, now fully engaged in the conversation. "And you, Julia. This is not the time and likely not the place to respond to an earlier comment of yours. But good lord. Your intellect. Your education. Your passion for the environment. For children and their needs. How dare you say you fear the mantle of Molly Commander? You are the most qualified… the most…," Billy's voice broke. Walker reached up to touch Billy's forearm lightly. "You are the most qualified person alive to assume the 'mantle' – those are your words – of Molly Commander. You may not want the job. You may not accept the job, but don't ever tell me again that you can't do the job." He paused again. "I'm sorry. I've cast a pall on an evening I meant to be entirely celebratory. The man loves you. I can only imagine the courage it took to broach the subject with you, in this way, at this time."

An uncomfortable silence settled momentarily over the group. Julia reached for her glass still sitting in front of Walker. As she did, Walker unconsciously reached for her hand and pressed it gently to his lips.

"I'm curious," Tommy Henning said from the entrance to the living room. "Is every night on the town with you guys like this?"

John Harleston laughed first. "Well, some nights are more interesting. This is just…," he laughed again, seemingly in spite of himself. "Ordinarily, for this level of drama, you'd expect Lucy to be in town. Maybe Billy's right. Maybe we have reached a new level of… a new level of…"

"Something… I don't know," Julia said quietly, her hand now resting on Walker's shoulder. "Without realizing it."

John Harleston sighed sarcastically, "You guys are wearing me out. I'm going to Canyon Ranch for the weekend."

"God, you are such a debutante," Walker said, bursting into laughter. "Make it a week. I'll go with you."

Billy pulled Julia to him and held her for a moment. "I think he's willing to sign off on the deal," he whispered. "Maybe you should give him a chance."

Julia stood up, wiping her eyes. "For god's sake, Walker. If it weren't for bad manners, you wouldn't have any manners. Tommy's standing there with no drink and no clue where things are. And you," looking at John Harleston, "is it your plan to let Charlotte ring the doorbell another five or six times before you get off your lazy ass to open the door?" She stopped in the door to the living room and rising slightly on her toes, kissed Tommy Henning on the cheek. "I'll be right back. Billy?" indicating by her tone of voice that he should begin to take charge of the evening.

Chapter Twenty-Eight

Julia was seated on the corner of the rear seat in the black town car provided by Billy's car service, almost on Tommy's lap. In the end, they had sent back the second car Billy had ordered. Charlotte had laughed, punching him on the arm. "It wasn't that many years ago that we had to wait for a van or an old Checker, so we could split the cab fare six ways. We'll all crowd in. Just don't sit on my dress. If the market doesn't come around soon, you'll be seeing this one again at Dr. Henning's ball."

Julia was listening to Charlotte, squeezed in between Tommy and Billy in the back seat, as she recounted the story of the night they had seen Hugo Lesesne in New York. "I was kind of in love with Hardin for a while. How could you not be?" Julia laughed. "But it was headed nowhere. Cute as he is." Changing the subject, she asked, "What were you going to do, Billy? Punch the chairman of Continental American in the middle of McMullen's? On a Friday night?"

Billy grinned, raising his eyebrows and looking up at the roof of the car. "You dog," he said to Charlotte. "I'm going to spread rumors about you at the Frick. Fake art credentials and the like…," throwing his hands up in mock defense when she reached out to tease him.

"Walker!" Charlotte said, tapping his shoulder in the front seat. "Are we going to Athens? The Fulton Club is only a few blocks from the Peachtree Club. Julia and I are starving."

"*Regardez, mademoiselle, nous arrivons.*"

"Oh, god, he's even beginning to sound like Lucy." Charlotte finished, as the car pulled under the porte cochere at the club. Two attendants immediately opened the doors and they could hear the music drifting out from the terrace overlooking Piedmont Park.

"The band's outside," Charlotte said with obvious delight. "However did they do that the first of April?"

John Harleston extended his hand to help first Julia, then Charlotte out of the rear seat. "For you, we would have heated the entire park."

"Julia! Come on," Charlotte insisted. "For once in our lives, it's not beach music."

Julia allowed herself to be pulled along to the terrace, which was indeed heated, covered with a white tent and banked with thousands of white blooms in terracotta pots. The deep resonance of a Barry White sound-a-like filled the space.

Julia laughed. "Charlotte. Stop," she said the moment before they ended up on the dance floor. "We're not in college anymore."

Walker came up behind the two girls. "We have a table in the bar, just inside the terrace doors, so you girls can rush out to the dance floor anytime."

The evening progressed in the comfortable surroundings of friends and acquaintances, many of whom stopped by their table to say hello, clearly delighted to see Billy out and about again.

"That's her, isn't it Charlotte?" Billy asked quietly some time later, leaning closer to her at the table.

Charlotte casually followed his line of sight toward the bar.

"The Oryzantia girl from McMullen's that night with Hugo?"

Charlotte nodded, keeping up the appearance of a conversation with John Harleston to her left. "Please excuse me for a minute," she heard Billy say to no one in particular.

Charlotte lightly placed her hand on John Harleston's forearm, signaling a pause in their conversation, "Billy?"

"It's okay. I left my dagger in South Carolina," he grinned, rising from the table.

"I left my heart in San Francisco," she retorted sarcastically. "Don't get into this tonight."

Billy had already walked away.

"Walker," Julia heard Charlotte say with a guarded tone in her voice. Looking up from the story Tommy Henning had been telling her, she saw Charlotte indicate the bar with a tilt of her head. She glanced casually toward the bar as she picked up her wine glass and saw Billy approaching Cynthia Morelli.

"What's he up to?" Julia said turning to Walker.

Tommy was amazed at the sudden, but extremely subtle change in the conversation, marked by a sharp increase in the level of tension, of which most people casually observing the scene would have been completely unaware.

"Give it a minute, Walker," he heard John Harleston say quietly. "Give it a minute."

"Nancy called last night," Charlotte filled in even as she continued to watch Billy at the bar. "She said to tell everyone hello, and you, Dr. Tom, how much she is looking forward to the Indigo thing. Bless her heart, I think she's been on a plane more than anywhere else for the past two months. But, success follows success. Anyway, she can stay with me at Mother's – unless we decided to make a house party of it. Wouldn't that be fun? Commander House is probably open, don't you think, Julia?"

"Of course. What a great idea. How stupid of me not to think of it. I'm sure Billy would agree. Tommy, don't you think…," her voice trailed off momentarily.

Billy studied Cynthia Morelli as he approached the bar at the opposite end of the room from the terrace doors where they were seated. She was standing with her back to the bar, gazing across the room, her elbows resting on the bar in a way he knew neither Julia nor Charlotte would have ever stood. Billy ordered a drink, signed the chit given him by the bartender and then turning to face her said, "I'm Billy Commander. I don't think we've met."

"I know exactly who you are, Mr. Commander," she replied, rather coolly he thought as she continued to allow her gaze to wander around the room.

"Billy's fine. Mr. seems a bit… well. You seem to know a lot of bankers."

Turning to face him, toying with the rim of her glass, she replied, "I know a lot of everybody. It's my job. I'm a development officer. But, of course, you already knew that," finishing her drink and placing the glass on the bar.

"Here," Billy said. "If you'll permit me."

"Ah. So you're a member here, then? But then, how could you not be? Tell me, Mr. Command...," she stopped herself in mid-sentence. "Billy. Do you ever grow weary of frequenting only those places the appeal of which seems to be keeping others out?"

"Like the Inman Society, for example, Miss Morelli," he said with emphasis on the 'Miss.'

"Ummmm...," she said turning around to face the mirror behind the bar and running her forefinger over her lips, as if she were in some way repairing her lipstick. Picking up her drink, she said, "Touché. Or should I say 'cheers'? I see nothing has changed much with you since college."

"Actually, quite a lot has changed since college."

"The Four Tops, was it not?" Cynthia interrupted, inclining her head slightly to indicate the music just finishing. "It's the Same Old Song..."

"Old friends and family trouble you? Or maybe it's the..."

"Nothing much troubles me. I didn't grow up in your coddled, accommodated world."

"Yikes. How did this conversation take that ugly turn? Usually it takes girls a couple of dates to figure out I am both coddled and accommodated," he said, sarcasm mixed slightly with the apparent good humor of his reply.

"Is this some kind of date in your post-fraternity mind?"

"Hmmm... suppose not. I just walked over to grab a drink. I'm curious, if you don't mind a professional question?"

"From another professional?"

Billy let it go. Turning back to face the mirror behind the bar, looking at her reflection as he placed his glass of wine down, he drew imaginary lines on the bar with the index finger of his right hand. "Where do the interests of Oryzantia, Alderlay Development and the Continental Bank intersect?"

Despite her carefully constructed, cool demeanor, Cynthia Morelli was obviously taken aback. Glancing around the room in an effort to buy herself some time for response, she answered him, "Am I being deposed, counselor?"

Billy responded, deadly serious. "I'm a member in my own right of the Inman Society. I seem to recall a document I signed which stated in part that 'members of the Inman Society are partners in the mission of Oryzantia, the modern investors in the future of the institution, inheritors of the tradition of Harrison Inman…'" He tapped his forefinger on the bar at the imaginary intersection of the lines he had traced. "As an investor, I'm curious."

At that moment, Charlotte walked up to Billy, slipping her arm comfortably through his.

"Cynthia," she said without extending her hand. "Charlotte Trapier. The Frick. We've met…"

"I know," Cynthia interrupted. "Chapel Hill. I'm sure I'll be seeing you at the Development League meeting next month in Boston."

"Yes. Of course." Charlotte began twisting the strand of pearls she was wearing with the fingers of her free hand, her other hand still comfortably hooked through Billy's arm as she leaned casually, ever so lightly into his side. "And, welcome. Can you even imagine? Dinner at the museum, in the midst of the Gauguins. George Ford must be having a fit. Not to mention André what's-his-name from the Louvre. Still, Eddie Bascom's got a fifty million dollar capital campaign coming up next year, and he'll need all the help he can muster."

Cynthia started to reply.

"Billy, you absolutely won't believe it. Elizabeth Wingate is outside and dying to see you. Julia and I haven't seen her in ages. She's got to leave in a few minutes. They're going on to some other thing at the High Museum. You must… Cynthia, you'll excuse us, won't you? It's just so seldom any more that we actually… well, never mind. See you in Boston?"

"Absolutely. Oh," she said to Billy, "thanks for the drink."

Billy grinned. "Sure. Don't mention it." Tapping the bar again with his finger, he said, "I'd still like to know about those lines sometime."

Billy caught up with Charlotte as she walked across the bar. "How'd that go?" she said looking at him with amusement. "Never mind. Come on. Let's dance. You have to save me from Timmy Rhoades. I just can't discuss a department store sponsorship of a Frick exhibition tonight. They probably would want to set up a sales counter in the galleries…"

"Unlike the Frick's own sales counters in the galleries."

"Oh. Funny. I need that from you like I need a headache. Never mind. It's different. You said you'd dance with me. I love this band."

Billy laughed as he studied her face. "What's different about you?"

"Nothing's different about me. Nothing." She took the glass from his hand, put it down on their table and led him out toward the dance floor.

"What's the Development League?"

"What?"

"You said you'd see her at in Boston, but you said it in a way that made it seem as if she had toilet paper stuck on her shoe."

"It's nothing. A private association of development officers for major museums. We get together twice a year. Talk. Trade ideas. She's ambitious. She got Inness Chapman to lean on some of the old girls to get her in."

"Well you certainly let her know she didn't quite belong," he said teasing her.

"Funny. Hilarious. You're giving me grief about exclusivity, standing here on the terrace of the Fulton Club. That's rich. Come on. Here comes Timmy Rhoades."

Chapter Twenty-Nine

The morning's *New York Times* and *Atlanta Journal* were scattered about the counter in Billy's kitchen with an assortment of coffee cups and breakfast items. Julia heard her cell phone ringing somewhere in the pile of papers.

"Julia? It's Lucy."

"Lucy. How in the world…"

"I'm fine. You probably are too. Let's don't deal with that now, Julia. I have to come to South Carolina. Daddy's not doing well. He says his life in Greenville bores him. I said that was redundant, or at least assumptive. Anyway. I'm worried. I've never thought he sounded old before. Have you?"

"Your dad's over eighty, Lucy. I haven't seen him since Molly's funeral. That's probably not a fair moment for assessment."

"I thought I'd bring him to the beach for a while. I only have four mares, and they're all bred. My yearlings ship to the consignor next week, so I could get away…"

"What a perfectly wonderful idea."

"Well, of course it's a perfectly wonderful idea, Julia. But that's not why I called. I've got to bring his driver and a cook down – and that won't work in his condominium. I could kill mother for selling her house.

"Lucy. Your mom's dead."

"A minor point right now. What am I to do?"

Julia listened to Lucy with mild amusement. Typical Lucy, she thought. 'What am I to do?' in the midst of a conversation where the implication was clear that Julia should be forthcoming with alternative proposals for resolving her staffing dilemma. But there was something else this time in Lucy's voice, an uncharacteristic tone Julia did not recognize.

"Is everything all right Lucy," she said in a softer tone of voice. "Talk to me."

"I don't know, Julia. I guess. Talking to Daddy made me sad. Hubert's in Paris at his mother's. I haven't talked to him in two days. 'Busy,' he said. 'You know, family stuff.' Like none of the rest of us have 'family stuff.'"

"He's quintessentially French, *ma chère*. You knew that when you started up with him."

"He is French. And I know I knew it. But it doesn't make it any easier right this minute, Julia."

Julia changed the subject quickly, struck with an idea, "Lucy, let me call Anne Evans. You know, she has that apartment on the ground floor of her house near the chapel. Maybe she'd rent it for your dad's driver and those?"

"Could they walk up to the pier?"

"Well, sure, I guess. I mean it's only about ten houses."

"Do you mind calling her? I don't know them."

"Of course not Lucy."

"Tell her I'll take it for a year if she'll let me. "

"A year?"

"He's old. And not going to live forever. He loves the beach, and if I can find a place for the help, he can go back and forth. What will she charge us do you think? Never mind. Whatever it is, it won't be as much as buying a house. I'll call Walker and have him send her a check. Do you think this will work, Julia? Julia?"

"No. Yes. I'm here, Lucy. I'll call Anne. I need to talk to her about the Indigo Ball anyway."

"Indigo Ball? What in god's name is the Indigo Ball. I don't remember any…"

"When are you coming over Lucy? It's a new thing. Benefits the hospital in Georgetown. Tommy took a table and we're all going."

"Tommy? Tommy Henning? You're pals now?"

Well… I've seen him some. We're all in Atlanta now actually."

"Atlanta? All of whom?"

"Walker had a meeting. Billy wanted to get his car. Tommy and I went over with him. Charlotte was in town working on something with the High. John Harleston…"

"Tommy and I, Julia? So it worked? You guys are itemized now. And Charlotte just happened to be there?"

"Lucy, this is not quantum physics. We all went out. It was fun. We even ended up at the Five Paces one night. But Tommy and I are not an… an itemette," she concluded.

Lucy burst out laughing. "I'm willing to wager Tommy sees that differently. Never mind. Can you call Anne? Let me know how much. I'll have Walker send her a check for the year regardless of what might…"

Julia heard Lucy seem to clear her throat.

"I mean regardless of what it may cost. Now," recovering her composure, "tell me about this ball thing. I had planned to come over Thursday or Friday before Billy's birthday. When's the ball? And who's going. You're not telling me much about the arrangements."

"You're not giving me much of a chance," Julia said smiling to herself. "Tommy took a table and asked me to help fill it. He wanted to support the hospital but didn't know ten people…"

"I hate ten tops at a gala, " Lucy commented. "So it's you and Dr. Tom, Walker undoubtedly. Who else?"

"John. Charlotte and Nancy are coming down with Walker. Mimi and Julius Irving. And, of course, Billy. And now you Lucy. That makes it perfect."

"Eleven won't work. And I can't crash Tommy's table."

"Eleven will work. Ten is huge. Fitting in one more is nothing. You and I have done it a dozen times."

"But Tommy…"

"Oh for heaven's sake, Lucy. Tommy's devoted to you. Talks about you all the time. It's incessant. Non-stop. Everyone will be delighted you're here."

"Who's the ball chair?"

"Kathryn LaBruce. She was at Sweet Briar when…"

"Oh good grief, Julia. I'm in France not Mongolia. Why don't we call Kathryn and tell her I'll take a table and then donate it – make it available somehow to the advancement office for the hospital. Let's do it that way."

"I have a better idea. You do that. I'll call Kathryn and ask her if they will give us two eight-tops. We'll put Mimi and Julius with your dad, Mother and Daddy, Walker's parents and maybe John's parents. And then we can sit next to them."

"You're a genius, Julia. But let Daddy buy that table. No...," she cut Julia off, as she started to object. "The changes are because of us. You're dear... it's the least we can do. Will Walker know how to send the money? I'll talk with him next. Maybe you could follow up with him about Anne's apartment? Do you mind? I need to call Daddy and get organized to get out of here. I am probably going to go down to Paris Tuesday, find something to wear. Get Billy a birthday present..."

"Oh, you're right, Lucy. For heaven's sake I'd forgotten. Maybe Tommy won't mind if we celebrate his birthday before the ball. Can I do anything to help with your dad? How long are you staying, Lucy?"

"I need to stay long enough to see that Daddy is going to be okay. I'd like to spend some time with you. With Billy. Walker even. Everyone. I have to be back over here the first of July for the two-year-olds-in-training sales at Chantilly. I don't know." Lucy listened for some response from Julia. She thought for a moment that the trans-Atlantic connection might have been broken. "Julia?"

"A lot's happened, Lucy. They think Molly's death may not have been entirely accidental. There was a fire at Asylum. Billy was trapped inside. I... uh... A lot's happened," she concluded quietly."

"I know. Walker tells me everything. He said Charlotte was at dinner with Billy in New York."

"I think Hardy put together a group on the spur of the moment. You know how he is."

"And she's in Atlanta with all of you, and now the ball?"

"What's your point?"

"Charlotte and Billy... oh, never mind. Let me talk to Walker then."

"He's not here."

"But you just said..."

"Billy went for a run. Tommy's back at Emory. Walker's downtown at Morgan's office. You could call him there or ring his cell – but call him this morning. I think he's going back to New York after lunch, and we're driving back to the beach this afternoon."

"With Charlotte?" Lucy said sardonically.

"Lucy. Leave it." Julia noticed Lucy was no longer on the line, disconnecting her own cell phone.

Chapter Thirty

A week later, Billy was reading the morning papers in the glass loggia at Molly's house when Thomas walked in with a stack of red leather bound books in his arms.

"I think these are the books you asked about, Mr. Commander. At least, these were the ones on the shelf in her closet."

Excellent, Thomas. Excellent," Billy said, privately regarding the stacks of books on the table with a growing sense of trepidation.

"Thomas, you know Mrs. Ferguson at the bank in Atlanta?"

"Yessir, of course. She was Mrs. Commander's assistant…"

"Exactly," Billy interrupted. "Mildred told me that they sent papers, correspondence and things from the bank in Atlanta to the bank in Georgetown for Molly."

"Yessir. Would you like some more coffee, a diet coke, or anything?"

"Thomas, it must have been a lot of stuff. Boxes or files or cartons of some kind. Do you have any idea what may have happened to all those files?

"No, sir, I don't. Let me pour you some more coffee."

"Please, that'd be great if you don't mind, and if you are going that way," Billy said picking up one of the red volumes and beginning to thumb through its pages.

Thomas returned a few minutes later with a fresh cup of coffee on a tray. "You know, Mr. Comman…," he began.

"Billy. Thomas, it's Billy."

"Yessir, of course, sir. When the bank moved from downtown to the new building out on the highway, Mrs. O'Steen called and said what did we want to do with all Mrs. Commander's things that had been in storage in the basement. Mrs. Commander's Georgetown office was to remain downtown. She did not want to move out to the new building…"

"Thomas?"

"Anyway, Mrs. Commander was in Europe with Mrs. Coggeshell at Mrs. Collins' house, I think. I had not heard from her – Mrs. Commander, that is, in several days, but that was typical when she was in France with Mrs. Coggeshell and Mrs. Collins."

Billy tried to remind himself that the wandering response was in some way tied to Thomas' own way of working through the loss of Molly and that he needed to be patient.

"Mrs. O'Steen called back and said something had to be done. I told them to send the things here. The bank sent a van with about thirty boxes and I put them in the basement. When Mrs. Commander came home, I asked what she wanted to do with them – the boxes, that is – and she said we'd make it a rainy day project. But…," his old voice faltered slightly, "we never got to it. The boxes are still downstairs."

"Thomas. Unbelievable. Will you show me? How heavy? Can we start bringing them up to the dining room? And I need a phone…," unconsciously patting the pockets of his robe.

Thomas handed him the portable phone from the kitchen.

"Julia. I need Julia."

Thomas extended his hand for the phone, "Mr. Commander, if you'll permit me?"

"Billy. It's just Billy, Thomas," beginning to realize with resignation that the familiarity would never occur.

Billy turned his attention back to Molly's daybooks to allow Thomas to complete his task and he heard the phone ring before Thomas could dial Julia's number.

"Mrs., … excuse me. Mr. Commander's residence," a moment later handing Billy the phone. "It's Miss Julia."

Billy eagerly grabbed the phone. "Jules, are you ready for this? Thomas found all Molly's daybooks and that's great. But here's the thing. All the correspondence folders from the bank. The stuff I told you about that Criswell had Mildred send over under the radar screen."

"Yes, what?"

"It's all here."

"All where?"

"Here in the basement."

"Bank correspondence in Molly's basement?" Julia said, the incredulity obvious in her voice.

"They screwed up, Jules. They're downstairs," he said, slapping his thigh at the thought. "D'ya believe it? Monumental stupidity."

"Billy. Those boxes have got to go back."

"I know they have to go back, Jules, but not until after we've read what's in them."

"Where? At Molly's?"

"Sure. Command central."

"All right. I have a couple of calls I need to make and some letters to sign but I can be there by one."

Two hours later, Julia walked into the dining room at Molly's house, looking with amazement at the quantity of material Billy had already assembled.

"Those boxes along the wall are the correspondence files from the bank in chronological order from left to right," Billy said pointing toward a row of record center boxes lined up two deep down the wall in front of the windows looking onto the terrace.

"Those," indicating two stacks of leather bound daybooks on the dining room table, "are Molly's agenda."

"Okay. So, do we have a plan here? What is it exactly we are looking for?"

"I dunno, Miss Pringle. You're the one with the practice discipline. I, on the other hand have no discipline. I've been lounging about in France."

Julia smiled at his re-emerging sense of humor. "So I've heard. So I've heard. Speaking of, Lucy's coming for your birthday and the Indigo Ball. Did I tell you that?"

"Lucy? Here?"

"She called me in Atlanta."

Billy walked over to the large windows overlooking the courtyard in front of the house, and, in the distance, the Atlantic Ocean.

"Billy? Billy?" she said, the second time more insistently. "What is it?" Deciding to drop the matter, she surveyed the boxes. "All right. I guess we read to get some sense of what Molly was looking at in the weeks or months before her accident. And then see if there is some… what?"

Billy nodding his assent, flipping a pencil up and down on the table as he listened. "Some indication that something was amiss?"

"OK. I still am not sure what it is that we're…"

Billy interrupted her. "I say we go back as far as we can. One of us skims the correspondence file – the other the daybooks. Then we compare. Trade jobs maybe. Look for patterns. No not patterns. A red flag. An indicator of 'wait a minute, what the hell is this'?"

"And legions of Hardy Boys' fans will rise up and call us blessed," she quipped laughing.

"Indulge me," Billy responded, clearly not amused.

"I'll start with these," she said, beginning to thumb through the leather daybooks, rearranging them in chronological order. Julia turned her attention to Molly's disciplined record of meetings, telephone calls, conversations. Rather quickly, she not only began to find Molly's rhythm but also began to decipher her cryptic references to the elements of her day – abbreviations uniquely her own for telephone calls, telephone conferences, meetings, plane schedules, dinner engagements and the like. Within an hour she found that she was able to begin to visualize Molly's days.

"When did Lucy call?" Billy asked quietly.

Julia looked up to find him staring out the windows overlooking the pool. "The last morning we were in Atlanta," she replied, waiting to see where his inquiry might be headed.

"Ummm… I wonder," Billy began and then fell silent.

Chapter Thirty-One

Julia waited, unsure what to say, and then watched as Billy rose slowly from his chair and walked out through the open doors onto the terrace overlooking the marsh.

"Give him the space he needs to talk things out if you really want to help," her mother had said the night before. "You all live in such a whirlwind. I wonder sometimes when you have time to reflect upon things, darling. Life is defined as much by the quiet spaces as it is by the frenetic progress of one's career, the glamorous aspects of one's social exposure. Solace may not be a thing you choose to embrace. Lord knows, it's not a regimen I could ever see working for any of you, Julia." Dot Pringle had paused. Leaning slightly toward Julia she had continued softly. "You are all Billy has right now. It may remain so."

"What do you mean? Billy is surrounded by people who care about him. John Harleston. Walker. Lucy."

"John Harleston can't figure out where he fits into his own life. Sweet though he is he needs more from all of you right now than he is able to give. Walker will marry someone from New York, whatever that means these days. She will rapidly seek to disassociate the two of them as a couple from the hometown crowd. She will be unwilling to be the ancillary figure in what she perceives as Walker's ancillary role in Billy's life. Walker has, or will have, plenty of his own money. She will use it to separate, not co-exist."

Dot continued, "Lucy's in love with Billy. She has been since she was twelve. It began the summer her mother bought her house at Pawleys. Everything in the interim with Lucy has been just that – interim. Fill up space until… well, until."

"Mother. How did you know all this?" Julia said with amusement.

"You thought I wasn't listening? All those years of carpools and supervising your activities build listening skills that are sharp enough to gather subtlety, innuendo, and inference from your conversations later in life. Plus, you forget dear, I have a magna from Smith," she had laughed. "I'm teasing you a bit. I think insight comes with being a mother. God sends us – all of us – what we hope is wisdom commensurate with our several challenges. That's where we started, darling. I worry that you don't have the quiet spaces in your life that allow you to hear that voice when it speaks."

"When we were in Atlanta, Billy told me I was the most qualified person alive to assume the mantle of Molly Commander."

Dot Pringle put her hand on her daughter's shoulder, recognizing the non sequitur in her comments. "All right."

"All right? You mean you agree?"

"No. I mean all right. I'm listening. I heard you."

"I don't know what that means. The mantle of Molly Commander."

"No?" her mother had asked with a touch of amusement in her voice.

"What?"

"Julia, you can't be this blind to your own actions, your own decisions. You were a Morehead and a Phi Bete at Chapel Hill, second in your class at Yale. You had law school internships at Debevoise followed by Cravath. You were offered a federal clerkship. And, wait," her mother went on chuckling softly "do I not recall a Morehead internship at the U.N.? You turned down a Fulbright to work at the EU one summer. And, you came back to Georgetown."

"And, your point is?"

"My point is, dear, you could have gone anywhere. You chose to come home. None of your friends did. Charlotte is at the Frick, Nancy at the Met, Walker at the bank. You? The only logical conclusion is that at some subconscious level you sought this involvement, this particular manner of influencing your community. That, I think, is what Billy calls the mantle of Molly Commander."

"You think I compromised?"

"Julia, you've made certain choices in your life. You have chosen to make a large impact in what your friends might consider to be a small environment, rather than participate in the somewhat larger…"

"And you think I made a mistake?"

"No, dear. Not at all. We all make these choices. I'm certain I could be running Bergdorf had I stayed in New York. I chose another path and I have loved every step along the path I've chosen. No regrets."

"But a mantle?"

Dot Pringle laughed again as she patted Julia's hand. "Metaphors are often difficult to grasp in the face of day-to-day reality."

"I can't help wondering if Molly was aware of her… her responsibilities, the impact her actions had on her community? When did you meet Molly? Do you recall?"

"Your father's plane from Houston is delayed. There's a problem in Atlanta. Would you like to have dinner? We could go to Eddie's. Run up to the beach club. Or, I suppose take our chances in the refrigerator. I'll take my chances at home if you will."

It had been Julia's turn to laugh. "Mother, neither of us can cook."

"Darling, it's not as if we've asked ten people to dinner and promised them beef Wellington. We can cobble something together with no help. Tell you what. Let's find a bottle of wine that seems to stand up to this conversation and see if we can't find something that will keep body and soul together until tomorrow."

Julia tried to control her amusement as she watched her mother open both doors of the refrigerator, staring into the interior as if observation alone would cause supper to appear. "Okay. Let me tell you what. I'll make this easy. You have all those little sausages Isabelle sent from Aix last month. Cornichons. There's bound to be a wedge of cheese or two. Here is some smoked salmon. Let's boil some eggs, make some toast points and… voila. We're done."

"Brilliant, darling. Just brilliant."

Julia handed her mother a bottle of sauvignon blanc from the refrigerator door as she balanced the elements of dinner. "Open this one. Sit there and talk to me while I do this," Julia said, indicating a stool at the counter. "Do you remember when you met Molly?"

"I do. I was going out with your father at the time. He was at Davidson, as Jim Commander had been, and we were at your grandmother Commander's for lunch one Sunday. I was at home on some break from St. Mary's. I was always a bit terrified of Mary Brewton, even though I had grown up around her. Thirty years of being in the Pringle clan had failed to dim that Commander willfulness. Molly and Big Jim were there. Mary Brewton asked me what I was studying at school. I began telling her about my European history course and she exclaimed 'History! Spending all your daddy's money up there in Raleigh to learn history. I could teach you history at home for nothing!' I was so taken aback I couldn't think of a reply, polite or otherwise. Molly looked up from her Bloody Mary and the *Times* and said as dryly as one could imagine 'thus establishing once again that those who do not understand their own history are bound to repeat it.' The idea of anyone who could not only stand up to Mary Brewton but also date and marry her brother was an amazing accomplishment to me. Molly was an anomaly."

"An anomaly?"

"Yes, I think that's the right word. Something different, not easily classified. She came into this cloistered society we call the Lowcountry with an independent base of power: her mother's money, style and powerful family connections and her father's presence in the community because of his investments. She was… what would it be? The ultimate outside insider. She knew everybody from day one. She was part of the legendary group that included Isabelle Barrett, Mimi Fraser, and Gardiner Blackwood." Dot Pringle paused, sipped her wine and laughed. "The four of them, I am told, wore out more debut party dresses by the time they were twenty-one than most of us ever owned. To be around Molly was… I don't know. For a young girl from a small town, it was captivating, energizing. Molly's the reason I went to Smith. Did you know that?"

Julia had finished arranging the elements of dinner and pulled another stool up to the counter, across from her mother. "No, I just assumed it was a result of the St. Mary's college counseling process."

"The St. Mary's college counseling process back then, darling, was to send you to Chapel Hill to marry a boy from the Deke or the Phi Delt house. Molly asked me if I intended to be a four-year girl at St.

Mary's or leave after high school. I told her my parents wanted me to go to Converse, thinking that might score some points with her. You must remember, I was shy, uncertain about myself."

"Let me guess," Julia smiled. "Molly boomed at you – 'well, what do you want to do?'"

"She did. She did. I told her I wanted to go to one of the Seven Sisters. She asked if I had a reason. I didn't. I had read about schools in the northeast and seen pictures in the magazines of debutante parties in Greenwich and Westchester. Summer houses on the north shore, Fisher Island. It all seemed so elegant, so cultivated. Unlike Pawleys and Georgetown in the old days. Molly said one place was like another unless you understood why you were part of this community as opposed to that community – and unless you developed a commitment to make whatever community of which you became a part a better place."

"'So, I should go to Converse?' I asked. 'You should go to Converse if your analysis leads you to believe they will contribute to your development, and you will contribute to theirs more than anywhere else,' she said. I said I was not sure my parents could afford to send me to school in the North with all the associated expenses. She said I should ask them. I asked my mother about Smith, and she said that all good schools were expensive but that I should not worry about the cost. It was the point at which I began to understand having money and the convoluted behavior that often surrounds it."

"You asked me, commented rather, about the mantle of Molly Commander. That must be Billy's phrase – slightly melodramatic." Dot Pringle paused, tilting her wine glass slightly to swirl the liquid around the bowl, studying the legs as if she could divine some meaning from the wine. "I don't know. She often saw what the rest of us missed. She used to quote Lucia Baker's work all the time, insisting that we seek the intersection between education and community, and that at that intersection would we find meaning in our own lives. Community for Molly was a kind of communion, not a geographic concept. The idea of being in communion with one another as opposed simply to sharing space somewhere. In that regard, she was the antithesis of a limousine liberal. More the embodiment I suppose of Robert Kennedy's liberal optimism: 'I see things that never were…'"

"… 'and ask why not?'" Julia completed the statement.

"She had a passion for change that I am not sure Billy shares. A dedication that implies responsibilities I am almost certain he doesn't want," she finished.

Chapter Thirty-Two

"Jules?" she heard Billy say, pulling her back to the conversation.

"She called Monday afternoon. Well, afternoon her time anyway. You know Lucy. Time is calculated from wherever she is. You were out running." Julia tried to sound light, casual.

"Lucy doesn't call me."

"Do you call her?"

"Is that the point?"

"I'm listening."

"To what?"

"To you."

"I… I don't…," Billy stopped. "I don't have anything to say really."

"About Lucy?"

"What do you mean about Lucy?"

"Billy, I'm willing to go along here. You brought it up."

"So what do all of you think about Lucy?"

Julia propped her elbow on the table, cradling her chin in her hand. "All of us don't think about Lucy in the way that you ask. She's part of our shared landscape. It's a view to which we are accustomed. Your question is what do all of us think about you and Lucy?"

Billy took a deep breath. "Okay. Tell me."

Julia ran her fingers through her hair while she collected her thoughts. "We've never had this conversation."

"I've never asked. I'm asking."

"Lucy's your danger zone."

"Danger zone?"

"I know. It's stupid. It's not my concept. It's Walker's.

"Are you serious?"

"I suppose he has a point. Lucy tends to push the conservative envelope in which the rest of us live. It can be trying. You find it invigorating. Scary."

"Scary?" he questioned.

"I think Lucy scares you in a way. I think it's part of why you married Caroline."

"Are you cr…"

Julia laughed softly. "Caroline was perfect. No. Wait. She was perfectly predictable. She was the ultimate achievement of all our mothers. I loved Caroline, Billy. Make no mistake about it. But she and Lucy are polar opposites."

Billy put aside the memory of Caroline for a moment and asked, "When Lucy called, what…"

"Hard to say. Ostensibly, it was about her dad. I think she wanted to know if you were okay. She's heavily invested in you. I think she also wanted to know what's up with you and Charlotte."

Billy wheeled around abruptly. "Charlotte?"

Julia gave him a gospel wave with her right hand. "She talks to Walker every day. Everything that enters Walker's head falls out of his face fifteen minutes later. You know that."

Billy turned back to the windows overlooking the marsh. After a moment he said, "Caroline was…"

"Billy, we don't have to do this."

"She seemed like a solid, quiet place. I felt buffeted about. Lucy and I had a brief fling, you know?"

"I know. When you were in law school. Everybody thought you were the rest stop between Alex McPherson and the Park Avenue guy. What was his name? All I can remember is 1050 Park Avenue."

"Hamilton Stuyvesant."

"Right."

"I was a rest stop?"

"It was a metaphor."

"A colorful one."

"I don't know. Maybe we should get back to the files here."

"Where are you chronologically?" Julia asked, thumbing idly for the moment through the book in front of her.

"Some of this box goes back fifteen, sixteen years. Memos about the acquisition strategy for the First South North Carolina Atlantic deal. Pro forma models of the savings from back office consolidation – one run printed on green bar paper. Seems archaic, doesn't it?"

"I'm just wondering. Doesn't it make more sense to start…"

"… closer to the present? I agree. If something here is informative, it's bound to be recent, not buried in the events of twenty – even ten – years ago."

Julia became absorbed in scanning as rapidly as possible through the entries in Molly's daybooks. At one point, she noticed Billy wandering back to the kitchen, a file folder in his hand. Returning with two diet cokes, he resumed his place across the table, stacking what seemed to be a year's worth of correspondence files in front of him.

"January, five years ago," she said finally.

Billy gave her a mock groan, rocking his chair back down on all four legs and going to the row of record center boxes underneath the windows. Pulling a box out, flipping the lid off, he ran his finger across the file folder tabs. "January, five years ago," he concurred. "January 15th. Faxed memo from Criswell about a meeting in Florida. Acquisition of Gold Coast Savings it looks like. Says she has to come down."

"January 15th. She's at a Baker Endowment meeting in Charlotte. Wait… what's this line drawn across the page? Did she leave early?"

"This must be it," Billy said scanning through several pages of correspondence. "Criswell says they're close on the Gold Coast deal. He needs Molly to wrap it up. There's a fax from Molly," glancing at the confirmation page, he continued, "sent from the Baker offices it looks like. Her handwriting in the margin. Can't come. Annual meeting. Committee meetings… and so on."

"Here's a phone conference with Criswell in her book on the afternoon of the fifteenth."

Billy flipped through another two pages. "Seems that Warner – who's Warner - is trying to hold up the deal for a larger premium on the stock and another twenty mil in his parachute. Criswell wants Molly to hit the board members… so…," turning back to another page. "Flight itinerary from Mildred. They sent the plane to pick her up in Charlotte on the afternoon of the 16th. Georgetown?"

"What?"

"The plane made a stop in Georgetown on the way up? Why?"

Julia laughed.

"What?"

"Clothes," she answered.

"Clothes?"

"She was in Charlotte in the middle of January and had to go to Palm Beach. She didn't have what she needed for dinner and meetings in Palm Beach. I'll bet the plane stopped in Georgetown to pick up a bag from Thomas, got Molly in Charlotte and then back to Palm Beach."

"Why would they do that?"

"One. You think Molly Commander would walk into the Everglades Club with the wrong shoes and jewelry? Two. It was a 700 million dollar deal. What do you think?"

"I'd have given the Florida boys another point on the deal and skipped the drama."

Julia shook her head in mild disgust.

"I'm starting to see your point," he added, handing her a photocopy of a handwritten note from Molly to Criswell Burnett.

"What's this?"

"Hand it back, then, if you're not going to read it. She sat next to the chairman of Gold Coast at dinner. That's our boy Warner. Asked what he saw as the single greatest opportunity for institutional growth. He says real estate finance… large developers, understanding the needs of large complex development companies and developing the array of financial products and services they require to service their customers."

"Whose customers?"

"Huh? Wait…," Billy gave a low whistle as he turned the page. "Are you ready for this?" he continued summarizing excerpts from the document as he talked. "Molly says here 'and which corporate clients do you see figuring most prominently in that strategy' and he says – the Gold Coast guy – the list would have to include Alderlay Development. Aggressive. Forward thinking. Great ideas. Huge market. Big need for financing and innovative financial products." Billy scratched his head.

"Now she asks 'Are there others similarly situated?' Gold Coast says WSI over on the West Coast… blah, blah, blah… but Alderlay could be the category killer. Molly says she'd like to meet their chairman… Warner says he will set up a meeting. She says no – only him, Criswell, Molly and the Alderlay guy. Six p.m. at Chuck and Harold's." Billy looked up abruptly. "Chuck and Harold's?"

Julia laughed again. "Of course. Perfect. Completely under the radar. No one there at six on a…," she looked back at Molly's daybook, "yep. Here it is. Six o'clock on a Friday evening. Happy hour."

"Molly went to happy hour?"

"No. Silly. She had the meeting at Chuck's knowing that no one would be there but college kids and whatever random twenty-something upper east-siders had just arrived for the weekend at grandma's. Yet another example of Molly's perfect pitch."

"And then nothing here until the 28th of January. Copies of memos about… not relevant. Anything there?"

"Nothing. Wait. The next day she called Isabelle. There's a question mark and then 'Barrett Cable – slash – AldDev.' What?" She looked up.

"I hope when I'm seventy-five I'll still be calling you every day to talk things over."

Julia appeared puzzled.

"Molly. Isabelle. Mimi."

"Billy, don't look now. Some things don't seem to change. Happily," she added as an afterthought. "Get back to work."

"Mr. Commander. Miss Julia." Billy heard Thomas say from the door to the dining room. "They just called from Mrs. Coggeshell's and said Miss Julia's office told her she was here, and could you and Miss Julia come for drinks at six-thirty and then go to dinner at the beach club?"

Billy shrugged his shoulders, as he turned to Julia as if to say 'what do you want to do?'

"Sure. I can run by Mother's and change. Tommy was coming out anyway. Daddy's in New York."

"Thomas. Do you mind calling Mrs. Coggeshell back and tell her we are delighted and that, if it's not a problem, we'll be five for drinks – Mrs. Coggeshell, Julia, Mrs. Pringle, Dr. Henning and me. And then,

I would be pleased if she would allow me to take everyone to the beach club. Can you work that out?"

"Yessir. I'll call right now. I think Mrs. Collins is also in town."

Billy turned back to the file boxes. "Okay. Financial stuff. Board meetings. Here's a nugget. March 10th same year. In-house memo announcing appointment of Hugo Lesesne to… something. Can't read it. Molly annotates the memo in the margin. Sends it back to Criswell. 'Are we absolutely certain Hugo has the discernment required for such a sensitive post?' Criswell sends a note back the next day – he thinks his discretion is equal to the task. Molly replies with a copy of her original note underscoring 'discernment' twice – yikes – adding an exclamation point and then 'not discretion – it's a different concept.'"

Julia laughed. "What did Criswell say?"

Billy searched. "Nothing apparently. But then I would have run for cover too…"

"Ummmm… Molly's in New York. Some GCA thing."

"GCA?"

"Garden Clubs of America. She and Mimi were… never mind. After the thing, she and Mimi went to Le Relais, and it looks as if Hugo is there with the Alderlay guy – Lawrence. No further comment. Wait. The next day there is a telephone call to Isabelle – no <u>three</u> calls and a note. 'See Mia Hld bz section tomorrow dash Ald.'"

"What's the date?"

"April 17th."

"Okay," he said, making a note on his legal pad. "We'll pull the business section of the *Miami Herald* for that day."

"Why?"

"The *Herald*'s part of Barrett Media."

"She had a heads up from Isabelle about something that would break with reference to Alderlay. But why would Isabelle…"

"Molly went to her with a 'what do you hear about these guys?' I'll bet Isabelle was in Miami when Molly called here, probably at the paper. Isabelle was not only a CAB director, but she was also watching Molly's back."

Julia reached for her wrist, twisting her watch around to find the time. "Good lord. I forgot to call Tommy. He's likely on the way."

"Why don't I pick you up?" Billy looked down at his own watch. "How long do you need? We only have 45 minutes."

"Mother will be dressed. She always is. I'll go like this. Let me scoot. Pick me up in 30 minutes," she said closing the daybook in front of her and collecting her bag and keys. "Billy?"

"I'm going. I'm going. Throw some water on my face. Brush my teeth. We're eating on the terrace though. I'm not dressing."

Julia rolled her eyes as she walked out. "Thirty minutes!" As she closed the front door, she heard Billy in the background. "Thomas?"

Chapter Thirty-Three

"So much for a quiet night at the beach with your mom," Tommy Henning said with a grin to Julia twenty minutes later standing in the kitchen of Dot Pringle's house.

Julia pretended not to hear him as she transferred some of the contents of her handbag to a bag more suitable for evening. She heard her mother respond.

"Why, Tommy? It will be just the same. Mimi and Julia and Billy will get caught up in some issue or another, and you and I will have all the time in the world to visit. Just as if we were here," she concluded with a soft laugh. Dot Pringle glanced in a mirror as she casually draped a pashmina around her shoulders, retrieving her bag from the console. "Besides, you've not met Isabelle Collins I don't think. She's a stitch." Casually slipping her hand around his arm, she moved the three of them toward the front of the house. "I had no idea your mother was Ella Campbell's roommate at St. Mary's. They were several years ahead of me… Julia, I'm certain that's Billy's car out front."

An hour later, Billy had everyone arranged comfortably at a table on the terrace overlooking the ocean at the DeBordieu Club.

"This was a wonderful idea, Billy. The terrace." Mimi said. "I've not been out here since they put up the wind screens. The candles all over the terrace make this a different environment entirely – lovely. Just lovely. She continued, holding up her wine glass. "Here's to Isabelle, safely returned from… where was it, dear? Of course. Buenos Aires. And to Dr. Henning. What a great pleasure to get to know you. Billy, thank you for making the arrangements. Now…," as she turned her attention back to Tommy and Dot.

Billy heard Isabelle resume the conversation with her right hand resting comfortably on his forearm. "You were still at St. Bart's, I think. Richard was so sick. He was in and out of Sloan Kettering for a year. There was no hope from the beginning. From the initial diagnosis. Still, one tries to believe otherwise. We tried everything. The last weeks at Sloan were grueling. There were press everywhere. We had just completed the Arkwright Cable merger. Some reporters had even gotten through on the phone in Richard's room. Molly finally called Edward Malcolm, the head of the hospital board. They re-routed the phone lines to a security desk, closed half the sixth floor. You couldn't get in without a pass, for god's sake. I thought I had influence," she smiled broadly in the soft candlelight, straightening up in her chair. "In the end, Molly was the voice of loving realism. She came into the solarium near the ICU one afternoon. 'Isabelle,' she said. When Molly said my name it always sounded like 'Izbull' kind of slurred together. 'This is not going to end well and we both know it.' She was wearing a suit Bergdorf told me they could not get for me, I'm sure because Molly had it, and they knew we went so many places together."

She laughed lightly at the thought and went on. 'You have a job to do,' she said. 'It's unavoidable. Your company… no… the economic fortunes of many people in your company depend on your actions. The continuity you are able to establish is vital to their security. You and Richard have built a remarkable business on the legacy of your father's enterprise. Richard went into areas no one had thought of. He is slipping away from us now. You are letting the press mold the story. We cannot afford for his legacy to be diminished by any perception of corporate uncertainty. Moreover, we need to keep the mind of the press focused on the story we wish to tell, not some fluff into which they will easily descend without readily available information. We need to send your plane now for Johnny Barnes, schedule a conference call with the principal business editors, release a preliminary statement to the press about Richard's condition along with the appropriate biographical and corporate c.v. material, and then set up a conference call with the major investment advisors, hedge fund managers and so on… 'The passing of

Richard Collins, a giant in the world of media appears inevitable. While we mourn the loss not only of our leader but also one of the legendary businessmen of our time, life goes on, and so on, and so on.'"

"Molly, I just can't, I remember saying. 'I know,' she said. 'But I can. Give me your book. What's the name of that girl that manages for you in Atlanta?' she asked. Four days later we buried Richard. I could not have made it through without her."

"Molly seemed to have been the rock for all of us," Billy commented reflectively. "I wonder. After my grandfather died, my parents… who was Molly's rock?"

Isabelle patted his arm softly. "You were, Billy. You were."

"I was eighteen when my…"

"You were the promise of the future. I'm sorry. I know that's horribly trite, but I've just come from South America. I think I am a bit too tired to put it more elegantly."

"Isabelle. This may be a long shot. Four years ago Molly was in New York. Julia says some gardening thing."

"GCA fall trustee meeting," Julia supplied turning her attention to Billy as she overheard the change in the topic.

"She called you. It looks like at the offices of the paper in Miami. You called her back. She made a note in the margin of her daybook to get a copy of the next day's *Herald* along with what looks to be an abbreviation – A L D," he spelled the letters.

"Yes?"

"Do you remember the call? What she wanted? Was it about Alderlay Development?"

"It was bank business, Billy."

"Well, likely so. But can you tell me…"

Isabelle Collins picked up her wine glass, looked directly at Billy, and repeated herself.

"But…"

"Billy, I think what Isabelle means is that it was an official call between two directors of the bank and to divulge the substance of that call…," Julia began.

"Would be a breach of her fiduciary duty." Billy completed the statement.

She looked at Billy calmly over the rim of her glass, with her elbows propped lightly on the table. "One of the things I love most about my tenure on the Credit Committee for the bank is the attempt at deciphering the various financial filings public companies are required to make. I even took a class, did you know that?"

"You went back to school, Isabelle?" Dot Pringle asked with amusement.

"I did, Dorothy. I truly did. I took a forensic accounting class in financial statement analysis at Emory. Kind of a new discipline in accounting, I think. I made Gardiner go with me. Tuesday and Thursday afternoons. And then we'd go to Everybody's for pizza after class with some of our fellow students." Isabelle laughed at the memory. "Gardiner even had a beer one night, which I thought rather crossed a line."

"Oh, my word," said Mimi. "What I would not give for a picture of Gardiner Arrington in a pizza place with a beer in her hand."

Julia noticed Billy beginning to look around the terrace. She nudged him gently under the table to bring his attention back to Isabelle.

"It was interesting. Conversation with students. Not only to hear their opinions but also to get a sense of their motivations, their anxieties, fears, hopes, aspirations. Critical aspects of understanding one's young colleagues that certainly does not come across in a job interview, or rarely in the context of one's professional association. We fell into a regular Thursday evening pattern that semester. It became stimulating – trying to decipher the corporate behavior that resulted in a particular financial event. For example," she put her glass down and turned toward Billy. "Why would a company borrow money from a bank toward the end of an operating quarter to buy T-bills… and then sell the T-bills within the same period?"

"Well, it sounds like an interesting experience, Isabelle," Bill commented noncommittally.

"Ummmm. Yes. Why would a company do that do you think?" she said, tapping her forefinger insistently on his arm. "Anyway. Do you know they package and distribute wine in boxes now, Mimi? That's another thing Gardiner and I learned at the pizza place. Boxes. With this spigot on it where you fill up the glass," she said seeming to change the subject while still looking intently at Billy. Turning to Tommy she then began, "Now, Dr. Henning. You must tell me…"

Julia stood up excusing herself as the conversation resumed a less focused pattern. As she leaned over to put her napkin on the table, she put one hand on Billy's shoulder and said quietly into his right ear, "Pay attention. She's drawing you a road map."

Billy smiled as if Julia had made some private joke, rose slightly to acknowledge her departure, and when he sat down, re-focused his attention on the table.

Chapter Thirty-Four

"My law firm is beginning to wonder if I actually intend to bill any time ever again," Julia said as she walked into Molly's dining room the next morning.

"I called Hardy."

Julia didn't follow his comment. "Hardy has an answer for the senior partner in my firm about my lack of billable hours? That's brilliant."

"No, wise ass. I called Hardy to ask him why a company would borrow money to buy T-bills and then sell them within the same quarter."

"So you were paying attention."

"Of course, I was. Everyone we know speaks in code. He said it depends."

"Meaning?"

"They could be inept. Financially stupid so to speak. I know," he held up his hand to stop her. "I said the same thing. Hardy said you'd be surprised at some of the things CFOs of major corporations do."

"The interest spread?"

"Nah. Never happens within the same quarter. You'd have to buy billions to make a nickel. But… he said that if the company engaged in regular trading activity of some kind, it might be possible that the loan and the sale could become disassociated financially."

"Disassociated?"

"If the company is regularly trading some commodity – oil futures – say. The sale of the T-bills could be classified as…"

"… trading revenue," Julia supplied.

"Exactly."

"And… it would impact their cash flow from operations rather than…"

"Right. And the loan would get lost over on the balance sheet among all the other short-term borrowings. You got it."

"Billy, the situation with my firm is serious." She changed the subject and sat down.

Billy noticed the change in her tone as Thomas appeared at the door.

"I'll have another coffee, Thomas. Julia?"

"Please. The same for me, Thomas. Thank you."

"I need you, Jules. I want to know if Molly was murdered. If someone tried – is trying to kill me. It's important to both of us. I don't want to live the rest of my life looking over my shoulder every time I go out to get into my car. Neither do you. We have complementary skill sets." He paused for a moment. "Do you really want to practice law as an associate – or even a partner – in a small law firm in Georgetown, South Carolina?"

"That's not really the instant point."

"Well, let's make it the point. There's a chance – probably a substantial one – Tommy's going to Emory. You and I both know it. Why would he not?" Tapping his index finger on the table, he added another point. "You're twenty-nine."

"Thirty next week."

Billy grinned devilishly. "I know."

"What are you up to?"

"Nothing. Nothing," he said putting his hands up to deflect the legal pad she tossed at him.

"You have your own money. Plus the ten mil from Molly. The combined yield, conservatively invested, is a minimum half-mil a year. That'll buy a lot of shoes, babe. Walker's doing an AmeriJet deal this week for us, coupled with a car service and this new thing with the Ritz. Some program that's more sensitive to security concerns. Different entrance. Name doesn't appear in the registry. Elevator only from a secured space."

"That's crazy."

"No. Careful. You were a car-length away from getting killed. Because of me. It's appropriate. And, it's an intermediate step before a security detail takes over. The law firm, I don't know. Do what you want. See where the relationship with Tommy goes." Julia wiped the developing tears from her eyes.

"Julia. If I started tomorrow, I could not spend the money I've got. I may never have children."

"Billy, that's…"

He held up his hand to stop her. "I may not want to do the marriage thing again. But even if I did, it's unlikely my children could spend the money they would have."

Billy paused at the soft knock on the dining room door.

"Thank you, Thomas. Here is fine. I think we're good for now. Maybe we'll have some lunch in a bit."

"Jules, look. We can change the paradigm. How we live. How others do. I've been thinking about this a lot in the past few days."

"Paradigmatic change because I have a jet? Now there's an in-depth piece for *Town and Country* if I've ever heard one."

"No. Paradigmatic change because you can focus your energy and considerable talents on big picture issues where you can precipitate paradigmatic change."

"Like what?"

"Like saving Winyah Bay. That river school thing Molly loved. I don't know. Or maybe you just go to Atlanta and become Mrs. Thomas Waterman Henning if you want."

"Meanwhile, you'll be doing what?"

"I dunno. Go back to France maybe."

"Well, there's a paradigm shift. So you think it was Alderlay engaging in the T-bill trades?"

The abrupt change of subject caught Billy by surprise. "No… or rather, I'm not sure."

"Did you tell Hardy that? I don't know if I still have his number." Julia said as she reached into her bag for her phone. "212-…?" she said looking at him.

Billy shuffled through the yellow legal pads on the table. "555-9212. That's his direct."

"Yes, it's Julia Pringle in Georgetown for Hardin Murrah, please." She paused, removing her earring as his assistant answered the phone. "You may. Please tell him I am calling about the possibility of the government of France acquiring the General Motors Corporation." Julia rolled her eyes, looking at Billy and mouthing the word "stupid." Speaking into the receiver, she continued as Hardy answered, "I should think if there is to be a wall between you and the business community – a structure we will discuss at another time, mind you – that Rémond Moncrif could at least afford you the services of someone clever. 'Can I tell him what this is in reference to?'" She gently mocked his administrative assistant. "You're probably right. And would that we were having a Pernod on the roof of the Plaza Athénée right now. How are you? I know. Billy said it was great. I'd love that. Maybe next weekend. Billy and the boys are going up to meet Mimi Coggeshell for the opera. Naked baritones are involved, I am told. About which, at this particular moment, I could care less. But I may grab a ride and come up to shop." She laughed again, characteristically twisting her pearls with her free hand. "No, I won't stay with you. But I will let you buy me a drink one afternoon. Now listen. Be serious. Tell me about these T-bills. Can you walk me through the transaction step-by-step?" She listened for a moment. "Assume you were a large real estate developer."

Billy went back to the file boxes, allowing the one-sided conversation to recede into the background, confident Julia would get what they needed from Hardy.

"Listen to this," he said after Julia hung up. "A memo from Molly to Criswell February 16th. Where was she?"

Julia found the page in Molly's daybook. "On the way back to Georgetown from Palm Beach, on the bank's plane."

Billy read from the sheet in his hand. "'... several things bother me.' Some comments about the meetings. '... while others chased higher fee-based business, we have always focused on serving the retail customer, including the communities in which they live.'"

"Municipalities?" Julia queried, slightly confused.

"No. I don't think so," Billy responded as he continued to scan the document. "Here it is. 'Small to medium-size businesses without the access to capital markets available to publicly traded corporations.'"

"Sounds dated by contrast. Vaguely old-fashioned."

"She goes on. 'Over the past five years our operating margins and return on capital have both been significantly better than the big New York banks. Our stock is up 10 per cent in the past twenty-four months. The big banks have risen by comparison an average of around four per cent over the same period.'"

"But can't a ten per cent increase in value in an institution with, say, a capital value of 5 billion dollars pale in comparison to a 4 per cent increase in an institution with a capital value of 30, 40 billion?"

"Well, therein lies the dilemma." Billy traced the typed words down the page, scanning Molly's comments quickly. "She quotes Hugo, from a recent speech somewhere. '… eat or be eaten.' 'I don't normally embrace such inelegantly put articulation of strategic planning – but he has a point,' she says. Last year's acquisition of BMW…"

"BMW?" Julia said with marked surprise.

Billy leafed through several pages in the folder on the table in front of him. "Bank of the MidWest. I don't remember that one."

"Oh, sure. Big credit card issuer. That's the one that made CAB the largest issuer of credit cards in the country."

"Anyway," Billy continued, "'good fit' she says. Essentially a retail endeavor. Consumer credit, properly managed, allows individuals and families to accomplish certain goals. Properly managed internally… excellent margins.' Here's where we get to the heart of it. Listen. 'Several things bother me about the Gold Coast deal. Our attraction to Gold Coast lies principally in their strong presence in the residential mortgage business – a notable weakness in our organization – and the possibility we could draw on their expertise to expand our own mortgage business in other regions. However, last evening Warner spent a lot of time talking about building bridges to large corporations to become more of a full-service financial institution with a particular emphasis on those rapidly growing companies pushing the geometric growth in coastal Florida, South and North Carolina.'"

"Curious leap. Joe Homeowner to Mega Corp."

Billy continued to quote from the memo. "'This strikes me as inexperienced if not clearly naïve.'"

"Ouch," Julia exclaimed.

"'… and the premium they want in the deal. It seems to me the fact that Synovia paid a 30 per cent premium for New England Marine could not be more irrelevant. Most of the recent deals sold on the basis that the 'market' will realize the synergies of combination and not discount the stock for paying a premium tend to result in the need to slash and burn to pay for the premium. The numbers I've seen indicate to me that we might consider a premium of a couple of points based on some incremental profits from their mortgage division. But, they've got a problem with their higher risk and underperforming mortgages, which they tried unsuccessfully to securitize earlier this year. I can't think we'd want to go any higher than 5 per cent. If you want me to go back down and deliver the news, I can go on Thursday.'" Billy looked across the table at Julia. "Curious, don't you think?"

"Why?"

"Major acquisition for the bank. And yet, no mention of what do you think, Cris. Just a here it is, you want me to wrap it up?'"

"Undoubtedly, the basic structure of the deal had been approved by the Board. Molly was likely the only one who knew how sick Criswell was. I think they probably had an understanding. She had been involved at the very highest levels of negotiations since First Texas. And, too, they were old colleagues – similar outlook, history, philosophy. She knew without asking that Criswell had reached the same conclusion she had. Remember, he called her to come down in the first place because of the premium their Chairman was demanding."

"Did she go back to Florida?"

Julia turned to Thursday in Molly's daybook. "Looks as if she was at the beach. Drinks at Mimi's – dinner at the beach club Saturday. Lunch with Loudoun Smith on Sunday. Wait. Here. Tuesday. They sent the plane from Atlanta to get her. Isabelle was with her. She must have stayed at Isabelle's in Palm Beach. Meeting the next morning at ten, Gold Coast Tower in Lauderdale." Julia paused.

"And then what?"

"I don't know. It looks as though she is back in Atlanta on

Wednesday. Lunch at the Fulton Club. Meeting at the bank that afternoon. Drinks with Gardiner and then some reception for the new executive director of the symphony."

"This looks like a printout of an email from Criswell to Hugo, Richy Concannon and Barrett Holmes in legal, with a copy to Molly. 'Gentlemen: Mrs. Commander called me from the plane a few moments ago en route to Atlanta. Gold Coast has now agreed to all the major deal points outlined in Hugo's and Richy's memo of 3rd February. She hammered out a final price of $68.00 per share, thus a premium over yesterday's close of slightly less than five per cent. Mrs. Commander has a signed letter of intent in hand. Let's wrap this one up. Please consider this as your authority to proceed with the appropriate documentation. By copy of this message, I am requesting Liz Patton in communications to schedule the appropriate conference calls and announcements. I will personally call the governors of Florida and Georgia, the chairman of the Senate Banking Committee and the chairman of the SEC. Hugo, I would like you to call the Comptroller's office…' and so on."

"It was Criswell's last deal," Julia commented quietly.

"Did you go to the funeral?"

Julia smiled. Billy noticed her close Molly's daybook, unconsciously trailing her hand back and forth across the leather binding. "Daddy and I took the girls – Molly, Isabelle, Gardiner and Mimi. Mother was in California for some reason. He was buried in Walterboro at the Presbyterian church. The bagpipers from The Citadel played. A choir from the local AME church sang "Precious Lord, Take My Hand, Lead Me Home" a capella. The chairman of the Fed read the most unusual thing for a eulogy I've ever heard."

Billy said nothing, allowing Julia to work through the memory that held some particular significance to her he did not yet understand.

"It was a passage from Thomas Wolfe," she continued. "*The Web and the Rock*, I think, commenting on the influence of Southerners in the 'cold canyons' of the North. 'They brought you… a warmth you lacked, a passion that God knows you needed, a belief and a devotion that was wanting in your life, an integrity of purpose that was rare in your swarming hordes…' It was the only time I'd ever seen Molly cry. I can see them now – all four of them in black. Mimi stooped, leaning heavily on her cane. Isabelle had her arm around Molly's waist. Gardiner stood slightly apart, her hand on Daddy's arm for support. None of them seemed able to move or speak. We stood there under the trees after everyone else left, just the six of us. Two ranks of Citadel cadets stood at perfect and unmoving attention, almost as if they knew some era was passing. The bagpipers played 'Scotland, the Brave' in the fading light." Julia wiped her eyes.

"Sorry. Where were we?"

"What's the Doc up to?" Billy subtly shifted the conversation away from the funeral of Criswell Burnett and the Gold Coast acquisition. "I've not seen him in a while."

"Work. Work. Work. Allen Fleetwood has been on vacation. They're short another ER doctor. I think he has been working double shifts, to tell you the truth. He called me earlier. Home sleeping now, I think. And, he's off tonight."

"Perfect. Let's do something. Unless I'm horning in on some romantic evening you have planned."

"Billy, please."

"Okay then. What are you up for?"

"You think it's too late for oysters?"

"Murrells Inlet, you mean?"

Julia nodded.

"Probably. They'd likely be Louisiana oysters."

"There's a new fish place up there, right on the water."

"You have a number? Name?"

"Fins, I think."

"Thomas…"

Chapter Thirty-Five

"You're going to the opera with Mimi Friday or Saturday night?" Julia asked after she hung up.

"Friday, I think," Billy replied, flipping a page in his own daybook. "John Harleston is going up from Atlanta. We're going with Mimi and Julius from Georgetown Friday after lunch, if that suits you."

"Hardy wants to go to dinner Saturday night then."

"Okay. I don't know when Mimi's planning to come back, but we can get home somehow, I guess. You want to call John Harleston?" Billy turned back to his reading. "Curious file, this one," he commented after about twenty minutes.

Julia looked up. He turned one open palm up in a gesture of confusion while flipping through the photocopies of newspaper articles with his other hand. "Almost random. Different from Molly's typically disciplined, orderly approach to information. Articles on exurban development in Florida and South Carolina."

"Exurban?" Julia queried, pausing in her own file review.

"Yeah. Apparently socio/developer-speak for large-scale development built on an urban planning model, but lying outside an urban area. In the boonies. This place near Tampa – five thousand new homes over a five-year period, but right now miles from the nearest grocery store, fifty minutes from a shopping mall. Ex-urban as opposed to sub-urban. A series of articles about U.S. timber companies – trouble competing with cheap Canadian softwood. Some project St. Stephen Paper Company is doing in the Florida panhandle, out in the middle of nowhere. The 'New Ruralism' says the *Times* and St. Stephen. 'Live with nature. Have a tractor. Watch the birds and alligators," Billy efficiently abstracted key points as he continued to thumb through the articles in the file.

Julia laughed but began to follow along more carefully.

"The impact of mad cow disease on cattle ranching in Florida. Here's an article about the impact of feed lot operations on traditional open-range grazing. Population growth or decline statistics for Charleston, Dorchester, Hampton, Jasper counties in South Carolina. Similar articles dealing with the southwest and south central parts of Florida."

"Is there a mention anywhere of the bank?"

"No."

"Gold Coast?"

"None that I see."

"Alderlay?"

"Again, none that I see."

"Give me the dates."

"The articles are in subject matter order, not chronological."

"Molly rarely collected random information. She was amazingly focused and analytical. What if we re-arrange the articles chronologically and see if anything emerges?"

Billy stood up and began to sort the articles into piles on the table. "Okay. The earliest appears to be February…," his voice trailed off momentarily. "The month she…"

"Met the Gold Coast guys in Palm Beach." Julia shot both her hands up emphasizing the look of 'see, I told you' reflected in her eyes. "Left to right?" she asked, joining him on his side of the table.

The reorganization took almost twenty minutes because of the number of articles, each of which had been meticulously photocopied with the name and date of the newspaper or magazine in which it had appeared superimposed at the top left corner of the first sheet in a batch.

"Get the correspondence files and I'll get the daybooks and we'll see if anything emerges."

"March 10th article from the *Times* about cheap Canadian timber flooding the market and its effect on stock prices of U.S. companies with timber operations."

"She was at a Southern Atlantic board meeting in Atlanta all day Friday. The article was likely distributed at the meeting as part of some background materials."

"But why did it end up in this file?"

"Keep going."

"Another. Same subject. *The Journal.* Thursday, same week. RJR announces plans to buy over fifty per cent of its tobacco crop on a contract basis, avoiding the major auctions in northeastern South Carolina and eastern North Carolina. Related article the next day in the *News and Courier* purporting to analyze the economic effect of RJR announcement, now joined by Brown and Williamson, on tobacco producing counties in South Carolina."

"Nothing significant here," Julia commented. "In her office in Atlanta. Back to the beach that weekend."

"Review from the Sunday *Times* of a book just translated into English from the French. Sociological and economic ramifications of the flight of young people from villages in the South and West to Paris, Lyons, Lille."

"That's a stretch."

"What?"

"To think anyone would willingly move from Provence or the Languedoc to Lille. Molly left for New York Monday morning."

"What's his name?"

"Who?"

"The author guy. The Frenchman."

"Uhh… let me look. Wait. Here. de Mowbray. Jacques-Louis de Mowbray."

"Yes." Julia said somewhat triumphantly. "He was in New York. One of those author night events at the Empire Club library. You remember. Drinks, comments by the author, meet and greet. Isabelle was in town, too. They went."

Billy shook his head, trying to find a connecting thread. "Look at this. Now, talk about random. A *Journal* op-ed piece reacting to a report released by the U.S.D.A. about orange juice concentrate. Overall decline in production. Weather issues. Growing demand for fresh squeezed, organic, etc., etc. Feature piece about a family selling their orange groves to a real estate developer."

"Where?"

"Central Florida."

"The developer?"

"Some LLC. Camellia Properties. They're only a footnote, so to speak. The article is about the end of a family tradition. What happens to family connectivity, traditions. No more Thanksgiving in the orange groves. She circled Camellia."

Julia looked up at him questioningly.

"Molly – or somebody – circled the name Camellia Properties LLC. Obituary from the *Times*. Jessie Kirk Stephens."

"In Florida?" Julia asked reaching for one of Molly's daybooks.

"Right."

Julia found the entry. "They all went. Molly, Isabelle, Mimi, Gardiner… look at the article. I'll bet she went to Converse."

Billy scanned the obituary. "Yep. Here it is. From Georgia originally. Class ahead of Molly. So they all flew down to Jacksonville for the funeral of an old college chum. Not surprising, considering two of them had jets. But why is it in this file?"

"Billy, she and Isabelle stayed. They had a meeting the next morning at St. Stephens' offices?" Julia tapped her finger on the relevant page in Molly's daybook for emphasis. "I wonder why?" Moving to the opposite side of the table, she said "Why don't you go find us a diet coke?" as she began flipping quickly through the monthly piles Billy had sorted. "Billy," she said, stopping him at the door. "Toss me the daybook that's on the floor by my bag before you go. Please."

Billy slid the book down the polished surface of the table, knocking one of the article stacks onto the floor. Julia shook her head in mock derision. "Thanks, sport."

When Billy came back into the dining room, soft drinks in hand, he noticed Julia had rearranged the file slightly. "She met Criswell in Palm Beach in February when? Second week? The Gold Coast deal?" pointing at another daybook at the far end of the table.

"Nineteenth," Billy supplied.

Julia looked back at the first stack of photocopied articles. "The first of these is dated March 5th, three weeks after she first met the Gold Coast-Alderlay crowd at Chuck and Harold's."

"You think all this is related somehow to Gold Coast or Alderlay?"

"I didn't say that. But if we are to assume that there is some significance to this accumulation, there may be some significance to the fact that these items, topics, events or whatever only began to interest her after she realized Alderlay was – or was about to become – a significant client of the bank."

Billy came around to stand by Julia, regarding the neat stacks of photocopies with renewed interest. "We need a phone," he said, patting the pockets of his shorts. "A cell phone, not a land line."

Julia reached across the table retrieving her phone.

"Mildred. But make it a law firm call. Official business. We don't know how they log phone calls."

Julia scrolled through the contact numbers on her phone and pressed the call button. "It's Julia Pringle from Smythe, Russell and Yearick in Georgetown for Mrs. Ferguson, please."

Billy was impatiently flipping the eraser end of his pencil up and down on the mahogany table. Julia cleared her throat discreetly while looking at him with raised eyebrows. "Mildred? Yes, I'm fine, thank you. I hope you are? Can you talk discreetly for just a moment? All right. Hang on for just a second," she said, passing the phone to Billy.

"Mildred, everything okay with you? Excellent. I'll be quick. Did Molly keep a regular reading file of some kind? You know, random accumulations of current newspaper or magazine articles she would read or review at some point in time after publication?" Billy listened intently. "Never? The entire publication… and then you did what? Was there any method… no, not method. Organizing principle? Instructions? Where?" He picked up several articles from the closest pile. "Bottom right, last page? I see it. 'da.' Da? And you assigned the codes? She did? Were there duplicates, like with the correspondence files? I see. No, go. I'll see you soon." He handed Julia her phone.

"How about some lunch?" Billy crossed to the double doors into the hall. "Thomas. Oh, sorry. There you are. Any chance we could produce something for lunch? Or, Julia and I could run up to the beach club."

"No sir. It's not a problem. It will only take me a few minutes. Maybe a salad with some vegetables. A glass of wine, Miss Julia?"

"No, no. Not for me Thomas. Water will be fine. Maybe a Pellegrino?"

Yes ma'm. Mr. Commander, do you want to eat in here on a tray or perhaps on the terrace? It's a beautiful day."

Billy looked at Julia for a decision. Julia smiled at the old gentleman and said, "The terrace would be lovely, Thomas, if it's not too much trouble. Why don't you let me …"

"It's fine. Thank you. I'll bring you another coke in a minute and get things set up for you outside," he finished, as he pulled the doors closed behind him.

"So. What did she say?" Julia asked, referring to his phone call.

"There was no duplicate. Molly marked articles after she read them and then sent the entire publication to Mildred to be photocopied."

Julia surveyed the boxes on the floor. "She must have done it for years."

"Everything in a file had to do with one topic," Billy interrupted. "A category assigned by Molly herself. They're marked. Coded." Billy turned to the last page of a three-page photocopy on the table in front of him, pointing to the letters in the bottom left corner. "I thought these were some sort of secretarial initials, indicating who assembled the document."

"'da'?" Julia asked.

"Let's look at the rest of the articles before we eat." Billy sat down indicating they should swap roles. Smiling broadly at his cousin, he gestured with his hand for her to proceed.

"Okay. Okay," she laughed. "Let me see. After the Stephens obituary, some more stuff about the effects of mad cow on domestic beef suppliers. The shift to feedlot cattle raised in a more controlled environment. An article from *Vanity Fair* about the disappearance of the Marlboro man."

"Marlboro man? Is this related to the tobacco articles?"

Julia shook her head. "I think it's a metaphor. Disappearance of the western rancher. Typically American cultural idiom disappearing. Some ads."

"Ads?"

"Condo hotels. Miami Beach. Miami proper, Coconut Grove actually. Las Vegas. One at Hilton Head." Julia looked at him ironically. "I would have more easily believed Molly was looking for a condominium in Iowa."

"So there must be a...," Julia interrupted.

"Theme. Unifying precept of some kind."

Julia ran her fingers through her hair, surveying the stacks of papers stretching the entire length of Molly's dining room table. "Exurban development. Cheap pine trees from Canada. Some benighted return to Walden Pond but in the Florida Panhandle. Mad cows. No orange juice. College classmates dying. Rural flight in the south of France. The Marlboro man retires. From all of which we deduce that we'll buy a condo in Vegas."

"Julia," Billy began hesitantly. "The last several months, while I was in France was Molly... okay? Collected mentally?"

"She was as cogent, focused, compelling at the Inman Society dinner as at any time I'd ever been with her. She engaged Julian with a riposte about the negative aspects of development in environmentally sensitive areas that was as accurately brilliant as it was funny. She had the whole table laughing about some gaff the chairman of American Motors had made that week in an investment analyst conference call. He seemed to forget for the moment that his company made a particular brand of SUVs."

Thomas appeared at the door just at that moment. "Mr. Commander, whenever you are ready, sir."

"Thank you, Thomas. We are on the way. One second, Julia. I just want to look at..."

Chapter Thirty-Six

"Wait a minute," Billy exclaimed suddenly, interrupting Julia in mid-sentence as he put his glass of water down abruptly on the luncheon table. "The return to Walden Pond in the panhandle – the exurbia near Tampa. Who was the seller ?"

"I...," Julia stumbled momentarily.

"St. Stephen Paper. I didn't make the connection. And the largest single shareholder of St. Stephen was..."

"Jessie Kirk Stephens," Julia supplied.

"Look at it, Jules. Decline in traditional agricultural mainstays: citrus, cattle in central Florida; tobacco in North and South Carolina; soft timber in North Florida, Georgia and South Carolina. She meets the guy who's analyzing the sociological impact of the decline in rural life, flight to the cities in France."

"Billy?"

"Millions of acres, the highest and best use of which is changing. The U.S. population is shifting to warmer climates, but now at the speed of light."

"Okay."

"Broad economic shifts in efficient markets. Markets now characterized by the instant availability of data, information. What happens?"

"Billy. I studied art history. I struggled through freshman economics at Chapel Hill. If it had not been for Stiles..."

"Julia!" he said insistently. "Think. Eighteenth century. One market declines. Nobody sees the trend or counter-trend until years, decades maybe, later. What is one of the counter-trends of a modern economic decline in a market?"

"I… uh… an opportunity?" she said uncertainly.

"Right. Who benefits here?"

"From?"

"Decline in market value or economic value of millions of acres. St. Stephen, which stock is publicly traded, is watching the value of its core asset steadily diminish, probably already affecting its stock price. Similarly, the per acre yield of a cattle ranch, orange grove or tobacco farm declines to the point that it is economically unfeasible to continue. It costs more to operate the farm than the land can produce. Families give up. Indigenous farm population erodes. But what of the land? Simultaneously, modern urban life is taking its toll. The baby boomers mature and get ready to retire. Rich city dwellers…"

"… rediscover Walden or the Luberon," Julia completed his thought."

"'Simplify my complicated existence,' they say. 'Give me a tractor or a street with front porches and sidewalks.' Who benefits?"

"Who benefits?"

"Think, Julia. Someone has to broker the change. Allow the farmer to move to town. Facilitate the urban retreat to the land."

"Developers," she said finally. "They buy…They acquire… what? Product?"

"Inventory," Billy answered. "Inventory, the present economic value of which is in decline, the future economic value of which has not yet begun to be realized, which can likely be acquired at depressed prices based on its prior utilization. They begin to alter the utilization of the asset – now making it a product, and sell into a new market in a way not previously conceptualized."

"Ok. I follow you so far. But the nefarious part of this process would be what precisely? It sounds to me like the operation of efficient markets you have been so laboriously describing for my benefit."

"Perhaps. I think I am beginning to see what caught her eye here. Maybe even see the unifying elements in this collection of information. What if someone – a developer or a development company – sees the trend, and is in a position to capitalize on it. But, it's tens of thousands of acres, acreage which may be acquired for a fraction of its ultimate value if the trend analysis is correct. If the demographic movement is, indeed, in the direction we surmise."

Julia shook her head, perplexed. "But what's the connection? Molly was the voice of anti-development. To the right of a conservationist in some ways. A preservationist, even. It had to be something else," Julia replied.

"It was a bank file. Not some personal accumulation of information of a curious, inquisitive mind. The bank was one of the institutions Molly served, in the mission of which she believed. If she assembled a file on paradigmatic shifts in real estate development, it had to be an issue that affected the heart of the bank. She was chairman of the Executive Committee not some junior credit analyst, remember."

"Would you hand me the daybook I asked you to bring?"

Billy reached down by his left leg to get the book as Thomas came out onto the terrace. "Thomas, thank you. Everything is wonderful. Well done. But, despite my cousin's reticence, I believe I will have a glass of white wine. A *salade niçoise* – I can't not attempt to enjoy vicariously a moment in France," he said convivially.

"Look at you," Julia mused. "Sitting on your terrace, barefooted, having a glass of wine in the middle of the day… laughing. You seem, despite all the contra-indications, almost happy. Or at least content."

Billy looked up.

She continued. "It's kind of a new color for you. Suits you rather well, I'd say. Oh, what the hell. Thomas, pour me a glass as well. The connection?" she prompted him as she settled back in her chair.

"Thousands of acres of opportunity at depressed prices based on potential use."

"Yes."

"Means a purchaser would have to get in there quickly, quietly and before the other guys figure it out. Large purchases within a small window of opportunity – or so they must have reasoned – takes…"

"Big financing," Julia supplied. "Because you'd need to get in fast with all cash offers. Consolidate your positions to develop critical mass in an area to maximize all the aspects of development."

"I thought you studied art history."

"Not in law school, Skippy. It would take a source of financing – maybe even the third largest bank in the country."

"Precisely. Molly saw what they saw."

"Who saw, by the way?"

"I dunno," Billy shrugged.

"Look at this." Julia opened the daybook Billy had retrieved from the terrace by his chair. "It's a month after the last of the articles in the 'da' file." Billy looked at the letters 'AldDev' circled boldly surmounting the notation 'MiaHld 25Apr'. "I think Molly had Alderlay in mind as she was assembling this file."

"But why?" Billy asked. "Alderlay was the fair-haired child at Gold Coast. One of the bank's biggest clients. Their roots were in second home development, a huge growth opportunity for Continental. Real estate financing, at either the retail or development stage, tends to be very straightforward. Look, if you skip the tax-driven limited partnership craze of the late seventies – early eighties – real estate financing is largely a numbers game. A property appraises for X. Bank advances Y per cent of X. Or the financing is taken off pre-construction sale contracts. Very formulaic. Junior loan officers can handle even large accounts. In fact, they typically do."

"I'll be right back."

Billy rose instinctively from his chair as Julia stood up, and then he walked over to the edge of the terrace overlooking the marsh.

"Here. I thought I remembered this," he heard Julia say a few minutes later behind him. She had a reduced full-page ad from the *Miami Herald* edition of April 25th on the table.

"Condo hotel at Little Pine Key." Billy shrugged his shoulders.

"Look at the bottom of this ad for Little Pine Key, the tiny print you can hardly read because of the reduction," she said.

Billy picked the sheet of paper up to look closer. "A project of Alderlay Development."

"Remember when we were in Atlanta, and you said Oyster Island had to be involved in this somehow… and I told you that you were grasping at straws? Land with incredible resort potential – the 'next new place,' I think you called it. Depressed prices based on prior utilization.

There has been a county moratorium on septic systems and an EPA ban on crossing the river with septic lines. Thus, no development…"

"Without a treatment plant," Billy completed her sentence.

"Which needs two things."

"Space and money. Lots of both. So now you're trying to forge a connection among Molly's death, the bank, Alderlay, and Oyster Island?"

"I don't know. You started the thread that afternoon in my conference room downtown. Does it stretch credibility to think Molly stumbled upon something, the awareness of which was sufficiently important to someone or some group that the knowledge became a threat to her?"

"Bank officers… or corporate real estate executives… bumping off old ladies? Jules…"

"Henry II."

"What?"

"Henry II. 'Will no one rid me of this troublesome priest?'"

Billy finished the wine in his glass. "I need a break. You want to go to the beach?"

"Billy!"

"I'm serious. Why not? Let's sneak another glass of wine out in a toter. Go sit on the beach," he finished, gesturing toward the front of the house.

Julia laughed. "My undoing is complete."

"Why? Because we go to the beach on a Tuesday afternoon? How many weekends have you worked on client matters that were inconsequential?"

"Many. But the matters were consequential to my clients."

"Congratulations. You fulfill your oath as a lawyer. How about your commitment to your own goals? We're going to the beach."

"I'll have to go to mother's first," she said, giving up. "To get a suit and a coverup."

"Go up to my room. Grab a pair of boxers and a t-shirt."

"Are you crazy? Out on the beach at DeBordieu in May in your boxers and a t-shirt?"

"Yeah," Bill said with an grin, teasing her. "Get going."

Chapter Thirty-Seven

"What are S – P – Es?" Billy asked Walker, spelling rather than pronouncing the word.

"SPEs?"

"Yeah."

"I dunno. In what context?" Walker doodled the letters on the pad by his phone.

"There's a reference in a couple of Molly's daybook entries to 'SPEs.'"

"No clue. Let me do a quick search," entering the three letters into a search engine on his desktop computer. "Hmmm. Not that. Nor that. Some college fraternity, likely not that. Here. Special purpose entities ring a bell by any chance?"

"Maybe. What are… "

"Special purpose… it's a financing vehicle of some sort. You'd be better off calling Hardy on this one. We're a trust outfit, not a deal shop."

"That's another phrase that is starting to turn up with some frequency. What's that imply – being a deal shop?"

"I've always understood it to mean the more aggressive side of investment banking – not an advisory role but the people who actually hammer out, in the sense of structuring, the more arcane aspects of corporate finance. Richy Concannon runs the deal shop for CAB. Remember that… "

"… night at McMullen's."

"Structured Financial Products – the proper name of Concannon's division – seems to be the darling of corporate finance these days. Financing vehicles or methods that are uniquely tailored to a corporation's needs – and I am guessing that S – F – Ps depend on SPEs." Walker laughed at his pun.

"Cute. Do you have a bed for me this weekend? I can always go to the Empire Club if it's a problem."

"Billy. Billy. Are you kidding me? As long as I have a sofa bed, you have a place to sleep. Seriously, don't ever think about staying at the club. My place is yours. You're coming up Friday afternoon with Mimi?"

"Yeah. That's the plan. Mimi and Julius, Julia, me, maybe her mom."

"Great. Mimi will be so pleased with all the company, that is to say, all the attention," Walker laughed. "Where is Jules staying?"

"I guess at the Harriman Club with her mom. Maybe the Junior League rooms at the Waldorf."

"I'd rather her be at the Harriman. Better security. Oh, by the way. Your AmeriJet deal should be completed by the end of the month." Walker paused, waiting for some response from Billy. "Billy? Are you okay? Anything up with you I should know about?"

"Nah. I'm all right. I don't know. Julia, Tommy and I were at this new place in Murrells Inlet for dinner last night. Do you know Eric Robinson?"

"Sort of. Charlotte went out with him a couple of times one summer while we were still in school. I think his mother has a house at Litchfield or somewhere."

"Whatever. I don't know. He said an odd thing to me."

"He's an ass, Billy. Whatever he said, don't…"

"No, wait a second. He came over as we were leaving. Julia introduced me, and he said he'd heard I'd bailed out at Howell Raines. Added some snide remark about CAB money and no need to work."

"Billy. He's a reasonably smart guy. First or second in his class at Georgia, I think. But he's an ass. Forget it."

"That's not the thing, Walk. His date came up, and as they began to leave he said, 'Did you ever think you'd see the day when the incredibly conservative corridors of the Continental American Bank would lead to the biggest deal shop on the street?'"

Walker sat up abruptly in his desk chair, removing his feet from his desk and taking Billy off the speakerphone. "Say that again."

Billy repeated himself.

"Lead to? Or, had become?"

"What?"

"Tell me exactly what he said."

"'Lead to.' I'm almost certain. As in the sense of down the hall to…"

Walker fell silent.

"Walk. What?"

"Eric's in the Atlanta office of Frederick, Myerson."

"Creative bunch."

"That's polite. Among other things they were named in the collapse of that natural gas pipeline company a year or so ago. El Paso Mexicana or whatever it was."

"Named?"

"Well, not sued. But implicated. Slapped on the hand by the SEC. Two partners were disciplined by the bar. Four associates and a junior partner took the fall and lost their jobs."

"Point?"

"Billy. Got to run. This is a call from Europe I have to take. Call me when you're on the way? I'll round up Hardy."

Chapter Thirty-Eight

"Can you meet me on the corner at Bergdorf at 11:30?" Billy heard Walker say, as he answered his cell phone.

"We're going shopping?" he laughed.

"No. Continental American just moved into their new derivatives trading floor on West 57th Street. Todd Cahill works there. He was a year behind me at Darden."

"Who?"

"I don't think you knew him. Nice guy. From Missouri, I think. Kept a low profile, not big on the party circuit. He worked in the b-school library at night. I thought it might be nice if we paid him a courtesy call. New digs and all that. They're in the old Northern Guaranty space, remember? Take him to lunch at the Empire Club. It's right around the corner."

"Sure. I guess. Why this sudden burst of business cordiality?"

"Structured Financial Products – Richy Concannon – is part of derivatives."

"SPEs?"

"SPEs."

An hour and fifteen minutes later, Billy was leaning against the corner of Bergdorf Goodman, his head buried in the current issue of *Fortune* magazine.

"Where're the 'No Loitering' signs when you really need them?" Walker joked as he walked up to his friend.

Billy grinned. "I thought loitering was what Bergdorf was all about. Loiter a while, spend some more."

"But you're at the Van Cleef corner. Different rules."

"Why did Jules go back?"

"Work, she said. Some big protest Winyah Bay Conservancy is filing with the EPA or the Corps of Engineers this week. So what's the drill here?"

"No drill. Chat. Listen. See what we hear." Walker noticed the puzzled look on Billy's face. "Frederick, Myerson has been counsel to some of the most… let's say progressive corporate finance offerings in the past several years. For one of their deal-doers to comment blithely – as if it were common knowledge in financial circles – that the bank has become a deal shop. Let's say, I think it's worth a visit. So does Morgan. And my family."

"But what if Concannon…"

"He's out of town. I had Byrd Smithfield call and ask him to a luncheon given monthly by some of the senior partners at Morgan. His assistant said he was in San Francisco until Thursday."

"You're sure?"

"We called The Huntington to leave a message. He's there."

"Do they have some kind of CIA training for you people at Morgan?"

"We deal with a lot of situations every day, Billy, most of them demanding extreme sensitivity and confidentiality. We live in an information age dominated by CNN *et cie*, who have to fill up twenty-four hours a day with something that sells ads. We can't afford a misstep. Not with our client list. We're here," Walker said, as the elevator doors opened onto a glass atrium on the ninth floor of the building.

"Good lord," Billy said in amazement. "Ricardo Mongiardino meets Renzo Piano."

"I know. With an unlimited budget. Look, Todd knows we're old friends. You're up from the beach. Sorry you never met at UVA. Came along for lunch. Blah. Blah. Got it?"

"Gosh, Mr. Coggeshell. It's my first business lunch in a big city. Is my tie okay? Jackass," Billy muttered under his breath as Walker began to speak to the receptionist.

"Billy Commander and Walker Coggeshell to see Todd Cahill. Thank you."

"What's his name, Billy?"

"Whose name?"

"The guy we're going to see. You're terrible with names."

"I'm not terrible with names. It's Todd. Missouri. Show me. Worked in the library and could never get off to go to parties or something." He lowered his voice. "I'm surprised we used our real names, given the critical sensitivity of our mission."

"Stop." Walker said as he noticed Todd approaching the reception area from the trading floor.

"Walker. What an incredibly nice surprise. How unexpected. Billy, Todd Cahill. I'm sorry our paths never crossed at Virginia. I didn't really travel in the fast lane with you and Walker."

"Walker was in a fast lane? Quite a revelation. At the time, living with him, it seemed more like life mired in a rut. I'm sure your experience was much the better for avoiding us – or at least me," Billy said with the disarming charm that characterized his public demeanor. "So this seems to be the capital of technology. What do you guys do here?"

"Let me give you a tour. Do you know much about derivatives?"

"Abstract expressionism is somehow derivative of cubism. That's about my limit," Billy commented, appearing to casually survey the banks of computer screens, racks of servers, bundles of cables, while absorbing the non-stop sighs of dozens of laser printers.

"Derivatives are financial instruments – contracts, really – the value of which is tied to or dependent on fluctuations in the value of the underlying asset. There is a market for them but they lack the incidence of ownership in an enterprise – the company."

Todd chuckled sympathetically at Billy's obvious confusion. "A simple example would be securitization of the mortgage portfolio of a mid-size S&L. They wish to convert a portion of their mortgage portfolio – which has a lower than market yield – and re-invest the cash in new mortgages at a higher yield. We monetize the asset – turn it into cash for them – splitting it into pieces that can then be sold to other investors."

"Monetize their assets?" Billy queried.

"Right. Convert an asset with a long-term payout into current cash. One guy wants to convert – monetize – to move into another opportunity, which he perceives to be more attractive. Another wants to pick up a couple of points above current money market rates without assuming a long-term investment risk. We structure a vehicle that accomplishes both goals – and create an aftermarket that lets the first guy avoid having to hold the underlying asset for its full thirty-year life. It's a market phenomenon, largely enabled by instant access to all sorts of new information sources. Initially, derivatives were a hedge against a specific risk. More recently, we've seen speculators – traders if you will – buying them."

"And, the bank profits how?" Walker asked.

"Investment banking fees from the S&L itself, in my example. Advisory fees charged by our analysts to fund managers or smaller brokerages without their own analysts. Commission fees from the sale of the monetized asset to the customer."

"Sounds to me the bank is on three sides of the same deal simultaneously," Billy volunteered.

"Theoretically, there are firewalls, separations between the various divisions. Financial management has become complicated in a deregulated environment. Banks provide many services these days."

"And bankers wear many hats," Walker said matter-of-factly.

"You guys enjoy a luxury at Morgan that we do not, Walker."

"What's on the second floor, behind the glass wall?" Billy inquired.

"Structured Financial Products. Richy Concannon's shop. Innovative as we are, our products are merely generic compared to theirs, in the sense that our products are available to any qualified customer of the bank. They build special vehicles for investment banking clients."

"Special purpose entities might you say?" asked Billy.

"I guess. Definitely special purpose. I don't know about the entity part."

Walker interrupted, changing the subject rather abruptly Billy thought. "Todd, you'll join us for lunch, won't you? We'll just go 'round the corner. Close, if that's okay?"

The sidewalk on Fifth Avenue was too crowded during the noon hour for easy conversation. The walk down to 54th Street was more an exercise in dodging tourists and shoppers than a conversational stroll. Billy paused in the vestibule of the Empire Club to sign in. "We're going up to lunch," he said cordially to the doorman. Indicating the way to the elevator bank for Todd and Walker, he allowed them to precede him across the marble lobby.

A few minutes later after Billy had dispensed with the lunch orders, Walker said, "Now tell me, Todd, I don't think I know in what part of town you are living?"

"East seventies, Walker. Seventy-second between First and Second, actually."

"Ah. Great. We're not too far apart."

Todd laughed. "No. It's a long way from you Walker. I live in a second floor walk-up above a karaoke bar. You live on Fifth Avenue with a view of the park. I have come to know the words to every Bon Jovi song ever written. You likely cannot hear the traffic below from your living room."

"The East seventies is very…," Walker began.

"You're a relationship manager at the most distinguished private bank in the country. Hugo Lesesne would give you his left ball for just a look at your client list. And you," turning pleasantly, in no way aggressively, to Billy, "are, or will shortly become, the fifth largest individual shareholder of the bank where I am a sub-altern toiling away on the derivatives trading floor. We lived twenty minutes apart in Charlottesville and never had a beer together. Yet, here we are," he paused momentarily taking in the two-story height of the room "in the often photographed Stanford White dining room on the ninth floor of the landmark McKim, Mead and White Empire Club. I didn't clean my silverware with my napkin nor react with obvious confusion when we had to fill out our own lunch orders with those little miniature golf pencils. What's up, guys? What's going on?"

Walker seemed at a loss for words, attempting to bridge the moment by looking for a waiter. Billy placed both his hands on the table, almost as if he were preparing to leave. Then, lacing his fingertips together and leaning forward, he said, "A junior partner in the Atlanta office of Frederick, Myerson said to me the other night 'wasn't it surprising that the conservative halls of the Continental Bank led to the biggest deal shop on the street.' I think it was a significant statement, but I don't know what it means. Neither does Walker. Walker thought you might be able to shed some light on the matter. It seemed an inappropriate question for the trading floor. Forgive me. Us. We intended no subterfuge. Certainly, no attempt to patronize you with a hidden agenda. There is growing evidence that…"

"Billy," Walker interrupted with a cautious tone in his voice.

Billy held up his hand. "There is some reason to believe my grandmother's death was not entirely accidental. Two incidents threatening me and my family now appear to be less that coincidental. I…"

"'Lead to' or 'has become'? Which did he say? The guy from Frederick, Myerson."

"Walker asked the same thing. I'm almost certain he said 'lead to,'" Billy responded.

"Frederick, Myerson numbers among its principal clients a real estate development firm – a firm with regional if not national ambitions. This firm is also a client of the bank, for which company I hear the bank has begun to structure a number of, shall we say, aggressively innovative financial products."

"Structured financial products?"

"Yes."

"Which could include some sort of special purpose investment vehicles?"

"Yes."

"Investment entities which perhaps push the envelope?" Walker asked.

"Perhaps."

"From Concannon's shop?"

"Yes."

"Todd," Billy began. "I don't suppose you'd care to share the particularities of these SPEs? The name of the client?"

He wiped his mouth with his napkin. "Collegial reminiscence is one thing. Career updates. What you're doing. What I am. Breach of fiduciary duty is another."

"I'm sorry. I didn't mean to…," Billy began.

"It's okay," he said holding up two fingers of his left hand to make Billy stop. "It's okay. I need to get back if it's all right," he said glancing at his watch.

The boys were silent in the elevator down to the lobby. As they reached 54th Street, Todd shook hands first with Walker and then with Billy. "You know the boys upstairs in SFPs have begun calling the last Friday in every quarter Paddy Murphy Day – hats, Guinness, Bushmill's – the works."

"Paddy Murphy day?" Billy asked with some confusion.

"Yeah. You know. The SAE's favorite Irish dad." Todd paused. "Let's do it again sometime. Thursday night is Bon Jovi night. You guys should come over," he said grinning.

"I like Bon Jovi," Walker said as they parted company at the corner of Fifth Avenue.

"Hardly the point," Billy replied.

"Well it sounds like more fun than that Irish pub day on the trading floor."

"Alderlay."

"What?"

"Alderlay. The code Molly used for the file with the news clippings I was telling you about was d – a. I thought it might be the initials of Alderlay Development reversed. It was 'da'. The diminutive form of reference to one's father or dad in Ireland. Paddy Murphy day. Molly knew. She had figured out something was going on in Concannon's shop that involved Alderlay and she was watching him."

"You put all this together over lunch?"

"It's too coincidental to be otherwise. You don't yet know everything Julia, and I have learned."

"Well, maybe it's time you tell me?"

"I don't want to expose you to any…"

"What? Danger?"

"I suppose," Billy replied dismissively.

"Asshole," Walker said angrily.

"What?"

"You heard me. When did you get to be Superman and the only one at risk here?"

Billy took a deep breath, glancing up and down 54th Street as if someone might be watching them. "When the bank built its new building in Georgetown, Molly's files ended up at the house rather than in storage. Julia and I have been going through the files, indexing the activity indicated in the files with her daybooks. I think she knew something was up with Alderlay and she was preparing to blow the whistle."

"Oh sh… are you telling me you have the personal files of the chairman of the Executive Committee of the third largest bank in the country…"

"And transcripts of a lot of her intra-bank telephone conversations."

"… at Julia's firm in Georgetown?"

"No."

"No?"

"They're on the floor in the dining room at Molly's house at DeBordieu."

"With a seventy-year-old black man exercising custodial control?"

"Thomas? Yeah, I guess."

Walker quickly retrieved his cell phone. "Rebecca. Put me through to Anthony Burgess, immediately… and stay on the line." Walker waited, somewhat impatiently. "Anthony," he finally said, while Billy wondered what in the hell was going on. "We have a client residence in South Carolina we need to secure. Yes, the owner is out of town, and valuable items are in the house. The address is 555 Sabal Court, Georgetown, South Carolina. In the DeBordieu Colony. I will call the gate right now with instructions." Listening for a moment, Walker said, "No. Listen to me. Now. Immediately. Dispatch a team at once. Yes. You may assume it is critical."

"No CIA training?" Billy queried.

"It's the environment in which we live. I'd rather have you explain how you came into the possession of the files than explain how you lost them." Walker closed his phone with a snap.

"Is Alderlay's stock traded?" Billy changed the subject.

"I don't know. We could go back to the office and check."

"Maybe I'll just run back up to the library here. They're bound to have research tools, wouldn't you think? If the stock's registered they have to make SEC filings, even if there's no real trading activity," Billy mused aloud. "There's likely also EDGAR access in the library, too. Dinner?"

"Sure. I'm playing squash with Hardy at 5:30. Meet us at the Racquet Club? Or maybe the Sleave?"

"Sleave at 7:00," Billy said pointing his finger at Walker and pulling an imaginary trigger. "Thanks for lunch."

"You signed the tab, buddy. Not me."

"Okay. Then you can buy dinner," Billy joked. "Let's keep it just the three of us. Will that be cool with Hardy?"

"Well, you know he's not happy with fewer than six people in tow."

"Tell him we're going somewhere new. Not sure how it will be."

"New? Us? Amazing." Walker playfully slapped Billy on the shoulder, turning back to signal the doorman for a cab. "Later, gator," he quipped as he ducked into a cab that whipped over to the curb in front of the club.

Billy watched his friend turn right on Fifth Avenue, already flipping open his cell phone, reestablishing contact with his professional world. Ten minutes later Billy was back upstairs in the reference section of the Empire Club library.

Chapter Thirty-Nine

"You must be a graduate student," Billy commented congenially to the younger man who was trying to assist him. "NYU?"

"No, sir. Columbia."

"So, is this an internship for you?"

"More of a part-time job."

"Impressive," Billy replied. "Well, good luck and thanks."

"Thank you sir. If there's anything else, I'm Derrick van der Horst. We... uhh... we don't wear name tags on the fourth floor."

Billy nodded, then crossed the reading room to take a seat in a leather arm chair in front of a computer terminal. He keyed in the phrase "Alderlay Development" and was directed to its home page. Billy followed the published corporate history of Alderlay online, flipping serially through the pages orchestrated by a PR firm to paint its history in a light that was simultaneously nostalgic, romantic and economically dynamic.

The catalogue of Alderlay's accomplishments unfolded before Billy's eyes in a continuum of sunrise beach walks, mid-day tennis matches, sunset marsh vistas, revealing front porch moments among neighbors interspersed with glimpses of rare water fowl indicated by the outstretched hand of someone's precious grandchild, images evocative of what Madison Avenue was currently branding and selling as the good life in America.

"No books anywhere in their houses," Billy thought as he scrolled through page after page extolling the virtues of life in an Alderlay development. "Nobody seems to do anything. The purposeless life examined. It's advertising," he reminded himself, "not reality. No mention of a mortgage payment, let alone maintenance, taxes or cutting the grass. I need to call Hardy."

Walking back over to the reference desk, Billy said, "Excuse me. Derrick? Is there a place I can use my cell phone?"

"Sure. We use the old pay phone cabinets. Down there against the rear wall, near American Lit. You'll see the Copley drawing of an officer on horseback. Turn left into the stacks."

Finding his way to the north side of the library, Billy found the small oak-paneled enclosures. Practically an antique he thought, looking at the 1970s vintage pay phone, still labeled with the distinctive blue and white logo of the American Telephone and Telegraph Company. Scrolling through his contact list, he located Hardy's office number. "How long did it take Julia to get all these numbers in?" he wondered. "I'll have to get her something. Oh, right. Sorry. Yes, Billy Commander for Hardin Murrah," he said to the receptionist at Rémond Moncrif. "No, not a problem. Let me just have his voice mail then, if you don't mind."

He completed his message quickly, returning to the computer he was using. From the website of the land records office for Georgetown County, he found his way to an outline map of the county. Clicking his way through successively more narrowly defined areas of the county, he came to the rough outline of Oyster Island in the middle of the Waccamaw River. Clicking the mouse on a tract of land he thought was Asylum Plantation, the name and address of his grandmother popped up on the screen, from which Billy was able to quickly trace the descent of Asylum Plantation within his family. Double clicking on the tract to the north of Asylum revealed the Oryzantia chain of ownership as he expected, based on his recollection of the maps in Julia's conference room. "Jules. I need to call Julia," he thought.

South of Asylum, his ownership search revealed the public ferry dock leased to the State of South Carolina by Oryzantia. Moving farther south, he began to run into individual lots in the village of Ruinville, registered in one of the identifiable family names of many of the African-American families on Oyster Island. Immediately south of the village, an ownership reference to Azalea Properties LLC caught his interest. Moving backward in the chain of ownership, he found the prior ownership descending through members of the Deas family until the acquisition by Azalea two years prior. Azalea's address of record proved to be a post office box in Columbia. Two more clicks on the map revealed another transfer from a local family to Azalea Properties. And then a third. Billy pushed back slightly from the desk at which he was sitting. 'Why would…' He clicked on the outline of a large tract of land at the very southernmost point of Oyster Island. 'Alderlay Development Partners II LLC? What's this?' He clicked on the prior ownership link and stood up in search of a coffee while the computer was doing its work.

"Derrick. Is there any chance of getting a cup of coffee up here?"

"Yessir. Of course. I'll call the dining room for you. Anything else, Mr. Commander?"

"Billy. It's Billy, Derrick."

"Yessir. Of course. If I might have your member number, Mr. Commander, I could advise the dining room and save you the…"

Billy smiled. "C879," he said, turning to return to the computer desk.

'Whoa. What's this?' he said to himself after resuming his search. In the blue letters indicating an active link, the previous ownership of tract IX-24032-02 appeared in the name of Azalea Properties LLC. Billy clicked the internet screen forward to make sure he had not made a mistake. There it was. The current owner of the tract was an Alderlay entity. He moved forward one screen again to the information that Alderlay had acquired the tract from Azalea thirteen months previously. Clicking on the active link to discover the owner from which the tract had been acquired by Azalea, he watched as the name Alderlay Partners III LLC appeared.

"Excuse me, sir." Billy turned to see a club porter with a coffee tray. "Oh perfect. Thanks. Here is good. Let me just sign the chit. There you are. Thanks again." Ignoring the coffee tray, he reached for a legal pad. Clicking one more screen back to find the owner from which Alderlay Partners III LLC had purchased, he saw the name of an old but inactive timber company appear. "Wait a minute," he said to himself, beginning a linear diagram descending on the legal pad. "McCaulay Northern Timber to Alderlay Partners III LLC. Alderlay Partners III LLC to

Azalea. Azalea to Alderlay Development Partners II. What the hell is this?" he muttered under his breath.

Billy clicked his way back to the outline of Oyster Island. Choosing a smaller tract on the southwestern edge of the island, he went to the ownership screen. 'Camellia LLC. Okay. Let's go back one more,' he said to himself. "Albert and Rhea Washington… and before that what looks to be her family." Billy returned to the Oyster Island map, continuing his search process for another hour without discovering anything as noteworthy as the Alderlay-Azalea transfers, when he was interrupted by a soft tap on his shoulder.

"Sorry, sir. Library services closes at five. The reading rooms will remain open, but we shut down the server and the research terminals."

"No problem. I need to go anyway. What time are you here tomorrow?"

"Nine o'clock, Mr. Commander."

"It's Billy. Thanks again," Billy seemed to pause for a moment.

"Derrick."

"Right. Derrick. Good. Okay. Thanks for your help." Billy tore the sheets of paper with his notes off the legal pad on the table and slipped them into his jacket pocket. As he exited the club down the 54th Street steps, the outside doorman asked him if he wanted a cab.

"No, thanks. I think I'll just walk a while. Nice day, you know?" Billy turned left at the corner of Fifth Avenue and headed uptown toward Walker's apartment building. Browsing mindlessly through the bookstalls near the entrance to Central Park, he soon found himself at the corner of Fifth and Sixty-Eighth, lost in thought. He stood on the corner through two traffic signal sequences and finally managed to throw off the reverie, recovering some sense of purpose. Greeting the doorman in Walker's building, he headed straight for the elevators. The phone was ringing as Billy unlocked the door to Walker's apartment.

"Where is your cell phone?" Walker demanded. "I've been calling you."

"Sorry. Still off. I was in the library. You know the rules inside the club. What's up? Sure. No that's cool. Seven o'clock then. I'm going to grab a shower and change. No, I know where it is. Seagrams building, diagonally across from the Racquet Club."

Chapter Forty

"I forget about this place," Billy said an hour and a half later as Walker and Hardin took a seat on either side of him at the bar at the Four Seasons.

"Martini, huh," Walker observed. "Real grown-up drink."

"I've had a real grown-up day," Billy replied. "Plus it seems to match the sophistication of the room. You know, I've never been able to figure out what makes the stainless steel curtains move."

"Interns from Random House and Goldman. They keep 'em downstairs and when major deal-doers gather, their job is to make the curtains subliminally whisper 'pay more, pay more.' I'll have the same," Hardy said to the bartender, indicating Billy's glass. "Here's the stuff you asked about." While Walker was ordering a drink, Hardy lowered his voice, handing Billy an envelope. "End of each quarter, three times a year, four years. I don't think any of the analysts on the street have ever noticed. How did you stumble on this?"

"A little bon mot fell on my plate at dinner one night," Billy replied with a wink. "Thanks."

"Champagne for me. Call me a wuss," Walker said brightly. "Where were we?"

"So, Bill. Walk says you've been holed up in the library all day. Boning up for the New York bar or something?"

"Funny. I ran across something interesting. Tell me what you think of this." Billy took a napkin from the bar tray and reached into the pocket of his suit jacket for a pen. Holding the napkin with his left hand he continued. "Company A acquires a piece of land, sells it to an LLC, which may or may not be related, which entity in turn, sells it on to a third entity, clearly related to the first."

Hardy rotated the napkin to the right so he could see Billy's diagram. "Over what period of time?"

"I'm not sure. I wasn't really focusing on the dates. Relatively short-term, I think. Definitely not a long-term hold."

Hardy shrugged his shoulders. "Hard to say. Here. What if you change your diagram from a linear chain to a circular one?"

"What?" Billy asked.

"Company A and C are clearly related?"

"It would seem."

"And you're not sure where B fits into the picture."

"Except to say that B is showing up everywhere A and C seem to have entered into a transaction like this."

"Look." Hardy flipped the napkin over and, taking Billy's pen in hand, sketched a circular transaction. "A to B and then back to C, which could actually be A," he suggested with particular emphasis on "back to C." "What is the incidence of common ownership in A and C?"

"I don't know."

"Check the corporate filings with the Secretary of State in the jurisdiction. Where is all this taking place?"

"South Carolina," Billy replied. "Oyster Island to be specific."

"Look at this, Walk," said Hardy, indicating his circular drawing. "It looks oddly like those forward prepays from the energy debacle in the late nineties."

"A what?" Billy asked.

"It's a financing mechanism. Vehicle. Not unlike commodity futures. Depends on the particular circumstances. There was some significant abuse of the concept some years ago. We were still in business school. It was one of the activities that brought down Trans Sedona, that big west coast accounting firm and, ultimately, El Paso Mexicana. Remember?" Walker picked up the diagram. "A agrees to deliver a fixed quantity of something, natural gas let's say, to B at a fixed price. B agrees to buy and then simultaneously enters into a delivery contract with C for the same quantity but at a slightly higher price. The producer – A, in this case –

gets cash up front and avoids its commodity risk. B builds in its profit margin in the delivery contract to C, and so on. Forward prepays is what they are called. They're derivatives," he concluded, tapping Billy's arm with his forefinger.

"But that's an open-ended transaction," Billy observed. "More like my diagram. The original owner bails out at the sale to B."

"Right."

"Look at your diagram," he said, turning the napkin over. "In your example the item comes back to an entity related to the original seller."

"Well, that was the abuse," Hardy interjected. "The sales were sham transactions put in place only to boost reported operating cash flow and earnings. They were actually disguised loans…"

"Which, when they did not show up on the balance sheet created a falsely favorable picture of the company's financial situation," Billy finished.

"Yep. But they got caught. Companies and the banks."

Billy shook his head. "I dunno. Seems irrelevant anyway. Your example deals with a commodity item, the underlying assumption of which is that one unit of the commodity is indistinguishable from another. The subject of this transaction was land."

"I suppose land could be a commodity," Walker volunteered.

"How?" Billy asked. "The value of land seems to be tied up in, or at least largely affected by unique characteristics. Not indistinguishable characteristics. Location. Topography. Underlying resources."

"Oceanfront property," Walker suggested. "When they opened Prince William, every ocean front lot – and every river front lot, as well – South to North. Same price. Large tracts of timber, how about that?" Walker turned to see who had just entered the room.

"What did you say?" Billy signaled the bartender for another drink, pointing at his own and Walker's mostly empty glasses.

"I said I thought for a minute that was Nancy."

"No. Before that."

"I don't know. What? Timberland. Why can't the land that produces the timber be a commodity – just like the timber itself is a commodity? Trace the money. That'll show you why they did it, if that's what you're trying to discern."

Billy looked at Walker. "Sometimes you can be so not blonde." Addressing the bartender, he said, "Have you a pad or something other than a napkin we could use?"

"Company A buys a piece of land for $100, sells it to B pursuant to some contract for $110. How is the $10 gain recorded?"

"Well. It depends," Hardy said, now signaling the bartender to refill his own glass. "On how the asset was booked initially – by A."

"Go on."

"Most land is carried as a capital asset at its purchase price. A non-depreciable asset. The gain would be the amount paid over the purchase price, either short or long term depending on the holding period. But if you are a developer, for example, land may be treated as inventory and the nature of the gain could change. To ordinary income, possibly."

"Operating income," Billy commented.

"Yeah. Sure."

"And any debt associated with inventory acquisition?"

"… would likely show up on the balance sheet as some kind of general liability related to operations rather than long-term debt. Remember these gunslinger types tend to live or die on this quarter's profits." Hardy concluded.

"We, on the other hand, live or die on the selection of a place for dinner," Walker began. "Where's it going to be?"

Chapter Forty-One

Billy sat in front of the huge 54th Street windows in the reading room of the Empire Club library in the early morning sunlight, forgetting for a moment the proscription against cell phone usage.

"Jules, it's me. What's up?" pausing to listen to Julia. "No, calm evening actually. Walker, Hardin and I had drinks at the Four Seasons and went on to the Veau d'Or for dinner. Do you remember that place from a hundred years ago?"

"Billy, I'm kind of pushed here. I want to hear about dinner, but maybe…"

Billy paused for a moment. "Remember the flower partnerships we ran across in Molly's notes? Camellia. They're all over the property records for Oyster Island, trading land back and forth among themselves and with various Alderlay partnerships. I think Alderlay is trying to assemble Oyster Island."

Julia was stunned. Of course, it made sense. "I need to call you back."

"Jules, I…"

"Billy. I need to call you back. Stay where you are. I'll be back to you in fifteen minutes."

Bill disconnected the call, mildly irritated. "What is all this?"

Julia grabbed her bag and headed for her office door. "Susan. Please call Judge Irving's office at once and tell him I am on the way over. It's critical."

Billy thumbed idly through the magazines on the library table waiting for his coffee and for Julia to call back. A club porter approached with his coffee on a tray as his cell phone rang.

Derrick, who had just come in to work, looked up abruptly from the library desk with a disapproving look. Billy signaled with his right hand that he was headed back to the phone cabinets. "Jules?" he said in a half-whisper.

"What's wrong with you?"

"I'm in the Empire Club library and the phone gestapo will get me if I am not in a phone booth. Okay. What?"

"I'm in Julius' office. I'm going to put you on the speakerphone, okay?"

Billy nodded.

"Billy, I need you to say it's okay."

"Okay. It's okay. Geez, Julia, such legal…," he caught himself when he heard the voice of Julius Irving through his phone.

"William?"

"Judge Irving. How are you, sir?"

"I am well, William. I trust that you are. Julia has rather quickly brought me up to date on your recent analysis, and the ties to Alderlay that you've stumbled upon."

"Yes, sir."

"It's a rather curious matter, is it not?"

"Judge, I think that Molly may…"

Julius Irving cut him off. "Now is not the time for that conversation. Nor is this the appropriate manner in which to discuss it. Julia has been put in harm's way at least once."

"Julius. Billy," he heard Julia begin. "That's not why I'm here. I didn't come to Julius out of some concern for my own welfare but rather to get his advice on the … on the next step." Julia seemed to be grasping for words."

"Julia," Billy heard the judge say. He could envision the rising level of tension in his office. "Listen to me, both of you. This is a serious matter. Not one for amateurs."

"You think it unwise that we ask too many questions about Alderlay or the acquisitions on Oyster Island?"

"I do. In view of the circumstances, I think it unwise."

Billy paused, unsure how to continue. "There is one other thing, while we are all here, if you have a moment, sir?"

"Go ahead."

"The two LLCs involved in the Oyster Island acquisitions were Azalea Properties and Camellia Properties, both of which show up in some … some…uh, correspondence I've seen in Molly's files. Anyway, both LLCs show the same registered address – 1207 Main Street, Columbia."

"What?" Julia said sharply. "Did you say 1207 Main?"

Billy repeated himself.

"1207 Main is the Continental American building in Columbia. It's the South Carolina headquarters of the bank," Julius Irving said with a tone of depressive resignation.

"Maybe it's the offices of a corporate agent?"

"William, the bank occupies the entire building. There are no other tenants at 1207."

Billy stared at the wall of the small booth, stunned. Taking a deep breath and shaking his head slowly, he said, "Jules. I'll be home tomorrow or Thursday. I'll let you know as soon as I get my arrangements made. Judge Irving, thank you as always for your advice and counsel. I will look forward to seeing you toward the end of the week."

"William, I wish…"

Billy disconnected the call and immediately pressed the speed dial icon for Walker's office. "Billy Commander for Walker Coggeshell, please," pausing while the call was transferred by Walker's assistant. "Walk. Are you alone? Anyone in with you just now?"

"What's up, Billy? It's just me. Want me to grab the door?"

"It might be better if you do." When Billy heard Walker pick up the receiver, he continued. "Alderlay's SPEs, the LLCs involved in the chain of acquisition at Oyster Island…"

"Yeah?"

"The registered office for each of them is the bank's headquarters in Columbia."

"Continental's offices in Columbia?" Walker asked, the incredulity in his voice obvious to Billy. "Who is listed as the registered agent?"

"Hang on. Let me look back at my notes." Billy thumbed through the legal pad, trying to balance his tiny cell phone between his shoulder and ear without dropping it. "Sidney Lancaster. S-i-d," spelling the first three letters of his name for clarification.

"Wait. Gimme a second here. There it is. Assistant General Counsel to Continental American, Columbia office."

"Lancaster is?"

"Yep. I'm in their online staff directory. Maybe this is not necessarily irregular."

"Walk. It's not like having your phone bill sent to the trust department for payment. Cahill practically told us they were setting up special purpose financing entities for Alderlay. Now we find out that the bank is not only involved in creating the legal entity itself but is also serving as agent for the entity?"

"Billy, are you sure about this?"

"The records of the South Carolina Secretary of State reveal that the registered corporate address of an entity acquiring land, likely with bank financing, is in fact the bank itself. And, that the registered agent for the corporation is a bank employee. How irregular can it get? This is not a situation involving stock transfer powers or some other back office corporate service. It's a specific set-up that requires, among other procedures, a stated communications protocol that dictates how the bank handles items coming in to the attention of the LLCs, which means that…"

"Someone in a position of authority within the bank authorized the procedure, which was itself the result of planning and discussion," Walker completed his thought. "The underlying activity may not in and of itself be irregular but it goes to the heart of the bank's complicity in whatever is taking place among the related entities."

"Right."

"This is serious. Morgan manages millions of shares of CAB stock. I can no longer avoid going to the senior people in my office and letting them know what we have found."

"Walk. Let's talk this through some more. Tonight? When are you headed home?"

"I have a meeting at five. Last probably thirty minutes. I was going to meet some guys from Citibank's new wealth management department for a drink but I can blow that off. Why don't I meet you at the Sleave at 6:15, 6:20 or so?"

"No. Let's make it back at your place. We can sit on the terrace and sort through this. No crowds."

"Okay. You'll get home before I do. There's a menu card by the phone in the kitchen. Gourmet-to-go or something equally clever. But not bad food. Why don't you call them and order something? Oh, and pop in Sherry Lehman on the way uptown for some wine. You know where it is? Madison and 61st?"

"Got it covered. See you later. I think I'm going to go for a run. Try to shake some of this off." Billy returned to the desk where he had been working to retrieve his shoulder bag and other legal pads. Dropping everything into his bag along with his cell phone, he headed to the elevator lobby.

"All through, Mr. Commander?" Derrick inquired cheerfully from the library desk near the entrance.

Billy laughed. "I don't know, Derrick. Answers seem harder to come by these days despite the proliferation of information. I'm giving up to go for a run. Thanks for all your help."

"Good call. See you soon."

Chapter Forty-Two

Billy took the elevator to the basement, signing in at the fitness center desk. "I'm sorry," he said to the attendant. "I seem to have forgotten my locker information. I've been out of the country for a while."

The attendant quickly checked Billy's member number next to his signature on the registry and flipped open a ledger containing the location, contents and instructions related to members' lockers. "This way, Mr. Commander. Let me show you."

Billy changed into the running gear that he had left at the club and fifteen minutes later went through the service entrance doors and up the steps from the basement to West 54th Street. As he began stretching his calf and hamstring muscles, he noticed the usual line of black town cars outside the club entrance; from out of the most recently arrived stepped Hugo Lesesne.

"Billy. What a pleasant surprise. Going for a jog? Or just finishing?"

"Just starting, Hugo. How are you?" Billy responded as he shook Lesesne's hand. "Thought I'd drag my lazy self around the park."

"Excellent. Excellent. I have a meeting inside in a few minutes but afterwards I'd be so pleased if you'd allow me to buy you a drink? Shall we say around five?" Hugo said, glancing at his watch. "In the Oak Room, how will that be?"

Billy knew he had no excuse. "That'd be great, Hugo. Five it is. I'll look forward to it."

"Okay my boy. Have a good run now. Careful."

Billy began jogging west on 54th Street toward Sixth Avenue, where a right turn and three short blocks would lead him to the entrance of Central Park across from the Ritz-Carlton.

An hour later, following a vigorous if uneventful run through the park, freshly showered and dressed, he walked through the double doors into the second floor men's bar to find Hugo Lesesne exchanging pleasantries with other similarly suited, senior executives. He saw Billy come in and began to excuse himself from the group standing at the bar. "John," Billy heard Hugo remark to the maitre d', "Mr. Commander and I would certainly enjoy one of the corner tables," as he gestured toward the rear of the room. "If that's not a problem?" He extended his right arm to Billy indicating that he should precede him as they followed the maitre d' to the back corner of the darkly paneled room. Hugo spoke cordially to other members of his acquaintance as he passed among the tables, choosing to sit with his left side to the room when they finally arrived at their table in the corner.

"Be all over the street tomorrow," Hugo commented congenially. "Billy Commander and Hugo Lesesne seen having drinks at the Empire Club. What deal can be in the making there? What are you drinking Billy? John. John, this man has just run completely 'round the reservoir and is in need of sustenance."

"A Perrier for me right now, Hugo. Maybe a drink in a minute. You go ahead."

Hugo dispatched the waiter with their order, appearing nonchalantly to survey the room as he did, and then turned back to Billy, a serious look on his face.

"Billy. You know, of course, Molly is irreplaceable. Personally and professionally. She and Criswell were – well almost founders of the bank. Mac and Niall Wright. We will never be able to replicate their generation."

"Thank you. Kind words. I…"

"But the institution goes on, fulfilling the legacy of its founders. We have a responsibility to build on their success, wouldn't you agree?"

"It's an abstract concept, Hugo. I am neither a director nor an officer of the bank, so I'm not sure what…"

"Thank you," Hugo interrupted as the waiter placed their drinks on the table. "Billy, you're sure water is enough. Let John get you a glass of wine maybe? John, bring Mr. Commander a glass of the Rhône wine we had at that French tasting last week," holding up his hand to silence Billy's objection.

"The point is the bank is at a critical juncture in an area affecting our market dominance and future success, an area where you are uniquely situated to wield a positive influence to help the bank."

Bill was partially slouched in his chair, idly twirling one of the cocktail coasters on the table with his finger, trying to look casual, relaxed despite the tension he felt growing internally. As the waiter returned, placing a glass of wine in front of him, Billy shifted in his chair, crossing his legs and sitting up straighter.

"I'm not sure I follow you."

"We sit at the helm, you and I, of the third largest bank in the country. We are facing increasing competition in our retail markets from the other large banks even as they seek to consolidate their control over corporate customers for investment banking purposes. Consolidate in a way, I might add, that at once seeks to prevent CAB's growth in large commercial banking and threaten our retail strongholds."

Billy attempted to chuckle with what he hoped would be perceived as congeniality. "Well, notwithstanding the huge compliment, I'm not sure I sit at the helm of anything other than my boat – and that, not as often as I'd like these days."

"You know I was devoted to your grandmother. She was one of my mentors both within and without the bank. The tragedy following the Inman Society dinner was doubly hard for me as it was Molly who had proposed me for membership in the society and who had nominated me to the Oryzantia Board."

Billy was amazed at how blithely Lesesne seemed to ignore the particular circumstances surrounding Molly's death. "And it was you who let her drive home alone, you son of a bitch," he thought to himself.

"But your grandmother, while critical to the success of the bank in its formative years did not fully grasp, I think, many of the demands of modern banking."

Lesesne moved his chair closer to the table, leaning toward Billy as if to indicate the level of confidence into which Billy would be drawn. Waving the drinks waiter away, he spoke quietly. "You are one of the largest individual shareholders of the bank. Your family association with the institution carries significant weight with many of the other large shareholders, like you, themselves descendants of those whom we might regard as founders of the modern Continental American. The bank has acquired new clients, among them clients who can rapidly begin to reposition the bank as a leader in emerging areas where we can consolidate a position of market leadership. Your support of our efforts to accomplish those strategic goals could be powerful," Lesesne concluded, tapping Billy on the forearm confidentially.

"Leadership in what kind of markets?" Billy inquired, as he discreetly removed his arm from the table and Lesesne's reach.

"Real estate development, particularly in resort areas. Mortgage financing activities up and down the entire chain of resort development from the retail consumer to commercial lending. Just to name one area, of course," he concluded.

"Well, it's way over my head. Corporate finance and strategic planning in law school had none of the emphasis on practical implementation that you guys enjoyed in business school." Billy signaled the drinks waiter for a check. "The success of the bank is legendary, Hugo. I am confident that the appropriate stewardship of that legacy will result in continued success. I'm told that if your numbers hold for another quarter, you could be one of the five most profitable corporations in America."

He uncrossed his legs and moved to push back from the table. Lesesne reached across the table to take hold of his left hand with which he had been pushing back from the table, a bit too strongly, a bit too aggressively, it seemed to Billy.

"I want this to be the beginning of a new basis of dialogue between you and me, within which we will forge new areas of cooperation."

"I'm thirty-two years old. In the midst of a career change and some might say an identity crisis. I am neither a director nor an officer of the bank and have no financial management experience." Billy stood up. "I'm certain you can find more effective, if not more powerful allies, than I."

Billy signed the chit presented by the waiter, dismissing Hugo's protest with a wave of his hand. "My pleasure. My pleasure entirely. I really have to run. It was great to see you and, well, thanks again for the kind words about my grandmother."

Lesesne accompanied him out of the second floor bar and down the broad marble stairs into the lobby, asking casually about Julia, where things stood with Howell, Raines, giving the appearance of a congenial business discussion between two colleagues despite their age disparity. Billy felt Lesesne's hand tighten uncomfortably on his right elbow as they reached the street. "May I give you a lift? My car is right here," indicating the third black town car in line near the portico.

"Thanks. I'm going to meet some friends just down the street," Billy replied disingenuously. "I need to get a car service, though. Do you recommend yours?" he asked, changing the subject.

"This is a bank car. I'd be glad to make arrangements for you to use one of our cars whenever you are in town. Just let me…"

"Thanks. There's always the club's service, I guess. Not really a big deal. Interesting device on the bumper," Billy said, noticing a royal blue, scarlet and yellow decal on the front bumper of the bank car.

Hugo laughed heartily. "Something Criswell developed years ago. Part of his Scottish heritage, I guess. I'm not much of a history scholar. Some kind of armorial insignia of the Scottish Royal Treasury. He insisted that it be used to identify all the bank's vehicles and moveable equipment."

Hugo clapped Billy on the shoulder as his driver got out to open the rear door of the car. "Costs me fifty thousand a year now to keep them updated on all our vehicles," he said laughing, shaking his head in mock disgust.

"All of them?" Billy inquired, as he bent down to take a closer look at the decal.

Hugo threw his hands up. "You know tradition and CAB. Every last one of them. Are you sure I can't give you a ride now?"

"No, I'm fine. Thanks."

Lesesne lowered his voice. "Let's talk again soon Billy. I'd like to count on your support. Cooperation."

Billy smiled noncommittally. "I'm not sure of my schedule over the next few weeks. I was thinking about going back to France. I'll keep in touch," he concluded, shaking Lesesne's hand in a gesture of farewell. "1603," he said.

"1603?" Lesesne replied with some confusion.

"The unification of the Scottish and English crowns following the death of Elizabeth I. It would have marked the beginning of the merger of the Scottish Royal Treasury into that of England, thus causing the disappearance of the armorial device Criswell chose for one of the bank's insignia. It was a comment on the merger activity of the bank. That was his point, I would guess."

Hugo Lesesne nodded his head, a perplexed look crossing his face as he ducked into his waiting car. As the car pulled away from the curb, merging into the late afternoon rush hour traffic, Billy reached into his jacket pocket for his cell phone.

"Mrs. Ferguson please, if she's still in the office," Billy said into the phone trying to glance at his watch at the same time. "Yes. It's… uhh… tell her it's about her car." When Mildred came on the line, Billy quickly said, "Mildred, it's Billy Commander. Sorry about the subtle deception. Walls have ears sometimes. Have a minute?"

Billy waited for a moment while Mildred obviously went to a more private location, noticing as he waited how many other pedestrians had cell phones to their ears. "I'm fine. In New York actually. Hope you are okay? Good. Good. Hey listen. Any chance you have a buddy – a rather low level buddy in the Georgetown Operations Center? Someone who might have access, say, to routine maintenance logs, sign-out sheets for bank vehicles, that kind of thing?"

Billy listened carefully to her response and then said, "It's important this remain completely *sub rosa*. Okay. Let me think a minute. Can you arrange for a generic courier pickup from Howell Raines? There must be dozens of deliveries going back and forth each day and this would likely not raise any particular suspicion. Call Sally Adamson – she's my assistant, or was – thirty minutes before you send it down, and tell her she needs to request an expedited pickup. I'll give her a call and let her know to expect a call from you. Mildred, thanks. We should hang up, okay?"

"Walk," Billy said when Walker answered his cell phone after several rings. "Get this. Every Continental American vehicle has a numbered decal on the front bumper."

"Billy, what's the significance here?"

"The number on the decal must create both a utilization and a maintenance log. It has to. You couldn't manage otherwise. Dated sign-in, sign out sheets and so on."

"Go on."

"The car that hit those people from Atlanta at Oryzantia came from a bank repossession lot in Georgetown. A bank security officer keeps showing up in odd places around me and Julia. If the car that hit Molly at Laurel Hill was a bank vehicle, the utilization logs may show who checked it out – and, if it sustained damage to the bumper, the maintenance log might indicate the repair."

"We need to get the logs…"

"I'm on it. Mildred Ferguson is getting the logs. Nominally because she is doing a survey for some director of various types of operating costs. Very pedestrian. Way under the radar. Copies of the logs will go to Atlanta and Mildred will courier them over to Sally at Howell Raines. Here's the thing. Hugo alone knew that Molly would be driving home alone from Oryzantia after the Inman Society dinner. He came to the house to persuade her to acquiesce to some course of action. Thomas said they argued before they left. He overheard both of them discussing something with raised voices. Julia said the tension at their table was palpable, relieved ultimately only by Georgia's arrival and the social deftness that she and Molly brought to the subsequent conversation. If the car…"

"You're on a bit of a roll here, bud," Walker interrupted. "Where are you? Where have you been?"

"Hotboxed by the distinguished Chairman of the Continental American Bank for the last 45 minutes in the bar at the Empire Club. I'll tell you about it when I get home. I'm almost at Sherry now. See you in a few, okay?"

Chapter Forty-Three

Billy was standing in Walker's kitchen, re-arranging the dinner items just delivered by the take-out service when Walker came through the front door.

"We're having a beach party?" he commented, noticing Billy barefooted in khaki shorts and a polo shirt.

"They're yours actually. Hope you don't mind. It's 78 degrees. I couldn't find any flip-flops. I thought we'd eat on the terrace. What dya think? Beer? Wine? Drink?"

"What'd you find at Sherry?"

"A Spanish white, Albariño. Gorgeous blond girl – Galician, I think – was there. Having a tasting."

"You've never been to Galicia and only once to Spain."

"Okay. She told me she was Galician and that we should try the wine."

"Is she coming over later?" Walker laughed.

"I ordered tapas, paella and an arugula salad. I'll admit the arugula salad doesn't really fit but it seemed like a good idea at the time. You think I got caught up in a Spanish moment because of the girl?"

Walker grinned at his friend's momentary insecurity. "Hardly matters. Dinner sounds great. Let me change - ditch the suit. I take it the discussion with Hugo was not without its own tension," he tossed over his shoulder as he headed back to the bedroom.

"I should get someone to fix the terrace, don't you think?" he asked a few minutes later as he joined Billy outside, reading the label on the wine bottle after he poured himself a glass. "Plants. Proper table and chairs. It's really quite a view. She was cute?"

"Who?"

"The Galician wine seller."

Billy ignored him. "Who's that guy? He's in the Inman Society. Degree in landscape architecture from some hotsy-totsy place. Made a name for himself doing urban terraces – you know small space gardens. He was on the cover of the Oryzantia magazine about a year ago."

"Oh, right. He did Isabelle's terrace down the street, I think. I'll call her. Tell me about the estimable Mr. Lesesne."

"Hugo pisses me off."

"Admittedly. Is there a specific reason here?"

"I dunno. He has this compelling, expansive CEO personality that makes people feel as if he is totally focused on their insight, their input. In reality, I suspect he is a master of the hidden agenda. Somehow, subsumed in all that ebullience, was the assumption that I'm some kinda fuckin' idiot, incapable of grasping the subtleties of higher intellectual processes. He rolls out this huge pitch about cooperation, mutuality of interest. He even told me that we – mind you, we were the only two people at the table – were at the helm of CAB."

"Colorful metaphor."

"Exactly. The pitch was how I could help the bank by becoming an advocate for its attempts to, among other things he added as an afterthought, become a major player in resort development and all the associated financing activities. Up and down the financial chain to use his words. And if, by the way, I could bring along all the other shareholders descended from the founding families who are unable to grasp the complexity of modern banking, as Molly had been unable to grasp them, well, that would be groovy too."

Walker burst out laughing, reaching back to retrieve the wine bottle.

"Transparent hardly begins to describe the meeting," Billy went on. "He actually grabbed my arm at one point. Even the drinks waiter noticed. It was not a pretty moment."

"Here," Walker said extending the wine bottle to Billy.

"What are we doing here, Walk? Isn't this a lot more complicated, a lot more unpleasant than we wanted our lives to be?"

Walker said nothing, looking out across the park in the fading light.

"I'm thinking seriously about going back to France. Buying an apartment in Paris. A place down south." Billy stood up, refilled his wine glass and leaning back on the terrace railing, put one foot on the chair where he had been sitting. "You're not saying anything."

"Did your dad ever talk to you about what you should do with your life?" Walker asked.

Billy struggled to follow the apparent abrupt shift in their conversation. "I was only nineteen when mother and daddy… we were still at St. Bart's."

"My dad runs the brick plant. Has his board seats. Eats lunch with the same bunch at the Palmetto Club almost every day he is in Columbia. Travels some because of his responsibilities with the museum. I think his life has been consistently the same in its essential detail for the past thirty years. Do you know, I've never asked him if he feels a sense of purpose about his life. He's never suggested there should be one in mine."

"Your dad's your dad," Billy commented rather noncommittally, turning around to face the park and the riot of architectural styles reflected in the towers of the apartment buildings in the distance along Central Park West. "I think he must be typical of his generation. They seem to internalize matters, force their emotional response to life into some sort of congenial submersion. It seems to us that they are distant, removed, unconnected. That they place a premium on doing rather than feeling, certainly action rather than explanation. They seem at times to be uninterested in helping us make sense of things. But what do I know? I never knew my dad. When I was little, in Atlanta, he was gone all the time, traveling on business. I went to St. Bart's a year before you did. Ninth grade. I was fifteen. In the summers, we were at the beach. He came over on weekends from Atlanta. He'd get in late Thursday evening or after lunch on Friday. He and Mother were busy most weekends. Molly was the real caregiver in my life, you know that. Your dad is cut largely from the same cloth. It's probably why you are as close to Mimi as you are."

Walker joined Billy at the edge of the terrace, leaning forward with his elbows on the railing. Billy had rarely seen his friend as contemplative, almost melancholy. "Lost in thought?" he wondered. "Or at a loss for words? And, if so, why?"

Walker dropped his head down, running his left hand through his hair. It struck Billy as one of the saddest moments he had ever witnessed in connection with Walker. Struggling simultaneously to conceal any obvious emotion and choose the right words, he turned to look at his friend.

"Walk, I need some help here. I'll sail down any channel you want, but I need to be able to see the same navigational buoys you're looking at right now."

Walker was slowly spinning his wine glass between his hands. He took a deep breath. "Maybe you're right, Billy. Neither of us can spend the money we've got, or will have. Maybe what's left is some neo-expatriate existence between Paris and the South. The modern legatees of Gerald and Sara Murphy. Great wine, food. Get laid every night because we're rich good-looking Americans. Why not? It's not like I have anything to keep me here."

"Are you serious? The soul of Morgan Brothers Cadwalader talking to me about bailing out?"

"It's your movie, man. I'm just living in it. Ditch whatever responsibility we might have, however small, however inconsequential. Find a place in the Seventh. A villa in the Dordogne. Trade DeBordieu for St. Jean de Luz." Walker shrugged his shoulders as he turned to face Billy. "You told John Harleston not long ago that you couldn't envision a day without him in it. The pool at Molly's."

"How did you know about that?"

"Billy, how long have you known me? It takes me thirty minutes and usually no more than three phone calls to get the news on Monday morning. I don't know where to go here. The navigational…"

"Buoys," Billy supplied with a laugh.

"I'm not John Harleston with the collateral confusion of…," Walker seemed to stumble.

"Life in gayland, although I'm certain he would not describe it thusly," Billy supplied.

"Perhaps. I can't imagine a day without you in it. Julia either."

"Do you think we're odd?" Billy asked

"I don't have to reach the question of odd. We are what we are, and odd or not, it's our life."

"It's our life?"

"What?"

Billy laughed. "It's Thursday, right?"

"Yes."

"Bon Jovi night on 72nd Street."

It was Walker's turn to laugh.

"Call Cahill. Tell him we're coming over."

"We'll have to change."

"Not much. 'It's my life,'" Billy mouthed while Walker was making the call as they walked into the apartment. He threw his arm around Walker's shoulders, "'and I ain't gonna live forever.'"

Chapter Forty-Four

"What's your afternoon look like?" Billy asked Julia when she answered her cell phone the next morning.

"Not bad. I have a luncheon meeting at twelve-thirty. Some people from the Lowcountry Land Preservation Trust. Nothing really pressing after that."

"Can we spend some time together after that, this afternoon? We need to finish the boxes. I have some other stuff to show you. Tell you about. I'm coming down on the Morgan plane this morning."

"What time? I'll need to come pick you up."

"Nah. I'll call Thomas. It's okay. Jules, do you think Susan could find us a copy machine?"

"A copy machine?"

"Yeah. I want a copy machine with a document feeder and a collator, sent out to the house. I don't know how to get that arranged or paid for."

"What are we… never mind. I'll take care of it. When do you want the…," she paused listening to Billy. "All right. Sure. I'll get it done. Oh, I almost forgot. I had a nice chat with Sally Adamson this morning. She called to tell me she had sent me a package of documents overnight, which by the way is here. What do you want me to do with it?"

"Can you run copies at your firm with a generic or unidentifiable client number?"

"What?"

"I need you to make a copy of the contents of the file but I don't want an internal record that ties it to you or me."

"I have a billing file and expense code associated with what I call daily administrative matters for Molly. I've converted it to the estate. Copies would show up without a specific matter reference. Kind of a housekeeping account."

"Good. Ask Susan to make a copy of the documents Sally sent you. Do you still have the access codes to my safety deposit boxes at the bank?"

"Yes. Billy, what's the mystery here?"

"Take a copy of the file Sally sent you to the bank. Bring the other to the house. I'll see you around two or two-thirty."

"Billy?"

"Jules. I have to run. I have a car downstairs. I can't make the Morgan guys wait. I'll see you after lunch."

Chapter Forty-Five

Billy heard Julia entering the house, speaking to Thomas at the front door. "Mr. Commander is in the dining room, Miss Julia. Can I get you anything?" Thomas was saying.

As she came into the room, he folded his arms around her, tightly. "Do you look this good every day at work?"

Julia allowed the moment to linger. "I look like I look. How long have you been gone? A month?" Assuming a more business-like tone of voice she continued, "The copier will be here by four. Here is the file Sally sent. We took a copy to the bank. What is this?"

"I don't know. Maybe nothing," he said, while taking the file she offered.

Julia turned as Thomas entered the room. "Maybe a coffee for me, if it's not too much trouble? Billy?"

Billy was engrossed in the file she had handed him, flipping through the pages as he ran his finger down each sheet of paper.

"Thomas, Harbor Office Supply in Myrtle Beach is going to deliver a copier this afternoon. It's about the size of a washing machine. Have you an idea where we might put it?"

"Maybe the utility room between the laundry room and the garage, Miss Julia. There's nothing in there really and it has a long counter you might find useful as a work space."

"That'd be perfect Thomas. Thank you so much."

When he had closed the doors behind him, Julia turned back to Billy. "What's in the file from Sally."

"Every CAB vehicle carries a numbered decal on the bumper. I had

Mildred dig up the maintenance and utilization logs for Georgetown. Look. Here," Billy pointed to a page of notations for the week following Molly's accident. "Front bumper replaced on a navy blue Ford Crown Victoria sedan, ID number 6432."

"How did you…"

"Here's the rest of it," Billy interrupted. "Same car, same ID number," handing her another log sheet. "Signed out to pick up Mrs. Hugo Lesesne at DeBordieu Colony and take her to Oryzantia on the night of the Inman Society dinner. And, then take the chairman and Mrs. Lesesne home at 11:45. What was the time of Molly's accident?"

"Around 10:15, maybe 10:30." Julia flipped between the two sheets in the file. "You're saying that you think a CAB car, driven by a bank employee, picked Georgia up at DeBordieu, took her to Oryzantia, left the grounds to follow Molly home, causing a collision at Laurel Hill that forced her car in the river and then returned to Oryzantia to pick up Hugo and Georgia and just… just drive them home," she sputtered. "Billy. This is beyond circumstantial. This is fantasy. The log, presuming we could produce the original, records a parking lot incident resulting in damage to the bumper of the car. The log would presumably be supported by testimony establishing its accuracy. And you're going to argue that an employee of the bank of which Molly was a director followed her off the grounds and forced her car into the river?"

"Yes."

"There's no evidence here. Certainly not with enough weight that you could even consider implicating people as powerful as those you… this is like a conspiracy to commit murder and you are proposing to go after the chairman of the third largest bank in the country with a bumper repair ticket?" Julia stopped talking when Thomas entered the room with her coffee. Waiting until he left, she turned back to Billy, "What were you and Walker drinking this week?"

"Correct me if I'm wrong. Standard operating procedure among the staff at Oryzantia likely provides that any event that results in potential liability of any kind for the museum requires a written report? Probably called something like an accident report… a…"

"An incident report."

"The parking lots for the Inman Society dinner were under the control and supervision of the senior security staff, undoubtedly."

"Go on."

"If there were a parking lot incident involving damage to the vehicle of the chairman of the Continental American Bank, himself a trustee of the museum, I can assure you, there will be a written report."

"If you are correct, we can get the reports through Julius. He's chairman of the committee for the board at Oryzantia that would have an interest in such matters. But what then, Billy? It seems we are accumulating stacks of inadmissible evidence that leads where?" She paused for a moment.

"Walker said you're going back to France. Buying a villa in the Dordogne or something. Do you want to tell me what's up with that? And at what point in time were you going to get around to telling me?"

"Jules, it was just an idea. An almost random thought."

"Which, when expressed by a guy with twelve dollars is one thing. When expressed by my cousin, a guy with the financial wherewithal to do whatever he wants at a moment's notice, it must be taken somewhat more seriously. I'm sure you can follow this logic," she concluded, the anger in her voice obvious to Billy.

"What exactly is your irritation here?"

"Bluntly put?"

"Yes."

"The idea of your waltzing off to France, to loll around in the sun with Lucy, even Walker. Because you don't have to worry about things here. Because I have ten million from Molly, and I should be happy to, expected to look after things here."

"Julia, I never…"

"Never? Don't tell me never. You call me to get a new car for Thomas to drive. You call me to get your stupid copy machine. Photocopy and secure documents, which action alone probably violates ten ethical canons of the bar. And for what? To enable your eventual neo-expatriatism. I think that was the phrase Walker used."

"What do you want from me?" he asked throwing up his hands. "I'm having a hard time getting my arms around this responsibility you seem to think I owe you. Owe everybody. I'm not Molly."

"It's becoming clearer to me you are not."

"Have I missed a step here? In the last seventy-two hours how did everything that happens in the Lowcountry become my responsibility?"

"Because in seventy-two hours you can change the paradigm. Your words, not mine. Because in seventy-two hours you can put in place institutional change that begins to make a difference in the lives of people who cannot help themselves. Because in seventy-two hours you can see that huge parts of an irreplaceable environment are not bastardized by the greed and rapacity of guys like Alderlay. Because in seventy-two hours you can see that the retirement years of people like Mildred Ferguson are not threatened by the greed and rapacity of men like Hugo Lesesne and Richy Concannon. Or you can go back to France. Rejoin the BCBG. Marry a Nappie. Marry Lucy. Move in with Walker. I don't know what you want. I can't… never mind." Turning she picked up her bag and walked out of the dining room into the hall, slamming the door behind her as she went.

Billy stood for a moment, unmoving, stunned by Julia's intensity, taken completely by surprise. He caught up with her in the hall, as she was fumbling in her bag for the car keys.

"Wait a minute," he began, angrily. "You can't slam the door and walk out like that. This is not some Nora moment."

"And this is not a doll's house," she snapped back. "It's the real world, Billy, a central point that you seem to be increasingly unwilling to confront. Your dad, your mother, Molly," she exclaimed, "would be saddened if not ashamed to realize this is where you've ended up. Another rich, indolent American. It is so antithetical to everything they… forget it."

"Do you have a plan?"

"A plan?" she echoed, obviously caught off guard.

"Yes. A plan. A vision of the future. Because I need to tell you I don't have one," he concluded, anger in his voice and tears of frustration beginning to well up in his eyes.

Julia caught her breath, studying the marble squares in the entrance hall as if some response would miraculously sculpt itself from the white stone. She looked up, wiping her eyes. "I have the makings of a plan. And the courage to pursue it."

"The makings of a plan? That's the best you can do?" A smile began to creep across Billy's face as he approached his cousin. "You want me to turn my life upside down, forego the sensual pleasure of a life of indolence, a life of indolence in France, mind you. And the best you can do is, 'I have the makings of a plan'? I don't know. Give up living with Walker? Rhône wine on tap. Blonde Galician girls." He was almost laughing as he concluded, "you're gonna have to do better than 'the makings of a plan.'"

Julia put her car keys and bag on a console in the entrance hall. Running her hands through her hair, she started back to the dining room. "Tell me what you learned last week. Start at the beginning. The day after I left. Don't leave anything out and try and keep things in sequence. Wait a minute. Let me find a legal pad."

Chapter Forty-Six

Billy settled into the chair at Molly's dining room table that he had occupied since the beginning of their survey of the bank files. Taking a rather deep breath he began. "Follow this. Tell me where, at any point, you think the logic breaks down."

Nodding, Julia resumed what had become, over the last two weeks, her customary place at the table.

"Alderlay had its roots in high-end resort development, not necessarily the most difficult or complex part of the development game. Its early success was built in the rather old-fashioned way of identifying an area that would become popular largely because of its proximity to other established resort areas. The conversion of a formerly tourist class area on the beach near Jacksonville into an upscale resort because it shared a common border with the elegant but mature development of Ponte Vedra is an operative example. As the company grew and prospered through the 1970s, it learned to go beyond simply beautifying and making desirable that which lay in the path of growth to making desirable an area that lay outside regional growth vectors. Here's the break through. Or at least one of them. In 1985, Alderlay assembled a five-hundred acre tract of hurricane devastated timber land on the upper reaches of the bay north of Captiva and Sanibel Island. It became the Port Charlotte Yacht Harbor, forty miles and almost an hour from a grocery store, let alone Saks or Neimans. Yet it became home to million-dollar yachts, three condominium communities in which the lowest price unit began at 500k. And now that they have added some additional infrastructure, begun to achieve some critical mass, they are starting to develop waterfront estate lots. Starting price? One mil. For the lot."

"Successful, step-by-step, incremental growth." Julia turned her hands up. "How do you get from there to corporate monster?"

Billy smiled at Julia's metaphor. "Companies with a steep growth curve – or the aspiration to a steep growth curve – depend on gunners."

"Gunners? That's a law school term?"

"No. A Wall Street term, I think. Guys whose modus operandi is what we used to call runnin' and gunnin'. Deal doers. Financial gunslingers."

"Go on. I'm intrigued with the twenty-something testosterone."

"Stop." He laughed. "Be serious. Corporate life in that environment is buoyed by success, enthusiasm. The rate at which one is able to close deals begins to eclipse even the size of the deals. No real focus on quality. It creates a climate of confidence, invincibility. An engine of growth that can only be sustained by more growth."

"And thus, the monster?"

"Well, a beast. A beast that must be fed."

"By more deals?"

"Yes. Remember Molly's file? The one we could not understand? The one with all the news clippings that seemed so random. Seminole River Township near Tampa. The timber estates in the panhandle?" Not waiting for her response, Billy continued, "Alderlay stumbled upon two dynamics. First, the wealthiest generation in history beginning to reject their acquisitive past for the simpler times of Walden Pond."

"Or the beach," Julia supplied. "Coupled with the money to accommodate their fantasy."

"Their reality," Billy corrected. "And second, available land of sufficient desirability and in sufficient quantity to enable the achievement of that reality. Remember the boomers are not only the wealthiest but also the <u>largest</u> generation in U.S. history," he said, tapping the table for emphasis.

Julia interrupted him. "Competition from cheap Canadian timber, ten years of devastating hurricanes in Florida and coastal South Carolina, demand for organic farming, reverse urban flight. It's beginning to make sense to me."

Billy picked up the thread of his argument. "Alderlay saw the opportunity to gain control of hundreds of thousands of acres that their burgeoning confidence tells them that they can profitably flip to the boomerazzi. They need to consolidate huge real estate positions before other developers figure out what their intuition and research has told them. Still with me?"

Julia nodded.

"But it's today. Guys are no longer willing to work over a long term for an eventual payoff. Life among the deal-doers demands a big payoff today, not twenty years from now. Immediate gratification for the breakthrough idea. All of this came together at Gold Coast, an organization that had become in equal parts aggressive and impatient. And then enter Richy Concannon and the vehicles to monetize Alderlay's assets, enable their growth and do it in such a way that the effect on Alderlay's stock was entirely positive, hiding the real fact of the massive debt Alderlay was incurring. CAB had no significant presence in either investment banking or mortgage banking – two weak spots in the edifice Hugo was building. Coastal South Carolina, North Carolina and Florida were the bank's largest markets prior to the acquisition of First Texas and First America. Hugo knew he had to become a player on a national stage or risk an earnings stall that would result in Wall Street torpedoing his share price. A lag in the stock price would not only cause his personal portfolio and his retirement package to decline in value, but also threaten his future performance bonuses. But here's the thing."

Billy held up his hand to halt Julia's response. "Worse yet, at least for Hugo, he runs the risk of losing his place at the big boys table. Wall Street dislikes poor performance from one-time stars. Hugo saw the future and Alderlay was it. Land Alderlay, use them as a referent point to pitch the bank's strength, market savvy and service to other similar companies, and become the preferred resource for all the large developers in newly emerging areas across the South."

Julia shook her head in amazement. "Criswell dies. Hugo and Concannon enter into what they must have regarded as a marriage made in heaven."

"In fact, it was a relationship brokered by the devil."

Julia stood up and walked over to the tall windows looking out on the marsh, absentmindedly fingering the silk curtains as if the contact might produce a manageable continuum instead of the storm of information that was rapidly spinning out of control. Quietly, she said to Billy without turning around, "What are you going to do? We... I mean... What's the next step?"

"I'm not sure."

"If our analysis is right, it does not paint a pretty picture for the bank. Who knows what you've found?"

"You're really the only one with the whole picture. Hardy. Walker. Each of them has part of the picture. Both have said any additional information will compel them to go to their superiors with the story. Heads up on a looming disaster and all that."

"Is there any possibility anyone in the upper reaches of the bank is aware of the information you've assembled and the direction in which it now seems to point?"

"I don't...," he paused. "How would I know that? What's your point?"

"You said that Hugo saw the future and Alderlay was it. Molly is dead. There have been at least two attempts on your life and one on mine. Hugo strong-armed you the other day in public, or at least in the presence of others. Maybe it's time to revisit Julius' recommendation for a security detail?"

"Isn't that the point of this exercise? That we resolve things in such a way that we avoid living the rest of our lives with security. Can you imagine walking into any of the places we frequent in New York or Atlanta with men in black suits and earphones. Why don't we just slap an 'asshole here' sign on our forehead?"

"Billy, I think you are overstating the situation..."

"Do you? Things will change the minute security shows up. This is not the end, Julia. You may marry the doc. Move to Atlanta. Do you want to live in fear that all that stands between a fake note and your child getting snatched out of the carpool line at the Speech School is a hired gun? Because some weirdo, unrelated to the bank, noticed that everywhere you go you're surrounded by black suits like a rock star. And sees it as an opportunity to cash a check. Only with your child. Where do you want this to end? Because unresolved that's where it's headed. Your child. The carpool line."

Julia began to cry. Billy had never seen his cousin cry. In an instant, he was heartbroken that he was the reason. "Jules. I'm sorry. I didn't think. I didn't mean to…"

"No. You're right," she said through her tears. "I don't really care about myself, but what if something ever happened to Tommy because of me? Because of you? What would I say to his mother? She was at St. Mary's with Mother, for god's sake." Trying to wipe her eyes and compose herself, she continued, "the worst of it is, as you say. What if, like Molly, I had to bury my own child. I can't even begin to… I'll be back in a minute," she said suddenly, walking out of the room.

Billy began to realize the degree to which he had come to intellectualize the emotional aspects of his life. He felt in his pockets for his cell phone and not finding it looked down the long table. "Where the f…," he began. He whipped open one of the double dining room doors. "Thomas." He called loudly, his voice reverberating through the otherwise quiet household. "I need a… I can't find a goddam phone." Standing in the loggia, he saw Thomas coming toward him a telephone in his hand. "I need my cell phone. I want to talk to Walker. Mr. Coggeshell. I don't know his number. It's on my…"

"It's not a problem, Mr. Commander. Just a minute."

Billy watched him pressing one of the keys on the phone, followed almost immediately by, "It's Mr. William Commander in Georgetown for Mr. Coggeshell. A matter of some urgency, if you don't mind." And then, "Mr. Coggeshell? Just a moment for Mr. Commander, sir," and he passed the phone to Billy.

Billy was unable to talk. Walker heard what he thought were deep breaths on the other end of the line. "Billy? Billy, are you there?" Receiving no response, he keyed another line on his phone to summon his assistant, scribbling a handwritten note as she came into his office: 'Get me the security detail responsible for 555 Sabal Court, Georgetown, the Commander residence. On the phone. Now!!' Billy?"

"Walk. Things are coming apart here. I don't know what to do… I… Julia's in tears…"

"It's okay. Everything's going to be okay. You need to tell me what's happened. Talk to me, B." Walker waited, trying to sound calm, trying even harder to actually remain calm. "Julia is with you?"

"Yes. Well, somewhere. I made her cry."

"But she's all right? She's not been harmed?"

"No… it's… it's not that…"

"Billy. I want you to put Julia on the phone."

"But," he started to protest.

"Bill. Put Julia on the phone now."

Billy heard Julia coming down the hall from the kitchen. "It's Walker," he said simply, handing her the phone.

"Thomas, it's okay," she said trying to sound reassuring. "Walker?"

She opened one of the French doors onto the terrace and walked out toward the pool, moving one of the chairs so that she could sit facing away from the house, her back to Billy.

Chapter Forty-Seven

"Mr. Commander, that was Miss Julia on the phone," Thomas said as he came into the loggia with Billy's coffee.

"Let me guess. She's ditching me." Billy retied his bathrobe, reaching for the rest of the morning paper. He caught himself, realizing the inappropriateness of his comment. "Sorry, Thomas. What did Julia have to say for herself?"

"She says she really has to stay downtown today and is that okay?"

"Sure. Do I need to call her or anything?"

"No, sir. She said she was just sayin'. And if there is a problem I should call her back. I think she may have thought you were not up yet."

Billy smiled, thinking about Julia's early morning circumlocution of direct contact. Any comment from him would have undoubtedly elicited the response, "Billy, I talked to Thomas. There was no reason to bother you about such a…" 'Do we all do this?' he wondered to himself.

"Mr. Commander?"

"Nah. It's cool, Thomas. No problem. Do you think I could have some eggs? Maybe some juice if we have some?"

"Of course. It will only take me a minute or two."

"Tell you what. I have a million things to do and if Julia's not coming, there's no reason for me to shave and dress. How's that?"

"Yessir. That's fine. On the terrace then? Mrs. Commander always liked to take her breakfast on the terrace this time of the year. After she was dressed."

"Right here's okay, Thomas," Billy began and then Thomas'

comment sunk in. "You know what. The terrace would be great. Thank you for reminding me. That'd be perfect. I just need a few minutes to get dressed," he said, starting up the back stairs to his room.

Twenty minutes later, Billy heard the house phone ringing as he came back downstairs.

"Mr. Commander, it's Mr. Murrah in New York." Thomas handed him a portable phone.

"Hardy. What's up, bud? Ridin' the wide open range of Eurobonds today?"

"Billy boy. Sent you the Alderlay stuff you asked about. You should have it by ten this morning. Even in Georgetown," he laughed.

"What'd you find?"

"It's all the SEC stuff plus their annual reports for the past two years."

"How's it look?"

"If I had not had the conversation with you, I'd have never seen it. The company looks solvent. Roaring along even. But when you look at the detail, isolate the transactions that appear to be related to the partnerships – LLCs actually. I think it tells a different story. You told me about the Azalea and Camellia LLCs. There are actually more. Dogwood, Lantana. Rhododendron. It's a whole flower garden of subterfuge. Anyway," he said with emphasis, "when you isolate the financial activity dependent on the LLCs… I think they're suckin' wind, Billy."

"How are the banks going along with this then? Is there no credit evaluation taking place? I mean a man who wants to open a pizza joint can't get a loan without completely collateralizing the loan and personally guaranteeing the credit. Alderlay borrows zillions of dollars with illusory assets?"

"CAB collected 46 million in banking and other fees last year from Alderlay. And that's just the amounts I can ferret out from published information. I'll bet there's another twenty million on top of that I can't find. I'm guessing the boys at the top said it would be cheaper to pay the fine if it blows up in their face than forego the income."

"Are you…"

"I think they're attempting to disguise loans as operating income.

It looks like to me, piecing together what you've told me and what they reported, that they are taking down money from CAB that both functionally and in accordance with GAAP standards is a loan. But by running it through these LLCs they accomplish what amounts to an accounting conversion from debt to operating cash flow. If, as you say, CAB has crossed the line and actually participated in the subterfuge, I think they have some real exposure here. The amazing thing – or one of the amazing things – is that this is the conduct that brought down two of the big energy companies in the late nineties, resulting in hundreds of millions of dollars in fines for First City, AmeriBank. It's…"

"And you think the bank made the loans and didn't check how Alderlay was accounting for the loans?"

"I think they made the loans and didn't care."

Billy let Hardy's statement sink in. "How did it ever get through credit?"

"I think all those transactions were handled on the investment banking side which applies a different kind of credit evaluation. But you're missing the point, man. Alderlay didn't book the advances as loans. They threw up this convoluted network of partnerships that were swapping the land back and forth. The system made the advances from the bank look like cash flow from operations. There are some variations here – but it's almost exactly what El Paso Mexicana and those other guys did back in the nineties… and it's possible that CAB aided and abetted the process. I think Richy Concannon may have built the vehicles, put up the money… walked 'em right down the garden path. Do you have any idea how many acres in Florida and South Carolina Alderlay has taken down in the past twenty-four months?"

"No, I…"

"I do. I added it up. I had to back into the numbers, so it is by no means an audited calculation," Hardy paused and Billy could hear the rustling of papers on his desk. "I think they have bought over a 100,000 acres of undeveloped land in central and southwest Florida and coastal South Carolina."

"Using the flower partnerships as vehicles."

"Yep."

"How did you get at this?"

"I've burned some midnight oil recently. Off the clock, so to speak. I'm invested here."

"What do you mean?"

"You forget, Billy. My dad held a lot of First Texas stock. We're now sitting on a pile of CAB stock because of the merger. Nothing like the Commander interests but a chunk of change nonetheless."

"If all this is true, where does it lead? Perhaps there is nothing amiss here. Isn't it possible that the structure developed by Concannon was accurately reported by Alderlay? I mean couldn't the bank have provided funding through the investment banking side that was… I don't know how to describe it. Not, in fact, a loan?"

"I'd check the tax returns. See how they treated the transactions for tax purposes. I'd also check the ownership of the various land partnerships – the flower partnerships."

"To look for what?"

"See if any familiar names turn up in the ownership lists."

"Where does it lead? Another round of corporate meltdowns? How…"

Hardy interrupted him. "I think Molly got to this point too. My experience with her, limited though it was, is that she missed nothing. You have her files right?"

"How did you…"

"Never mind that now. Narrow the search. See if you can find any indication that Molly stumbled on a discrepancy in the tax returns and financial statements. Look for any mention of the ownership of the flower partnerships. Let the rest of it go for now. If she uncovered that… Look, I gotta go. When are you coming back up?"

"I'll call you."

"I need to run. Got a meeting. John Harleston called. He's in town. Drinks and stuff tonight."

"I haven't talked to him in a couple of days. I didn't know he was in New York."

"Billy. Somebody said… well, I heard that… that John might be playing for the other team."

Billy fell silent, not sure how to respond.

"Billy?"

"Tell me we're not having this conversation. John Harleston's your friend. As am I. We go way back. Talk to him if you feel the need."

"Point taken. We'll call you from drinks tonight. We gotta get you a place up here, man. Ditch the one in Atlanta. Lots more happening here."

Billy laughed. "I'll call you. Take care of yourself."

Hardin lost his prevailing jocularity for a moment. "Watch your back, bud. There's a lot of money that could be at stake here. Can make guys do crazy things." And with that, he hung up.

Thomas came out of the kitchen as Billy hung up with Hardy, extending his hand to take the phone and return it to its cradle. "Would you like breakfast now, Mr. Commander?"

"If it's all right with you Thomas, I think I'll go for a run. Skip breakfast maybe."

"Yes sir. Miss Julia called back while you were on the other line with Mr. Murrah and said can you go to Oyster Island with her this afternoon at four o'clock and then go to dinner at Mrs. Pringle's? She said she'll pick you up here at 3:30."

"I guess. Why does she… never mind. Sure. Call her back if you don't mind and tell her it's okay." Billy started up the back stairs to change into his running clothes and then paused at the bottom step. Sitting down he ran his fingers through his hair, attempting to find the appropriate words. "You know. You don't have to sort through all these messages and things. I can talk to Julia or whomever."

Thomas straightened up imperceptibly as Billy was talking. "It's my job, Mr. Commander. It's my job," he said hesitatingly. "If I am not doing it to suit you…"

"Nah. That's not it. I guess I feel slightly uncomfortable…"

"Mrs. Commander always told me that the execution of my job had the same economic contribution as a bank officer. She had a lot of responsibilities, and my doing what I did enabled her to do what she did. I am well paid. I have a retirement plan, insurance, a car. It's my job. But if I am not doing it to please you…"

Billy held up his hand. "Thomas. Stop. I don't know what to say except I'm sorry. You do a great job. Knowing that you feel good about it helps. I think I'm having a hard time adjusting to Molly's not being here. This was always her house." Billy stood up and started up the stairs.

"Yes, sir. And now it's yours."

"What did you say?" he abruptly turned around.

"And now it's your house, Mr. Commander. You are not a guest here."

"Yeah. I guess it is. I'll be back in about forty-five minutes."

Chapter Forty-Eight

Fifteen minutes later Billy called Julia on his cell phone before he began to stretch his legs.

"You're going out running with your cell phone? You're spending too much time in New York."

"Not exactly. I'm going running but not with my cell phone technically."

"So you're calling me from what? A pay phone on the beach at DeBordieu?"

"No. But it's not…"

"Billy. What?" she said with a hint of exasperation in her voice. "I'm not playing bridge or something here."

"I had this conversation with Thomas. I got all twisted up about whether or not I wanted eggs."

"Eggs?" There was silence from Julia's end of the call. "Billy. It's ten o'clock in the morning. I have a stack of… forget it. I have a lot to do and we're having a conversation about you and Thomas and eggs. Do I really need to be here for this?"

"It's a larger issue, Jules. The idea of someone looking after one's personal needs."

"It's a job, Billy. A job. He is extremely well paid. Trust me on that point. But that's not the issue. He chooses to do this job in the face of other options. There is no emotional indenture or symbiotic relationship held over from prior generations."

"He seemed concerned that he might not be doing things in a manner that pleases me."

Julia took a deep breath, searching for patience, a sensitive response. "A logical concern in view of the fact that you do effectively sign his paycheck."

"That's not it Jules. It's the larger issue of the parochialism…"

"Paternalism," she interrupted impatiently.

"What?"

"Paternalism. Parochialism is the wrong word. Look, we can't resolve this now, certainly not on the phone. Listen to me. Here is what you're going to do. You're going to go for a run. Then you're going to take a shower and get dressed. Have lunch. Work on the boxes. I'm going to pick you up at 3:30 and we're going to Oyster Island. Then we're going to dinner at Mother's. I think Isabelle is in town and some friend of Mother's from school. And then we'll start over tomorrow. I'm hanging up."

Billy heard her phone click off. The bright spring sunshine caused the ocean to have those brilliant points of reflected light on every surface ripple stretching out to the horizon. He sat down on the beach to stretch his legs so that he could keep the view of the ocean in front of him. Leaning back on his hands he tried to identify the feeling with which the events of the morning had left him. A sense of loss, certainly. But more a sense of displacement. Coupled with a lack of concern, enthusiasm for the future. "It's normal," he told himself. "Consistent with the emotional residue of grief. You work through it. Face the feeling. What was it Molly used to tell him? 'In returning and rest, we shall be saved.'" He stood up, repeating the phrase to himself, pushing off with his left foot to start up the beach.

Billy accomplished the circuit from the dunes in front of Molly's house to the inlet at the north end of DeBordieu and back in about thirty minutes. "About four miles all told. Not bad for as fat and out of shape as I have become," he thought crossing the road and walking into the forecourt of Molly's – now his – house.

Molly had moved to DeBordieu after his grandfather died, leaving the old house on the river at Sewee Hill substantially as it had been when they lived there together. She had bought four lots: two on a slight rise on the west side of the ocean boulevard and the two lots on the beach directly in front of them. The elevation of the interior lots, which was an unusual topographic feature of land so close to the ocean, and the ownership of the contiguous beach lots assured her an unrestricted view of the Atlantic. Her house, designed by the legendary Atlanta architect, Philip Trammell Schutze as one of his last projects, was a triumph of Georgian classicism and orderliness amidst what Molly had once politely termed the exuberant architectural inconsistency of newer beach communities.

He sat down on the low brick wall supporting the wrought iron fence that surrounded the front courtyard, his back to the warmth of the morning sun, and studied the façade. He had never considered making what had been Molly's rooms his own until this moment. To have done so would have recognized the change that had taken place, the unresolved tragic circumstances that lay behind it and confronted his vague sense of uncertainty about the future. It occurred to him that he had not had what he might regard as his own space since he had been fifteen – the year he went away to school.

He had moved to Molly's after his parent's death, to the small upstairs bedroom that had been furnished originally as a guest room. College and graduate school had been a succession of comfortable but somewhat impersonal places relieved by the addition of a couple of small Italian paintings that had been his father's and photographs of his family and closest friends. His first apartment in Atlanta had been a tiny carriage house in the rear of a Peachtree Battle mansion that Molly had furnished simply but quite beautifully with items retrieved from storage that had been in his mother's house in Atlanta.

He had bought the Habersham Road condominium almost a year before he and Caroline were married. While he liked the apartment and certainly appreciated the value of the underlying real estate economics that inured to his benefit, he always thought it was rather impersonal. "Kind of like living in a decorator show house," he once commented to Caroline.

Billy leaned back into the fence and closed his eyes as if confronted by the enormity of the task that lay ahead. Unavoidably, images of Caroline and the two years they had spent together in Atlanta began to penetrate his conscious memory for the first time since the day they had stood in the sweltering July rain and buried her.

He had been in depositions all day on the day she had left for Georgetown, unable to find the time during his only break to call her. He was standing in the living room simultaneously trying to reach Caroline on her cell phone to make sure she had arrived in Georgetown safely and find CNN on the television, when he heard the front door open. He was surprised to see Julia and John Harleston appear in the arched opening at the entrance to the room where he was standing. It had been exactly like the morning eight months later when he had looked up and seen Lucy walking down the hill to the round pen on her farm in Normandy. He knew in an instant something was gravely wrong.

"Billy," Julia had begun. "Caroline's been in an accident." And he knew it was over. Caroline Coachman had been one of the girls boys like Billy Commander were supposed to marry. Of impeccable background, nicely educated and beautiful in a rather cool, serene way, she had been a comfortable adjunct to the Buckhead life that had begun to define their daily existence.

Within three months after her arrival in Atlanta as Mrs. William Bradbury Commander, Caroline had been accepted as a volunteer at two of the most significant institutions in Atlanta, beginning to mold a subtle but nonetheless pronounced social presence among a society that was an odd mix of old families and new arrivals clamoring for acceptance. Her initial volunteer activities positioned her noticeably in the subtle hierarchy of the Atlanta Junior League, resulting in a coveted placement within the annual Atlanta tour of the Metropolitan Opera. Eight months later, she was accepted into the Peachtree Garden Club and her ascension in distaff Atlanta was secured.

"The Peachtree Garden Club?" Billy had questioned with surprise one night over dinner at Capital City. "We have four pots on a terrace."

"It has nothing to do with gardening, Billy. Clearly. I was nominated by Isabelle Collins and seconded by Gardiner Arrington and four more of their friends. Do you want to tell Isabelle, let alone Molly, that... what? I'm too busy? I don't think so."

Yet amid all the ostensible glamour of life in Atlanta, she had brought a comfortable realism to their relationship. Billy recalled driving down Peachtree Road one night on the way home from a dinner party, decrying the conversation in which he had been ensnared with a girl he had thought of as an empty-headed charity ball chair. "It's more like the absence of any intellectual activity whatsoever," he had retorted in response to a more benevolent comment from Caroline.

"I think she's just doing the best she can."

"Is that a South Carolinianism? An excuse for being dull-witted?"

"Life in Atlanta for a lot of girls is hard," she had replied.

He remembered the beauty of her profile and sleek blonde hair silhouetted by the lights of Peachtree Road sliding by outside her window.

"Her husband is from somewhere in Mississippi but not Jackson and not the Delta. He's on the partnership track at Lord and Van Allen. They have everything at stake and nothing secured. Can you imagine what that must be like? The ball chair thing is a big deal for her and you – or rather your background – terrified her. I think she's doing the best she can," she had concluded calmly, smoothly rebuking him without seeming to do so.

Deftly changing the subject, she continued, "Betsy Little asked us to Sea Island next weekend. They're going down on the Everette Development plane, and she said we could ride with them if we wanted. Cynthia Ingersoll said they've taken a place near Grasse the last week in July and the first two weeks in August. She asked us to come over for a week. Or a few days even," Caroline added as an afterthought.

Out of the corner of his eye, Billy watched her toying absentmindedly with the diamond earring in her left ear lobe. "I think Cynthia is a bit unpredictable. Richard is sweet enough, though. Everybody loves him."

"You seem remarkably unenthusiastic about either opportunity," he had observed.

"It's Sea Island and Grasse, Billy. Two of the places commonly acknowledged to be on anybody's short list of the best places in the world. What do you want me to say? I don't want to go? I'd rather go to Pawleys Island?"

"I dunno. I just thought that. Never mind. Sure. Let's go."

"I'll take care of it. I suppose we could go over a few days early if you want. Spend a few days in Paris. We could run up and see Lucy or maybe she could come down to town. Anything to avoid that tiresome LaGardiére. I'll call Cynthia and Betsy tomorrow."

She found him later, after she had changed for bed, reading in his small dressing room. "Are you coming to bed?" she asked, kissing him first on his cheek and then more romantically on his lips.

He had not wanted to make love that night for some reason he could not recall, continuing to read while she went to sleep alone. She had left for Georgetown the next morning.

Billy felt someone shake his right shoulder gently. Opening his eyes, he saw Thomas.

"Mr. Commander, I saw you come in from your run but I didn't hear you come into the house. I brought you some water, sir. Are you all right?"

"Fine. I'm fine," he said as he took the glass of water Thomas offered. "Day dreaming a bit, I guess. I need to get going here. Thanks again. No. You first," Billy finished indicating the front door to his house.

Chapter Forty-Nine

"I'm pulling into the courtyard right now," Billy heard Julia say through his cell phone, "so get your cute behind out here."

"I'm wearing shorts and flip flops."

"We're going to Oyster Island, not the Fulton Club," she laughed, watching him come out the front door talking to her on his phone.

"Can I hang up now," he joked as he got in the car.

"Look at those legs. Hubba. Hubba," she continued teasing him.

"You're in a good mood this afternoon."

"It's been a good day. The conservancy's objection to further development on North Island has been largely upheld. There will be another 3,000 acres going into a conservation easement and the size of allowable development will be limited to less than 50 acres, none of it near the sensitive wetlands over there. All in all, a good day."

"So we're headed to Oyster Island? The reason for this trip would be…?" he questioned.

"A different point of view."

"For whom?"

"You."

"You assume I have a point of view about Oyster Island?"

"Yes."

"And this would be a different point of view from the one you are assuming, with shockingly little basis I might add, that I currently hold?"

"Yes," she said playing along with his little verbal game.

"Even though you really don't know what my current point of view may be?"

"Exactly."

"Brilliant. Thus proving once again that in the hands of a clever lawyer, even an unknown hypothesis can be disproved. They taught this kind of dialectic at Chapel Hill?"

"I've had additional training."

"I haven't been over there since the house at Asylum burned," Billy said suddenly serious.

"We're not going to Asylum."

"Where, then?"

"Mt. Arena with Alabama Deas."

"Who?"

"Alabama Deas. She was a friend of Molly's. Her family were Oryzantia people, native to Oyster Island. They were among the first freedmen to buy land over there. She'll tell you."

"Do you have a point you are trying to make? Or a cause you are advancing?"

"Indulge me. I need to go over there and look around. There's a matter that is before the Conservancy. Never mind. We're going."

Chapter Fifty

Julia pulled into the parking lot at the Oyster Island ferry dock and parked her car just as the river boat was docking. The Oyster Island ferry was a sixty-foot diesel-powered river launch with its aft deck fitted out with six rows of benches, partially covered by a canvas bimini. Clear plastic curtains, rolled up and snapped into the edges of the canvas cover at the moment, could be let down and secured on the gunwales in the event of inclement weather. Emblazoned down the hull of the boat on each side were the words "School Boat" in the same black lettering that identified the buses of the South Carolina public school system.

Waiting on the dock was an elderly African American woman, dressed in a royal blue silk suit, leaning on her cane and gazing across the river toward Oyster Island.

"Dr. Deas," Julia greeted her as they approached. "How nice to see you and thank you for your time this afternoon. I'm not sure you know my cousin. Allow me to introduce to you Billy Commander. Billy, Dr. Alabama Deas."

Alabama shifted her cane to her left hand to shake Billy's hand. "William, I've not seen you since you were a child. How lovely to see you. Julia, congratulations on the decision you got today," offering her cheek for Julia to kiss. "An important accomplishment I'd say. David Denby called me from the hearing room with the news."

"Thank you, Alabama. Are we ready?"

"JJ is just waiting for us, dear," she said, waving her cane to the boat captain as they boarded through the stern gangway.

"Now, William," she turned her attention to Billy. "I must tell you that your grandmother honored me with her friendship for over forty years. We would be the same age, Molly and I. You have no idea how much I already miss not only her counsel but also her uplifting spirit. Our world is poorer for the loss of Molly Commander."

"Thank you, ma'm. We miss Molly as well," he replied helping Alabama to sit down on one of the benches.

"Do you know much of the history of Oyster Island?" she inquired, as she settled herself.

"Some. One of the few places in South Carolina where former slaves were able to buy land. Became freeholders. The resulting entrepreneurship enabled the only sustainable rice cultivation in South Carolina – up until when? The 1940s as I recall."

Alabama nodded. "The development of Oryzantia by Harrison Inman coincided with the decline in the economic feasibility of the cultivation of rice. Those who planted and grew rice learned to make bricks and other building blocks composed of local materials. They progressed to becoming builders, landscapers, and artisans of various kinds, whatever Inman needed to complete his vision at Oryzantia. This brief interregnum of prosperity ended with the death of Mrs. Inman in 1959. Still, life went on. Natural resources were abundant: fish, especially shad migrating inland to spawn, game birds, water fowl, wild turkey, wild boar, and deer. Most of the families maintained a vegetable garden. Life proceeded much as it had for a hundred years.

"Harrison Inman founded a school on the island in the '30s which continued to operate until 1965 when the state authorized a school boat to connect with the school buses on the mainland – and the children were able for the first time to attend Georgetown County schools. That service continues to this day. Look. We're here." Taking Billy by the arm, she continued, "Would you go for a walk with me?"

The road leading from the school boat dock to the village of Mt. Arena could actually no more be called a road than Mt. Arena could be called a village. The tiny settlement centered around the Mt. Horeb Baptist Church, a beautiful Greek Revival structure, the construction of which had been funded by the Inmans in the forties. Facing the church was a matching, complementary building, which had housed the Oyster

Island school and a small medical clinic until 1965, and now was used as a community center.

Alabama held onto Billy's arm for support as they walked down the sandy lane between the two structures.

"Electricity and running water came to the island in the mid-sixties. Telephone service followed about ten years later. Life is still quite slow here by modern standards, I suppose. There's no crime. People feel safe in their homes. Some of the younger children earn spending money by carrying groceries or other supplies from the boat dock to people's houses. Social life, such as it exists, centers around the church and its activities."

"It seems idyllic, almost a throwback to simpler times," Billy said, gazing about the small collection of whitewashed houses, most of which exuded a general air of tidiness. He could see evidence here and there of window air conditioning units and television antennae, both tokens of a connection with the world across the river.

"Yes, well, that would be a romanticized vision, don't you think? Let's walk over there," she said, indicating a small wooden frame house situated on a hill overlooking the river in the shade of two huge live oaks.

Alabama announced their arrival by thumping her cane on the boards of the front porch. Billy noticed the tiny porch seemed to shake under the tapping of the cane and the addition of Alabama's weight. He observed that the house, which appeared to have a certain rustic charm from a distance, actually had a depressing air about it when seen at close hand. Modern windows had been installed in the old structure, but poorly and he could see gaps between the window frame and the exterior wall of the house in several places. Two of the three windows on the front of the house had no screens and the screen on the third was ripped and rusting in places. One set of the hinges on the screen door had rusted and broken, causing the door to sag and move back and forth in the breeze coming off the river.

"Aunt Cora, it's Alabama. Are you home? May we come in?"

Billy heard nothing from within the house, but Alabama opened the door and walked in nonetheless, beckoning Billy and Julia to follow her.

Addressing an ancient African-American woman seated in an old rocker, she continued. "Aunt Cora, I'd like you to meet two young friends of mine, Mr. William Commander and Miss Julia Pringle."

The old woman acknowledged their presence, silently nodding her head up and down before turning her attention back to the fuzzy broadcast of an afternoon soap opera playing on a small yet modern television.

"Poor dear, she's over ninety and no longer hears well," Alabama commented quietly to Billy and Julia. Raising her voice again she said, "Aunt Cora, where is Mattie? Is she home yet? I thought I saw her at the boat earlier."

Not waiting for a response, as she knew there would be none, Alabama crossed the small living room to call into the rear of the house.

"Mattie. Mattie, come here dear. It's Alabama. I've brought some friends to see you."

A moment later she turned back toward the room with her free hand holding the hand of a tiny black child who appeared to be six or seven years old.

"Mattie. This is Billy. And this is his cousin, Julia."

Julia stooped down to address the child at her eye level. "Hello, Mattie. Look at your pink pants. Is that a pony on your pocket?"

The little girl shyly fingered the embroidered patch on her pants, looking down at the floor, avoiding eye contact with Julia.

"Is this one of your school books?" Julia asked, noticing a book in the hand hidden behind Alabama's legs. "Could you read it to me?" Julia sat down on the floor, indicating a place next to her for the little girl to sit.

Alabama gave Mattie an encouraging pat on her shoulder. "It's okay, sugar. Julia likes to read to little girls."

As the little girl sat down next to Julia and began to open her book, Alabama said to Billy, "Perhaps you'd like to see the interior of the church. It's actually quite beautiful."

"Sure. I mean, whatever you'd like," Billy responded, still unclear if there was a purpose to the afternoon, and if so, what it was that he should be gleaning from the experience.

"Aunt Cora, I'll come back to see you later in the week," Alabama said, patting the old woman's arm and rearranging the thin blanket covering her knees.

"Thank you, William," she said, availing herself of Billy's outstretched hand as she descended the steps. "A real estate developer has offered Cora 75,000 dollars for her house, and offered to pay for her transition expenses, as they termed it, to a state-operated nursing home in Andrews."

"If she is unable to care for herself, perhaps she would be better off," Billy began, more out of the need he felt to participate in the conversation than out of any real analysis, let alone conviction.

"Cora hasn't left Oyster Island in probably ten years. This is her world," Alabama said gesturing slowly about with her cane. "Everyone she has ever known is right here. Why do we think she would be better served in the final years of her life to be in some antiseptic institution, surrounded and cared for by strangers?"

"Is the little girl her granddaughter?" Billy asked in an attempt to re-direct the conversation.

"Mattie is her great granddaughter actually."

"Where are her parents?"

"Her mother, Cora's granddaughter never married her father. I am told he was from the mainland, not the island. Letitia had to drop out of high school in the tenth grade when she became pregnant with Mattie. She is unable to pursue her education because she works seven days a week changing beds and cleaning rooms at one of the hotels in Myrtle Beach. Tuesday through Saturday she gets up at 5:30 so she can take the school boat to the mainland at 6:30. If there is no one on the boat with her who keeps a car parked at the landing, she has to walk almost a mile to Highway 17 to catch one of the green and white buses that transport hotel workers from as far away as Williamsburg County to the beach. She is required to be at work at 7:30."

"The reverse process in the afternoons means that she does not get home until almost 6:00. She works what is called a half-day on Sundays and Mondays, but even so does not get home until 2:00. She is not here to fix Mattie's breakfast, get her ready for school, or pack her lunch. By the time she returns in the evening, her child is hungry, not to mention starved for attention and affection. Even if she were sufficiently educated to be able to help Mattie with her studies, weariness and lack of time take their toll. She has supper to prepare, laundry to do. Her mother's life, her aunts' lives were largely the same. She can envision no change in her own life and gave up hope years ago of affecting a change in the life of her child.

"If she has a moment before she goes to sleep, she sees on television the stories of unreality, fantasy, which somewhere in her subconscious mind she believes to be truth." Alabama shuddered. "As I said, her own lack of education prevents her from helping Mattie with her studies even if she had the time available to help. Letitia is herself a product you might say of this system. Her pregnancy occurred, in part, as a result of a general lack of supervision because her mother was compelled to work a similar schedule, also cleaning rooms at one of the hotels."

"But who looks after the little girl? Her great grandmother cannot be much help."

"No, this is true. Letitia must provide for both of them. She pays one of the neighbor children – a little girl in the seventh grade – $20 a week to come in and get Mattie ready for school."

"Here we are," she said pausing in front of the church. "The architect for this church and its companion structure was Horace Trumbauer."

"The Philadelphia Museum of Art?"

"Harrison Inman was from Philadelphia, as you know, and commissioned these buildings as part of the development of Oryzantia. You likely notice they are roughly based on – or inspired by – I suppose one should say – the Greek temple at Agrigento in Sicily.

"Shall we go in?"

Billy was struck by the elegant simplicity of the interior of the church as they went in.

"The plaster was mixed on site using local river sand and crushed shell. This delightful pale ochre comes from the materials themselves. It has never been painted. The floors and woodwork, including the railings and the pulpit, were made from cypress trees logged and milled here on the island. The windows were made in the old cabinet shop at Oryzantia. Oh my word. Let's sit down for a minute, do you mind? I'm certainly getting too old for this."

Alabama sat down in one of the rear pews and looked silently around the church for a moment.

"My grandfather sang in the choir in this church."

Billy looked around, absorbing the details of the workmanship in the church. "Did you grow up on Oyster Island?" he asked quietly.

"My mother's family lived on the island. My father's family was from Washington. He was an educator. A professor and later the president of a small black college in Baltimore."

"How did he…"

"… meet my mother?" she said with a soft chuckle. "In the depths of the Depression, Mr. Roosevelt sent teams from the War Department, as it was then known, to various regions in the South to map – to improve the quality of maps for military purposes. It actually may have been part of the broader public works initiatives that were central to the New Deal. Anyway, my father taught geography among other subjects, and he took a summer job as a supervisor on one of the crews that came to South Carolina. He met my mother in this very church. He and some of the others had learned about the recently completed Trumbauer project and came over to see the church. They fell in love. He arranged for her to go to an all-black, all-female school in Washington on a scholarship. Several years later they married."

"Unlike Mattie's mother, my mother was able to break the cycle of working poverty and illiteracy that afflicts so many people in our area. I suppose that makes me one of the lucky ones. I don't know."

Billy rested his chin in his hands, his elbows propped on his knees as he listened to Alabama. She watched the young man contemplating the church, wondering what was running through his mind. His grandmother had been one of the first to grasp the incrementing desperation of the working poor along the Waccamaw Neck.

"The bank can't help with jobs, Alabama," she recalled Molly saying. "Even tellers are required to have more than a high school diploma these days. And to hire more people for jobs like that held by Thomas' aunt is not the creation of economic opportunity. It is the perpetuation of the cycle of the lack of economic opportunity grounded upon the lack of education. You and everybody else are approaching this in the wrong way. I've been saying that. Fix the education process first.

Economic opportunity will become the principal, if not the immediate, by-product."

Alabama turned her attention back to Billy. "Do you know much about the labor demographics of the Waccamaw Neck?"

"No, I've… I was about to say that I've been away. A truer statement would be I've never lived here."

"Nationally, only about one in four working families is able to survive financially. A full-time job at the federal minimum wage level is inadequate to keep a family of three above the poverty level. Over the last thirty years, real wages for those who did not complete high school have actually declined by nineteen per cent. Here, along the Waccamaw Neck, the majority of the available jobs – cashiers, maids and janitors, landscape workers, waiters – are low-paying jobs. A prominent think tank recently looked at the issue of regional economic mobility and concluded that over seventy-three per cent of workers with jobs, the wages from which keep them at or below the poverty level, are unable to lift themselves out of poverty. Unable. Over seventy-three per cent," she repeated for emphasis.

"Letitia is in the majority, not the minority. The average number of hours worked along the Waccamaw Neck indicates that those who have hourly jobs are working the equivalent of one and one-half full-time jobs, rendering the prospect of economic advancement based on additional training or education impossible. That's the circle of their existence we seem unable to break."

Alabama stood up and turned to go, waiting for Billy to precede her into the aisle. Putting her hand on his arm for support, they started toward the door. "America has long espoused the dream that continued hard work will lead to the achievement of a brighter future. That dream is becoming harder and harder to realize for a large segment of our community."

She paused as they reached the porch of the church. "We lifted our light beside the golden door of opportunity. We exhorted the world to send us their tired, their poor, their huddled masses. Doesn't it strike you as sad that a little more than a hundred years later our exhortation has become send us your tired, your poor and they shall remain so? Look. Here's Julia."

"We read five books," Julia said laughing as she rejoined Alabama and Billy. "The billy goats gruff story was her favorite," she teased Billy. "Did the two of you have a nice visit?"

"Poor boy. He's been stuck with the nattering of an old woman, I fear. William, you were a dear to keep me company and allow me to run on so. You children should go along now and do something fun. I'm going to stay and have dinner, and then J.J., the boat captain, will see me back to my car." She put up her hand to silence their protest. "No. No, I insist. I'll be fine. I've been doing this for years."

"Thank you for a lovely afternoon. It is a very touching place," Billy commented as he shook her hand.

Julia kissed her lightly on the cheek, squeezing her hand warmly. "Let me take you to lunch next week. Promise?"

Alabama smiled. "Go. Go. You're going to miss the 6:00 ferry run."

Twenty-five yards down the sandy road, Billy stopped. "Give me a second, would you, Jules?" He turned and walked briskly back up the slight hill to where Alabama was still standing, watching them walk toward the ferry. She regarded Billy quizzically as he approached. Julia could see her listening intently to something Billy said. Tears came quickly to her eyes as she saw her cousin reach down and embrace Alabama with both his arms, holding her closely for a moment, then kissing her on the cheek he turned to leave and join Julia.

Chapter Fifty-One

"I think Isabelle is going to be here," Julia said as they drove into the courtyard of her parents' house. "And a friend of Mother's from school," she finished, parking her car and leaning back against the headrest. "I'm exhausted. Aren't you?"

"Where's the doc these days? He's been a mystery man."

"Didn't I tell you? He had a long weekend and he met Celia and his mother in Morehead City. He asked me to go up with him. I just couldn't get away."

"How long are they staying?"

"He just drove up this morning. 'Til Sunday I guess."

"You're going tomorrow."

Billy, I…"

"Walker said the AmeriJets thing is done. You're going up tomorrow morning. No arguments. I'll call Thomas from inside. Walker gave him the number. It's written down at home. Call the doc. Tell him you're on the way.

"Billy…"

Billy held his hand up to silence her. "Pack your bags, babe. Tomorrow you're sittin' on a different beach under a sky that's Carolina Blue," he laughed. "Let's go meet the mystery friend. What's her name?"

"Whose name?"

"The mystery guest."

"Demetra Adams. She knew Mother when she was at Smith. She knew your mom and dad, too. Through Mother, I guess."

"Why do I sense there is something you're not telling me?"

"They were all friends in college. Mother thought you might like to…"

"Like to what," Billy interrupted. "Are you handling me?"

"To listen."

"To what end?"

"Perhaps to see a side of your parents you didn't know existed."

"Your mother's organized a dinner party to help me know my parents better?"

Julia leaned her head back on the headrest of her seat, idly fingering the steering wheel of her car.

Glancing up at the sky through the open sun roof, she said, "Do you know what your parents believed in? Were passionate about? Do you know what their summer jobs were? Who your mother's boyfriends were? Your father's girlfriends before they married? All of those were questions you would have asked when you were twenty-one or twenty-five. Only you couldn't. Because they weren't there. And you and Molly had this…"

"This what?"

"This way of talking around one another instead of to one another." Julia got out of the car dropping her keys into her bag. "Go home if you want. I think you should stay, but what the hell do I know?"

Billy watched Julia walking into her mother's house. "Can this day get any more bizarre?" he thought.

"Billy!" Isabelle Collins exclaimed, as he walked into the entrance hall alone. "How wonderful to see you and how wonderful you look. Dorothy's man has made these divine gimlets. Divine. Won't you have one? I'm sure you will. Evan. Let's get Mr. Commander a… oh, see it's already here. Come with me. I want you to meet Demetra Adams. I don't know where Dorothy is."

Billy fell into the familiar rhythm that began every night between six and seven o'clock among certain kinds of families. Molly observed once that, among polite people, the cocktail hour marked a transition between the business day, and the requirements and privileges of a life in society. "Such subtle but important changes are the hallmarks of civilized behavior," he remembered her commenting. "Otherwise, everything just runs together in a big mess."

"Billy. Here you are. How did I miss you when you came in?" he heard Dot Pringle say as she came out from the kitchen. "Did you meet Demetra? Isabelle?"

"Yes. Yes. Good lord, Dorothy, do you think we just let him wander around by himself?"

Dot Pringle slipped her arm comfortably through the arm of the tall, elegantly dressed African-American woman to whom Billy was being introduced.

"Dr. Adams," Billy stammered. "What a…"

"Surprise?" Demetra responded with a bright smile.

"No, m'am. An honor. I didn't make the connection. I have known you by reputation, of course, at Atlanta University but I had no idea you knew my parents," turning to Dot Pringle for some explanation.

Demetra laughed. "Later, William. Later. We'll tell all those old stories. For now, I need to refill my wine glass. I understand you've been to Oyster Island today with Julia. I want to hear all about it."

"Dorothy," he heard Isabelle exclaim from the doors to the terrace. "You must come see the moon. It is a full orange moon over the ocean. Very unusual. Demetra, don't try to monopolize that boy. He's not giving you any money. At least, not until I tell him he should," she said with a smile.

Several minutes later when they were all settled on the terrace with a view of the ocean in the distance, Billy said to Demetra, "I'm sorry. I missed the connection. You knew my parents through Dot and Lowndes?"

"Yes," she seemed to hesitate and turned to Dot for reinforcement. Billy noticed Dot avoid eye contact with Demetra by attending to the drinks glasses and exchanging hors d'oeuvres trays with her houseman.

"But you were at Berkeley, then UCLA for grad school," he continued, "as I recall from the articles in the paper at the time you assumed the presidency of the university. Not Smith. There was a certain amount of comment in the African-American community when you came to Atlanta about your west coast antecedents."

"I suppose."

Billy looked around the group assembled on the terrace. Isabelle was chatting quietly with Julia, while Dot was sitting with her head resting on the back of her chair, listening to Billy and Demetra and watching the moon over the water. He sipped his gimlet, thinking again, "What the hell is going on here? What was the relationship in the sixties between two rich white women at one of the east coast Seven Sisters schools and an African-American woman at the west coast epicenter of the student protest movement?"

"Please, go on. You were telling me how you knew my parents," he said.

He observed the obvious pause in the conversation as Demetra looked at Isabelle Collins for what could only have been construed as consent. Nodding almost imperceptibly, Isabelle picked up her cocktail glass and turned her attention to the conversation taking place between Billy and Demetra.

"Dot has some pictures of all of us together. I'd like you to see them," Demetra commented with a pleasant nonchalance in her manner.

"Pictures?

"Snapshots. From a long time ago."

Dot retrieved an old photo album from a console by the doors, handing it to Demetra.

"Come sit by me," Demetra said, indicating a place next to her on the sofa.

As he sat down, Billy began to study the photographs in the book open on her lap.

"This looks oddly like Miami Beach. A political rally of some kind. That's my mother," he said pointing to a beautiful young blonde woman. "And Dot, next to her?"

"Yes."

"What is this?"

"The 1968 Republican Convention."

"Republican Convention? Mother and Dot?"

"We both worked on the Rockefeller for President campaign." Dot explained. "Rockefeller people recruited heavily within the Ivy League and the Seven Sisters. You must recall this was before the advent of personal computers. It took a lot of young staffers to assemble and manage all the information necessary for a national campaign. I was a… how would you describe it, Isabelle, in current terminology?"

"Rather like a fact-checker, I'd say. One who assembles, verifies and analyzes a particular body of information."

"Exactly. Thank you. I had the responsibility of delegate information for three southern states – Georgia, South and North Carolina. Your mother was part of the advance team, making the arrangements for the candidate's appearances. We worked initially in the New York headquarters office and then went to Miami about three weeks prior to the convention."

"The '68 Republican convention?" Billy queried with amusement. "I couldn't be more surprised."

"The party was in disarray, shambles, after the Goldwater disaster in sixty-four. The country was embroiled in debate over Vietnam, the civil rights movement. Johnson had announced he would not seek re-election, throwing the Democratic party into a leaderless tailspin. Dr. King was assassinated in Memphis in early April. Robert Kennedy in California in June after winning the California Democratic primary. Rockefeller seemed like the logical, responsible, liberal voice."

Demetra continued. "Nixon was nominated on the first ballot, as you may recall. The non-Nixon delegates were split among Governors Rockefeller, Reagan and Romney. John Lindsay from New York. The majority leader – Gerald Ford. Nixon was able to assemble the required number of votes based on the party's emerging southern strategy and the confusion that ensued among the supporters of what many considered to be the other four equally strong, viable candidates. I was working in California for Eugene McCarthy, who was at the time the most outspoken critic of the war in Vietnam. Within an hour of the first ballot in Miami handing Nixon the nomination, I was on a plane from San Francisco to recruit former Rockefeller staffers for the McCarthy campaign. It had become quickly apparent that the Nixon camp was going to turn to Governor Agnew for the vice presidential slot, instead of one of the better known governors or even Mayor Lindsay. Our logic was that we became the only choice for the liberal social principles that had been a hallmark of the Rockefeller campaign. I had a friend from Berkeley in the West Coast Rockefeller office, who introduced me to Dot and your mother, whom I recruited."

"We went straight from Miami to the Democratic Convention

in Chicago. I thought my parents were going to have a stroke," Dot chuckled at the memory.

Demetra turned through several pages in the album to find an eight-by-ten black and white photograph. The picture was an archival newspaper photograph of a protest, replete with signs and placards decrying the war, police in riot gear confronting a mob of mostly young protest marchers, wisps of tear gas creating an almost otherworldly cloud hanging over the crowd. She continued the story.

"Michigan Avenue, Wednesday evening, August 28th, 1968. It was the day the violence reached its zenith. Mayor Daley would not allow any protesters near the convention center. The party had turned to Hubert Humphrey, whom the liberals identified with LBJ and the government's policy on the war. We – the McCarthy staffers – felt defeated, disenfranchised, powerless to influence the course of government policy that was allowing the murder of young people abroad, unable to extend the most fundamental of constitutional protections and civil rights to black people at home. We joined the protesters and began the march from Lincoln Park to the convention center that became known as the Battle of Michigan Avenue. That's your mother," she said pointing to a young woman in jeans and a white shirt.

There was a man next to her leaning over to help another young woman pick herself up from the pavement, where she had clearly been shoved by a policeman in full riot gear, standing over her with a billy club raised threateningly in the air.

"And that," pointing to the man, "is your father, helping Dot back to her feet after she had been knocked down by a police officer. Molly and your grandfather had become concerned about Frances and Dot. They allowed Motte to come to Chicago to bring them home. He had been working that summer in a voter registration program in Mississippi."

"Motte arrived in town the night the platform debates were concluded." Dot continued the story. "Not only had the party rejected the peace plank, but it had also refused to move forward with a civil rights plank. Motte was enraged. He had been part of the student group that shut down Columbia in April in protest to the war. He had himself been the victim of protest-related violence that summer in Jackson."

Isabelle leaned toward Billy, putting her glass on the cocktail table. "Molly and I were in New York at my apartment when we saw the first reports of the violence on the news. There was a tape delay because Daley would not allow live broadcasts from outside the convention center. The paper's plane was in Kansas City at the time. I sent it immediately to Chicago to get your mother and father and Dorothy. A lawyer from Shearson Pearsall, who represented both the bank and the newspaper, got your dad out of jail and managed to find Frances and Dorothy, delivering all three of them to Midway Airport around five in the morning."

Dot Pringle wiped her eyes as she recalled the events of that night. "Your dad still had blood all over his face. Your mom was wearing a t-shirt calling for death to the pigs under a white oxford men's shirt. My arms were bruised from the police officer who had grabbed me, and I had blood clotted in my hair from where I fell. We were a sight," she laughed in spite of herself at the memory.

"So you were in Lincoln Park that night, also," Billy asked Demetra.

"Yes."

"You were part of the movement?"

"Yes."

"And my parents?"

"Yes."

"But you sit on the Coke Board with Isabelle. The Emory board with Gardiner Arrington. Two of the three traditional pillars that hold up Atlanta."

She nodded.

"You brought down the government. Ended the war. You picked up the remains of the civil rights movement and enabled the feminist movement and the gay rights movement. You were a principal participant in a movement that transformed American society, and you…"

"Sold out?"

"I would not have said that."

"You were going to say that I… we sold out. How? I sit at the helm of an institution that daily transforms the lives of young African-Americans, many of whom have no educational alternative. But because I choose to do so in a designer suit and beautiful shoes and have drinks here with you at DeBordieu, you assume I may have in some way compromised the integrity of an earlier period. Your father was a partner at the most prestigious law firm in Atlanta, and you grew up on Arden Road. Do you think they sold out? Did Dot?"

"I… I don't…"

"Billy," Dot took a deep breath to compose herself. "Molly said revolutionary change was part of the American experiment. We were sitting in Isabelle's kitchen in New York getting our dings and dents patched up. She said that by many processes, including sometimes protest, the inclusion of everyone in 'We, the People' must become manifest. She reminded us that we, unlike many others, were able to march, secure in the confidence that we would be able to eat, finish school, go on with our lives regardless of the outcome of the march. She said the day after the revolution succeeds someone must pick up the reins of government, the reins of social institutions and corporations or the gains of protest would never be consolidated."

"You knew about this?" Billy turned to Julia.

"Pretty much," she nodded.

"How long?"

"I guess all my adult life."

"And you never…"

"I just did."

Rather abruptly, Billy stood up. "I'm a bit more tired than I realized. If you don't mind, I think I'll go home. If that's all right? Dot, is it possible I could have copies of the pictures that…"

She crossed the room to hug him. Kissing him on the cheek, she said, "You already do. On the top shelf of the linen press in Molly's bedroom are a series of leather bound albums. It's all there."

"Dr. Adams. Isabelle," he said preparing to leave. "Thank you. Dot, I'm sure…"

She shook her head, obviating the need for any further comment.

"Let me drive you home," Julia began.

"I'm gonna walk. Thanks, Jules. Walk'll do me good. I'll call you tomorrow."

"I'll see you to the door, Billy," Dot said, placing her glass on the cocktail table as she rose. Walking down the hall, she slipped her arm through his affectionately. "Are you sure I can't change your mind?"

"I hope you won't find me rude. I think I want to go home. I feel like I've been ambushed twice today by Julia … I'm not sure I understand…"

Dot patted his arm. "Billy, some of us are given the gift of teaching, some healing, others preaching. Some are given great wisdom. Some can only try to keep the lamps of hope burning. And then, some of us are given the special gift of building, creating opportunity where there was none." She reached up to kiss his cheek as they reached the door. "Sleep well."

"A diversity of gifts. But one inspiration," he commented from the steps.

She paused as she was closing the door. "One might say."

"St. Paul versus the Corinthians."

Dot laughed softly, nodding at him.

"Interesting case, that." He started down the steps. "Thanks. I enjoyed being here. Oh, tell Julia I'll call her tomorrow with the information about the plane. Goodnight."

As he turned onto the beach road, he sensed that Dot was still watching him. Without looking back, he threw up his hand and waved to her.

Chapter Fifty-Two

"Curious," Billy thought, pausing as he read the morning papers, "how comfortable I am beginning to feel in these surroundings. Even sitting in the same chair every morning."

"Mr. Commander, would you care for some breakfast? I have fresh local melon, the first this season actually. Probably an indication of a hot summer. There's some local blueberries, too, that the vegetable man brought. And, the new bacon came yesterday."

"New bacon?" Billy asked with marked curiosity.

"Yessir. It's a bacon-of-the-month thing. A Christmas present to Mrs. Commander, I think. This month is smoked Big Sky bacon. I don't know what that is."

Billy chuckled. "That sounds great Thomas. Fruit and some Montana bacon. Perfect. Do you have Mrs. Ferguson's number at the bank in Atlanta by any chance?"

"Give me just a minute, sir."

Billy turned his attention back to the *Times*. A moment later he heard Thomas coming back into the loggia. "Mrs. Ferguson in Atlanta, Mr. Commander," he said passing Billy the phone.

"Mildred? I asked Thomas to get me your number and he was kind enough to place the call for me. How are you?" Billy nodded his thanks to Thomas, as he went back into the kitchen. "Good. Good. Yes, everything here is fine, thank you. Hey look. I was wondering. Do you have any vacation time? Any chance you'd have an interest in getting out of Atlanta for a few days? Now, before you answer, I don't want to be guilty of flying under false colors, so let me tell you what I had in mind. I could use some help sorting through Molly's things. Some bank related, some not. The overnight bags you recall. Anyway, I have to go to New York the first of next week, and I thought maybe you could come over, help me out a bit and then you could hang out here at the beach while I am in New York. Stay here at Molly's… uhhh… my house. Thomas is around to look after you, keep you out of trouble." He laughed again. "Any chance you'd have an interest in doing that?" Billy paused, listening. "Really? That's great. A whole week? Okay. Great. I'm going to send the plane to get you. What day can you travel?" Listening again, he then continued. "No. No, I insist. You're doing me – us – a huge favor. I'll call you back with the arrangements. Thanks again. I know, me too."

"Mr. Commander, your breakfast is ready. There's no breeze this morning so the no-see-ums are going to be bad outside. I set you up at the kitchen counter if that's all right."

"Wherever it's convenient is fine. Fine. Thomas, Mr. Coggeshell sent some stuff down about how I book the plane. We did one of those AmeriJet deals. Do you happen to know where that information is?"

"His assistant called me from New York and explained the procedure. I think they were concerned that you don't have your desk organized yet."

"That sounds like Walker talking," Billy commented with good humor.

"Would you like me to take care of it?"

"You know how to get this done?"

"Yessir. It's not that hard," Thomas said grinning uncharacteristically as he placed Billy's breakfast dishes and a fresh cup of coffee on the counter.

"Awesome. Okay. Julia needs to go to Morehead City this afternoon, and we need to get Mrs. Ferguson over here from Atlanta on Saturday morning. I need to go to New York on Tuesday. I guess I should call Mr. Coggeshell and Mr. Murrah in New York, and I need to track down Mr. Read." Billy paused as he picked up a slice of bacon with his fingers. "Do you enjoy doing this kind of planning?"

The older gentleman smiled. "Yessir, I actually do. I did a lot of this kind of thing for Mrs. Commander. It's not only my job but I like it.

She always said I had a very logical mind. No, that wasn't it. Sequential. That was the word."

"Tell you what. You work it out. Don't take any grief from Julia. Tell her she's going to Morehead this afternoon, and we don't want to hear any protest from her. Mrs. Ferguson's coming over for a few days to help me out with the file boxes in the dining room, and then she's going to hang out here for a while, enjoy the beach, while I'm in New York."

"Do you want me to put Mrs. Ferguson in the green room or the blue room upstairs?"

"Whatever you think is best. I leave all of this in your very capable hands."

"Thank you, sir."

"I need to get organized," Billy said to himself. Much as he did not like to admit it, he didn't even have a desk at which he could work, make and return phone calls.

"Thomas, I've been thinking about our conversation the other day. You know, when you said it was my house. I was not a guest here."

"Yessir."

"Well, I was thinking. If you don't think it's too soon, I thought we'd make some changes. Maybe I'll move into Molly's rooms after all. Would it bother you in anyway if we… I dunno… changed the curtains, bedspreads, upholstery, stuff like that."

"No, sir. Not at all. I think it's probably what your grandmother would want you to do."

Billy sat back comfortably in the bar stool at the counter. "Okay. I'm going to go run and then get dressed. Thanks for breakfast."

An hour later, Billy was in the dining room, thumbing through the files in the boxes containing the most recent correspondence and information. Sitting cross-legged on the floor, he was fixing small yellow post-it notes to various files and documents that seemed germane. Thomas appeared at the door with the phone in his hand.

"Mr. Read for you, sir."

"Hey, hey. John Harleston. How's it going? Where are you? I see. We have the plane coming over Saturday morning sometime if you want to grab a ride. I called 'cause I need a favor. Some advice actually.

I'm thinking of making a few changes around here. Moving into Molly's rooms. I don't want to screw things up but at the same time I was hopeful you might know someone – a decorator – who could help. But a guy who can produce – I dunno – something a bit more masculine than what we have here now. Does that make sense?"

"Sure, Billy. There's a ton of guys out there who can do that."

"But can you recommend someone?"

"Here? In Atlanta? Or at the beach? I don't think you're going to find anyone at the beach. I'd look here or in New York, if I were you."

"New York's cool. I'm going up Monday or Tuesday. Any chance you'd go with me? Translate?"

"Translate?"

"Yeah. I am a little uncomfortable in that I don't really know the lingo or the drill – how one would approach this. I don't want to sound like an idiot, nor do I want to make a mess of Molly's house."

John Harleston laughed. "Sure. I'll go along. Translate, so to speak. You know McMillen helped Molly with her house originally. There's a young guy who just left them to go out on his own. Doing a lot of work for guys. Hedge fund managers, you know. His work looks good. We're publishing a loft he did next month. I'll see if he's available. He would likely be knowledgeable about what they did for Molly and certainly respectful of his firm's work. Not want to throw everything out and start over. Know what I mean? I think we have some pictures of Molly's house around here somewhere. We shot it a couple of years ago. I'll see if I can find those. Invent some business in New York so I can tag along."

"You have no idea how much I'd appreciate it. I'm thinking this becomes my place and Julia takes Commander House. Maybe the same guy could help out there, too. It really does need some sprucing up."

"Well, look. Let's take on one house at the time, okay? I'll grab a ride on Saturday morning, and we'll hang out at the beach and then go up to New York the first of the week. I need to spend some time with my mom and dad anyway. I missed Mother's Day. Maybe I can make up for it by being there for Father's Day." John Harleston stopped abruptly. "Billy, I am so sorry. Just not thinking. Really, I…"

"It's okay. Don't think about it. I'll call you with the plane details. I think they go out of Peachtree DeKalb. Need to run here."

"Later."

"Gator," Billy said, laughing as he hung up.

Thomas appeared at the door, diet coke in hand. "Miss Julia is going to North Carolina at 2:00. She said to tell you she will call you from the plane. Dr. Henning will meet her at Morehead City. Mrs. Ferguson will be here at around 11:00 on Saturday morning. I will be glad to pick her up in Georgetown, if you like."

"Sure," Billy grinned. "You're the man in charge. Mr. Read is going to grab a ride over with Mrs. Ferguson. Can you call his office and let his assistant know the details? I'd have likely screwed this whole thing up: sent Julia to Atlanta, Mrs. Ferguson to North Carolina and forgotten John Harleston entirely. Thanks for the coke," he said turning back to the file boxes.

"Friday night," Billy thought. "Julia's gone. John's not here until tomorrow." Reaching up to the table, he retrieved his cell phone and found Walker's number in New York.

"What?"

"That's how you answer your phone now? What?"

"I knew it was you. It comes up on the screen."

"Julia's going to Morehead this afternoon to hang out with the doc and his family."

"I know she just called me."

"She just called you?"

"Yep."

"She didn't call me."

"Maybe I'm missing something here, but I'm guessing she figured out you knew she was going, since she's going up on your plane."

"Can we call it something other than my plane? I'm not sure I'm comfortable having a plane."

"Well, you don't really have a plane, as you say. You have a piece of a plane, but if it bothers you, you could say you have access to a plane, I guess. Or, you can tell everybody it's my plane, and I just let you use it."

Billy laughed. "Okay. Whatever. John Harleston's coming over Saturday morning, and then we are coming up together Monday or

Tuesday. He said he'll go to the Empire Club. I thought I'd stay with you, if it's okay."

"Of course, you know it is. I'm going to get you keys made this time." Walker wondered, "What is up with this?"

"So, what are you doing tonight?" he heard Billy say. It hit him all of a sudden. Friday night, Julia's gone, and Billy has nothing to do.

"I'm going to meet Hardy, Nancy and Charlotte after work for a drink. Then we're going to something at the Asia Society. Anniversary. I think one of the Rockefellers is giving the party."

"Um, I see," Billy replied noncommittally.

"Billy?"

"Yep."

"What's up?"

"Nothing. Just checking in. The New York thing next week, you know."

"Okay. What are you doing tonight?"

"I... well... I don't... no real plans, I guess."

"Nothing to do?"

"What?"

"You have nothing to do tonight – is that it?"

"I guess."

"Gimme a sec here." Billy could hear the rapid click of keystrokes from Walker's computer as he waited "All right. Here's your night. There's an opening at the art co-op up at Litchfield. You know the one. In there, next to the grocery store and all that. Works of grad students from Chapel Hill and Carolina. Looks pretty good actually. Check out the paintings. May see something you like. Then hit the bar at Eddie's. There'll be a crowd by then. It's Friday night at the beach, for heaven's sake. You can fall in with a bunch for dinner. Then go home early and go to bed."

"You're planning my evening?"

"You brought it up, sport. Wasn't me whining about nothing to do." Walker laughed. "Call me tomorrow. I have to go."

Chapter Fifty-Three

"Thomas said I would find you in here," Mildred commented as she came into the dining room on Saturday morning. "What a beautiful room. I haven't been over here since shortly after your grandmother built this house. How many dining rooms would one find with this view of the Atlantic ocean?" she questioned rhetorically.

"Please, please. Sit down. Let me get you a chair. Your flight was okay?" Billy had stood up immediately when she entered the room and then moved one of the armchairs back from the table to make it easier for her to sit down.

"William," she addressed him rather formally when she was settled in her chair. "I understand you want me to help you review certain files of information your grandmother accumulated over the last several of her years with the bank, accumulated as you know, with my assistance."

"Yes." Billy was not sure of the direction of her conversation.

"You have terminated your relationship with Howell Raines, as I understand it?"

"I've talked to Bunky Sanderson several times. I notified him in writing last week of my resig…"

"But you are still a practicing attorney, a licensed attorney, one might say."

"In Georgia and South Carolina. Mildred, where is this…"

"Very well. I should like to retain you to represent me."

"Represent you?"

"Yes. I assume that, if you represent me legally, the substance of our discussions can never be disclosed, even in the context of a legal proceeding. Is that correct?"

"Largely. There are few, if any, exceptions to the attorney-client privilege."

"Would you consider a retainer of one hundred dollars sufficient?"

Billy looked at the check Mildred placed on the table in front of him, drawn on her personal account and payable to the order of William B. Commander, Attorney at Law. "Mildred, what's bothering you?"

"Is my retainer sufficient? May I consider you retained?"

"Sure," Billy grinned at the older lady, thinking he would indulge her penchant for confidentiality.

"The accumulation and shipment of those documents," she glanced at the boxes lining the wall, "was authorized by the then CEO and chairman of the bank for a specified purpose, in contravention of written bank policies. I assume he had the authority to act in such a manner. I have no confidence the current chairman would see this action and my involvement in the same light. I intend to help you glean what I think it is you want to know from your grandmother's files. I wish to do so without the knowledge of the current bank administration – and I want the additional assurance of privileged communication between us."

"I have to tell you that this is no guarantee that the bank will not take issue in some way with…"

"Well, certainly the events of the past several months have shown us that there are no guarantees in life of any kind, wouldn't you agree? Our arrangement may not be a belt and suspenders, as they say," adding a pronounced emphasis to 'and,' "but it's better than no belt at all."

"You're a crafty old bird, aren't you, Mildred?" Billy smiled at her with growing affection.

"Now, I presume you have reviewed the contents of these boxes." She raised her hand slightly. "And, I would assume that you have made some notes as you went along."

"Yes."

"I'd like to review those notes before we start, if I might. For me to know where you are in your analysis may allow us to complete our task more efficiently."

"Sure. Let me just find…," Billy rose and began extracting yellow legal pads from various stacks of files and piles of paper. "There are my notes and Julia's, and some stuff Hardy Murrah assembled in New York…" He quickly arranged the pads and files into a semblance of order and moved the new stack of information across the table to her. "I'd reverse those. The first notes we made are on the bottom and then… most of them are dated with the day we made the notes. I think you'll be able to follow along."

"Wonderful. Why don't you give me an hour or so to thumb through these, and then we can reconvene? If that's an agreeable process?"

"That's great. My laptop is there, at the end of the table. If you want anything, there's a buzzer on the floor somewhere…" Mildred laughed as she watched Billy get down on his hands and knees to find with his fingers the buzzer that sounded in the kitchen. "Here. By the back leg of the pedestal. I never understood how Molly could find it with her foot without looking."

"Years of practice, my boy. Years of practice. Run along now and let me read."

Billy closed the door to the dining room behind him as he went out into the hall. Entering the kitchen, he retrieved a glass from the cabinet and opening the refrigerator began to fill it with ice.

"Mr. Commander? I thought I heard you. What can I get for you?" Thomas asked, as he came in from the butler's pantry.

"Thomas. I can get my own diet coke. My action in doing so expresses no dissatisfaction with you or the discharge of your duties. It means simply that…," Billy faltered a bit. "That I can get my own diet coke."

"Yessir"

"I think it's time we start cleaning out my grandmother's bedroom. Her clothes and personal things. Do you think you feel up to removing those, sorting and indexing all that somehow? It's maybe the one thing I'd rather not do."

"It would be my pleasure, sir."

"Let's send her jewelry to the bank for the time being. Even the pieces she kept in the safe here. I don't know what we'll do with her clothes, shoes, bags – that kind of thing. I may call Mrs. Coggeshell and ask her what to do."

"Yessir. Shall I get them on the phone for you?"

" No. I've… wait. Mrs. Ferguson is going to be busy for a while. If you don't mind, call up to Mrs. Coggeshell's and ask them if she could see me for a few minutes. I'll be up in my room."

Billy took the steps two at the time, forgetting he had a full glass in his hand until it began to splash over the rim onto the carpet. "Sh…," he thought. "Molly's gonna kick my ass." He could not suppress the laughter that accompanied the subconscious response from his teenage years.

Chapter Fifty-Four

Billy gave a low whistle as he glanced over the document Mildred had just handed him. "If I didn't know better, I'd swear you were a lawyer."

"A paralegal."

"What?"

"A paralegal. Most of the work I did for the chairman, the board and later for Mrs. Commander struck me as essentially the same as litigation support. Mastering facts about a particular situation, organizing and managing files, quickly retrieving information necessary in the advocacy or refutation of a certain point of view. Mr. Burnett, with the support of Mrs. Commander, allowed me to go back to paralegal school about twelve years ago. The bank paid my tuition and covered the cost of my books. But I went at night, on my own time," she concluded matter-of-factly.

"A woman of so many talents," Billy complimented her.

She laughed softly. "No, sir. Just a working girl trying to keep her job. I agree with the analysis you developed with Julia and others. Alderlay's involvement with the bank precipitated a chain of events that led to a growing disagreement between Mrs. Commander – and I think the Executive Committee – and Hugo Lesesne and his principal lieutenants. You found the first intra-bank indication of their growing predicament – the T-bill transactions. Concannon's department began to build more creative methods to accomplish similar goals. Look at this email from one of the bankers in his division." She indicated an entry on page one of her document. "The comments within the brackets are my annotations."

> Email from Scott Tarver [one of four Vice Presidents in Investment Banking Div. (mf)] to Richard Concannon: Alderlay loves these deals. Who wouldn't? The ability to create cash flow – and lots of it – without the big d [I think he must mean 'debt' at this point (mf)] torpedoing their balsht [balance sheet? (mf)]

"Mrs. Commander learned about the T-bill transactions and started watching the emails with reference to other Alderlay entities. At one point she asked to see the documents establishing two new LLCs – Azalea and Camellia. Here, and again here," she said again referring Billy to her document. "Mr. Lesesne's response was that he didn't want to trouble her. Look at the transcript of this telephone conversation."

> Transcript of t/c MBC and HL, Tape No. 124:
>
> MBC: Well, Hugo, I appreciate that, but on the other hand I've been looking at documents my entire life. I'm certain a few more won't hurt.
>
> HL: We'll put together a package for you, Molly. All the documents aren't even drawn yet and it may hamper the efficiency of the process to review drafts in progress. MBC: Don't drag this out, Hugo. It's an important issue and within the bounds of my oversight.
>
> HL: I think this is really an internal matter and as I've already told you have my assurance that… [garbled on tape]
>
> MBC: What does that mean? You don't have the ownership lists of these flower llcs?
>
> HL: … [reply garbled again]
>
> MBC: … then is the bank advancing funds to an entity the ownership of which is unknown or uncertain? Doesn't that violate the Patriot Act and place the liability squarely on the bank?
>
> HL: It's complicated, Molly. We've been assured by Alderlay that there is no risk to the bank in funding the partnerships. Alderlay guarantees performance of the obligation.

MBC: … and did they guarantee us a get-out-of-jail-free card as well?

HL: Molly, sarcasm really has no place here.

MBC: I was not being sarcastic, Hugo. I was making a point. I want the information I asked about. If it doesn't come from you, I'll go straight to Richy Concannon.

"Mr. Lesesne finally sent the documents she asked about. She apparently found them to be weak. Look at this email from Mrs. Collins."

Email from Isabelle Collins to Molly Commander: Molly – lovely to hear from you. I still cannot get used to a couple of old warhorses like us using email. Of course, I can't type and I'm sure you can't either. I write my messages out by hand and then someone else accomplishes the transition to email. It's all gobbledy gook to me. And, to think I was invited to Richard Devlin's 'leaders of technology' summit meeting in Sun Valley this summer!

Anyway. In re: Alderlay. Nothing has come through my credit committee involving Alderlay or its subsidiaries. I would assume, as I would hope, that means that if we have advanced funds or established a credit facility for them, it falls within the established guidelines of loan authority granted by the board to senior loan officers. Why not have a glance at the minutes or records of the internal credit committee itself, if you are concerned? Or I could ask. Let me know how else I can help. I'll be at home in PB tonight. Call me on land line. 305/555-1212. Need to chat.

"Mrs. Commander made a note in her daybook about the call. Would you hand me the blue daybook just there? Here," opening the book she pointed to the same date where a notation had been inscribed in Molly's handwriting:

t/c I.B.C. in PB. Issy also wary of Concannon and SFP shop. Where is internal supervision of this ops? Lesesne. Fox supervising henhouse?

"Three weeks later she began to suspect that Oyster Island was one of Alderlay's acquisition targets. Where is it? Here. Look at this."

Email from Cynthia Morelli [Chief Advancement Office at Oryzantia] to Richard Concannon:

R – confirm my discussion today with Dir/Ory [Director of Oryzantia? (mf)]. Ald will have coop and support of Ory w/ref to Oys land in consideration of matters we discussed in your office last week. Regards. C.M.

"I don't want to drag this out unnecessarily…," Mildred hesitated.

"No. No. Go on. This is amazing."

"That same week, it looks to me like she found the first indication of how the bank was cooperating with Alderlay. These emails are a bit lengthy, but I think instructive."

Email from Richy Concannon to Risley Lawrence (CEO Alderlay Development): To confirm our t/c this day, CAB will advance 100% of the money you project Camellia will need for land acquisition; and will provide a rev l/cr [revolving line of credit (mf)] in an initial amount of $15M USD for preliminary infrastructure development. I have instructed my team to start preparing the deal documents

Cc: H. Lesesne

Barrett Holmes, Legal

Email response from Hugo Lesesne to Concannon, same day:

Richy: That's fine. I realize this generates substantial deal flow fees for CAB (for which, congratulations and thank you, btw) but when are we going to ask Risley for the IB [investment banking (mf)] order?

"Then there was a second exchange of emails that same day, which are… yes. Here."

2d email from Lesesne to Concannon, later that same day:

R: Clarification needed here. CAB funds the LLC 100% in effect becoming the de facto equity owner of the land – but certainly not the record owner. 1) Are we confident about the underlying valuation? 2) How does CAB get cashed out?

Email response from Concannon, one hour later:

H.L. 1st, recall that we are forming Rhododendron LLC simultaneously. CAB will have in place a contract with Rhodo taking us out of Camellia at a 25 % cash-on-cash return.

> Rhodo is secured by Ald stock with a trigger if stk declines. Rhodo is being sold to other investors. Beyond that. Bit tricky. Especially since advance to Camellia is secured by the land. There is no appraisal. Would rather not explain this to I.C.'s committee. To do an appraisal that passes cr comm [Credit Committee of the board chaired by Mrs. Collins, I believe (mf)] review would alert every owner on Oyster Island to the land assembly – and drive prices up substantially as they began to hold out.
>
> So we are advancing funds not as a real estate loan but an IB [again, investment banking (mf)] and taking the collateralization on the land as part of the deal docs.
>
> We stand to make over 14mil on this one and don't forget o'ship [ownership? (mf)] of Cam [Camellia? (mf)] Where else am I going to generate internal returns like that and allow Ald to tk care of our frnds [Alderlay to take care of our friends? Who are? (mf)]

"Mrs. Commander emailed the chairman the first of the following week. Page twelve. I summarized the email as it was lengthy and not entirely germane."

> Summary of email from MBC to Hugo Lesesne:
>
> M. Comm says NO! What they are doing is no more complicated than letting cash roll in the door without accounting for it as debt. She asks HL if he has seen tax returns. Tax returns for Ald clearly report most of these advances as debt. She wants explanation of financial statements apparently taking a different position.

"Later that week she received an answer from Concannon, which she found less than satisfactory. That's the exchange of emails and faxes you see here and on the following three pages. She continues to ask for the opinion of counsel letters for the Alderlay credits. They continue to demur. At one point, returning from a luncheon, Mr. Lesesne apparently questioned whether or not her questions about Alderlay lay within her duty. Look at this notation in her daybook. No, the red one now. [date]." She pointed to an entry, again in Molly's handwriting. "She followed up with an email."

Email from MBC to H. Lesesne: Are you aware that one of the congressional sub-committee findings in the collapse of El Paso Mexicana was that its Board failed in its fiduciary duty to the shareholders? Attached is what my office tells me is the "link" to the transcript.

"By the last week in February, it looks like to me the discussions between Mrs. Commander and the chairman are rapidly disintegrating. Have a look at this email."

Email from Hugo Lesesne to Richard Concannon:

Richy – just got off the phone with Molly Commander (again) She is on the warpath (again) over these Alderlay loans and the documentation and the way they are treating the advances for accounting purposes. Can no one rid us of this meddling and let us run the bank. What is our response to M.C.? Will you please take care of this today?!

"There is another telephone conversation, the first part of which was completely garbled. I remember typing the transcript. I don't know what was the exact reason for the call, but here is the end of the conversation."

Transcript of tel conversation between M.B.C. and Lesesne:

MBC: Do you remember Glass-Steagall? It separated commercial banking from investment banking seventy years ago? Do you know why?

HL: Of course I remember Glass-Steagall. It's an archaic…

MBC: Archaic? It was put in place to protect investors, not to mention customers of the bank from being sold the bank's own products. And now here we are seventy years later confronting the same situation. Loaning Alderlay money and the boys up at Continental American Securities recommending the stock while we are preparing to manage a public offering for them?

HL: It's a very competitive environment out there Molly. If we don't do it, First US or Merriwether Barnes will…

MBC: If Harrison Martin [CEO of Lincoln Aerospace

and the Chairman of Executive Committee at First US (mf)] wants to put his neck on the line over such an issue, let him. I see no reason to leap off the building holding hands.

"Reading for context, it seems to me that Lesesne must have said something to her to the effect that the Board's Credit Committee had no objection to the Alderlay. Ipso facto, why should she? Here is her response."

Email from M.B.C. to Lesesne, next day: Are you insane, Hugo? Did you actually authorize this? The Board's Credit Committee has not objected because they know nothing about this activity. Did you think I would not talk to Isabelle? The careful segmentation of the advances because of the various Alderlay entities involved does not in any way lessen the bank's total exposure with Alderlay.

Isabelle and I are calling a joint meeting of the Executive and Credit Committees for Tuesday morning in Atlanta. I'd like you to be sure that at least one of the bank's jets is available for shuttle duty Monday afternoon and evening.

I want a full report on the bank's relationship with Alderlay. Isabelle and I are each sending official notice of the meeting later today as prescribed by the by-laws and the Board rules.

This is a serious matter, Hugo. Treat it accordingly.

"I'm guessing that's when it hit the fan as you young people say. Here. Page 21 of my document, Hugo tells her he made her rich. She reminds him she was rich when she was born; he had nothing to do with it. He says they'll continue the discussion when he comes over for the Inman Society Dinner. To Page 23. Lesesne emails Concannon again that afternoon."

Mrs. Commander is once again all over my unowht [assume he means you know what (mf)] about Alderlay. Can we not defuse this some way? Do we have a plan? I have to see her tomorrow night. [emphasis added (mf)]

"There's an email you apparently missed. Here," she said indicating a new sheet inserted following Page 23.

Confidential email from Richard Concannon to Hugo

> Lesesne: Barrett Holmes in legal just cm. Learned that (1) CAB <u>not</u> Morgan becomes trustee of Molly Commander's estate if Billy Commander dies without exercising certain options that come to him under the terms of the will. All relevant copies of the documents are on file in the Trust Department with the appropriate instructions.

Billy sat back in his chair, running both hands through his hair, clasping his hands behind his head as he considered the full ramifications of Mildred's explanation.

"William, there is one document I believe to be significant that you seem to have overlooked. I have some hesitation in giving you this document as I fear the subject of the information may have been unaware of its existence."

Billy raised his eyebrows as she passed him two sheets of paper stapled together, the first of which bore the logo of the Continental American Bank but a different heading: Continental American Trust and Banking Corp. (Cayman) Ltd.

"An offshore account. A CAB subsidiary? This looks like some kind of account set-up information card."

"Exactly so. A copy of the back and front. Do you see the name of the account owner in the first section of the first page?"

Billy found the section. "Oleander Land Company LLC. A flower. One of the Alderlay flower partnerships?"

"Yes. Caymanian banking regulations, while maintaining statutory confidentiality about account transactions, require the disclosure of the entire ownership of a foreign corporation. This document was furnished to Mrs. Commander through the offices of a local director of the Caymanian subsidiary of Continental American. Look at the ownership of the LLC, on the second page."

Billy flipped the top sheet out of the way and began scanning the second page. "Okay. Alderlay. Risley Lawrence. All the usual suspects. Whoa. What's this?" He looked up abruptly. "Georgia Lesesne? Georgia was one of the owners of an entity that benefited…" Billy fell silent contemplating the ramifications of the disclosure.

"Benefited from the relationship between the bank and Alderlay. Yes. That's my analysis exactly."

"How did…," Billy absentmindedly scratched his head.

"Hugo says to Georgia, 'I've put some things in your name recently. In case anything ever happens to me, they would come to you outside my estate' and so on, and so forth."

"And as casually as that, fraud becomes embedded not only in commercial but also in domestic life?"

Mildred laughed. "I'm only a paralegal. You're a lawyer. It's entirely within your purview to reject my analysis." She twisted the watch on her arm around so that she could see its face. "My word. It's almost 6:00, William. You don't suppose Thomas could summon up a glass of wine for us, do you?"

"Sure thing. Let me just go dig him up."

"There's another thing," she said. Billy paused on the way to the kitchen. "When you read my entire summary, I think you'll agree that matters had come to a breaking point between Mrs. Commander and Mr. Lesesne."

"Okay," Billy said quizzically.

"In addition to the information found in the files, do you not think it would be helpful to know the substance of their conversation here, the evening of the Inman Society dinner. I know Thomas is the very soul of discretion, but if he had overheard anything… well, I'm sure you see my point."

"I asked him once before and he was a bit non-committal. I thought it might have been because his memory was fading and he was embarrassed and I dropped it. Maybe I'll come at it in a different way. Give me just a minute."

Walking into the kitchen, Billy picked up several of the cashews Thomas was placing in a silver bowl. Tossing them into his mouth, he said, "Hey, Thomas, Mrs. Ferguson thinks she might enjoy a glass of wine. Do you think we could…," Billy paused as he observed the elements of the drinks tray Thomas was assembling on the counter.

"I thought she might like a glass of the white Bordeaux that seems to be a favorite of Mrs. Collins. Would you like to be on the terrace?"

"That'd be great. Can you let Mrs. Ferguson know? I'm just going to pop upstairs and wash my hands."

"Yessir. Will you have wine as well, or do you prefer something else, Mr. Commander?"

"Wine's good for me. Thomas," Billy paused considering carefully his phrasing. "The night of the Inman Society dinner, where did Molly and Mr. Lesesne have drinks?"

"Right here in the loggia," he replied, indicating the oversized armchairs by the terrace windows where Billy had become accustomed to taking his morning coffee. "Mrs. Commander said set up for drinks in the hall, as she always called it, because she didn't want him to get too settled in."

"And where were you?"

"In and out of the kitchen to check on her. Mostly out in the pantry polishing silver."

"Polishing silver?"

"Mrs. Commander was having a brunch the next day, Sunday morning after the dinner at Oryzantia. We were using white flowers, and she wanted only silver and white on the table. I was making sure everything was ready."

"Did you hear her conversation with Hugo at all?"

"No, sir."

"But you were ten feet away," Billy said with a growing amount of frustration in his voice.

"Yessir."

"And you heard nothing?"

"It was not my place to listen to Mrs. Commander's conversations."

"Thomas, I know that's…," Billy tried to prevent his frustration from beginning to sound like anger.

"Give me a minute, please sir. Let me get Mrs. Ferguson looked after."

Billy nodded, mystified. "Okay. Sure." Then said to himself as he jogged up the steps two at a time, "I don't get it. How hard could it be to…"

Several minutes later he joined Mildred on the terrace, where she was shuffling through her compilation of information from the files. Thomas, carrying a silver tray, came out onto the terrace as soon as Billy sat down. He placed a small square linen coaster on the table next to

Billy's chair, followed by a glass of wine. Straightening up, he extended the tray toward Billy, on which remained a mini-cassette of the kind used in dictating machines.

"What's this?" Billy inquired, looking up.

"It's the tape of the conversation between Mrs. Commander and Mr. Lesesne the night of the Inman Society dinner. I put it in a drawer in the kitchen when I was cleaning up the morning after... well...," Thomas paused with obvious difficulty. "Her accident. I forgot about it until just now. I'm very sorry, Mr...."

"She taped it?" Bill interrupted him incredulously.

"Yessir."

"How? Or rather why? This is..."

"Perhaps I could help William," Mildred began. "With your permission, Thomas?"

"Yes ma'm. Of course. Mr. Commander, if you don't need me?"

"No. No, we're good. We'll probably just run up to the beach club for a bite. I'll see you tomorrow. Thanks for everything."

"Yessir. The play back machine is on Mrs. Commander's desk in her bedroom. The headphones are in the drawer. I left the wine in the cooler on the counter. Thank you, sir."

"Good night, Thomas," Billy said, Mildred echoing his words.

"About five years ago, Mrs. Commander began having headaches that took longer and longer to subside. The CT scans and other tests revealed nothing. Her doctors put it down to a busy schedule at an advanced age and recommended that she slow down, drink only red wine and begin an exercise program."

Mildred smiled as she remembered the sequence of conversations. "She told them she could not slow down – 'I'm Molly Commander, for god's sake,' she said. 'Did you miss that on my chart?' She asked if he was – the young internist as I recall – 'insane'. 'Would anyone trade single malt scotch for some silly red wine?' And she added that she got plenty of exercise walking to the door of her car and up the steps of her plane."

Billy could not help laughing. 'Once again, vintage Molly,' he thought.

"Nonetheless, the experience alarmed her. She ordered several of those micro-cassette dictating machines and began to use them to record meetings, conversations that she thought were important. She said she didn't care so much about a record of what other people said as she cared about being able accurately to recall what she had said. The evening of the Oryzantia dinner, I would surmise the machine was positioned out of view on the kitchen counter, and I would imagine she turned it on when she heard Thomas admit Mr. Lesesne."

"Molly. You dog you," Billy mused as he rolled the tape over with his fingers.

"If it relieves your mind in any way, she did obtain an opinion from the bank's legal department before she began taping conversations."

Billy burst out laughing.

"I'm not sure I see the…"

"Hugo. Hoisted by the petard of his own legal department. Classic. Beyond classic."

Chapter Fifty-Five

"One more thing before I go," Billy asked. "Is it typical in your estimation for a director, a committee chair even, to exercise this kind of oversight?"

Mildred tilted her head slightly to one side, running her index finger lightly around the edge of her wine glass as she considered a response. "First, my estimation is delimited by my experience with only one institution, an institution that has been characterized by the active involvement of Molly Commander from the outset. Her authority flowed from contribution, her connections, her financial power, and, I think, in no small part, from her judgment. Don't forget, Mrs. Commander brokered the creation of CAB itself. Within the bank, they used to know that story all the way down to the teller lines.

"She did not have, as one might say, an M.B.A., but she understood the fundamentals of a profitable business as well as any man in banking. I'm sorry I characterized it that way. I suppose at the end of the day my answer would be 'I don't know.' Mrs. Commander and CAB were a unique phenomenon. She was a powerful voice on other boards, to be sure, but her participation on other boards never achieved the level of respect and authority she enjoyed within the bank. She understood that the financial needs of modern corporations had changed. She understood that the fundamental expectations of the bank's core customer – a working couple raising their children, trying to carve out a better existence for themselves – had not."

Billy's voice wavered with uncertainty as he spoke. "I don't know what to do. I'm thirty-two years old. I've no training, no experience for this kind of a matter."

Mildred rose from her chair and went into the house, returning in a few seconds with the bottle of wine Thomas had left on the counter. She sat down next to Billy, re-filling first his and then her own glass.

"Surcease for a weary soul. William," she said distinctly. "Thomas Jefferson was a year older than you when he wrote the Declaration of Independence. Jay and Adams were only slightly older than you when they wrote the Federalist Papers. Martin Luther King was only two years older than you when he delivered his I Have a Dream speech. Your mother and father were only in their twenties in Chicago in 1968.

She paused for a moment, studying her wine glass, as she collected her thoughts. "The history of this country is replete with youthful, principled involvement."

"What do you think I should do?"

"I don't know. I'm an old woman, but I do believe that there is no such thing as coincidence in the life of the faithful." She paused, laughing softly. "You know, Samson picked up the jawbone of an ass and began to slay Philistines. I need to freshen up a bit before we go to dinner. Why don't you listen to the tape? I have some sense that's a thing you need to do alone."

Billy stood up and helped Mildred with her chair. Accompanying her into the loggia, he indicated the stairs with his left hand. "Shall we say 45 minutes then?"

She patted his arm gently and started up the stairs to the room Thomas had prepared for her.

"Mr. Commander?" he heard Thomas calling him from the kitchen.

"I thought you'd left. Mrs. Ferguson is going up to change."

"Yessir."

"Mrs. Coggeshell called while you were on the terrace to say that she was having dinner with Judge Magrath tonight at Eddie Hazzard's and was there any chance you might join them? At eight."

Billy glanced at his watch. "I have an hour. Close to it. Do I need to call Mrs. Coggeshell?"

"No, sir. I'll take care of it. Mr. Read called and said he's at his mother's and asked about dinner."

"Well, maybe he could…"

"Mrs. Coggeshell said she'd be delighted, and they called Mrs. Read's from Mrs. Coggeshell's."

Without thinking, Billy threw his arms around the old man's shoulders in a warm embrace. "Thomas, I don't know how you do it. Thank you. The night sounds great. Although I see Walker's hand in the background here."

"Oh one more thing. Mr. Read said he may need to stay here. It seems Mrs. Read has the trustees from ETV at her house."

"Sure. That's fine. We have plenty of beds."

"I can put Mr. Read in the red room then."

"That'll be fine. Do you know where my phone is?"

Thomas retrieved Billy's phone from the pocket of his white jacket. "You left it in the dining room."

"Mr. Commander," Thomas said looking pointedly at his watch. "Mrs. Coggeshell said eight o'clock."

"I'm going, I'm going. Let me get my glass and I'm off."

"I'll bring it to you, sir." Thomas shook his head as he watched Billy walking barefooted down the hall toward his grandmother's bedroom.

Billy went first into the dining room to get a legal pad for his notes and then crossed the hall into Molly's living room, adjacent to her bedroom, for the first time since she had died. The blue silk curtains in the living room were pulled to keep the late afternoon sun from fading the upholstery, casting the room into semi-darkness. He made his way carefully across the room to the door of his grandmother's bedroom. Pushing the door open, he paused momentarily to survey the room. At the far end of the room was a large French writing table that he knew from his grandmother's stories had belonged to his great-grandfather Bradbury. It had been the only piece removed from the house at Tuscarora Wood when she moved to DeBordieu.

He pulled the Louis XV chair back from the desk and sat down, looking for the playback device for the dictating tape. Locating the machine in the center drawer he inserted the tape, pressed the play button and began to listen to the tape. Julia had told him that Molly had worn a gold and green brocade jacket over a black silk skirt to the Inman Society dinner. He was able to picture his grandmother as the sound of her heels clicking on the marble floors filled the room.

"Hugo. My word. You walked down from the villas? That can't have been fun in a full dinner rig," he heard her say, laughing.

Billy wondered if he would have some emotional response to hearing his grandmother's voice posthumously, but he felt calm for the moment.

"Here. What can we get you to drink? Thomas. Let's see after Mr. Lesesne. I know he's had a long day. Did you come over this afternoon?"

Lesesne's response sounded oddly muffled, and Billy was immediately concerned he would be able to hear only one side of the conversation. And then, suddenly, with complete clarity he could hear Lesesne's distinctive voice.

"Molly, you look wonderful as always. Wonderful. Great evening. Cynthia Morelli told me we not only have the largest crowd ever for the dinner but the largest number of new members being introduced tonight in the history of the society. Great night for the museum, wouldn't you agree?"

"Sit. Sit, for heaven's sake." Billy could picture them sitting down in the oversized chairs by the windows overlooking the terrace and the marsh just outside the kitchen.

"No. Thomas, the martini is for Mr. Lesesne. I'm going to have just a splash of that Woodford Reserve. Two fingers only. No more. Although we should probably rethink that. Did you see the offerings on the bar at the last Inman Society reception? Good lord. Ordinary does not begin to suffice. Rab Pritchard told the development girl – what's her name, Hugo? I can't ever remember that child. Right. Well, whatever. Anyway, Rab told her that she must have confused the plans for a general member's reception with the Inman Society because there was nothing on the bar drinkable. Of course, it being the beach, and summer, that didn't seem to slow most of the boys down."

"Molly, I'd like to ask you to change your mind about Tuesday's meeting."

Billy noticed the abrupt shift in the topic of conversation and Lesesne's tone of voice. He could almost see his grandmother attempting to avoid some appearance of recoil, remaining calm in the face of his aggressiveness.

"We are at a critical juncture in our relationship with Alderlay, which will in turn lend either impetus or dissipation to the relationships we are trying to build with other large developers."

"It seems to me that if the bank is at a critical juncture with regard to Alderlay and a new market, that's all the more reason to convene the Executive and Credit Committees."

"These are really matters best handled by the executive officers of the bank. The details of daily operations are not really within the purview of directors, wouldn't you agree?"

"No."

"No what?"

"No. I would not agree. Apparently you do not understand the meaning of the word purview. Because if you did, I think you would also agree as a director, that such matters lie absolutely within the range, the limit of authority and responsibility of the Board."

Billy heard Hugo raise his voice slightly. "Molly, Alderlay's business will generate close to forty million dollars in fees this year alone. That doesn't include interest and other transaction fee-based income from the relationship. They are considering naming Continental American Securities the lead underwriter in the public offering with which they intend to go forward in the fall."

"My point exactly, Hugo. We participate in a public offering where the information furnished to the SEC and the investing public is fraudulent… do you have any idea what that would do to the bank?"

"Oh, Molly, there's no fraud. We have Risley Lawrence's assurance. And an opinion letter from their auditors…"

"As did El Paso Mexicana."

"What?"

"You may recall that before EPM slid into the abyss, they obtained a letter from Roberts Keegan, opining that their books were clean. They were not. And now both EPM and Roberts Keegan have disappeared from the commercial landscape. They are lying. It's no more complicated than that."

"Now, Molly, all companies engage from time to time in accounting that is – well – creative."

"Creative? That's what you call it? Booking a transaction one way for federal income tax purposes and another way for financial statement purposes?"

"The rules of tax accounting and financial accounting are different. You know that."

"I know that I don't like a bunch of slick operators who try to split hairs over the fundamental treatment of balance sheet items. I didn't have to go to Harvard to learn that. Here, your glass is empty. Let me get you another drink. Thomas?"

"Mrs. Commander?"

"Mr. Lesesne will have another drink, Thomas. And so will I."

"Yes, m'am. I'll get those and then pull the car around to the front. I assume you want to take the Mercedes."

"That will be fine, Thomas. Thank you."

Billy heard Hugo interrupt, and he sat up in his chair, surprised even though he knew what was coming.

"Molly, I'll drive you to Oryzantia. Georgia's coming later and we can all come home together."

"No, that's fine, Hugo. Thomas will drive me. I would not want to inconvenience you and Georgia."

"I insist. Georgia was saying only yesterday that she didn't get to visit with you as much as she once did."

"That's lovely. I still prefer that Thomas drive me in my own car. If I should want to leave early…"

"If you want to leave early, we'll have one of the security guards run you home. It's settled. We can continue our conversation on the way up. Thomas, I'll drive Mrs. Commander… and thank you," he finished, as Thomas put his glass down on the table.

There was a moment of silence on the tape that Billy did not initially understand. He checked the tape to see if it was still turning in the player.

"Thank you, Thomas. That will be all for now," he heard his grandmother say. He envisioned the exchange of looks between them that resulted in the compromise.

"Molly, let's agree that we will postpone the meetings you and Isabelle called for a few months to allow things to settle down. What do you say?"

"I told you no."

Billy was amazed at the pleasant tone his grandmother was able to maintain as she relentlessly refused to concede.

"You don't want to precipitate a crisis within the bank… it would be inconsistent with your fiduciary responsibilities to…"

"To whom, Hugo? The shareholders? As I recall my fiduciary responsibility is to the shareholders of the bank, not to Alderlay Development."

"That's a complicated issue."

"Well, let me simplify it for you. I have no intention of standing by, given what I know and letting this continue. I see it not only as a breach of my responsibility as a director but also a breach of my fiduciary responsibility to the owners of the bank – the shareholders. I will neither abrogate my responsibilities to the bank nor abandon my duty to the shareholders. There is also the issue of personal liability. I assure you that I speak not only for myself but also for Isabelle and the other three outside directors on the Executive Committee. If you think for one minute that Isabelle and I are going to allow ourselves to become the target of an SEC investigation or, worse yet, trot up to Capitol Hill to testify before our good friend Denby Spencer, the Chairman of the Senate Banking Committee, and attempt to explain to his colleagues how we sat idly by and allowed yet another meltdown in the financial system in this country, you need to re-think this whole matter. You need to inform the board of the full extent of the bank's exposure with Alderlay. You need to express an opinion on whether or not it is appropriate that the bank reserve for any potential negative repercussions from the Alderlay relationship. You need to do this on Monday. If you do not, I can assure you that you will be confronted with a resolution out of the Executive Committee demanding such action. Let me suggest to you, that you don't want to go there. We need to go. I don't want to be seen dragging in as if we had three other more important things to do before the dinner. You and I are both trustees."

"Your mind is made up."

"Resolutely."

"How can you be so damn sure you're right about everything?"

"I'm not, Hugo. I'm not. I am willing to put matters on the table for full and open discussion. I trust the judgment of my colleagues. Thomas, where are the keys?"

Their conversation became muffled as they proceeded down the hall toward the front door. It was then that the sadness hit Billy with full force. Suddenly, he realized he was listening to his grandmother walk out of her house, never to return. He was momentarily overwhelmed. It never occurred to her that she would not come home safely, he reflected.

"It must have been the same for my dad," he thought suddenly. "He got on the plane in Paris thinking he would see me that weekend at St. Bart's." It had been the weekend of the state swimming championships, and his dad had planned to fly up and spend the weekend with Billy. Instead, Molly flew up to tell him he would never see his dad again. And now Molly.

"Son of a bitch," Billy muttered to himself.

He clicked off the tape player, glanced at his watch and hurried out of his grandmother's room to get ready for dinner.

Chapter Fifty-Six

Julia thought for a moment "Why do I have my phone with me sitting on the beach?" as she reached into the straw bag next to her chair. Glancing at the screen and realizing it was Walker, she traced her finger across the screen to take the call.

"Surprising developments at deb-wa-deux," he began, affecting an exaggerated if somewhat bastardized French pronunciation of their neighborhood.

"What?"

"It seems our boy has decided to get a life."

"What are you talking about?"

"Well, it seems that we are cleaning out Molly's bedroom, indexing, and packing her things. We're even cleaning out our room and disposing of cherished polo shirts we've had since high school. A virtual flurry of purpose and organization."

"How do you know all this?"

"Mimi called and said he came up there to ask her what to do with Molly's clothes."

"And she said?"

"The decision is the furs, those dinner jackets she loved so much, her pashminas all go to Julia."

"Walker!" Julia laughed.

"You have to go sort through her bags. Take what you want. Mimi did not think the Birkens, Kellys, Diors and their ilk should go to charity. The remainder is apparently bound for the thrift shop that supports the East Side Settlement House for Women. You know. It's a joint project of the Junior League and St. James. I think Charlotte and Nancy both worked there."

"They did. Wonderful idea. They have that outreach program that helps abused women get themselves ready to go back into the workforce – helps them get their clothes pulled together, practice their interview skills, confidence building and all that. I think Nancy still volunteers there. I'll write Mimi a note. Terrific idea."

"Yeah. Well, get this. He and John Harleston are coming up Tuesday, apparently to hire a decorator."

Julia sat up suddenly in her beach chair. "A what?"

"You heard me. Some hot new guy that worked for Kit Sherrill at McMillen. We're sprucing up at *chez guillaume* and apparently at Commander House, too. Billy says Commander House is yours, and you have to come up Tuesday with them. Otherwise, he's going to do the whole house in Florida bamboo prints and yellow furniture."

"But, of course, he's too busy re-organizing my wardrobe and my life to call to tell me about it. How do you know all this?"

"My usual Monday morning calls. Mimi. John. Then our boy himself. He said he's going to call you. Mildred Ferguson's over there, helping wrap up the survey of those bank files that we are not supposed to talk about. He's wrapped a little tight at the moment."

"Good lord. I leave for two days, and I have a new house and new pocketbooks. What if I don't want Commander House?"

"He said you'd say that. He said it's better than your condominium in Georgetown and you need to quit staying at your mother's. You're twenty-nine now. Plus, if you move to Atlanta, you'll need a beach house. That's what he said. John Harleston said the decorator guy is great. He was at Chapel Hill behind us. Then Parsons. Frankly, I'm not sure it's his design portfolio John has his eye on."

"Walker!"

"I'm just sayin', that's all. I'm just sayin'. You and the doc headed back today?"

"Tuesday. Tommy doesn't have to work tomorrow, so we had planned to drive back down Tuesday morning. Looks as though I'll miss the decorator express flight."

"Fun?"

"Yeah."

"Really?"

"Yes, Walker. It's been great. Where are you?"

"Hamptons. Along with eight million other people. I need to go back to town to take a rest from being fashionable."

"Please. You love it. It's your element. A sea of gorgeousness. I'm hanging up now. Tommy's coming with refreshments. They start happy hour a little earlier here than we do at Pawleys," she laughed.

"Jules, wait I…"

"G'bye Walker." She was still laughing when Tommy handed her a gin and tonic in a plastic beach cup. He leaned down and kissed her. "Tommy, your mother and Celia are on the porch."

Tommy looked at her with an air of mock quizzicality. "You think they think we're not doin' it. I hate to be the one to break this to you, sugar. You're not my first girl friend. Plus, be a shame not to use such great assets," he laughed, enjoying the teasing that seemed to keep Julia slightly off-guard. "Are you blushing?"

"No. I'm sure it's only the sun. Hand me my hat, would you?"

"Let me guess. Billy?"

"No."

"Walker?"

"Yes."

"Who called with news of Billy."

"He's in the Hamptons. Bored. Apparently Billy is beginning to take charge of his own life: re-decorating at DeBordieu, sending me to Commander House swathed in Molly's furs and carrying a dozen Hermès bags. That seems to be the plan. I guess he's going to sell my condominium in Georgetown," she said sardonically. "Maybe he'll get me a new car while I'm up here?"

"Good man."

"What?"

"I said…"

"I heard what you said. What do you mean?"

"Medically," he paused, as he ordered his words. "It sounds as if he is overcoming the dissociative effects of grief and loneliness and the healing process has taken hold." He leaned over and kissed her again. "Your boy's getting back in the game, Babe."

Julia closed her eyes, letting her head recline onto the high back of her beach chair. Sipping her drink, she reached over and softly slipped her left hand into Tommy's.

Chapter Fifty-Seven

Billy was on the steps of the Empire Club when he heard his phone ringing. Flipping it open, he saw Walker's number on the screen. "What's up?"

"I've got a call from Hugo Lesesne on the line. He's insisting I patch him through to you."

"Thus establishing that you can. I'm not crazy about that. Is it his office?"

"No. The man himself and he sounds hot about something."

"Can you stay on the line?"

"Sure."

"Okay. Put him through."

"Hugo. I've got Billy on the line. Go ahead."

"Thank you, Walker." Lesesne's voice came over the line stronger, more insistent than normal. "Billy, I just received a message from our security office that we are to retrieve twenty-six record center boxes of bank documents from Molly's house in Georgetown. Can you tell what in the h…"

Billy cut him off. "Excellent," he said cheerily. "And, thank you. That will let me get my dining room back in order."

"What?"

"I said, thank you. As soon as you send someone to get your boxes out of my dining room, we can put the room back in order and move on. I'm in New York with John Harleston Read to hire a decorator to spiff up at DeBordieu. Of course, it's hard to get started with piles of your stuff laying around my house."

Billy rattled on intending to defuse Lesesne's anger with confusion or at least, he thought to himself, a good offense.

"Do you know what's in those boxes?"

"Can't really say."

"You mean you don't know?"

"No. I mean I can't really say. I can't say I'm sufficiently familiar with bank communication protocols to say with any accuracy what's in them." Billy could have sworn he heard Walker stifle a laugh. "I thumbed through the boxes to determine if the material looked as though it might be related to my grandmother's personal affairs or my family's business. Looks like mostly bank files. I had Thomas stack them up as close to the front of the house as we could manage and call the bank to get them picked up. Since you seem to be personally involved, I'd really appreciate it if you could get them out of my dining room. This guy we're hiring is eager to start work?"

"This is a very serious breach of bank security. I hope you are aware of that."

"Not my breach, Hugo."

"A very serious breach for which there could be serious repercussions," Lesesne continued not seeming to hear Billy.

"Hey, hold it, Hugo. Let me straighten you out here. It's not my breach, nor is it my grandmother's. She was in Europe when your staff in Georgetown got all hot and bothered during the move to the new building about her files that were stored in the old CAB building downtown. They told Thomas, my grandmother's seventy-year-old houseman, that he had to do something about them right that minute. He was unable to reach my grandmother at Isabelle Collins' house in France. Your people loaded up twenty-six record center boxes and sent them out to the house, which action among other things compelled an old man to hustle twenty-six heavy file boxes down the steps into my basement. Quite frankly, I'm a little pissed about it."

"Excuse me," Lesesne said, the consternation clear in his voice.

"The bank's oversight and inattention have caused my houseman to be lugging a bunch of boxes up and down stairs. He's got no business doing that. And he doesn't work for you. He works for me."

"I trust you've made no copies of internal bank documents."

Billy forced a laugh. "You think we have a copy shop in the basement, Hugo? Have someone call Thomas. I'd appreciate it if you'd pick up your boxes. Make sure you send someone to load them into a truck, van or whatever. I've already told Thomas he is not to touch a single box. The original delivery ticket generated by the bank in Georgetown is with the boxes. I can't talk any longer. I'm at the Empire Club, and you know how they are about cell phones. I have to go." Billy severed the connection. Ten seconds later Walker rang him back.

"Lemme see. The best defense is what? An aggressive offense. I think I heard that somewhere. Jeez, Billy. It's not every day you back down a guy as powerful as Lesesne. Didn't you copy those files?"

"Of course, I did."

"Then you lied…"

"I didn't lie to him. He asked me if I had copied the files. I asked him if he thought I had a copy shop in my basement. He dropped it. His inability to extract the precise information he is seeking is not my problem."

"What did you find when you got through everything?"

"We'll tell you tonight at dinner. John Harleston's tapping his watch as if I'm time-challenged or something."

As Billy turned to join John Harleston on the steps leading into the club, he noticed two men he thought were limousine drivers leaning against a black town car parked at the curb. "Bit hot for black leather, don't you think?" he mentioned to John Harleston as he held the door open for his friend.

"Not to mention the wrong part of town," he replied, as he preceded Billy into the vestibule.

"Tripp Gregory," John Harleston said quietly as they crossed the marble reception lobby.

"What?"

"Tripp Gregory. That's his name. You're terrible with names."

"What is it with you and Walker and the name thing?"

"Kit Sherrill. McMillen and Company. They did your grandmother's house and her offices at CAB Plaza in Atlanta. You love their work. You're excited about working together. Blah. Blah. Blah. Those are the bullet points."

"Are they hiring me?" Billy teased his friend. "And I am not terrible with names."

"You asked me to come along and translate. Your words. This is how the game plays out at the top." John Harleston shifted his focus as they approached Tripp who was waiting by the fireplace in the main lobby. "Tripp. John Harleston Read. Nice to see you again. You know Billy Commander, of course."

"John, Billy. A pleasure."

The doors to the first elevator car opened as John Harleston pressed the up button, revealing a cab almost full of younger guys headed up to lunch from the fitness center in the basement.

"John, you go ahead," Billy said, indicating the crowded elevator. "We'll grab the next one."

John Harleston replied, "We're on nine. One of the small dining rooms to the left, down the hall from the main room."

A few seconds later the doors to the second elevator opened, revealing an empty cab. "After you," Billy gestured with his left hand. There was a moment of awkward silence as the doors closed.

"John's a big wheel at *American Interiors*. I was flattered he called."

Billy nodded.

"He probably told you to tell me how much you love my work. You admire the work my former firm did for your grandmother. You look forward to the project. Something like that."

"Something like that." Billy smiled and began to relax a little.

"Look, Billy. Ninety per cent of my current clients are younger guys, who are ambivalent at best about decorators." He laughed congenially. "Relax. It's become my forte. You won't end up with a keg in your bedroom and sports posters in the bathrooms, nor will you end up on the cover of *American Interiors* swathed in chintz with a poodle on your lap." Glancing sideways at Billy, he finished. "I promise. You don't like what I suggest, fire me. We'll have a beer afterwards, whatever happens."

It was Billy's turn to laugh. "Fair enough." The doors opened at the ninth floor where they found John Harleston waiting.

An hour later, Billy and John Harleston walked out of the Empire

Club onto 54th Street. "That went well enough, didn't you think?" Billy asked. "He seems keen to do what we want."

Billy looked down the street toward Sixth Avenue for a cab, noticing in his peripheral vision the same two men in black leather jackets he had earlier noticed leaning against one of the town cars parked at the opposite curb. His attention sharpened as the men sauntered across the street toward the awning-covered entrance of the club. Glancing back down the street, Billy saw no cabs approaching the club.

"Billy Commander?" one of them said brusquely.

"Yes," he replied calmly.

"We'd like to have a word with you.

"Really? About what?" Billy replied. "John, if you don't mind, perhaps you could step back inside and let the desk know that we are delayed – that we have been detained on the street, as it were," exchanging a knowing glance with his friend.

The second of the two men, the shorter and more muscular of the pair, moved uncomfortably close to Billy. "Tell me," Billy asked, attempting to sound casual. "I'm curious. How do you know who I am, and how did you find me? New York is a very big city."

"You seem to be causing a lot of problems," the taller of the two men said. "Too many problems."

Billy could not help being amused at the obvious aspects of comic parody in this encounter but was also aware at a deeper level that random street violence was still an occasional visitor even to the best New York neighborhoods. He glanced casually around himself, assessing his situation.

"Gentlemen. Is there a message here? From whom?"

"I think you know…"

Out of the corner of his eye, Billy saw two Empire Club security guards in navy blazers and grey trousers come out of the basement service entrance onto the street. They began walking rapidly toward the main entrance. Billy recognized the larger of the two guards as a former pro-football player that worked part-time at the club to supplement his coaching salary. The second of the two guards was already speaking into his wrist radio transmitter.

"You guys have to be kidding, right? You're not really serious about this gimme-a-message-on-the-street thing?" He forced a laugh. He had bought enough diversionary time to allow the club security guards to reach him.

"Mr. Commander."

"Jim. Hello."

"You have a phone call inside, sir. The porter said to tell you it was urgent and if you could come right in?"

"Of course. Thank you. Gentlemen, if you'll excuse me."

Billy turned to re-enter the building and one of the leather jacketed men moved to follow him. The larger of the two club security guards stepped immediately between him and Billy. "It's a private club. Members only. I'm sorry," and gestured toward the opposite side of the street, at once barring entry into the club and compelling him to move away from the steps.

Billy motioned discreetly to the other security guard.

"Yes sir?" the guard said quietly.

"Check the front bumper of the car they get into."

Billy passed through the double glass vestibule doors and heard with relief the electronic security locks activated from the porter's desk click into place.

"Thank you. Have you seen Mr. Read?"

"In the Blue Room, just down the hall to the left, past the Ladies Lounge, sir."

Billy found John Harleston talking quietly to one of the club's associate managers.

"Billy, are you okay, man? Do you want us to call the police? Contact anyone?"

"Freddie, hey. How's it goin? Nah. I'm all right. John Harleston seemed to get the cavalry there just in time. It's probably nothing."

The guard with whom Billy had spoken outside paused politely in the door to the room. "Excuse me just a minute, would you?"

Billy crossed the room to the guard. "It was a black town car, Mr. Commander. This is the license plate number," he said, passing Billy a small slip of memo paper.

"Thank you. Not only for this but also for likely saving my ass out there."

"Yes, sir. Of course. It's our job. The bumper?"

Billy waited for the additional information that seemed to be forthcoming.

"How'd you know about that? There was a decal. A coat-of-arms looking insignia in red, yellow and blue."

Glancing quickly at the guard's name tag, Billy replied, "Lucky guess, Ron. Thanks again. Good work. I won't forget it."

Turning back to the others in the room, he said, "John and I need to make a quick phone call, and then we're outta' here. Thanks again, Freddie." Billy was already reaching for his phone, impatiently waiting for it to power up, and then pressing the speed dial key for Walker's direct line.

"It was the bank," he commented quietly to John Harleston.

"What?" John Harleston thought he must have misunderstood Billy.

"Those two guys were… Walk. You won't believe this. It's like a bad movie. Worse than that. A really stupid movie. Two CAB goons just tried to shove us around on the sidewalk in front of the Empire Club. No seriously, it would have been comic, a real parody, if it had not been real. No, everything's all right. He's with me. Nah, the staff at the club was totally cool. Handled it all with such discretion I don't think any of the guys coming out for a cab even noticed."

Billy paused, listening to Walker. "Because the security guard saw the CAB insignia on the town car in which they drove away. On the bumper. Yeah, I have it. Hang on." Billy rummaged around in his pants pocket for the slip of paper given to him by the guard. He laughed aloud.

"You won't believe it. New York plates, 641 CAB. The irony of the license number is consistent with the stupidity of the confrontation. No. NO. Listen to me. They were waiting for us. We both saw them when we came in. I know. Okay. We'll be right here then. Are you coming uptown? Okay."

Billy turned his phone off as John Harleston asked impatiently, "What'd he say?"

"He said Hugo must be insane. Enforcers working for the bank. Is that a real word? Enforcers. I don't know about that one."

"Billy?"

"He said we should go upstairs and have a drink. He's coming uptown to get us in a Morgan car." Billy threw his arm around John Harleston's shoulder as they walked into the lobby. "Thanks, buddy. Just when you think nothing else can happen, huh?"

Chapter Fifty-Eight

John Harleston dropped his cell phone into his jacket pocket as the town car in which he and Billy were riding passed through the gates at Belmont Park. Billy raised his eyebrows as he glanced at his friend.

"Walker," John Harleston said.

"And?"

"He said your phone's off."

"And?"

"He wanted to know why we're going racing."

"That's why he called you instead of me. My phone's not off. I told him this morning we were meeting Isabelle at Belmont. She wanted to see the Stake today. I think she may have a filly that's a full sister to the favorite. I told him that he should go with us, that Hardy was going and that there would likely be more of his clients in the Turf Club today than downtown."

"He said 'we should be working.'"

"He's just being pissy. Here we are. Do you have your pin?"

"What pin?"

"Your TOBA pin. It gets you in the racetrack."

"I have to have a pin?"

"Molly's sent you your TOBA pin for Christmas for years. You wear it on your lapel. It lets you in any track in the world, basically. Is any of this ringing a bell?"

"Well. Caught by surprise, how the hell did I know you'd decide to go racing? You're lucky I had such a great tweed jacket with me."

Billy regarded his friend with a mixture of affection and

amusement. "Come on," Billy said getting out of the car and starting toward the entrance gates. "We'll go in the Clubhouse entrance. Maybe they'll overlook what a doofus you are."

Of course there was no problem.

"My friend changed his jacket on the plane," Billy said to the gate attendant as they went through the Clubhouse turnstile, "of course, leaving his pin on the other jacket." Billy raised his hands as if to say "what can I do?"

"Liar," John Harleston said under his breath, extending his wrist to the attendant to be stamped.

"Not entirely," Billy laughed. "Undoubtedly, on one of your two dozen tweed jackets is a TOBA pin. Probably long forgotten – or left on the floor someplace we don't need to bring up," he joked.

"Left on the floor? Not likely."

"Not likely?"

"You're thinking I'm a candidate for a situation that might result in clothes getting left on the floor."

"Really? Not a candidate huh?" Billy said, continuing to tease his friend as they walked out into the section of owner's boxes overlooking the track. "Look. Isabelle is already down there with Hardy in Molly's box."

"Your box."

"What?"

"It's your box now."

"I know." Billy turned to look at John Harleston seriously. "I'm trying to get accustomed .....nah, that's not it. Get comfortable with a box at Belmont in my name. A plane at my disposal. A house at DeBordieu. A New York decorator. This seems like Molly's life somehow."

"Is this so unpleasant for you? Today? Yesterday?"

"You mean, except for almost getting mugged on 54th Street? It's ok, I guess." He paused momentarily, gazing over the crowd filtering into the boxes for the fourth race. "Did you know my mom and dad, Dot, got the crap beat out of them at the '68 Democratic Convention?"

"Yes."

"What do you mean yes?"

"I mean, yes. I knew it. My dad told me years ago – when your dad died, actually."

Billy signaled a passing drinks waiter and ordered two glasses of wine, caught by surprise with the sudden realization that his parents' death had so affected his friends as well.

"Isabelle and Hardy are waiting…."

"Not really," Billy said glancing at the video monitor above his head. "They're watching them load for the fourth. Hardy, ever the king of charm, is fully engaged in his god blessed Texas routine. They're fine. Go on."

John Harleston accepted a glass of wine from the waiter, as he passed back down the aisle. "We came home on the plane from Virginia with Molly. My parents, Walker's, Julia's were all sensitive to how the tragedy had affected us. My dad sat in his library with me the night we got home. He told me how much he loved me, cherished me."

John Harleston looked up at the ceiling for a moment to compose himself. "Somewhat uncharacteristically for my dad. He said he was telling me this because Motte was one of his oldest friends and that he – my dad – could not get past the realization that, whatever was going through your dad's mind when the plane began to skid down the runway, the one thing that was paramount had to have been the desire to tell you one more time how much he loved you, how much he admired you, how much he cherished you."

The emotion of the moment overcame Billy. He turned away, ostensibly looking down the track toward the clubhouse turn where he saw the leaders in the fourth race heading down the lane toward the wire. He heard John Harleston continue behind him.

"Dad told me your dad had the greatest courage of his convictions of anyone in their group. That's when he told me about the student protest at Columbia when Motte was in law school. About the voter registration job in Mississippi that summer. About Chicago. The day we buried your mom and dad at St. Peter's I couldn't talk. Motte and Frances had assumed an iconic status in my mind at that point. I didn't know how you were going to go on. Julia was only fifteen. Walker was – well, Walker. That day at St. Peter's was the day I became aware of the complicated depths of my affection for you."

Billy turned back to face him. "Do you think this is the place?"

John Harleston glanced at the crowd milling around in their

immediate vicinity. "We spend our lives in these places, Billy. We think somehow that the privilege of wealth is privacy, but, in fact, we spend most of our time in one public forum or another. It often seems private because most people cannot wander in off the street into our midst. But when do any of us ever have a private moment, really?" He raised his eyebrows to emphasize the question. "I know you slept with Lucy the night after we were at Eddie's. I know Julia slept with the Doc the night we had dinner downtown in Georgetown. Walker." He made an upward gesture with his free hand to signify 'see what I mean.' "Nancy tells me about the guy from Idaho. Charlotte can't get you out of her……."

"Nancy's dating a guy from Idaho?"

"Jesus, Billy. Let it go. That's hardly the point."

"I don't know what to…"

"There's nothing you can say. It's my issue. We've got to go. It's Isabelle Collins we have waiting, not some. Well, whatever."

"I'm going to hit the head. You go on. I'll be there in a second."

"Billy…I…"

"I need a minute. Give me that, will you?"

John Harleston straightened up resuming the congenial demeanor associated with the environment in which they found themselves. "Okay. I'll get Isabelle and Hardy to go down to the paddock with me. We'll see you back at the box?"

Twenty minutes later, Billy joined the others in his box, kissing Isabelle on the cheek, and engaging in the obligatory polite chatter accompanying arrivals among friends. "Good lord. Two different agents tried to sell me the same horse on the way back from the men's room," he laughed. He sat down in one of the folding chairs along the front rail of the box, casually tying a knot in the shoulder strap to his racing glasses as he placed them on the shelf beneath the front counter of the box. "I'm sorry we're late getting here Isabelle. I'm sprucing up a bit at DeBordieu, and John Harleston was engaging me in some arcane debate about the relative merits of one Louis over another."

Isabelle looked first at John Harleston and then at Billy. "Are you all right? You look a bit drawn. You're among friends. Friends who love you," she reminded him lowering her voice.

"I'm fine, Isabelle. Fine." Deciding to change the subject and picking up the Daily Racing Form from the floor, he said to no one in particular, "Anybody feel strongly about one of these in the fifth?"

The afternoon at Belmont passed pleasantly, the casual conversation among friends and acquaintances with a common interest punctuated every thirty minutes by two minutes of racing. Shortly before the Sheepshead Bay Stakes, the feature race on the day's card, Billy turned slightly in his chair to address Hardy.

"Hardy, I need to pose to you an entirely – I repeat –entirely hypothetical question."

"Entirely hypothetical?" Hardy answered with a grin.

"A banking – financial management question."

"John Harleston, look." Isabelle Collins exclaimed. "I haven't seen Elizabeth Greenberg in ages. She looks wonderful. She's just down there, next to the Ardrey's box. Would you go with me?" She stood up, smoothing her skirt, and leaned over to kiss Billy lightly on the cheek. "We'll be back in a bit, or maybe we'll just meet you in the paddock before the stake. How would that be?"

Billy and Hardy immediately stood up as Isabelle and John Harleston left the box.

"Perfect pitch," said Hardy.

"What?"

"How – or where – do those old girls get it? I don't know any girls like that. If I did, I'd marry one of 'em tomorrow. As long as she was hot, too."

"What do you mean?"

"About gettin' married?"

"No..."

"She anticipated the question you were getting ready to ask me and realized that she couldn't hear it. She created a social diversion that saved the moment. Anyone watching, hell, anyone listening would never have caught it. Elizabeth Greenberg, my ass. She was in La Grenouille last night when we were. Isabelle went over and had a chat with her on the way to the ladies room. Perfect pitch."

Billy chuckled softly, shaking his head. "Hardy."

"Yo."

"Completely off the record. How does one minimize the impact – both in the markets and operationally – of the sudden resignation of the CEO of a major, global financial institution?"

Hardin turned abruptly to look directly at his friend, taking a sip of his diet coke. "A financial institution of the size and scope, shall we say, of the Continental American Bank?"

"For example."

"Oh sh…, Bill. We've known each other a long time. You were one of my mentors at St. Barts. My association with you, Walker and John Harleston is largely responsible for scrubbing the sagebrush and tumbleweeds off my Texas ass and allowing me to fit into the oh-so-rarefied atmosphere of the East Coast. You… you…" Hardin paused to collect himself. "You are aware that the biggest part of your money is tied up irretrievably with CAB's stock?"

Billy nodded.

"And that any hit the bank were to take impacts you personally – not to mention disproportionately."

"Go on."

Hardin rested his chin in his left hand surveying the crowd below them on the apron of the track. His voice assumed an objective, almost cold quality.

"If the CEO of a major financial institution is going to step down, and step down with none of the traditional warning signs, it becomes imperative for the institution to seize control of the sequence of events. Assume control of the story. The markets abhor uncertainty, let alone a vacuum. You develop a plan. Have the corporate explanation ready, crafted in advance. Schedule a call with the twenty largest investors, followed by a call to the ten most influential market makers. All the federal regulatory bodies – the SEC, Comptroller General, Senate Banking, maybe even the White House – get a heads up before any announcement. Then you leak it to the *Times* or the *Journal* to soften up the ground, and finally either call a press conference or issue a press release. You have a succession plan pre-approved by the board. It's tricky – risky – orchestrating everything in the background out of sight of CNN *et al* until you're ready to go public. There are forces at work in these things that lay beyond institutional control. I don't know…"

"How big is the hit we take?"

Hardin threw his hands up, running his left hand through his hair. "How big? I dunno. I'd have to talk to some people – run some numbers."

"How big, Hardy?"

"I don't know, Bill. Maybe ten per cent, maybe more."

"The after effects? If we clearly demonstrate we are managing the clean-up?"

"Clean-up? What… God, I'm a year younger than you. We're here at a box at Belmont, riding around on our family's money, our family's connections. And you're asking me questions about events, actions of national consequence? Geez, you can't be asking me these things, Bill."

Billy turned to him, furious. "Bullshit. Molly got killed because of these bastards. I almost did. Julia too. If not you, then whom? You think Molly or Isabelle ever backed down from a fight? Your dad? Your grandfather? I love you, man. Step up to the plate with the rest of us here – or get the hell outta my box."

Hardin stood up abruptly, knocking over the plastic drink cups on the box ledge. Buttoning his suit jacket, he turned as if to leave.

"Hardy?"

"What?"

"Where do you go from here? Back to Park Avenue? And then what?"

"And then what, Bill? When the hell did you get religion?"

"Last week, if you must know," Billy said rising. "Then what?" he said a second time in a tone of voice that could not help but uncomfortably begin to attract the attention of those in nearby boxes.

Hardin felt Billy grab his forearm as he attempted to leave the box. Looking around, realizing the multiple layers of difficulty in the moment, his gaze finally rested on a nearby clubhouse steward, whom he summoned abruptly to the box.

"We need a bottle of wine here. Something nice. A Chablis Grand Cru or a Chassagne something or other. Pretty damn quick."

He resumed his seat, appearing to watch the entries in the eighth race take the track. "Continental American's by-laws give tremendous power to the chairman of its Executive Committee. It was an amendment the Directors put through when Criswell was diagnosed with cancer and your grandmother held the chair. It was the simultaneous recognition of the needs of corporate governance and Molly's influence within the bank. Isabelle can now assume that responsibility. She can poll the outside directors. There will be no resistance. No one is going to tell Isabelle Barrett Collins no. She can be 11-0 before it ever comes to Hugo's attention. Dudley Ramsey is as good a corporate spinmeister as you'll ever find. He's here in New York. You need to bring him in off-campus, let him cooperate with Isabelle. Control the spin, manage the voice of the bank. Everything goes through her office."

The steward placed the bottle of wine in its silver cooler on the edge of the box and proceeded with the ritual of opening, tasting. "Excellent. Perfect," Hardin said. "Find another one just like that and be back with it in twenty minutes." Hardin saluted Billy with his glass.

"Someone will obviously have to confront Hugo. You'll have to develop a scenario that essentially makes it financially disastrous for him not to go along. Step down. The Hugo lieutenants – and I assume Richy Concannon – you just fire. Presumably there is enough documented culpability – emails or something similar – to justify a for cause dismissal. They are fired two minutes after Hugo is confronted and escorted by security from the building. Julius Irving will be able to craft the necessary corporate… uhh… resolutions whatever is needed. Someone will have to pull the trigger."

"Pull the trigger?"

"Orchestrate it. Not only. Confront Hugo. Force him down on the mat. Kick the shit out of him. You're going down big guy, and so on."

"Who pulls the trigger?"

Hardin laughed, holding his glass up, looking at the track in the distance through his wine. "I would say the fifth largest individual shareholder of the bank and the chairman of its Executive Committee."

"Me and Isabelle?"

"How'd you think it was going to go down, Bill? We just send Hugo a note during lunch period and he goes running out onto Peachtree Street?" he laughed. "Billy?"

"How did you… the bank will not soon forget the advice critical to its prosperity that Rémond Moncrif has…"

"Now it's my turn to say bullshit. That's not what's going on here."

Billy looked at him questioningly.

"Step up to the table? Molly, my dad? My grandfather," he repeated Billy's recent litany. "We have a huge history, me and you. All of that transcends some economic tit for tat. Don't drag me into this and then trivialize the moment with a…"

"Billy?" they heard Isabelle say from the rear of the box. "You didn't get to the paddock. What do we like here?"

John Harleston gave Billy a knowing look as she sat down.

"You know the eight horse is a half to that filly Molly and I bred last year with Martha duPont. Eddie Barclay said it worked a bullet six furlongs Monday. What do you think?"

Hardin reached across the box and ruffled Billy's hair, jerking his chin as if to say 'it's okay.'

"John, come with me. We'll go put the money down. Everyone in for twenty? I could have sworn you were talking to Braden Townes down there. Is she back in town? What's her story? Spare me no details. I know you know."

Isabelle propped her elbows on the edge of the box as the two boys headed toward the betting windows, watching the horses load into the starting gate through her binoculars. "Hardy had a solution?"

"A solution?"

"Yes."

"What do you mean?"

"Billy. I'm not stupid. I'm in line for the chairmanship of the executive committee because there is no one else who can continue Molly's stewardship. You are one of the bank's largest shareholders, yourself a lawyer and a confidante of Julius Irving, counsel to the bank. Increasingly there are indications of the bank's complicity, if not cooperation, in some scheme that involves Alderlay, about which you believe Molly had knowledge and Molly and I had conversations. You avail yourself of the counsel of Hardin Murrah, a developing insider at the leading investment bank in the country, who has the ear of Nathan Robinson, its chief dealmaker. You have – how shall we characterize this – facts in evidence that implicate Hugo or at least his judgment. And…"

"Isabelle?"

"Are you this naïve," she said, the charm obvious in her tone. "Pour me a glass of this fabulous wine Hardin ordered and undoubtedly charged to his father," she said winking at Hardy as they returned. "Tell me you do not believe acquiring a billion dollars happens without the ability to synthesize apparently unrelated information. You're ready to act to bring Hugo down. How can I help?"

"Isabelle, I… where were…"

"Where was I until now? Watching. The situation had to get to a certain point before I could take official recognition of what was happening. You have no idea how hard…" There was a catch in her voice for a moment before she recovered. "Molly never mourned the loss of her own child, so concerned was she for you. You've not mourned the loss of Molly, numb as you are emotionally after Caroline." Isabelle looked up. "Hardy, where is the wine?"

Isabelle continued. "You don't need an economic bulwark. If I had your money, I'd give mine away," she laughed. "You need an emotional bulwark. Listen to me. My own children are a mess. They not only don't need me, they don't want me around. A triumph of too much money and too little discipline early on. Molly and your parents pursued an importantly different course with you – all of you actually. If you need an emotional bulwark, however, you have it. Julius can give you the operating authority of my office – of the office I will shortly assume. I give you my… I've spent my life in the service of others. I am immensely rich because of the institutions my father built and Dicky expanded. To the extent going forward in the resolution of the bank issues, you need the imprimatur of 'Isabelle said so', you have it. I am not unaware of the influence of my name. Straighten it out, Billy. We may not be able to put away the guys who pushed Molly into the river, who tried to do away with you and Julia, who daily try to defile the financial markets, upon the integrity of which ordinary people should be able to depend. But there's different kinds of jail. Loss of position, power, for some is tantamount to bars. Pull the trigger. It has to stop. Look. It's the eight. Come on, girl." Isabelle snapped her fingers as the field turned for home. "Come on, girl. You got 'em. Yes. Yes."

Chapter Fifty-Nine

"Making out in a wine shop? In Georgetown? Would I love to add that picture to my Julia Pringle book of memories." Nancy Randolph said in the back seat of the town car on the way to the Winyah Indigo Society Hall the following night. "He's cute as hell, Julia. If you don't want him or, in typical fashion, can't make up your mind, give him to me. I'll streak my hair and move to Atlanta tomorrow."

"Julia was making out with the doc in a wine shop?" Lucy interrupted, taking interest in the conversation. "God. I go back to France for a month and decorum falls off the map in South Carolina."

"Kind of like Normandy, wouldn't you say?" Julia replied to Lucy, the sarcasm evident in her tone.

"That was a bit uncalled for, Julia. Neither of us has a really successful track record with relationships. Do you honestly think I don't realize that? I'm over there in a relationship, if one can call it that, where I'll never be accepted. Even if he were to love me completely, which will never happen, I will always be this American girl. And not even from a major family. From South Carolina, for god's sake."

"Lucy, I do think the people we know in France are more open minded than that…," Julia began.

"Oh, will you hush, the two of you?" Nancy said, mildly disgusted. "Lucy, you live in not one, but two of the most French – and that is to say the most rabidly un-American – parts of France. And, you're living with a boy whose family's title is so old they don't even use it, for god's sake. What did you think it would be like? Easy? And everybody knew he was going to ask you, Julia. Walker said so two weeks ago."

"Did you ever think in a million years you'd see a line of cars like this pulling up for an event in Georgetown?" Nancy remarked as she leaned forward over Charlotte's shoulder to see the entrance to the Winyah Indigo Society Hall. "Oh good grief. Look at that. Photographers. We'll look like out-of-towners for sure."

"Okay, girls, game faces," said Charlotte as she snapped the mirror on the car visor shut and reached for her bag.

The group collected on the plaza in front of the Indigo Society Hall amidst not only arriving ball patrons but also the confusing flash of the lights from the cameras of the assembled press. Hardin looked down the street as he helped first Nancy and then Julia out of their car, inclining his head slightly toward Julia as he did and then looking suddenly back in the direction of the waterfront. "Odd, isn't it? A macked-out Hummer with low lights in this part of Georgetown."

Julia turned, putting her hand on Tommy's arm as she casually followed Hardin's gaze. A level of her subconscious perception registered that something was not right with this scene. "Charlotte. Step back. Where is Lucy? Tommy… I…"

Billy, standing next to Walker watching the line of cars emptying patrons into the plaza, heard the discordant note in Julia's voice. Looking back down Front Street, he immediately sensed an uncomfortable incongruity. The car was moving too slowly, looked completely wrong for the surroundings. "Lucy, I want you to…," he began. In that instant he heard a 'pfft,' seeing out of the corner of his eye a tiny cloud of dust kick up from the oyster shell plaza. He spun Lucy instinctively around behind his back turning to face the source of the noise. As he turned, he saw the rear window of the car behind Judge Magrath's explode and its driver seemed to stagger, grasping the rear door handle for support.

His rational mind kept informing him that those could not be gunshots. Not in Georgetown. Not at a charity ball. His visual perception of the unfolding events began to transform itself into a slow motion sequence of reality.

Tommy Henning had pushed Julia to the ground beneath him as he fell. He forced her head back down into the ground as he watched the Hummer disappear down the street. "Bill. Billy," he yelled.

Billy looked back toward Tommy and saw beyond him Charlotte

half-kneeling, half-standing with her back to him. She slowly turned, a look of abject horror and shock on her face. As she did, Billy noticed a red stain on her hands, her left arm and another dark stain covering the skirt of her dress. She could not speak and seemed to stagger slightly as if she might collapse.

"Tommy. Behind you. Charlotte."

Tommy scrambled to where Charlotte had sunk to her knees. Beyond Charlotte, he saw John Harleston, lying on his back, a telltale red stain spreading through the skirt of his white dinner jacket, his eyes staring vacantly at the exploding fireworks. Charlotte began to scream, now noticing the blood stain on John Harleston's jacket and her own dress.

Tommy quickly pulled up the skirt of her dress to look at her leg in the area of the blood stain and found no wound. John Harleston had been shot. "Julia," he barked. "Take my phone."

Julia reached into the pocket of his dinner jacket, retrieving his phone and saw the full horror of John Harleston lying on the ground, the stain on his white jacket spreading.

"I… Tommy… I…"

"Give me the goddam phone," Tommy heard Lucy say. "What? WHAT? Talk to me."

"Call 911. Tell them it's Dr. Henning. My emergency code is GH 2042. Golf. Hotel. Two zero four two. I need an ambulance now with… never mind. Make the 911 call."

He looked back at Lucy pressing the numbers, as he found the gunshot wound in John Harleston's side. He ripped open his shirt to locate the wound and determine if there were more than one gunshot wound. Removing the handkerchief from the breast pocket of John Harleston's dinner jacket, and his own, he made a compress and began to apply pressure to cause the bleeding to subside.

He heard Billy at his side. "Thomas has been shot in the neck. I can't stop the bleeding. I think the driver of the car behind Lucy's may be dead." Billy saw John Harleston for the first time. "Oh god," he gasped as his voice broke. "No. No."

"Billy. Get a hold of yourself. Here hold this." Taking Billy's hand he guided it under his own where he was compressing the wound.

"Keep the pressure on it just like this," he said, pressing his hand down on top of Billy's. "He's going to be okay. The shot made a clean exit and I think missed all his organs. He's going to be okay."

Tommy noticed Billy's breathing was becoming increasingly shallow and rapid as the images of the past few minutes became real.

"Breathe," he heard Tommy say. "Deep breaths. You haven't the luxury of passing out now. Deep breaths. Look at me. Look at me, goddamn it," pulling back on Billy's shoulder. "Do you hear me?"

Billy nodded.

"Lucy, come with me." He started across the plaza to where he saw Hardin kneeling by Thomas, helplessly looking around. "Call 555-2128. Tell them it's Dr. Henning, and I am in-bound with one, no two gunshot wounds." He reached Thomas' side. "Move. Move," he said insistently pushing Hardin out of the way. "Tell them to find a thoracic surgeon and have him standing by. Lucy! Are you getting this?" He heard Lucy begin repeating his instructions into the phone. "And we are going to need an orthopedic surgeon before the night is out. Have them get Mark Hennessey if they can find him. Call 911 back and ask them where my fucking ambulance is?"

He looked up at Lucy. "Lucy, don't fall apart on me right now. Look around. See if everyone else is okay. Can you see Julia?"

Lucy heard the strident scream of the ambulance, now several blocks away. She surveyed the forecourt of the building wordlessly: Billy kneeling by John Harleston, Charlotte cradling his head in her lap. Nancy helping one of the older ladies to her feet from where she had fallen as the melee began. Dinny Washington speaking insistently into his cell phone. Beaufort Estes deploying his deputies into some semblance of control over the events, barking orders into his shoulder mike. She heard the sirens of other police cruisers approaching and had the irrepressible sense that life would never again be quite the same. Some sense of security in the world they had all taken for granted was violated and could never be reacquired.

An hour later Lucy sat in stunned silence in the small room at Georgetown Hospital to which they had been directed by Tommy Henning. Charlotte was crying softly on Hardin's shoulder holding the lapel of his jacket with one hand and his arm with the other. Julia's head was in Billy's lap, his hand absently stroking her hair. "This is the room where Tommy brought me the night of Molly's accident," she heard Julia say quietly to no one in particular, turning her face into Billy's leg as the tears started to flow.

Walker was on the phone with Julius Irving who was preparing to go to John Harleston's parents' house, the Reads not having been among the first arrivals for the ball.

"Let me send Malcolm in Judge Magrath's car. It's late. No, he's still here. I'll send him to get you and then you can go to Polly's. Yessir. I understand," he finished, snapping his phone shut.

"He's going to be fine, Billy. He'll be okay," Walker said squeezing his friend's shoulder for reassurance and pressing his lips to the top of Julia's head.

Lucy, for once, was speechless. She sat with her head resting on Nancy's shoulder. Hardin offered each of them small bottles of Evian.

Tommy came into the small waiting room, wearily removing his dinner jacket. "John Harleston's going to be all right. He lost a lot of blood, but nothing was damaged that cannot be repaired. He'll have a painful recovery, but there's no indication that he won't be 100%."

"And Thomas?" Julia raised her head from Billy's lap when she heard him talking to Tommy.

"Bill – it's still touch and go. The gunshot struck him from behind, penetrating his trapezius muscle and wedging near his cervical spine at C5-6. He's in surgery now. There's a very narrow margin of error in the removal of the bullet. A centimeter either way could result in the total severing of his spinal cord, causing paralysis from the neck down, ultimately impairing his ability to breathe. It's critical. He's no longer young…," Tommy's voice trailed off.

"Oh, god. It's because of me. All this is because of me." His voice cracked slightly.

"No. Billy, no…," Julia began.

Billy looked around the room at his friends, trying to catalogue the devastation that had been visited upon those closest to him tonight.

"… acts of random violence…," he heard Julia saying, half-listening. "There's no foreseeable connection…"

"Walker?" Billy said firmly. "Find Dinny Washington. And Julius. Set up a meeting. Anywhere. But now. Tonight."

"Julius is on the way to Polly Read's…," Walker began.

"Then after. Here. Walk – please."

Billy put his arms around Julia, pulling her close. "Luce. I want you to take everybody back to Commander House. Find Tommy. Get him to give you something for Charlotte. But you need to get Hardin and the girls out of here. Beaufort Estes will arrange cars to get you there."

"I don't want to leave until we know that…"

"Lucy. This is not the time to argue with me. Trust me, for once in your life. Please." His tone softened. "Do as I ask. Please."

Lucy stood up. "Julia. Come on. We're going. Come on. I have to get Charlotte." Crossing the small room to where Charlotte and Hardin sat, she continued her organizational efforts. "Come on, Tex. Help me out here. Charlotte, we have to go. I know you think you can't do it, but we have to get to the car. I've no idea what's waiting outside," she said looking pointedly at Walker. "No idea," she repeated as she helped Hardin lift Charlotte up.

"Wait. Luce," she heard Billy begin. "Where's Tommy? There's bound to be a back entrance, a service door of some kind that is beyond the view of the press."

"I'll find him."

"Luce."

"It's okay, Billy. I've got it. Nancy? Julia, you're coming with me. Hardy, time to saddle up. Charlotte?"

"Lucy, I should stay until Polly gets here."

"Julia. You're coming with me. Get up. Walker will be here. Billy needs to know that you're safe. Come. Now."

Billy watched them leave. Lucy. Sensitive. Confident. Solicitous of the needs of others. She looked back at him, as she guided the group out into the hall, pausing for a moment with her arm around Charlotte's shoulders.

He lifted his chin, nodding at her, acknowledging the weight of the moment. And then she was gone.

A moment later, Julius Irving entered the room with Polly Read. Dinny Washington was only two steps behind them.

"Billy," John Harleston's mother began. "How did this happen in Georgetown, for god's sake?"

"Polly, he's okay. He's going to be all right. Tommy Henning and his team – despite the fact that this is Georgetown – they're the best. He was at Hopkins… Yale," Billy's voice trailed off, at a loss for words. Tears clouded his eyes. His voice lost its presence. "I… I don't…"

"Polly, Dr. Henning will take you back now. Give me just a minute with Billy and then I will find you, if that's all right?" Billy heard Julius Irving say. "Polly?"

"Yes. Julius, whatever you say. Dr. Henning?"

"Mrs. Read. I'm Tommy Henning. John Harleston's going to be okay. If you would come with me…"

Julius was visibly shaken, sinking into an available chair.

"Bill," Dinny Washington began.

"Dinny. There's no time. We need to talk. Tonight was no accident. Let me tell you what I know," Billy began softly. "Five years ago Alderlay Development with the cooperation initially, and later the complicity of the Continental American Bank, entered into a carefully orchestrated program to finance the acquisition of property with resort development potential or what has become known as exurban development potential."

Walker rose to close the door to the lounge.

"Molly created three immovable roadblocks to Alderlay's scheme. First, she refused to sell any of the Commander Bradbury land on Oyster Island and began immediately to place the Companionville/ Turkey Run tract on the north end of the island – the only potential site for a bridgehead from the mainland – under a conservation easement. Second, she assembled a coalition of Oryzantia directors that blocked any possibility of Oryzantia's cooperation with respect to its Oyster Island land.

"And, third, she uncovered the complicity of the bank in Alderlay's financing scheme to acquire potential development property in North Carolina, South Carolina, and Florida. Molly's refusal to sell was one thing. It could be considered as economic. The crazy, green opposition of a rich woman. Whatever. The refusal of Oryzantia to participate – to sell – had political ramifications. Molly and her coterie represented a group that saw themselves not only as the inheritor of the legacy of Harrison Inman but as the conservators of a certain tradition, a certain attitude that directly influenced the pattern of development along the Waccamaw Neck. Thus, a political debate was raised."

"But," Billy paused for emphasis, "when she realized the full extent of the bank's involvement with Alderlay and threatened to expose it, Hugo had to act or back down."

Billy paused for a moment to get a cup of coffee from the small galley kitchen.

"An anomaly in the structure of Molly's estate was brought to the attention of Risley Lawrence, albeit inappropriately, by Richy Concannon, whose information could have only come from Hugo. The anomaly was that, if I died before I had the chance to exercise certain options, to change the structure of her estate after I inherited… it's complicated."

"Billy, if you'd rather have this conversation tomorrow," Dinny began.

"No. No," Billy said with greater emphasis the second time. "You need to know what I know tonight. The Morgan Bank manages for my family. Morgan is very circumspect about simultaneously representing the estate of a client and the heirs of that same estate. They consider it to be a conflict of interest."

"Bill, this sounds like a lot of what?… Wall Street stuff," Dinny asked tentatively.

"No. Wait a minute. Let me finish. I inherit from Molly, among many other things obviously, the control – what the outside world sees as – the disposition of Oyster Island. If I survive Molly, I can exercise those powers. I can decide what is the disposition of the Commander lands on Oyster Island."

"Billy?" Dinny started to say.

"Stay with me for a minute. Molly dies – and if I happen to die before I exercise the options that give me complete control over her estate – including the power to dispose of Oyster Island – the power falls to the bank."

"Morgan?"

"No. Continental American."

"CAB?"

"Yes. CAB becomes the trustee of Molly's estate under the terms of her will if I die. And can then dispose of property in her estate as it determines to be in the best interest of the estate. It created a window of opportunity. Alderlay was playing a shell game with its shareholders, the markets, to an extent with the bank itself. The bank was not only complicit in the scheme, but they had, in fact, also participated in the structuring of the financial vehicles that enabled Alderlay's deception. They attempted to co-opt Oryzantia's management into the deal with promises of corporate support. Molly began to understand, piece together actually, what had happened. The customized financial product – SFPs as they were called – put together by Concannon's deal makers. The bank began to realize that if Molly prevailed, and Alderlay's financial house of cards came down, the bank could not avoid significant damage, large fines in the collapse. The most senior officers feared criminal charges. As surreal as it may sound, they conceived a plan to take first Molly and then me out of the picture. Both the scheme itself and the accompanying chain of authorization went all the way to Hugo's office."

"William," Julius interrupted. "I must caution you. These are very serious accusations, which you are making in the presence of a prosecuting attorney for the government, which will have an interest in these matters. Your own personal finances…"

"They killed Molly, Julius. Molly found out what was happening."

"How can you be sure?" Julius interrupted again.

"You have proof of all this?" Dinny Washington asked incredulously.

"I have the proof I need."

"What do you mean. Will it convince a grand jury?"

"I don't need to convince a grand jury."

Julius stood up abruptly, crossing the room to answer a knock at the door. Realizing it was Tommy Henning, he glanced over his shoulder to find Walker. Walker and Tommy talked quietly in the doorway as Julius resumed his seat. A moment later Walker re-joined the group. "Polly's going to stay with him. He's heavily sedated but Tommy says he's going to be all right," he finished wearily.

"Thomas?" Billy asked.

Walker put his hand on his friend's shoulder. "It's not looking good. He's still in surgery."

Julius turned to look at Billy. "Who else knows the scenario you have described?"

"Julia. Walker and Hardy to an extent. Isabelle."

"Is all of your evidence, if we are to call it that, anecdotal?" Dinny asked.

"Mostly documentary… well, written I'd say. I have her daybooks. And, the bank screwed up. They delivered close to thirty storage cartons containing intra-bank correspondence including four years of emails to Molly's house instead of to the record storage center when the bank moved in Georgetown."

"And as chairman of the Executive Committee she had access to anything she thought…"

"Was germane to the exercise of the duties of her office." Billy completed Julius' sentence.

"But, emails?"

"Criswell ran into a problem during the Gold Coast acquisition. Molly had to fly down at the last minute to help wrap up the deal. She gleaned from the chairman of Gold Coast that they thought Alderlay was one of the ascendant stars in their financial firmament. In the course of her visit, she met Lawrence, the head of Alderlay. She thought they were fast operators, possessed of a certain naïveté with respect to sophisticated financial management. When she returned, to Atlanta, she and Criswell instructed IT to blind copy Molly on every bank email – internal or external – that had the word Alderlay in the text or was addressed or received from any of their top executives."

"None of which would be admissible in the way you have obtained it," said Dinny shaking his head.

"Perhaps not. But the Senate Banking committee is not bound by the same restrictions as the district attorney. Nor is the SEC."

Julius Irving leaned forward lowering his voice. "Isabelle Collins told me tonight she is assuming the chairmanship of the executive committee."

"Yes."

"She asked me if I would consider taking a seat on the board of the bank – firm rules permitting."

"Yes."

"You knew that?"

"Yes."

"She said she needed an indication of my interest by Monday morning," his voice trailed off momentarily. Julius paused, studying first Billy's face and then Walker's. "You don't intend to bring this to Dinny. You're going to force Hugo out. Clean up the Alderlay mess internally. Why?"

Billy looked at Julius, holding his gaze intently.

"Why?" he repeated. Billy's logic began to dawn on him. "Because the 'mistress of this house' was Molly Commander. You're trying to save the bank. Avoid participation in another corporate meltdown, which this time could shake the very foundations of the U.S. banking system. Save your grandmother's reputation."

Billy continued. "Not to mention the thousands of employees whose 401ks, whose health benefits, pension benefits, the college education of their children depend upon the continued health of the bank – and, yes, avoid another corporate meltdown which would undoubtedly reflect poorly on my family but could also result in a larger collapse, a collapse that this time the financial system might not be able to withstand." He stood up. "I have a plan. You want to hear it?"

Chapter Sixty

Billy walked through the double doors into the suite of offices occupied by the chairman of the Continental American Bank, trailed by Julius Irving. Passing the paired desks of the first of Hugo Lesesne's three assistants without comment, he went directly to the door of Lesesne's private office.

"Mr. Commander? You can't. The chairman is in a…"

Billy paid her no attention, throwing open the door so abruptly it crashed into the paneled wall with a loud crack.

"Billy. I… what…," Hugo Lesesne began.

"You were responsible for getting my grandmother killed. Your goons tried not once but three times to kill me, in the process almost killing my cousin and my best friend. Stupidly, they tried to strong-arm me on the sidewalk outside the Empire Club. For what, Hugo? For money?"

"Billy. You're crazy. You're making completely groundless accusations," now noticing Julius Irving behind Billy. "Let's sit down and…"

"Groundless, Hugo? I'll tell you the ground I stand on." He tossed a document folder on Lesesne's desk. "There's the whole sordid story of the relationship between the bank and Alderlay Development from the first meeting with Molly and Criswell in Palm Beach. Azalea, Camellia, the other partnerships formed by the bank's own legal department. The deception, the complicity of bank officers at almost every step along the way. The damaged front bumper of the car that pushed Molly's car in the river. The car from the bank's repossession lot that killed Jack

Evans. In fact, a tie between the bank and everything that's happened, except the shooting at the Indigo Ball. Give me another week, and I'm sure I'll have that."

"As we speak Walker Coggeshell is in the anteroom of the offices of the chairman of the SEC. My cousin Julia is outside the office of the Chairman of the Senate Banking Committee. Dinny Washington has an appointment in fifteen minutes in Atlanta with the United States Attorney for the Northern District of Georgia. And Isabelle Collins just pulled through the gates of the White House on her way to the Oval Office. You're through. You step down now and you walk away with your parachute. No further options. No retirement. No ancillary benefits. But you get to keep your money and avoid being led away on the evening news."

Billy pulled his cell phone from his jacket pocket. "Interesting thing I have on my new cell phone. It's called group calling. Means with one button I can get as many as, say, four people on the phone simultaneously. What's it going to be, Hugo? I can tell Isabelle to tell the President 'hello' for me or I can pull the trigger on the whole story. My next call will be to Sidney Carrington at the *Times*. You're leaving, or I'll pull the house down around your head – yours and Richy Concannon's. It's your call, Hugo. You have thirty seconds."

"This is absurd. You are delusional. You have no…"

"Proof? You screwed up, Hugo. Criswell and Molly put in place an operating procedure that any email, internal memo, notes to a credit file, external correspondence – anything with Alderlay in it was blind copied to Molly. You overlooked it after Criswell died. When the bank moved in Georgetown, they sent thirty boxes of documents to Molly's house at DeBordieu instead of record center storage. The boxes you were nice enough to get out of my dining room. Remember? It's all there," he said, indicating the folder on Hugo's desk.

"None of which would ever be admissible in a…"

"The SEC and Senate banking won't care. The documents we have would be sufficient for hearings that would be brutal, at best. You now have ten seconds."

Lesesne sank into his chair.

"What's your assistant's name."

"What?"

"Her name, Hugo?"

"Marjorie… it's Marjorie."

Billy turned slightly, raising his voice. "Marjorie? Get Mildred Ferguson up here. Now. And get the guys from corporate communications up here, too. The chairman needs to make a statement."

Marjorie was standing in the door to the office. "Now," he barked.

Billy thumbed the key on his cell phone. "Isabelle?" he began. "Hey. No, I'm fine." Billy looked pointedly at Lesesne, raising his eyebrows in an unspoken question. He could not misunderstand the look of resignation that crossed the chairman's face. "Hey look, if you happen to see the President, tell him Julia and I said 'Happy Birthday.'" Listening for a moment, he continued, "Yes, ma'm. Next week then. Jules are you there? Walker? Jules are you going to grab the shuttle? Okay. Walker we'll meet you at your place around seven, okay? Sure." He laughed. "Best place for a drink on a Monday night. I dunno. Uptown or down? I'll have Nancy and Hardy with me. I think Charlotte went up this morning on the Morgan plane from Georgetown. Can you call her, Walk? Send a car 'round for her? Jules – you sure you're okay on the shuttle?" He laughed. "Yeah. Me too."

Turning, Billy said, "Judge?"

"William, I believe I am needed here, if you don't mind."

Billy embraced the older man with affection and respect. "Yessir. I imagine you are."

Noticing Mildred entering the Chairman's suite, he continued, "Mildred, Mrs. Collins is on the way down from Washington later today. Let's be sure her plane is met. She has polled the board and will be assuming the chairmanship of the Executive Committee. So, perhaps you could get my grandmother's…," Billy faltered for a moment, "if you could get Mrs. Collins' office ready. She'll be a busy lady this week."

"Judge, with your permission, sir. I have a plane to catch."

"Go. Go, William." Julius Irving regarded the younger man, tears starting to collect in his eyes.

"Yessir. I know. Thank you, sir."

Billy kissed Mildred on the cheek as he headed out the door and started down the hall to the elevator lobby.

Chapter Sixty-One

"Come," Julius Irving said barely concealing the irritation in his voice. It was the third interruption in thirty minutes as he was trying to proof an appellate brief.

"Judge Irving, Mrs. Coggeshell is here," he heard his assistant begin.

"Thank you, my dear. We would both like some coffee. Preferably strong. And then we wish to be left alone." Mimi Coggeshell marched into his office, one hand wrapped around her cane and the other around a leather portfolio.

"Mimi. This is quite a surprise. If there was something you needed, I would have been delighted to come to the beach. It's quite…"

"Oh, for heaven's sakes. I'm not an invalid and I certainly do not need to be patronized by someone half my age," Mimi said laughing. Now, Julius, we have work to do. How do we do this? Do you take notes on some legal pad – or do we get a secretary in to take notes?"

"Mimi, if I might know the reason… sit. Here, sit." Julius moved an upholstered armchair closer to the side of his desk.

"Julius. You have followed and been a part of the recent proceedings involving the Continental American Bank, Oyster Island and the Commander interests?" She held up her right hand to halt his response. "Of course, you have. What you may not know is that Julia – if I may say, upon my recommendation and that of the Morgan Bank – is assuming the seat formerly occupied by Molly on the Baker Endowment Board."

"Mimi, I had not…"

"Well, now you have. She will be the youngest trustee in their history. We are delighted. You do not need me to explain to you that she must forego all other trusteeships in educational institutions that may be potential beneficiaries of Baker funds during her tenure."

"But Julia is not…"

"Julius, you must allow me to complete a thought, please." Judge Irving chuckled to himself as he sat back and gestured to Mimi to continue.

"We are here to discuss the formation of the Commander School on Oyster Island. In time, it shall become a beacon in the darkness of the lives of those who have lost hope for their future and that of their children. We envision a boarding school primarily for young African American children and teenagers living on Oyster Island and in similar communities throughout the Lowcountry. While she might be an attractive choice, Julia cannot chair the board for the reasons I have just described. Billy does not wish to participate directly in the governance of an institution bearing his name and to which he is the primary contributor of endowment funds. Walker doesn't have the educational background for an undertaking of this kind. Last night, Billy, Julia and Walker came to see me and asked if I would convene the constituency locally to build – literally and figuratively – the Commander School. I agreed."

"Mimi, I…"

"Julius, I'm old. I've done my bit in my time, as have we all, but I always let Molly and Isabelle take the risky positions. I regret that." She reached for her bag, retrieving a sheaf of papers from inside. "You need to construct the organizational entity. By-laws. Board, whatever. I will chair the board initially. I am reliably informed that, if asked, Dinny Washington will assume the position of head of school. I would expect you to take a seat on the board. There is a list in those papers of those whom we should ask to join the board."

Julius Irving stood up to retrieve a legal pad from the far corner of his desk and started to speak.

She held up her hand to stop him. "I will be seventy-eight next month, Julius. I realized yesterday, as if it were the first time, that the status quo is not good enough. Billy said the buses have become invisible to us."

"I'm sorry, Mimi. The buses? I don't follow you."

"The green and white buses, Julius. Are you blind, too? The buses that take the black women from Oyster Island and elsewhere to work in the hotels in Myrtle Beach. Now, while work is commendable, these jobs come at a price. The price is yet another generation of young people, lost not only as productive members of society but also lost to the achievement of any sense of personal fulfillment or satisfaction. Why? Because no one is at home to make their breakfast or help them with their homework. Let alone make sure they stay in school. Those buses, Julius. Those are the ones that have become invisible. They just got visible. You and I are going to paint them a new color."

Julius took a deep breath. "Mimi, I am constrained to ask, is there… uh, do we have a…"

"A what, Julius? A budget? Whatever it takes. Whatever it takes. What is the price tag for the generations we have already lost, the generations we stand to lose in the future? What is the price tag for the damage those like Hugo Lesesne and his lieutenants are doing to our society? Shall we stand idly by while that bill is tabulated and presented? We begin to do whatever we can to reverse the conduct we observed recently at the bank. Whatever it takes," she said with finality.

"Billy will put up 45 million, half from his personal accounts, half from the foundation. He will additionally match at twenty-five cents on the dollar every dollar we raise above that in the first year. Here is my pledge for five million" she continued, handing Julius a separate sheet of paper. "Lowndes and Dorothy have committed a million dollars, payable over five years. Gardiner has matched Lowndes' pledge and Isabelle has matched mine. Julia herself is putting up 250,000, matched by an equal amount from Walker. Morall Magrath and Lucy have pledged a million between them. John and Polly Read have pledged a half a million payable over five years."

Julius Irving looked over the printed list Mimi gave him with some amazement. He heard her continue.

"Stinnett Ashton Associates is available to develop the design schematics for the campus. You may recall they were the lead architects on both the expansion at both Exeter and St. Paul's. John Harleston Read, who is facing a six-month recuperation at a minimum, has agreed to work with Stinnett Ashton to guide them in couching their plans within the Lowcountry vernacular."

"Mimi, I'm astonished," Julius began. "You have done this practically overnight for a concept that is yet…"

"That is yet what, Julius? Unformed?"

"I was going to say inchoate, but…"

"'There is a tide in the affairs of men,' Julius, 'When taken at the flood often leads on to victory,'" she chided him gently, in good humor.

"It's a lot of money for a young institution, Mimi."

"A young institution that will have an old board with years of experience. Beyond that, every institution of distinction in this country was at one point young, as you say." Mimi stood up and began to gather her things. "Alabama Deas has retired. She says she is old and tired. I believe otherwise. I think she is discouraged. If we were to staff to her weaknesses, she would be an excellent first Dean of Faculty. She will know whom to recruit and how to begin filling out the teaching staff. I think you should call her and have that conversation."

"Now, please tell your girl to get my car brought 'round, would you?" she continued, watching as Julius picked up his phone.

"Undoubtedly, there will be things we need to discuss. If I am to be down here frequently, I should also think the ability to produce a decent glass of sherry in the afternoon – or perhaps something stronger – will be important. I'm just sayin'," she concluded, giving her old friend a broad smile.

"You need to call Loudoun Smith, solicit his involvement and support. Billy wants the school to have an affiliation with the church. Might straighten them out, too, while we're at it. Can you come 'round to dinner tomorrow? Seven-thirty. Gardiner's in town. Isabelle will be there. I'll call Morall Magrath and see if he is up to it. Maybe some of the younger crowd as well. Thank you, Pam," acknowledging the information that her car was waiting out front.

Moving toward the outer offices of the firm, she paused in the doorway to Julius' office. "Walker has a song he loves, the message of which he insists must become manifest in South Carolina. Somebody

Dylan. I don't think he is from around here. 'The times they are a changing.' Julius?"

"Yes, tomorrow night. Seven-thirty. We'll get to work," smiling and shaking his head in amazement at the enormity of what had been accomplished within such a short period of time.

Chapter Sixty-Two

Loudoun Smith looked up from the small group of people with whom he had been casually chatting prior to the beginning of the dedicatory ceremonies at which he was officiating. Billy Commander and Walker Coggeshell were walking toward him across the lawn adjacent to the river at Asylum Plantation. The remains of the Commanders' River House had been razed. Thirty acres surrounding the site of the old house had been landscaped, and in about twenty minutes the community would witness the announcement of the new Commander School. The list of constituent support read like a veritable who's who of prominent, well-connected people from the Carolinas, Atlanta and New York.

"What a remarkable turn of events," he thought. "Two thousand acres of the Commander-Bradbury river land now subject to a conservation easement and secured in trust as the site of the new school. Dinny Washington stepping down as an assistant D.A., declining a partnership in Julius Irving's law firm to assume the position as the first Head of School at the Commander School, a 70 million dollar endowment at his command and an ambitious educational initiative focused on disenfranchised young people on Oyster Island and throughout the South Carolina Lowcountry."

The boys stopped on the crest of a slight knoll near a group of newly planted white *Camellias japonica* that had been Molly's favorite, shielding their eyes from the morning sun as they watched the preparations surrounding the small dais set in the middle of the grounds. Bishop Smith excused himself and began to walk over to where the boys stood.

Dressed in khaki shorts and polo shirts, one in boat shoes, the other in sandals, it was clear they were not planning to attend the ceremonies.

"Walker," the Bishop said shaking Walker's extended hand with affection. "William."

"Bishop Smith," said Walker cheerfully, greeting the sixty-five-year-old cleric. "How are you, sir?" Billy addressed the Bishop.

"Tom Henning told me Thomas is going to be okay. Thanks be to God."

"Yes, sir. He has a long road ahead as you might expect, but we're going to do everything possible to insure his full recovery."

"It's a remarkable thing you've done here, William. Both of you." Smiling, he said, "I take it from the casualness of your appearance you're not joining us this morning?"

Billy laughed and grabbed Walker by the back of his neck with one hand and the top of his shoulder with the other, giving him a playful shake, "No sir. We thought we'd go sailing…"

"Many people here today would like to recognize – indeed, honor – not only your particular generosity but your vision. Lives will be changed by your efforts, William"

Billy responded seriously but with the humility that typified his response to praise or recognition. "Thank you, sir. I hope so. We all do. But all I really did was get the ball rolling. Others did the heavy lifting – you, Dinny, Julia, Walker's grandmother…"

Billy's voice trailed off as the small crowd assembling on the platform shifted slightly, the participants greeting one another or beginning to take their seats. He saw Julia move to the front and say something to Dinny Washington. Behind her he saw the unmistakable silhouette of a familiar figure.

Turning to Walker, he said with surprise, "Lucy?"

The Bishop followed his gaze and said with amusement in his normally dignified and sonorous voice. "Yes. Miss Magrath."

"Lucy is here?"

The Bishop continued, adopting a rather formal tone of voice, smiling, "At the invitation of the Chairman of the Trustees, Miss Magrath has accepted a seat on the Board and has agreed to chair the

Committee for Institutional Advancement. Apparently she said that, having been a 'destroyer of money for most of her life' – I believe that was the phrase she used – that she thought she would try her hand at raising money."

Billy looked up at the sky, laughing. "Lucy," he said again.

"While it is certainly not my place to comment, I am told that last night during our Trustee dinner at Eddie Hazzard's, when asked how long she intended to stay, she was heard to remark that she was home, with no immediate plans to return to France."

"William," the Bishop continued in a more serious tone of voice, "I've known you since you were born, watched you grow in spirit and stature, and participated in both the joys and sorrows in your life. I am constrained to tell you that your absence from these proceedings here today may be misinterpreted. Your absence from these proceedings may result in important things left unsaid."

"Sir?" Billy responded with some surprise.

"You are the vital link between the legacy of your family and the future. That is unavoidable. You do not have the luxury of casualness that might be perceived as rendering insignificant or, worse yet, severing that link. Mimi Coggeshell is old; Dot Pringle is already on four other boards, two of which are national. Julia takes a seat – not just any seat mind you, but the seat at the Baker Endowment formerly occupied by Molly Commander herself – filled with anxiety if not trepidation – as she becomes the youngest trustee in the history of one of the most consequential philanthropic institutions in the country. Julius Irving, Polly Read, Isabelle Collins, Gardiner Arrington… the list goes on and on. They serve because like your grandmother they were taught to serve. They serve because the cause is right. But they serve to honor the memory of Molly Commander. Who acknowledges that sacrifice? That service? Me?"

Billy looked steadily into the aging cleric's eyes for a moment struggling with his own emotions. Turning back toward the podium, he saw Lucy comfortably chatting with other trustees as they waited for the dedication to begin. "Do you have a pen, something to write on?"

Bishop Smith reached inside his jacket pocket and produced a ball point pen and a small black leather note pad. Billy scribbled a quick note and, tearing the small sheet of paper out of the note pad, handed them back to the Bishop.

No one among the organizing principals of the Commander School had given much thought to Billy's absence from the platform party or his lack of participation in the dedication ceremonies. Julia had put it down to his natural tendency to avoid calling attention to himself.

Mimi Coggeshell had been more direct. "Who would want to bring upon oneself the media storm that attends large charitable gifts these days? Not to mention that feeding the media would undoubtedly dredge up coverage of Motte and Frances, Caroline even. Too painful."

It was with some surprise that Julia saw Billy start up the steps to the platform dressed as he was. As he approached the platform, he asked Julia quietly "Is the mike on?"

Julia tapped the head of the microphone as discreetly as she could, and they both heard the familiar echo sound indicating the mike was live. She glanced quickly at Lucy, who had taken her seat next to Julia's in the front row. Lucy gave a small shrug with her shoulders turning her palms slightly upward as if to say 'don't ask me.'

Billy appeared to take a deep breath, put both hands on the podium, and lean into the mike as if slightly fearful of what it might do.

"Excuse me." He paused as the people in the audience began to turn their attention to the platform with some confusion. Tommy Henning turned to John Harleston, whom he was assisting into his seat in the second row and uttered "What this? Do you know what's going on?"

Standing up straighter and with a more relaxed tone to his voice, Billy continued, "I'm Billy Commander." He paused, looking around, assessing the crowd in front of him. "I had not planned to be here today." A ripple of laughter went through the audience as people began to sit down. "I thought that the remarks about this project would be best made by others. That my role had been a tangential one. It seems I lost sight for the moment of the need to honor the efforts of those whose love, dedication, experience, time, talent, and ability have made the Commander School a reality."

Billy lingered slightly on each word, endowing otherwise overused concepts with special significance. "My good friend Loudoun Smith reminded me of that a few minutes ago."

"Please do not confuse the casualness of my appearance with the serious mission of this school. Please do not confuse the casualness of my appearance with the serious intent of those seated behind me."

Billy paused, collecting his thoughts.

"My great-grandmother Bradbury believed passionately that one person working in community could make a difference; that one hand outstretched to those less fortunate than oneself would ultimately be joined by other hands to build common cause. My grandmother Commander believed in the transforming power of education and its ability to create opportunity. She believed business should participate in the building and nurturing of the communities from which it drew its sustenance. Her life is a tribute to the struggle to achieve that sort of communion among us. My parents believed that the freedoms and opportunities guaranteed to 'We, the People' had to be extended equally to everyone for this communion and this community to survive and prosper. This then becomes, in part, the legacy of the Commander School."

He stopped, looking up at the cloudless sky and absorbing the landscape of Oyster Island as it fell away toward the Great Pee Dee.

"You know, Molly would have loved this school – 'a beacon of hope in the darkness of the Lowcountry swamps' she would have called it. That it is enabled by so many of those whom she loved and with whom she served on other projects must give her special joy as she looks down today upon these proceedings."

"There are many without whose efforts there would be no Commander School. None figure more prominently on that list than Mrs. Walker Evans Coggeshell, Sr. Mimi Coggeshell has been the relentless force behind us all – and generations of young people will be the beneficiaries of her efforts." Billy paused as a wave of applause swept over the audience and the platform.

Billy turned slightly to his right. "Julius, Isabelle, Dr. Deas, Dr. Adams, Dot, Polly, Julia, Lucy…" he continued solemnly calling by name each person in the platform party seated behind him. The undeniable weight of the moment obviated the need to catalogue the specific contribution of each individual.

"We honor you for your selfless devotion of time, talent, and energy to bring forward this wonderful institution. Your lives will become an example to every child who passes through the doors of this school."

"Mme. Chairman," he continued formally. "Thank you for letting me interrupt these proceedings without notice. I leave you to the resumption of your program."

Turning to leave, Billy dropped the note he had hastily scribbled on Lucy's lap. Leaning over he said quietly, "Some late breaking news for the new chairman of the Institutional Advancement committee." He kissed Julia on the cheek and paused to embrace Mimi Coggeshell at the head of the stairs. They exchanged a few quickly whispered comments and Billy descended to where Loudoun Smith was waiting with Walker to be introduced.

"Your turn," Billy said quietly. The Bishop chuckled, replying, "Godspeed and good sailing, boys" as he embraced each of them.

Billy responded, "Thank you again sir, for everything." He could hear from the platform the dignified voice of Julius Irving begin "Ladies and Gentlemen, the Bishop of the Diocese of South Carolina, the Right Reverend…"

"What was that about?" Julia whispered to Lucy, indicating the note in her lap, as Loudoun Smith began to make his way up to the podium. Lucy silently passed her the note without averting her gaze from the audience.

Julia flipped open the note, scrawled in Billy's handwriting.

"*Sunset drink, portent of a bright tomorrow. Deck at Dirty Dan's. 6 p. Chair on my left will be empty. Hope you'll be in it. B*"

Julia quietly slipped her left hand into Lucy's right, giving her hand a slight squeeze as she saw Billy and Walker walking toward *Convergent* in the distance.

Walker glanced sideways at Billy as they walked down the grassy lawn to the dock. "Big crowd. How you feeling?"

"Bit of reminiscent melancholy I suppose. Other than that, pretty good. I think my dad would be proud. That pleases me more than I expected."

"What's next?" Walker asked

"What's next?" Billy repeated as they reached the dock. "In the big picture we started sketching today? I don't know, Walk. What I do know is that we need to catch this tide if we're going to Charleston today."

Climbing aboard, Billy took the helm, cranking the Volvo diesel while Walker manned the dock lines, uncleating first the bowline, shoving the bow out into the river while beginning to let the stern line play out through his left hand. When Billy was ready, he stepped over the lifeline and onto the starboard coaming as *Convergent* slipped away from the dock.

Walker coiled the dock lines and secured the companionway hatch covers in the port lazarette, disappeared below and emerged a minute or so later with two diet cokes and the handheld VHF radio. He handed Billy one of the soft drinks and then activated the radio as the Wampee Marina came into sight off the port bow.

Billy waved to Buddy Cleveland, visible in the dock master's office of the marina overlooking the river. Walker keyed the hailing channel on the radio. "Dockmaster, dockmaster, this is the Moreland 32 *Convergent*."

"*Convergent*, this is Wampee dockmaster. Go to 63."

Walker continued, "Buddy? That you?"

"Yessir, cap'n. Who's that driving the boat? Looks like a rookie." They could hear the humor in his voice and Billy waved again as they began to pass the marina.

"Buddy, we're headed down to Charleston. Billy says thanks for everything. She looks great and feels fast back in the water."

"No problem. You boys have a safe trip. Should be smooth all the way down. Wind'll change some when you hit Bull's Bay. Come back and see us real soon." Buddy gave the boat a quick casual salute.

"Roger that Wampee. This is *Convergent*, out."

Twenty minutes later *Convergent* cleared the bay bridge and entered Winyah Bay. Billy set the boat on a broad reach for the south side of North Island.

Walker stood in the bow of the boat, one hand loosely resting on the jibstay, looking down the bay toward the ocean. "Best place in Charleston for a sunset drink," he began.

"Mt. Pleasant or Peninsula?" He heard Billy laughingly pick up the game.

"Peninsula."

"Cooper or Ashley side?"

"Ashley. It's a sunset drink, doofus."

"Too easy. Got to be the deck at Dirty Dan's."

"Got to be."

"So Lucy's back," mused Billy gazing up at the telltales on the mainsail. "Did you know?"

Walker replied, "I'd heard a rumor. But then you know Lucy."

Billy said nothing, continuing to gaze at the sky, one bare foot on the wheel.

"You need a phone."

"What?"

"To call Lucy?"

"Nah. I took care of it. I think she's going to meet us."

Walker noticed the cheerfulness in Billy's voice.

"Best place to be on a Saturday afternoon in May," he heard Billy say from the stern.

Looking into the wind Walker said quietly, "Right here, right now, Billy boy. Right here, right now."

The End

Acknowledgments

Through every moment of the work on this book, I have been the beneficiary of the quiet, and sometimes not so quiet, support, encouragement and faith of many people whose participation in the process has informed and improved the story – and changed my life in a way that the typical attainments of the life we were all educated and trained to assume could not.

Linda Ketron has edited and re-edited this book more times than either of us can recall. She was the first person to tell me that the story was good, the writing had merit and that, in time, I might find the voice of an author. Without her constant support, gentle criticism, guiding hand and unwavering sense of what makes excellent story, there would be no *Waccamaw Gold.* We have indeed found our way back to one another.

My brother and sister, Tommy and Amy, have continued to believe, at times with no rational support for their faith, that recovery was mine for the claiming. That faith and their willingness to allow me back into their lives have been a beacon in many dark nights for me. My daughter, Harriett Jordan Woodson, a reader with vision and insight far beyond her years, strengthened the characters in the book with her keen observations of the society and the dialogue of the twenty- and thirty-somethings who populate this story. Her simple affirmation that the book was a good one kept me working more times than I can recount. The way in which my son Harrison cherishes stories, experiences and relationships has been an inspiration for me to tell the story of the characters in *Waccamaw Gold.* His courage in seeking me out while I was beginning the complicated process of recovery and his refusal to give up on our relationship informs and reflects the depth of the relationships among the characters in the book.

Gayle Edwards, whose sharp sense of story and even sharper editing pen improved the book immeasurably, has believed from the first time she read the book that *Waccamaw Gold* deserved to find an audience and with her help, it has.

Jack Steele and I met in a swimming pool at Davidson College more than forty years ago. The intervening years have not dimmed the constancy of our contact or the encouragement he has offered for this book. Two landmark conversations with Jack overcame my insecurities as a first-time author and brought this book to publication. His abiding friendship and those like it with Jane Dunn, Jim Clamp, Kenny and Cindy Young, Walter Sprunt, Philip Powell and Felicia Furman, all of whom have read and re-read the book, offering not only encouragement but also comments and criticism, have strengthened the story and helped me to persevere.

This book would not have been possible without the memory of William West Woodson, whose love of story was exceeded only by his love of books; without the memory of Edwin Craig Wall, Jr. which gives rise to the hope that there may come yet another generation of leaders who emulate his sense of community responsibility, his passion for education and opportunity and his grasp of the connectivity that characterizes business and society; and without the memory of Martha Laurens Taylor, who taught us all a thing or two about friendship.

William Woodson
November 2013

P.O. Box 2884
Pawleys Island, SC 29585
www.ClassAtPawleys.com

CPSIA information can be obtained
at www.ICGtesting.com
Printed in the USA
FFOW01n0816131213
2632FF